THE WHISPERS SERIES BOOK TWO
WHISPERS

from the
CURSE
S.K MAY

HUMMINGBIRD EDITING

For those who fight when hope seems lost,

the fire within will always light the way.

CHAPTER 1

REFLECTIONS OF THE PAST

Nik

I looked out the floor-to-ceiling penthouse window, thinking only about how Larissa was still gone. I had not found her yet, but I knew she was alive. I could feel her through the bond. Her emotions ranged from fear, to worry, to love. I sighed; I had handled the situation with her incorrectly. I should have never called her my curse. She was right, I was hers. I had come into her life and complicated it. She never needed to know I existed, but fate brought us together, as it had done in the past. I leant my forehead against the cool glass, considering how the world had changed around me. I remember when I arrived in London in the eighteen hundreds, during the Industrial Revolution. The roads were made from cobblestone and the air was thick with pollution. Transport was a horse; the streets were covered in animal and human faeces. The women were more reserved. They married and birthed multiple children before dying young. Men; however, had not changed. They still fought for power and control.

Two hundred years later, the buildings were taller and covered in glass. Women wore minimal clothing and were loose with their motives. There was no saving your gift until marriage, it was for desire and need. Men were men, I would not deny that. I had remained the same. I viewed a woman as perfection, born to be worshipped, and mine. Now, men were being taught to respect women, who were strong and held onto their beliefs, but at its core, society had not changed. They still rejected what they did not understand, they still feared what could not be explained.

The day the bombs fell, Aurora and I had been together for barely a decade. I had turned her as I had done in the past. She never questioned my choices; she just loved me. She was no Larissa. She didn't fight every decision or question my every thought.

I sipped my blood. The more I had, the more I could feel her. I moved back towards the couch. The map on the wall glowed, tracking my history. I may have started in the Roman Empire but after it fell, I went in search of more. I ventured through the Visigoth Kingdom, which, while brutal, helped the Roman Empire crumble. But they had a different culture, which I respected. Roman and I enjoyed the change, the new world. In the Byzantine Empire, the art and architecture were beautiful, as were the women, but my eyes were only for her. My Liyana, my love. My favourite was the Ottoman, with their stories of Vlad the Impaler that turned into stories of Dracula. The way vampires were depicted was farcical; that we were creatures that had to hide from the light. The Moors, Prussia, Caliphate, Songhai Empire, Mongols, and the Tang Dynasty. Roman and I even ventured to the Americas but found it a bore and returned for more opportunities within London. The sun did not burn my skin. It did not matter where we landed, stories always spread. Humans had never grasped just how much power we had; we were the sons of a god. We were the beginning of supernatural creatures, both wolves and vampires alike, but our creations did not compare to what we could do.

They had no idea what our true powers were or how we lived. While we lived in plain sight, we could hide or compel when needed. Humans were oblivious to our existence until it benefitted us. Once they discovered us, it was always Liyana who fell first; her death had become inevitable. She became my weakness, and they hunted her. I questioned if it was part of the curse, whether there was an outside force that pushed for her to be taken from me.

Every time she was reborn, she kept her birth name. She never remembered who she was until later in life, and by this stage, she was so used to it that she kept it. There were some odd names, but she did not care, stating it was her life. Liyana was always pure of heart; she cared for others more than she did herself, and she would sacrifice all she had for those she loved. The day the bombs fell, her parents and brother were in France. She came to London to study in Oxford and we found one another when I visited for a lecture. The second we locked eyes, she remembered. We were inseparable until that day; she flew home to be with her family. I warned her it was too late, that the damage had already been done. If a bomb had not taken them out, the radiation would kill them. She refused to accept this; she flew before I could stop her. I followed her but she fell to the ocean from the radiation. She was not strong enough to heal from it. My heart broke at the sight of her falling to her death, especially knowing I could not stop it. I crushed the glass in my hand, the memory of it still fresh, still burning inside my brain, as were all of them.

CHAPTER 2
I FOUND HER

I SAT ON THE COUCH, REMEMBERING THE PAST WITH MY LOVE, ALL the ways I had lost her, and all the ways we had loved. I had one desire, but it would never be fulfilled. I always prayed to have a family with Liyana, but I was a monster who could not procreate. Roman had that chance but never took it. The elevator beeped; I could smell him before he entered the room. The scent of wet dog was not pleasing to the senses, but I loved my brother and that would never change. Despite our constant fights over trivial things, he knew she was my mate. Still, he would always love her. She was a beauty like no other, in every single way.

"Mr Silvia, it is a pleasure to see you," Maria spoke softly. He grunted. I listened as he walked over to the bar and poured himself a drink before he slumped onto the couch beside me.

"Any updates, brother?" I asked, taking another sip of blood.

"What do you think? The wolves are hopeless, and the Alpha is a dick."

I snorted. That had not changed. I never understood why Roman did not want to rule them when he was more than capable. But he preferred to stay out of sight, living his life in the shadows, and seemed to enjoy it that way. We were opposites even before my transformation into another creature. He sighed and downed his drink before standing to pour another. "Does she still live?"

"Yes, I can still feel her. There are varying emotions, I have no doubts that I will—" I cleared my throat, "that *we* will find her."

"How are you so calm?" He shook his head. I hated when he would hit at me in this way. I had to remain neutral.

"Do not start, Roman." I stood and poured myself another glass of blood with some whiskey. I was not calm, but I had no choice. I needed to focus on her emotions, to stay in control of the beast, or I would never find her. She was the goal. If I lost control, I might miss an opportunity to sense a change or sense where she was.

Roman threw his hands in the air. "I have men searching the entire city and you are sitting here, drinking blood without a care in the world," he stated, frustration clear in his voice.

I spun on him. "Don't assume I do not care. I am trying to keep my head clear. I need to stay focused on her ever-changing emotions. I need to focus on her scent to find her. I cannot give the monster power; she is my reason for staying calm. I will *not* lose her."

"Again," Roman muttered under his breath. I shook my head. We had been together for centuries; centuries of conflict, centuries of adventure, and we still fought and bickered. I would love my brother till the day we took our last breaths, whenever that day would come. It was never an option we had considered; we assumed we would rise to join the other gods when we were younger but when I was cursed, that changed. I changed my name and became another person. Remus was the man from the past. I became a Phoenix, a man who burnt his soul and survived. But as time passed, I became Nik, a name more accepted by society. I never felt worthy of our mother's name, Silvia, and instead found a name that seemed to fit in with London when we arrived.

I suddenly noticed a change in Larissa's energy—her fear had increased. She was angry and filled with hate, but terrified. I clung to the wall beside me and held my chest, feeling the fire burning inside her. She was trying to push through the barrier that held her magic back. There was another jolt to my system, and I could feel her magic brewing as it seeped into me. I had never felt a pull of this magnitude.

"Nik, what is it?" Roman asked as I focused on the emotions charging through my body.

"Larissa. Something is about to happen." Roman stood and finished his drink.

"I shall run through the city once more." I closed my eyes to push my limits, feeling the tiniest sliver of her. It was all I needed.

"Roman wait! I know where she is." I removed my suit jacket and pushed the door open, holding out my hand.

"You know I hate to fly; it goes against the wolf in me."

I snorted. Having experienced both flying and transforming into a wolf, the former was my preference. I did not have to remove clothing or feel my bones break and mould into a beast. I only felt the wind on my face as I sped through the air. The only downside was the birds. On the odd occasion, I would be pooped on. They were rather inconsiderate.

"Check your phone."

I took off faster than anything toward her. "I am coming, Larissa." I texted Roman the location, knowing he would not be far behind. We tested it one time, we were as fast as one another in the air and on the ground.

CHAPTER 3
WHERE IS MY MATE?

Nik

I COULD SMELL ASH BEFORE I ARRIVED. THE WAREHOUSE WAS burning, and it had been for some time. I clenched my fists in anger. Her smell lingered in the air, but she didn't feel close. Roman appeared beside me.

"Where is she?" he asked. She was close, but she seemed so far.

"Fan out and see if you can find anything." I could smell bodies burning, there seemed to be more than twenty. I turned the corner to find a cauldron and a stage with rope, which I approached with caution. Magic was never to be trifled with; it was ageless and dangerous, especially for those who practised the dark arts. I looked over the athame and crystals, the book was open to a spell: *'Transference of Power'*. I shook my head; Luce was trying to steal Larissa's magic. Larissa would have been furious, and I chuckled at the thought of her yelling at her sister. I could smell fresh blood, but it was not Larissa's. I followed it on instinct, searching for my brother, who would also be following the scent. Luce appeared before us, lying on the ground. She had minor burns to her arm. I moved the hair from her face; she was unconscious. I wanted to arrest her and bring her to justice, but I could not. Larissa believed her sister could be saved, she believed Peter was the cause of all this.

Roman came over and asked, "What do we do?"

I stood and rolled my sleeves, bit into my wrist, and allowed a few drops to land on her wound. Roman growled.

"It is what Larissa would want. I cannot arrest her; she would never forgive me. Either you take her in, or we let her go."

Roman scratched his chin, his eyes glowing yellow as I caught the same smell. My ears pricked at the sound of shuffling behind us. I ran at super speed, stopping before them.

"Hello, Peter." He pulled a gun from his pocket. "Have you not learnt that I am immortal? Your weapons can not harm me."

"No, but they can slow you down."

My eyes glowed in satisfaction; I pointed behind him. "Can they slow down him?" Roman had turned into his wolf and stood tall. Peter dropped the gun. The son of a god, Roman was larger than the average wolf and could make himself bigger again if he desired. I smiled in admiration; he was marvellous in this form. Roman snapped his teeth at Peter, a clear warning to listen or die.

"Come willingly and I shall allow you to live."

"Bloodsucker, I would prefer to die!" he shouted, yet his eyes darted to find an exit.

"That can surely be arranged for your crimes. But for now, I need you alive." He pulled a knife from his belt and stabbed himself. I rushed forward and pulled it out, slicing my wrist again to allow my blood to heal him. "You do not get to die; I will ensure you rot for your crimes."

"I will destroy you," he whispered in a warning tone.

"Where is Larissa?"

"You should know," he answered. Roman growled. There was no malice in Peter's answer, only truth.

"Why?" My brow creased in confusion. How could I possibly know?

"You took her." Peter passed out as I cuffed his hands together. I would interrogate him later and find out more about this rebel group. I looked towards Luce, but she had already run away, which made the decision of what to do with her easier. I exhaled. I had kept my promise to Larissa. Roman stood before me in human form.

"You took her?"

I shrugged my shoulders. "Was it another spell?" I asked.

"It was no lie."

"I know, Roman, you are not the only creature who can hear. I did not take her. Who has the power to change into other forms? Larissa would have known it was not me."

Roman clapped his hands together. "Not at first, she would have seen you and run before realising that it wasn't. She went with them. Shit. Which demon can do this?"

"Demons cannot enter topside; it is against the rules. You know this. This is something else." Unease spread through my body. Some demons could, under particular circumstances. We did not know who Larissa's father was, so a possible blood connection could allow him to enter this realm. I kept my mouth closed, Roman would not take kindly to this information.

"A witch, perhaps?"

"A witch would not have that much power." I looked around the area for a sign of lingering demon magic. I flicked on my vampire senses and allowed them to take over. There were no signs of any other magic, not even Larissa's.

"Larissa does," Roman mumbled.

"Larissa is not a pure wit…" my words trailed off. Whoever took Larissa knew exactly what she was, and they wanted her power. This was someone else, something else. My heart grew heavy in my chest. As we looked at one another, I knew Roman was thinking the same.

"Fuck, we may never find her."

CHAPTER 4
SOME SECRETS DON'T NEED TO BE TOLD

Larissa

I shot up suddenly and took in my surroundings. I lay on a huge golden bed in the middle of a room. The walls were made of what looked like limestone. There were no windows in the circular room, just one door. A breeze hit my face as I noticed a small opening above the bed. I slowly made my way around the room. There was not much of anything, just the bed and a dresser. I looked at the wooden door, hesitant to go through it, before turning the handle and pushing it open. The door creaked as I poked my head out, the corridor had torches lining the wall. I slowly took a step and ran my hand along the wall; it seemed surreal. The last thing I remembered was being rescued by a person who looked like Nik. I prepared to open my mouth before I stopped. If my kidnapper saved me by using Nik's face, it was probably not wise to call out for Nik. It could be his enemy more than a friend. I continued along the empty corridor before I found my way to a set of steps the same limestone as the walls. I tested the limit of my magic and found I could access it with no blockages. At least I had one weapon. I slowly descended the stairs, hearing a soft voice in the distance that sounded like chanting. With every step, the sound grew louder before I stopped at the landing, next to a room where the chanting was at its loudest, and put up a shield to protect myself. I walked in to see a person, a man, kneeling. He was wearing a black and red cloak.

He stopped and stood. "Hello, Larissa, it is about time you woke."

I could feel the evil dripping from his every word. He turned around slowly, his eyes glaring red, his thick black hair sitting perfectly atop his head, his tanned skin with the hint of a tattoo hidden beneath his black and red suit. I opened my mouth to speak but I was paralysed.

"I thought it important that we speak with no interruptions. Will you comply and be silent or shall I keep you paralysed?" He released the spell only slightly to allow me to nod my head—there was no use in fighting him. I had covered myself with a shield and he was still able to penetrate it.

"Good girl, come and sit."

I looked around to see a table and chair materialise from thin air. I moved and sat down; food and water appeared before me. "It is not poisoned, I swear it. I have no reason to poison you." I picked up the glass and drank the fresh, cold water before moving to the selection of fruit. I was starved, so I ate quickly as the man removed his cloak and sat down. "I am sure you have questions, please ask away. But if you become irrational, I shall place that spell upon you once again, understood?"

I nodded. "I suppose I shall ask the obvious, who are you?"

He chuckled at my question, inspecting his black fingernails as his gaze turned back to me. "There are so many ways to answer this. I have many names; they have changed throughout time and history, but I suppose you could call me the first evil being to walk the earth." His words sent a chill down my spine.

"What, the Devil?"

He scoffed. "Please, the Devil is a story designed to terrify children. It was put in the bible to keep those in fear, to follow the rules. I am a god. I suppose the God of all Evil. I am Malignus."

"So, the Devil was named after you, is what you are saying? Malignus is Latin for evil."

He smiled and lifted a glass to his lips. "I see you inherited your mother's intellect, but I suppose witches *do* speak Latin, so it is probably common knowledge." He shrugged his shoulders nonchalantly.

"You knew my mother?" I queried as cogs began to turn in my head.

"Quite intimately, I am afraid." His smile changed and I took a step back from the chair until I reached the wall. I felt sick at the realisation of who he truly was. We shared the same red eyes and olive skin; my head spun at the realisation. He stood, his eyes darkening as the room grew smaller and the lights dimmed. "I warned you not to behave irrationally." His voice projected as my knees threatened to buckle in submission.

"Forgive me for my reaction. I just discovered my father is the God of all Evil. Not something you want to discover or know. I wanted to know my father but now I am not so sure."

"Oh, come now, Larissa. We can share some quality bonding time. Your mother hid you from me since birth, so it is about time I get to know my living heir." The words made my skin shiver. What the hell had my mother done? Why did she sleep with the God of Evil? What could have possibly possessed her to do this?

I moved to head towards the staircase and back up to my room.

"You are forbidden from leaving this room until I allow it." I ignored his words until I collided with an invisible wall. I rubbed my forehead before I put my hands up to feel for any possible gaps, but of course, there were none.

I spun around and glared at him. "Let me out!" My magic was itching to be released, and I felt my eyes glow red.

"Well, well, well, you are stronger than I imagined. Quite powerful. And we share the same eyes! You inherited quite a bit from me. Excellent." He tapped his fingers together in excitement. His words only fuelled my anger and the urge to get away from him. The tingles intensified down my arms.

"Larissa, give me your best shot." He was baiting me to use my magic on him. My inner voice started to scream at me, *'Don't play his game, be smarter!'* I noted that the voice did not sound like my own. It almost reminded me of another, it was so familiar.

"Hit me, Larissa!" he screamed, his eyes black as night as he stood, prepared for an attack. I shook my head and allowed myself to calm down.

I exhaled a deep breath. "No! I won't be controlled or baited by you. I will take my leave now." I spun around again and held my hands up to his invisible wall, fire bursting from my hands. It seemed to help, or he lowered it, who knew? I was just grateful to be away from him. I needed space to process the fact that I was half-God. Was there an actual name for that?

"It is called a Demigod." He leant against the wall at the entrance to what I assumed was my bedroom.

"I said I was taking my leave and stay out of my head," I gritted my teeth; the man infuriated me.

"I did not permit you to leave and despite your display of fire to break through my spell, it will not stop the rules that apply." I smiled internally, the knowledge that I broke his spell brought me a certain joy.

"I am not a child," I rebutted, refusing to show him any weakness.

"On the contrary, you are *my* child, and you will follow the rules I set within my house." He glanced around the room to signify my prisoner status.

I crossed my arms and tapped my foot. "What are these rules?" I had a desire to roll my eyes, but I felt like it would only piss him off further.

"Number one, you will speak when spoken to." He held his finger up. "Number two, you will eat when food is provided, regardless of what it is. Number three, you will bow in my presence. Number four, you will not use your magic unless permitted." He paused counting his fingers. "Number five, there will be no contact with the outside world. And lastly, number six, you will listen and follow any instructions I give you."

"And what happens if I break any of these rules?"

His eyes glowed brighter than ever. "I am the *God of all Evil* Larissa; I am sure you can figure it out. Now, stay in your room until I say you are allowed to leave." He slammed the door closed and I heard his footsteps echo in the hall as he departed. I slumped onto the bed, trying to reach for Nik, but it was useless. I could not feel him, but I knew he was still alive.

"Find me, Nik, please," I whispered, looking toward the ceiling and holding my hands together in a silent prayer. My magic thrummed in my body but even I knew it was useless in this moment.

CHAPTER 5
FLASHES FROM THE PAST

I PACED THE ROOM FOR HOURS, TRYING TO PROCESS THE FACT that I was the daughter of a god. It was not just that, it was more the fact that he was the God of all Evil. I walked over to the door and pounded my fists against it. Before long, it swung open and Malignus stood in the door with anger written across his face. He exuded danger but I could not allow my emotions to show. He could hear my thoughts; he would know every move before I even tried.

"I want more answers," I demanded, but he simply shook his head.

"I am glad you listened to the rules." I processed his words, realising I spoke without being spoken to first.

"I apologise, but I need more answers. I cannot make sense of it. How was the relationship between you and my mother?"

He put his hand up to silence me. "You broke the rules, Larissa, and it deserves punishment." His eyes glowed brighter as my heart beat faster and sweat rolled down my back.

"Get over it."

He walked over but I refused to move. I had faith that he was not going to hurt me. I was his daughter. Surely, he would have a heart.

"You are mistaken, Larissa. You might be my flesh and blood but that does not mean I will not punish you." He scratched his chin. "I believe I have thought of the perfect punishment." He gave me a wicked grin before he snapped his fingers. I felt instant, excruciating pain.

I opened my eyes to see James standing over me, but he looked different. It was a different time. He wore a golden crown atop his head, his light hair was short, and his toga was clipped over his shoulder.

"This is for your adulterous behaviour, you whore." He held a sword in his hand, my blood dripping from the tip of the blade. He dropped my body as I saw Nik appear before me, so innocent-looking. He looked young and handsome as ever. His hair had curly rings, not perfectly styled as I had known it to be. He pulled me into his arms and held me close as the pain seared through my body. My body struggled to process what was happening; it shook, spasmed, relaxed, flushed, and sent bursts of pain. I was living and feeling my first death and my body screamed with every step Nik took. I could not talk; all I felt was a burning sensation tearing through my body. At my death, my eyes opened. I wiped the tears from my cheeks and looked back at him. It was Liyana's death. She died in Nik's arms. I barely registered his words at the end, only feeling the love he had for me before I took my last breath.

"For every rule break, I shall make you relive every single death your soul has had to endure."

"You are a monster!" I screamed at him from the floor.

"Yes, the God of all, in fact." He sat on the bed, holding his hand out for me. I walked over and slid my hand into his. I would follow his rules, for now. He took a deep breath. "Ah, yes, you are more powerful than I comprehended. Interesting that you smell of that creature." I squinted at him. That creature?

"You mean Nik?"

He scoffed, but his refusal to answer was what I needed. How did he know Nik? He pretended to be him, so there must have been history.

"You have access to your full power now, Larissa. I broke the remnants of the spell that was keeping it contained. Careful, use too much and you may become something other than what you are." His eyes flashed brighter. Did he want me to lose control?

———

Malignus left, and I had time to ponder what having access to all my power would mean now. Surely, I would have enough to escape this prison, so to speak. There was no light, which made it difficult to know which way was up. I allowed my magic to flow freely around the room, searching for any gaps in its shield. I pushed it further, wanting to feel Nik, to get a message to him. The boundary to him was thick but I pressed further into it, needing Nik to find me. The door to my room burst open.

"Nik," I whispered breathlessly. Had my magic worked? I ran over to him, wrapping my arms around his body.

"Larissa, my love." I looked into his eyes, but they were different.

"You piece of shit!" I pushed him hard as the façade dropped, and Malignus proceeded to laugh.

"What gave me away?" I wanted to kill him, anger burnt through my body, eating away at me. It wanted to take over, to destroy everything. Malignus smiled, I fought hard for control before settling down.

"Your eyes." I dared not to think about the tingle, so I closed off a section of my brain.

He turned his head curiously. "Interesting," he said, placing his hands behind his back and pacing around the room.

"What is?"

He smiled. "You put up a wall inside your mind. Interesting. I will break it down. You cannot hide from a god." His tone turned threatening over the fact that I had overpowered him.

He snapped his fingers, the room disappeared, and I was transported to another time. I looked down at my dress, it was a deep blue colour. My hands were covered in blood with a body lying at my feet. Blood spilt from his neck, his eyes open and lifeless. I wiped my mouth with the back of my hand. There was more blood.

'You bitch!' someone screamed as I turned to feel a stake being plunged into my heart. It was fast, and I only heard Nik scream before my heart stopped. It was a quick death but there was no pain. I did not feel it as I did the first, but what hurt was the memory of Nik screaming.

Malignus stood smiling, enjoying the pain he was inflicting. He was the God of Evil. It clicked. He grew stronger with my pain; he was able to feed off it. The torture was for his gain. But the bigger question was, why did I not feel that death?

CHAPTER 6

CONTROL IS SLIPPING

Nik

I RETURNED TO THE PENTHOUSE ALONE, BUT ALL I COULD SMELL was her scent. Larissa had been in every part of this apartment, her scent was in my clothes, my kitchen, my bed. I needed to be away from this space. She was alive. I hoped she was alive. I didn't know how or where but it was not possible to have lost her already. We were destined to be together and deserved to be happy. I roared as my monster simmered underneath the surface, all part of the curse. My wolf may have been removed but the rage and aggression that came from him never left. I was a different kind of monster. I no longer transformed; I just drank the blood of the living. I did the bidding of an evil creature, I had killed more people than I ever wished to, but I would do it again. *For her.* Larissa was…was…my everything. I could not explain how she was so different to Liyana, but the connection I felt towards her was stronger. I couldn't lose her.

I needed blood. I needed to rip into a throat to cage the monster inside or I would lose control completely. Roman appeared, worry etched in his features.

"I have never seen you like this before over her. Why is this time different?" His claws were ready to attack, on edge at my loss of control.

"Because *she* is different. I can't explain it. I don't know how. She is just everything. I can't lose her again. The thought of it is causing the monster inside to want to rip the world apart." My fists clenched as I punched through the wall in the kitchen.

"When was the last time you drank?" He shook his head as he remembered it was before I left for the warehouse. He threw a bag at me as my eyes zoned on the source of my hunger.

"Roman, it is past this. I need fresh." My voice hoarse as I held the bag in my hands.

"Nik, you know the danger when you are like this. How many times have I had to pull you back from the brink? You cannot afford to lose control right now, she needs you," he pleaded, trying to reason with me. "She needs us, not just me. I need you, brother. She needs you." I couldn't control it anymore. If I did this, I would break the rule I created to protect humans. I slammed my fists into the wall again, and it shattered under my power.

"Eat from me," Maria spoke, her voice quiet and filled with fear as she offered her neck. I could hear her heart pounding in her chest. I could see the vein throbbing. I dared not question it. It was not the first time I had drank from her. I tore into her throat, and the animal beat against its cage. Her blood did not compare. It was dirty, the taste changed by the number of preservatives inside processed food. It was almost tainted. I pulled back for a moment as I heard a soft voice. I moved for another drink, and a soft sob reached my ears, *'Nik, please. Find me.'* I pulled back and pushed Maria away.

"FUCK!" I couldn't be this person. I threw the door open and flew high in the sky where it was quiet. There was no noise, and I heard her once more.

'*I am sorry, Nik, please find me.*' The voice hitched at the end. She was scared. I wondered if she felt me feed from Maria. I knew she wouldn't like it, but I needed it. I blocked out all the noise.

"I will find you, Larissa, I swear it." I had to find her. She was different. I needed her.

When I returned to my penthouse, Maria was sitting on the couch with Roman. He offered her a glass of water, and I noticed her neck was still bleeding. My teeth ached for another bite, another taste, another chance to hear Larissa's sweet voice. Roman's eyes glowed, sensing my hunger. I moved to heal her neck.

"Nik, what happened?" He stood, putting himself in front of Maria. I smirked, knowing I would easily be able to tear her throat out before he could wolf out.

"I heard her." I averted my gaze as my eyes scanned the kitchen for a sign of her.

"Impossible."

I retreated to the kitchen and leant on the bench, my fingers digging into the stone. "I heard it as clear as I hear you now."

"What did she say? How?" Roman asked, moving closer at this revelation.

"I don't quite understand how. I could not feel her as she spoke, I only heard. She kept repeating, '*Find me.*' Roman, she was scared." A small rumble escaped his chest. He was as frustrated as I was. "We will find her, Roman."

CHAPTER 7
WILL I EVER FIND THE ANSWERS?

Larissa

I NEEDED TO PLAY THIS SMART. TO FIND MORE ANSWERS, I NEEDED to know what the game was for Malignus. Why had he decided to kidnap me and bring me to wherever this place was? I had to play the evil creature. I had to be like him. I could cast a spell, but Malignus would know. It was more about locking away logic. I opened the door to my room and walked down the stairs, where he was on his knees, praying or whatever he was doing.

He looked up. "Ah, my beautiful daughter, what brings you to my presence?" he asked as he stood, towering over me. I definitely did not inherit his height.

"If I am to be stuck here, I may as well get to know my father."

His eyes glowed brighter, they were terrifying. He smirked. "Would you prefer if they were my natural colour?" I tilted my head at him. I had assumed they were always red because he was evil.

"Do not be silly, Larissa. I was not born evil; no being is born evil. It is purely circumstances that create a person, especially in my case."

I contemplated his words, the same ideation existed in the human world. "That is interesting, I did not think…"

He interrupted my remark, "You could not process that I was once normal." He sniggered as a goblet appeared in his hand.

"Well, yeah, pretty much. You seem like an arsehole."

He chuckled. "That is your mother. She always was very straightforward in how she spoke. Come, let us eat." He snapped his fingers, and a large golden rectangular table appeared, covered in food with a chair on either end. I moved to sit down when he snapped his fingers again and I was suddenly wearing a beautiful black gown that flowed to my ankles. It had a soft neckline and covered my shoulders. It was modest.

"I have always believed that your clothing speaks more than the words from your mouth."

"But I did not pick this." The soft material flowed through my fingers. It was a stunning gown and fit my body perfectly.

"You can." He remarked as he took a seat, picking up a grape and popping it into his mouth, the juice spilling out as he licked it away.

I picked up my glass. "Malignus, just how powerful am I? I am at a loss on how you broke the spell and what I am capable of doing. I was told witches are separated into groups and…" He threw his fork onto his plate, the sound echoing around the room, startling me in the process.

"Witches and their nonsense. Your mother discovered this before her end. Witches put themselves into two categories when there is no need. All are powerful, but it is those who wish to push the boundaries that have the most power. You are the daughter of a High Priestess and a God; you are incredibly powerful. You could change your clothes if you wish. You can create from simple thoughts. Close your eyes and think of something, anything, start small, say a flower." I closed my eyes as he said and thought of a gold rose. "Think about the features, the stem, the thorns, the petal texture. Create it in your mind." I followed his instructions. "Perfect," he purred. "Now open your eyes and snap your fingers."

I did as he commanded and snapped my fingers. A rose exactly like the one I pictured appeared in my hand. The thorn sliced my finger. I dropped it and sucked on the blood.

"Holy shit," I whispered. I had done that—created an object out of thin air.

"Not quite holy, but yes. You have more power than you could dream of. I cannot wait to teach you more." His eyes seemed to sparkle with joy even with the blood-red colour of them.

"What are the conditions of this?" I leant back in the chair and crossed my arms, dubious of his intentions.

"I understand your suspicion, but once I discovered your existence, I knew I had to know my daughter." He cut into a piece of steak that honestly needed to be cooked a touch longer.

"How did you discover it? I mean, even I was clueless of your existence." I reached for some vegetables and chicken.

"Your precious Nik." He *did* know him, but how? I needed to be careful about how I treaded moving forward. I needed to block off that part of my brain and filter only small amounts to him.

"How do you know Nik?" He stood and smiled, and I took note of the fang hanging over his lip. "You were his creator. That is how you know about Liyana."

"Yes, I am the god who cursed him to an immortal life. Cursed him to love a mere mortal whose only value is to fall in love and die in his arms. It is poetic, really."

"If you call it that. I find it rather distasteful," I spat at him in anger. I *was* that mere mortal.

"Larissa," he growled in warning.

"I apologise. I will bite my tongue in the future. Did Nik tell you?" I asked, remembering his warning about being polite.

"Unwillingly, he didn't realise who the father of Katrina's baby was. Nik broke the terms of our agreement, refusing to do my bidding since the day Katrina died. I found you again the moment he fed you his blood. The more you shared, the more I was able to track you. When that pathetic creature bit you, I wanted to rip his head off. Not many can drink from you. There would be less than five, maybe."

"Why is my blood tainted?" I asked him, rubbing the spot where that vampire tore into my throat, the feeling still lingering on my skin.

"Ah, Larissa, it is not tainted. It is pure. Your blood is thousands of years old, untouched by evolution, or from the crap humans eat now. You have the blood of the first humans the gods created." Nik would be able to drink from me and not be harmed. The younger the vampires, the more of a threat I was to them. I raised my eyebrow, intrigued.

"How did my mother create me?"

He eyed me warily. "Come, I must show you something. Enough chatter about nonsense." He was hiding something. He seemed almost curt when he spoke about my mother. I wondered if he loved her or if she tricked him. I would never know. Malignus walked over and offered his arm, and I took it. I would play by his rules, become the perfect daughter, and when the moment was right, I would get out of here. My magic had no limits, and that freaked me out. I needed to find the limits or the grey area with this power. I refused to turn into something evil like him. My last name literally meant the sun and I would shine bright and not be tainted with evil.

Malignus pushed a door open as I snapped out of my brain fog, leading me onto the balcony. The sky was pink and red, and the ground surrounding us appeared barren. There were small sections on fire and screams that floated in the wind. A wind but there were no trees. The vast deadland made me feel sick. I was in hell, quite literally hell. I was never getting out of here.

CHAPTER 8
LONG LOST RELATIVE

Larissa

I COULD NOT SLEEP THAT NIGHT; IT WAS HARD TO STOP MY BRAIN from thinking. Malignus was the one who cursed Nik and Liyana. He was the one who hunted Katrina on that fateful day she died. He was like a missing piece, but it gave me no relief to know my father still lived. If anything, it caused more anxiety. I wished I had my medication to ease my constant thoughts. My fingers bled from the continuous biting and picking. I wondered if I was the daughter of a god, would I be able to heal? I didn't think even Malignus knew the answer to this, I believed he kept me close to discover more about me and what I could do. Or he was trying to steal more power for himself. Who knew? I doubted I would ever find the answer.

I shot up from the bed. If my brain refused to sleep, I would at least adventure around his palace. I was inside a literal castle that I had not explored. My door creaked but I did not care if Malignus heard. I needed to be out of that room. The limestone-covered palace was cold. I had not expected that from hell, but I supposed all I knew were stories. Not many people survived hell or could escape it. I kept trying to reach Nik, but it was useless. I could only feel that he lived. I sighed as I heard a soft cry in the distance,

"Hello?" I called out. I shook my head. It was probably one of his prisoners he was torturing.

"Hello!" the feminine voice called out, her voice weak and filled with fear. I froze in place. I could tap into my magic and find the voice, but I did not want to risk waking Malignus and having another death vision. I still wondered why I had not felt the last one.

I slowly crept through the palace when a warmth filled my body. I stopped and looked at the door, a bright light peeking underneath. I could not stop myself. I reached for the door handle and slowly pushed it open. The warmth enveloped my entire body, and all I could feel was love and happiness. My eyes squinted from the brightness before they adjusted to reveal a familiar brunette locked in a tiny two-metre by two-metre cage.

"Katrina." My voice broke—my biological mother. There was a thick black chain around her neck that glowed red on the inside against her skin. Her eyes were sunken, and her dark hair was scraggly, not like the woman I had seen in Nik's vision. She no longer appeared beautiful, but sick and tortured.

"Oh, my baby girl," her soft voice echoed in my head as a memory resurfaced. *I ran into her arms as she spun me around and we laughed before we collapsed into the garden of flowers.*

"But how? I don't understand, you are dead." She barely managed a smile.

"Oh, Larissa, there is so much for you to learn. You have only just started to scratch the surface of the supernatural world. I tried to keep it hidden from you, but I was naïve to think I could. Fate was working against me." She shook her head as she tried to move closer to the bars, but her neck glowed brighter.

"Katrina, I..."

She reached for me. I could tell she was in pain, but I moved forward and touched her.

"He found you, didn't he?"

"Malignus? Obviously." I looked around the room, and she smiled.

"Nik," she clarified. I nodded, and she muttered something under her breath as she clenched her fists.

"What was that?" I asked her, stepping closer again to hear more clearly.

"It is all wrong."

"What is all wrong?"

"You shouldn't be here. Why aren't you with Elizabeth?"

"You mean your sister? She is dead."

"*SHIT!*" It was obviously not part of her plan.

"Katrina, what is it?"

"This isn't what was supposed to happen. You were meant to stay in that small town. You were meant to stay safe. I made sure there was a backup plan. What the hell happened?" I could not help but laugh.

"What do you find funny?"

"Hell, sorry. It is childish but we are in hell."

"I know, Larissa." She clutched the bars in anger. "I have been here for decades, I am aware." The lightness in my heart sank.

"How did you end up here?"

She let her head fall against the bars. "I was stupid. I wanted to help a friend and… and I made a deal."

"With Malignus?"

She sighed. "Yeah, I cared for Nik. To see him suffer after he lost Aurora… it didn't matter how many times, it was still just as painful." My brain clicked on the time.

"Wait… but…" My head was scrambling.

"I was a High Priestess, Larissa, I did not age as a normal human. I knew Nik for over a hundred years and when I set out to break his cur—" there was a bang in the distance, "Go, Larissa. If he catches us, he will kill me. Come find me again."

"But I have so many questions," I said frantically. I needed answers and I wanted them now.

"I know, and I promise I will answer as many as I can, but he will kill me." Her eyes were pleading for me to go, and I could see the hurt behind them. She worried about what would happen to the both of us. How had she survived this long? I moved towards the door, but I couldn't take my eyes off her.

"I love you, my beautiful daughter, and I am sorry for all the hurt I have caused you. Go, please!"

My feet refused to move. The woman who birthed me was alive somehow. I had to save her. I *would* save her. Katrina touched her fingers to her lips and blew a kiss toward me, and all I felt was her love. I closed my eyes and enjoyed the sensation as it filled my body. I would have to block this memory from Malignus, and it would test my capabilities, but I was eager to see how far I could push myself.

CHAPTER 9
TIME PASSED SLOWLY

Larissa

EVERY NIGHT FOR THE LAST WEEK, I VENTURED DOWN TO Katrina. I started to learn who she was as a person; she was beautiful inside and out. Nik was right, she was one of a kind. She entranced me with the stories she told of when she ruled over the coven. She avoided speaking about Nik and the curse until she mentioned Aurora. Her face fell once the name left her mouth.

"You knew her?" I asked, wanting to know more about the woman who came before me.

"Who?"

I shook my head; she was trying to avoid the topic again. "Katrina, you cannot keep avoiding this conversation."

She sighed and sat down in her cell. "No, but I thought it was worth a try. I have only ever wanted to keep you safe."

"Start at the beginning, please"

"I met Aurora before Nik. She was the epitome of beauty. There were not many that could compare to her, but her exterior hid the true beauty inside. Aurora, like Liyana and all the others, sacrificed parts of herself to help those around her. She was empathetic and her heart was golden." A tear fell down her cheek. "She remembered who she was, but the day the bombs fell, I remember her call as clear as anything. I begged her not to leave, told her it wasn't safe, that the radiation would kill her. She did not care, wanting to save whoever she could. She cared more about the innocent. Her exact words were, *'What's the point of being an immortal creature if I cannot save those who did not deserve that end?'* Nik told me about her death and begged me to find a way to break the curse. It was always the same end for Liyana's soul. Always a tragic death, always painful."

She stopped speaking as she composed herself. She loved Aurora and she cared for Nik. Her fingers interlinked with one another, and she pulled on the chain around her neck. She wanted out of the cell. Katrina had sacrificed for Nik, that much was clear, but what specifically, I could not be sure.

"Mum." Her head snapped in my direction, and it was as if that word alone cleared the fog in her head. There was clarity in her eyes.

"You were never supposed to meet." Her words are filled with emotion but said with conviction.

"Who?" More tears fell from her eyes, the answer was clear, but it did not make sense. "Katrina, please. Can you explain how this has worked?"

She sniffed and calmed herself down before continuing, "Malignus created a sophisticated and complex curse. It is easy to break but also not. Once I figured out the intricacies, I knew I could destroy it. The only problem was Nik. I had to pretend I wasn't able to do it and let him think there was no option. The hardest part was lying to him. No, the worst part was tricking Malignus. I needed his blood, and I tried with just his blood at first, but I was never able to recreate Liyana. It was not about recreating Aurora. I had her DNA. It was about recreating

Liyana. She was the key. Elizabeth begged me not to do it, to leave it alone. She knew the vampires were not worth it, but Nik was not just a vampire. He was the first, the son of the god, Mars. He will never find his peace in life unless he can be with his mate."

Katrina's eyes flashed at me. His mate. I was his mate. Nik had said those words, and I did not believe them, but from the magnetic pull toward him, the tingle in my body when he was near, it was clear we were bonded. I glanced at the ground. I rejected him and picked Roman out of spite because I refused to admit what I felt for him. The intensity of the love I felt for him, it scared me.

"When did you first notice it?" she asked as my body shivered.

"The pull?"

Katrina nodded.

"When I first laid my eyes on him. He had not seen me yet. Part of me just wanted to hold him, give him comfort and make him feel better. I could not explain it. Once we spoke, it only grew. I began to dream of him and when he touched me, it…it…" I wrapped my arms around myself, missing his touch, his warmth, his comfort.

She smiled. "I wish I had felt that pull toward another. The love you share is infinite, it has no limits, and it is beautiful and untainted. I grew jealous when I watched them together. If either moved, they would track each other's every step to make sure they were safe. It was eerie and beautiful. That was the reason I wanted to break the curse. True love exists and I wanted to be the one to give this couple their happy ending." She cleared her throat. "Once I figured out that it was not about recreating Liyana but rebirthing her into this world, I set about trying to break the natural order. I needed the blood of Liyana and the blood of Malignus to bring you back. His blood would give you the strength to fight aspects of the curse unseen, and my blood would give you an advantage against the darker forces in this world. A form of protection."

"Katrina, how did Malignus agree to this?"

She smiled and moved the hair from her face, the same green eyes stared back at me. "I was beautiful once." She still was, there was no denying her beauty. We looked nothing alike apart from the green eyes.

"You still are." The word *mum* threatened to come out again, but I held it back. She was my mother, but I had missed out on a life with her. The memories I did have, I was too young to remember them clearly.

Katrina snorted at my comment. "I tricked Malignus using a basic enticement charm. I made myself irresistible. I came to ask questions about the use of black magic, which I had already accessed, but he was not aware..."

"Malignus can read minds though, how did you?"

She winked. "A magician never reveals their secrets. I had to time it perfectly, moments after our dirty deed. The spell was cast, and nature would take over. I was at the hands of fate."

"Is fate really behind all this?" I shrugged my shoulders at the idea that the gods existed.

"Never speak badly of Fortuna. She does not take kindly to it."

I chuckled. "Have you met her?"

"I have met the lower-level gods. The big guys, no. And I never wish to." Her body shivered in fear as she shook her head. I wondered if Nik and Roman had, but based on the stories I'd heard, I doubted it. There was a loud bang in the distance, signalling it was time to end the conversation. I stood up and dusted off my clothes, looking back at Katrina.

"One more question—what does it mean?" The one question that seemed to be plaguing my thoughts.

"What, sweetheart?" Warmth filled my body at the tenderness of her words.

"You were never supposed to meet." Her face froze, and I could feel something beside me.

"Yes, Katrina, my love, what does it mean?"

His eyes glowed red with small black pinholes in the centre. Fangs extended outside his mouth and evil filled the room. I could not breathe. My own magic pushed forward to harm him, but I could not use it. It was not natural; it did not feel like me. Katrina focused on me; her eyes never looked at Malignus.

"Return to your room, daughter," he ordered, his voice so low and threatening that the hairs on my arm stood up.

"But…"

"Larissa Solis, do as he says." Katrina's words stopped my thoughts. She was scared. I turned to do as she said. "Larissa, never forget." The words echoed through the room. It was like something was being burnt into my brain. I held my head high and walked towards my room.

CHAPTER 10
TESTING THE LIMITS

Larissa

Screams filled the castle, the screams of her torture. I held onto the bed, containing in my own rage. I wanted to protect her, my mother. She birthed me, she enlisted a whole town to keep me safe. She spelled Roman to look out for me, to keep me from Nik. The story was still missing aspects, but it was slowly coming together. Katrina knew how to break the curse but lied. 'You were never supposed to meet.' The words echoed in my head; it stung as my ears rang. I touched it as I looked at my finger and saw bright red blood, my mind returning to Katrina. She cast a spell but what would it achieve?

The door to my room burst open. Time for my punishment. I closed off part of my mind, not allowing him to access what memories I had. I saw his eyes before his body appeared, blood dripping from his chin. He drank from her. I sank to my knees in submission.

"Ready for my punishment, father." I bowed my head as I waited for the pain.

He smirked and closed the door, his long nails tapping against it. He was contemplating his next move, probably trying to get into my head. I kept myself composed, trying not to let him throw me off. I had to make sure I was stronger than him. A fog filled my head, and I pushed it out, forcing up a shield as an extra layer of protection.

His manic laugh echoed in the room. "You think you can overpower me? I am a god!" his voice boomed through the room, my ears ringing from the vibration.

I could feel him thundering on the shield, trying to get access. I held it for as long as I could, the fire in my body slowly losing its spark. His smile grew bigger. I focused on Nik, Luce, Katrina, Elizabeth, and Roman. I drew strength from those I loved, needing to win against him. It was a long shot, I knew that, but I had to test the bounds of my own strength against him. My power came from him, and I wondered if that was why he wanted me here—to have more power to control. He *was* evil.

"LARISSA!" His voice was a warning to stop and submit to him.

He yelled as my body struggled, but the shield held as I pushed myself harder. A pool of blood grew at my knees, it was intense. He pushed harder as the fog grew, and I could not hold on any longer. I let go as the full force of his power hit me, falling back onto the ground and hitting my head. I reminded myself to keep the lock on Katrina's conversation. He must never know.

I could hear his soft voice. 'There you are. I thought you were going to sleep the entire day.'

I smiled at seeing him. 'Morning, my love.' He kissed my lips as he stood at the entrance to the tent, his bare body on display. A skirt covered his bottom half, which frustrated me. I sat up and pulled the blanket to cover my naked body. 'Will it begin today?'

'Yes, the Persians will advance.'

'Are you sure we are on the winning side?'

He chuckled and turned back. 'I was right about you, my love.' The bond tingled with love and affection. I reached over and took the golden goblet of wine, taking a sip. It tasted funny as I put it down. My throat grew tighter.

'Remus.' I gasped for air as he rushed over.

'No, this cannot be happening. Not again. Hold on, Liyana. I will find some help.' He rushed from the tent as the air grew thicker. The world lost its colour, and it was not much longer until I heard the last beat of my heart.

I woke and found myself in the room with Malignus sitting on my bed.

"I am not sure which of your deaths I enjoy the most; your soul has had every death imaginable. It is like a reality television show."

I dared not tell him I did not feel this death, holding my throat to pretend like I had experienced the sensation. It was odd that I could not feel them. I felt Liyana's, but not the last two. What was this curse? What was the spell Katrina cast?

"I promise you, Malignus, I swear on my limited life that I will make you pay for this."

He laughed as he exited the room. It was pointless, but I wanted him to know I would destroy him. It was now time to push myself further than before, to test the bounds of my magic.

Chapter 11

SECRETS OF THE WORLD

Nik

I was no closer to finding Larissa; all I knew was that she was alive. I could feel her, but it was fading as my blood slowly left her system.

I entered the station, hoping Peter would have answers. The white-walled station had grey flooring and steel chairs, and large rectangular lights covered a majority of the roof. Roman was beside me; we were planning the good cop/bad cop routine with Peter. We needed answers. How was he able to hide? What resources did he have? Where would Lucianna hide? Everyone was quiet as we walked past, but that was the norm for us. We were the sons of a god and appeared rather intimidating to many other men. It was comical when we lived in ancient times; we were larger than men of that time. Not many were over six feet tall, but all were muscular. We blended into society as it changed but we had been and always would be outcasts. It was the reason I hid my true identity. No one needed to know I was the first vampire to walk the earth.

Roman and I stopped outside the interrogation room, both of us able to hear Peter's heart pounding in his chest.

"Did you eat before you came?" Roman queried as he rolled up his sleeves. It was normal for him to ask, always wanting to make sure I was fed before anything he considered important. It kept the monster satiated and under control but with Larissa missing, it didn't matter how much I was consuming. He wanted to take over, he was desperate to find her.

"Yes," I answered curtly.

"How much?"

"Roman, please."

"Answer me, Nik," he snapped, wanting to know just how much he would have to intervene if necessary.

"I had more than enough to keep myself calm. I promise"

He looked at me with suspicion. I had, but I would not be able to stay calm. There was too much on the line to keep in control. I closed my eyes to focus, then glanced at Roman and nodded. When we entered, I took a seat at the cold silver table and Roman leant against the wall behind me as if he had no care for the man before us. Peter's eyes were wide, his mouth agape, as he registered I was before him.

"Is there a shortage, or have they hired filth to run the department?" Peter remarked as Roman snorted behind me "What are you supposed to be, good cop?" Roman growled, his body shook, and he worried about me losing control. I raised a brow at him as my brother rolled his eyes.

"Peter, we can make this easy or hard, which would you prefer?" I asked him, tapping my fingers on the table.

"I would prefer to wipe you off the face of the planet, can we follow through with that?" He appeared cocky but his body told a different story. His brow was covered in sweat, his heart thumping rapidly, and his hands fiddled in his lap.

"Your words have no worth." I leant back in the chair to show I was bored with his useless information. Roman appeared and slammed his hands on the table,

"Why did you take Larissa?" Peter jumped as Roman's eyes flashed yellow. I put my hand on his arm to calm him, and Roman glared in my direction. He was no longer following the plan. Peter had barely tested his patience.

"Peter, what did you want with Larissa?" I kept my voice calm and even.

"Lucianna deserved her birthright."

I tilted my head at his comment. "What birthright?"

"When Elizabeth died, Larissa stole the family magic. She only wanted what was rightfully hers."

I laughed at his idiocy. The magic was not Lucianna's. Elizabeth inherited the magic when Katrina died and became the new High Priestess. When Elizabeth died, it returned to Larissa, with whatever was naturally Elizabeth's going to Lucianna. Magic was complicated but it had rules, and there was no way for Larissa to steal it. Larissa's magic was not pure witch, the other half of her magic was dark and evil. Lucianna was so wrapped up in this idea that she did not stop and think about the consequences. If they had succeeded with the power transfer spell, it would have killed her.

"Where did Lucianna get this idea from?"

Peter crossed his arms, exuding cockiness, like he had the upper hand in this interrogation. I would let him think he had it. "I know about witches."

I smiled at his belief that he knew anything at all. "Oh, I did not realise you were so well-versed in the supernatural world.

Please, tell me more." I gestured for him to continue, knowing I would hear nothing but nonsense.

"They are irresistible to vampires…" *Not true.* "They depend on the elements for control…" *Also, not completely true.* "Lucianna is very powerful; her powers are limitless." I stroked my face. The Solis bloodline had always been a powerful coven, but witches had limits. If this was true, there was something more about Lucianna, which I doubted.

"Interesting. What else?" I feigned interest in his useless facts that had no validity to them. He continued to tell me all about the witch world.

"Wait." I sat up straighter, as a thought popped into my head. "Who is the current leader?"

"Juliet Aqualis."

The last I heard of Juliet, she was a child, but it had probably been decades. Time was hard to keep track of when my love was gone. I focused more when she lived. Aqualis witches used to live near the ocean, and it was believed that not many were left after the fallout from the bombs.

"But the Aqualis coven were extinct. The bombs destroyed them."

"That is what you think?" He seemed so sure of himself.

I stood up. "You will tell me, Peter." No more games. I wanted answers and his face pissed me off.

"You cannot compel me. I take a concoction from the witches that protects me against basic compulsion."

Roman laughed behind me. "Oh, Peter, a basic vampire will not be able to compel you. But Nik is not a basic vampire."

"You are all the same," he scoffed.

"Nik was the first. Nik is a god." I listened to Peter's heart beat faster, and I moved closer.

"Now tell me, Peter, what do you know?" My voice purred with compulsion.

"The world is not vacant as the vampires want you to believe. Some places still exist. Some places survived the radiation. London is not the only surviving country."

"Nik?" Roman questioned. I shook my head, knowing nothing about this. I stayed in the shadows. I had power but I preferred for others to not know my true identity. It was too risky, but I was unaware of the world still existing. I needed to know more.

"What else, Peter?" I asked him, using a little more compulsion.

The door to the interrogation room opened. "Time's up, Dankworth." I stormed over and slammed the door shut.

"Roman, hold it." I could feel my control slip. I wanted to know more. Peter trembled; he should fear me.

"You want to call me a monster, here I am. NOW, WHERE IS LARISSA?" I roared at him. He would give me the answers I wanted.

"I don't know." His voice shook, terrified. I slammed my fists down on the table causing the room to shake.

"TELL ME or I will drain you of your blood and Roman will feast on what is left." My brother growled, and I sensed him shift slightly into his wolf. Peter screamed as men attempted to burst into the room.

"WHERE IS SHE?" I yelled at him again, but Peter stopped. He sat on the chair and crossed his legs. I found the sudden change in his attitude unnerving.

"She is safe. She is where she belongs." I did not need to ask to know who sat before me.

"How? You cannot cross the threshold," I asked, returning to the cold chair and looking at the face of the man who held my mate.

"Ah, Remus, centuries old and yet you are still so young. You will never learn." He glanced at his fingers as if I was not worthy of his time.

"Where is safe?" Roman shifted fully back to human form, his eyes trained on our enemy.

"Roman, lovely to see you. How goes the search for your mate?" Roman growled in response. I could feel my brother's anger.

"Pluto, tell me where she is," I demanded, using the name he refused to identify with. He grimaced at my words. He hated hearing his birth name.

"You will never see her again. She will be safe from *all* the dangers with me." Peter returned to his body. I pondered his use of all, what did he know?

"What the fuck was that?" He stood and jumped on the spot with jitters. Roman put his hand on my shoulder.

"We know who has her now. It won't be hard to find her, Nik. I promise. We will bring her home." His words echoed in my head. I closed my eyes, praying I would be able to hold her once more.

CHAPTER 12

I AM COMING FOR YOU

Larissa

THE DAYS HAD MELDED INTO ONE; I HAD NO SENSE OF TIME OR dates anymore. I spent my time working on mastering my magic. Sophia said the most powerful witches are those who are always in control. The magic was evil, I could tell it was tainted. Whenever I attempted to access all of it, a coldness would sweep through my body. I had two halves: the light and the dark.

I pushed the magic further as my nausea grew, refusing to let it control me. I was stronger. I had to be stronger. I pushed once more and as the evil magic flowed freely, it whispered to me. Its words were dark, *'That's it, Larissa. Give in to us. Give us control.'*

I stood and moved around the room, but it didn't stop the voices. A softer voice appeared. It was quieter than the others. I forced my focus toward this voice, *'I am here, baby girl. I will protect you. Find the love and follow it.'* Tears filled my eyes. It was Elizabeth, the woman who raised me, the woman I considered my mother for my entire life. I had only heard her voice once, when I laid in bed with Nik.

I took a deep breath, focusing on my shoulders as they rose and fell with every inhale and exhale. I thought of love and only love. The love of my mother, the love of my sister, the love of Roman. But the thoughts of Nik brought an instant calm. My body relaxed and I regained control of my magic. I replayed the memories I had of Nik; the good and the bad. All were filled with a form of love, the mate bond. Was this why Katrina combined the magic?

I pushed my magic all around the room to try and find a gap, forcing myself harder and harder again. I put everything into escaping this room. The room grew brighter with a mixture of red and golden patterns that reminded me of flowers, the true combination of light and dark, good and evil. It was beautiful.

"Nik, where are you?" I forced my mind to go somewhere it had never been. Stars filled my vision as I heard my father's voice yelling at the door. He pounded against it with all his strength, but I pushed myself further again, keeping the door shut with whatever my magic would allow.

"Larissa?" Nik's voice echoed in the room, barely a whisper, but I heard him. I cried at the relief and joy that I had found my way to him. "Larissa, hold on. I am coming for you. I promise with all that I have, I am coming."

I lost control for a moment, which was all Malignus needed to burst through the door. I would pay for this, but I did not care. Nik was coming. I could feel his love as it cocooned me with warmth. I let it all fall away. He would save me.

Chapter 13

THE PLAN OF ATTACK

Nik

I went a few rounds with the bag. I had it reinforced to ensure I did not break it or the room around me. Since discovering who had Larissa imprisoned, I had been searching for her. I knew that evil monster had her. I searched all my archives for any information on his hidden locations but knowing him, he would be in hell, protected. But how did he possess Peter? He had been cursed by the gods to stay in hell for his crimes against humans. I worried that he may be leeching power from Larissa.

I punched harder and harder with my mind, searching for Larissa. I smelt Roman as he entered. We had not spoken since we discovered who had her. I took the blame, knowing I never should have taken the deal. I should have listened to Liyana from the start and let her go. But it is impossible to consider living without your mate when you are forced to live forever.

"Nik, let it go." I ignored him, so he stood in my eyeline and wrapped his hands. He knew I needed a proper fight, a way to release all the excess power in my blood. This was going to be fun. Roman and I entered the boxing ring, my gym having everything a person could need, with a dark and moody interior.

"Are you sure you want to do this, brother?" I asked, loosening my shoulders, rolling them, and stretching them out.

"I believe our record is me in the lead by one." He smirked.

"Last fight ended in a tie," I reminded him with a smirk.

"Only because you cannot admit defeat."

I closed my eyes to access the monster inside, feeling my eyes turn red as I opened them. Roman's glowed yellow.

"Let the games begin." I charged at Roman, who ducked and spun to land a blow to my back. I jumped to avoid him before landing on his shoulders. Roman growled. He hated it when I used my ability to fly against him. It was not my fault he belonged on all fours. I threw myself backwards as Roman flew into the rails and bounced to the floor. He sprung to his feet and lunged. I landed a punch to his chest, and he stumbled before he moved with animalistic speed and took my legs out from under me. I fell flat on my back as Roman jumped and struck my gut. I groaned as I lifted my legs around his waist and spun him to the side, scrambling to get on top as I hit his jaw. It cracked under the pressure, and Roman roared in pain as he thrust me off him. He groaned as he forced his jaw into the correct position.

"Ready to admit defeat?" I asked. My vision went black as pain radiated through my head. "Argh!" I held my arm out and Roman took it.

"What is it Nik?" My fangs descended, and I felt an overwhelming amount of power. It was blinding before it settled, and I felt her. I smiled at the amount of love she pushed through our bond, closing my eyes to focus on her surroundings. I could not see her face, but I witnessed the sheer amount of power she was wielding. It glowed brightly in the room. I had been to this location with Malignus. He had her in Hell, a place I was not allowed to visit.

"Larissa, hold on. I am coming for you. I promise with all that I have, I am coming." I prayed with all my might that she could hear me. Our bond filled with relief; she had achieved what she wanted. A pounding echoed through the room, Malignus was attempting to burst through her door, but she held it closed. Katrina had created someone more powerful than a god, and he would punish Larissa for it. I broke contact as Roman refused to let go of my arm. I stood and beamed with excitement.

"Fight is over. I know where she is. We are going to need help to get her out." I unwrapped my hands as I left the gym. Roman followed as I walked through the house to the study.

"What happened, Nik? How do you know? What the fuck was that?" I could hear the fear in his voice.

"I don't know what it was exactly, but I believe it was her power. It was magnificent, it glowed with gold and red. The combination of her witch and demon power. I have never sensed something so intense."

"But how did you sense her?" he asked, knowing I had been trying for weeks to find her.

"She sought me. She used all her strength to push through his field and found me."

"Holy fucking shit." He appeared dumbfounded, his mouth hanging open.

"Yes, indeed. I know where she is. She is in Hell."

"How can he take her there when she still lives?"

"She has half his blood, so she can walk between both worlds. There is so much more to her than I ever realised." My mate, my powerful mate, would keep me on my toes with what she could do.

"We cannot enter Hell. How do you propose we go and get her?" I knew this to be true, but it was possible.

"I will distract him. He showed himself. I will go with some ridiculous deal to make with him while you get her out. Only one issue." I tapped the pen on my desk.

"Other than you being mad, what?" Roman threw his hands in the air. I could sense his apprehension, but I had to do it.

"We need a witch, but I doubt they will help me. I will try. I have to try. I will speak with Juliet Aqualis." I threw the pen down at the desk; it bounced to the floor.

"She wanted to help Peter and Luce. What could you bargain with to get her to agree to help us?"

"Roman, I am insulted. Am I not the most charming Lord in London?"

He scoffed at my remark. "I want no part of this deal. They will ask for something you cannot give. Tread carefully, Nik."

"I need my brother with me," I pleaded,

"You want to risk them discovering our secret? You have lost your mind. You have never been this reckless before. She will die and come back. Let it play out as it has for the past millennia." I picked up the pen and threw it at him, but he caught it.

"You dare leave her to die," I warned him. I would not risk her life.

"It is not something that we have not done in the past, why is this any different?"

"*She* is different. I cannot explain it, but this time I can feel it. This time we will be together." My head and heart told me this would be the final version of her.

CHAPTER 14
THE KEY TO BREAKING THE CURSE
Larissa

Since being able to hear Nik, I had a sense of joy. I knew he would come for me, that he would never leave me. It was but a glimmer of hope, but I would hold on tight to it. Malignus punished me with another life and death that I did not feel. I could not understand why I had felt the first death and none of the five that came after. Each one broke my heart. I would see Nik holding them as he cried and begged for his own life to end. The torture he had endured for centuries for his mate, and being immortal must have made it worse. I knew who had the answers, but I worried about seeing her again. He would punish us both. A dark thought entered my mind, and I considered the fact that he could only punish her, as I did not feel mine. I paced the room as I contemplated the idea of torturing Katrina, but I wanted answers, I needed them.

I snuck from my room, avoiding the use of magic. He knew as soon as I did. I ran down the stairs before sneaking through the halls and entering the room where Katrina was imprisoned. She looked worse, the mark on her face was deep but it was her eyes that shocked me. The rings around them had grown and the light had disappeared.

"Oh, my beautiful girl." Her voice broke, showing signs that she was close to death. She may have created me for a benefit, but I knew she loved me.

"Hey, Mum." I wanted to give her joy before her end, which I believed would not be far away.

"Why are you risking this visit?" she asked, clearing her throat, her attempt to show she was fine.

"I need to know more. I understand the purpose of my creation, but there is more to the story of Nik and Liyana. Please, can you tell me more?" She waved her arm to the ground before her. I took a seat, moving as close to the cage as I could. Katrina reached for me as pain flashed across her face and I raised my hand for her. She slipped hers inside mine and I sensed her love as my mind filled with flashes of her memories.

"I wish I could say that I regretted creating you but that is far from the truth. You are the reason I exist. I was born to give you life. Nik and Liyana deserve their happiness. When I discovered the trigger to the curse and how to break it, I knew I had to do it. I seduced Malignus to conceive you, but I have never felt so full of life as I did while I grew you. You are pure and warm. The hardest part of my journey was selecting a name that would suit you. I flicked through centuries of names before landing on Larissa. I wanted a name that started with the letter of your birth name. When I heard Larissa and discovered what it meant, I knew it was perfect."

"Wait, my birth name?" Katrina peered at the floor, my brain scouring for a logical answer, but it kept coming back to one point. "Holy fucking shit. I am not, please tell me."

"You *are* Liyana, not a makeshift of her. You are the original. I brought you back to the start. It was part of the plan. Remember how I said you were never supposed to meet?" I nodded as I moved away, my chest growing tighter, my breathing erratic.

"But if I am Liyana, does that mean I am cursed or not? This does not make sense."

"You were never cursed. You are caught in someone else's curse." I could see her eyes pleading, she was giving me answers I could not interpret.

"Nik's. But I still do not understand."

"Nik is the key to breaking the curse." The ground began to shake as the room filled with a thunderous roar. The hairs on my body stood in response. That was the call of a wolf, but the type of wolf was what worried me. "Larissa, you need to go. The castle is shaking because of an intruder, you must leave."

"But—"

"No, I worked too hard to mess this up. You need to go."

"I will come back for you. I promise, Mum. I will save you." Tears streamed down her ash-covered cheeks.

"I know, sweetheart." The words were cold as if she had already resigned herself to death. I refused to accept it; I would save her. I had to save her. I turned back one last time and blew her a kiss. I kept my eyes trained on her as I closed the door; her body fell to the floor. I did not know how much longer she would have, but I had to get her out. I overpowered Malignus once, I would do it again.

Chapter 15
HELL OF A TIME

Nik

Juliet had agreed to help on the condition that I bring Larissa into the coven to join the witches. I doubted her sincerity, but I agreed to the terms because I believed Larissa may *want* to join them. It would offer her more protection or more understanding of who her mother was. The token had been spelled to allow entry and exit into Hell for Roman and me. A third token was for Larissa to leave, if we found that she was not able to leave when we tried. It was a precaution and one I insisted on. I would not risk everything to leave without her. I was not sure how this plan would go, but I remained positive while Roman was the opposite.

I wore a black suit and covered myself in a red cloak as I crossed the border between the human world and the world of the dead; Hell. Roman entered after me to avoid suspicion of us colluding. The sky was red, with beasts swooping through the air. The dry ground was covered in cracks. I dared look into one of the slivers in the ground and saw lava bubbling underneath. I fed on plenty of blood before arriving, needing my senses and powers sharp. Every step toward the man who cursed me brought up emotions and feelings I had buried for so long. I was his puppet for centuries, doing everything he asked before breaking away and refusing to help with any more deaths or delivering more souls. His castle came into view; it was a marvellous site made from limestone, with ancient runes carved into it. They would be protection runes. I had not seen them before, but Pluto—or Malignus—was a lot older than I. He had been alive since the beginning of creation.

Every step brought more apprehension, but I could sense Larissa. A demon stood before me, wearing a dark cloak, black leather pants, and a chainmail top. His skin was grey with tendrils that hung from his chin. His eyes were black, representing the evil he had committed in his life. But the curved horns, I questioned. Demons did not need horns, so I wondered if he had stuck them on. His soulless eyes focused on me, and while any other man would crumble under that glare, I had seen worse. Roman in his wolf form caused more fear.

"I am here to see your Master." He moved closer and sniffed me. I laughed at this creature and his attempt to frighten me.

"I have seen far mightier than you. Your Master is waiting, and we know he does not take kindly to those who make him wait." The creature grumbled as he cut his wrist to open the door, an interesting entry I would remember during our escape.

Malignus stood in all his glory as the doors swung open. "I wondered when I would see you." An evil grin crossed his face as his eyes turned black. I sensed his power creep over my body, searching for a way to control or attack. I knew better now. I knew how to fight him. It may have taken centuries, but I could not be controlled by him anymore, not since the loss of Katrina.

"Master." I bowed my head in a sign of respect but did not mean it. He did not deserve any respect. He was a monster. "I have come for my mate, and I am willing to bargain."

His cackle echoed through the hall as the doors closed behind me. I was alone for now, but I trusted Roman would be able to enter with no issues. He spun, stalking away. I followed, observing the area and searching for places to hide or escape. I had to stay focused, or he would read my mind and discover my true thoughts. We entered his den, which smelt of rotting flesh and blood. The monster inside wanted to revel in this room as my feet squelched through the blood-soaked carpet. I could feel the creature stirring, wanting to feast, but I would not allow him. Whenever I let him out of his cage, it ended in disaster. I thought back to Pompeii, forever grateful for that volcanic explosion that hid the depravity I caused. I sat on the seat, listening to the screams of those who came before me.

"Don't you miss the trouble we caused through history?"

I held back my anger, my jaw clenching, before I plastered a smile on my face. "It would depend on which century you are referring to." He threw his head back in laughter as I dreamt of slicing his throat open and dancing in his blood. A momentary reprieve, but then I remembered he could not be killed.

"Yes, I supposed it would. You were always more entertaining when your precious Liyana was dead." I gripped the armrests tighter. This was his motive—he would push buttons to get reactions and feed off anger. I pulled myself in as I cleared my throat. "She was controlling as are all women, no?" He cracked his fingers and grumbled. I wondered to whom he referred. "What do you want?" His tone had shifted, and I realised I had hit a nerve without knowing or meaning to.

"I believe it is clear why I am here. I want my mate, Larissa. Hand her over." He leant forward, putting his head in his hand as he pushed his shoulders out to intimidate me. It used to work but I grew wise to his tricks.

"Why would I hand over my child? I need to groom her to rule this wonderful kingdom." He grinned, which only caused an involuntary shiver.

"I did not realise you were going to die soon."

"What does that mean?" he snapped at me, and my monster growled from inside at the shift in his attitude.

"Larissa would only need to rule if you were to pass on from existence, and for someone as old and powerful as you, I doubt that would happen." He moved back in his chair and crossed his legs. I had called his bluff. He smirked as if he knew I was missing an important piece of the puzzle.

"Nik, I have been curious about you since the beginning. You have had a singular focus, *her,* my daughter. Have you ever thought that maybe I took her to keep her safe?"

"How could you possibly keep her safe? You are the ruler of Hell, the man who punishes any who enter. She is light and pure, she doesn't belong in this filth," I spat out. I couldn't believe he did this.

"She deserves to be safe, and I can keep her safe from all the forces that want to harm her." I turned my head at him curiously. What forces could he be talking about?

"Here you are, twisting tales to suit your story."

"Remus." I flinched at hearing my name, but he only used it when he wanted to ensure I listened. "I don't understand how you have not figured this curse out yet. The piece that brings it all together. She *could* be the final version of Liyana, she could be your future, but you need to pull your head out of your arse. You need to put all the pieces together. There is another who pulls the strings." I needed the answers, and I knew this time was different. What would it cost me to know the answers?

"You are willing to risk it all for her, aren't you?" He stroked his chin as he listened to the thoughts in my head going crazy. I had made a mistake. I wanted to bide my time until my brother could get her out and take her to safety. I had been so focused on Larissa that I may have missed the signal. I would give it all up for answers, to never lose her again, to spend every day with her in my arms. I needed her to survive. Malignus knew. *Roman where the hell are you?*

CHAPTER 16
LOSS OF MY HEART

THE ROAR ECHOED THROUGH THE HALLS, CALLING TO ME. I COULD smell Roman's familiar scent, it was him. Nik and Roman had come for me. I allowed magic to flow a little more freely, dropping my shields to search for Nik. My body began to tingle, and I knew he was in the castle.

"Larissa!" Roman screamed, the sound shaking the walls. I ran towards it.

"Roman!" The floors crumbled and I lost my balance before a monstrous beast stood before me. For a moment, I froze before I saw his eyes. "Roman?" The wolf buried his head in my shoulder, reassuring me. Roman's wolf defied imagination. It was larger than the average bear, closer to the size of an elephant. His paws were so large that one strike would be fatal. I reached up and touched his fur, the deep brown colour reminded me of his hair. He nudged me with his snout as I stood. "Roman, I have to save Katrina." He tilted his head as if he had not heard what I said. "She is alive, please." He motioned for me to continue as I led the way.

We ran back to Katrina's room and Roman burst through the door first, growling. Katrina stood slowly as a smile spread over her face. "I have missed you, old friend." Roman put his snout between the bars and she stroked it. She scratched behind his ears before bending to look into his eyes. "Thank you for taking care of my daughter. I know lying to your brother would have been impossible." Roman made a guttural noise before stepping back to look at the bars.

"I don't know how to break them. If I use my magic on them, he will know." Roman shifted back to his naked human form. I loved his brother, but I forgot how hot he was. He gripped the bars before pulling back, his hand was red and smoking. I rushed over, ripping my top to cover the burn. He kissed my head and pulled me into his chest.

"I missed you, beautiful. We can only try your magic; your father is with Nik." I suddenly wanted to vomit over the idea of Nik in the lion's den. Every atom of my being wanted to run to him. I could not leave him alone with that monster. Roman caught my arm. "Larissa, he will be fine. Trust him and me. Try to break the bars."

I turned back towards them, glancing at Katrina. She smiled, her face lighting with relief over no longer being trapped. I allowed the power to flow through me, focusing on love and those I cared about. It filled the room before I turned my attention to the bars, feeling the ancient spell. I pushed a little further on the bars before a click echoed. When I opened my eyes, Katrina had left the cell. She cried as she ran and held me close.

"I thought I would never be able to hold you again. Even if this is my last day, it is my second best. The first being the day I birthed you into the world." Warm tears tumbled down my cheeks, only now releasing just how much this woman meant to me. Her memories were buried so deep by my mother, Elizabeth, that I did not even know what I had missed. Time seemed to stop as her beauty returned, the scraggly hair disappeared, and the spark within her reappeared as did the colour in her cheeks. She stood before me as I remembered her, the mother who would sing me to sleep at night.

"Hi, Mummy." She laughed as she wiped the tears from my cheeks, her touch made me feel like a little girl again.

"Let's get to safety." Her words did not match her face. She smiled, but her words seemed almost foreboding. Roman took my hand, pulling me towards the door as I took Katrina's. We walked through the hall before Roman shifted into his wolf form. Men came out of every corner, and Roman tore them to pieces. Katrina waved her hands as black magic shot from her fingers. I held a shield. I had no idea how to use magic for defence and the last time I did, I almost died from using too much of it. I had never felt more powerless in my life. Roman and Katrina did not allow any to get close to me. The tingle grew intense as I looked up, my eyes meeting Nik's. Malignus held a knife to his throat, and the room stopped.

I rushed forward. "Nik!" Roman caught me and held me in position. I pushed harder against him to break free. I needed to save him.

"Be smarter, Larissa," Roman muttered in my ear before his arms relaxed a little.

"Yes, Larissa, did I not teach you to use your head?" Malignus dragged the knife down before thrusting it into Nik's chest. I screamed as he dropped to his knees, but Roman's strength held me from running. He stabbed him once again as blood pooled on the floor. "I am intrigued by how you thought you were strong enough to defeat me. I created all this. I create evil and you wanted to walk into my domain and take what was not yours." He kicked Nik to the floor, who groaned from his wounds.

"Nik." I could feel every inch of his pain and I wanted to scream. I wanted to kill. My resolve was slipping as the dark voices grew louder. They pounded inside my skull, wanting to be free, to destroy, and in this moment, I wanted it too. "You will let him go."

"Or what, my traitorous daughter?" he asked as his eyebrow rose.

"I will kill you." I bared my teeth at him.

"You will die trying. Have you learnt nothing? I cannot be killed."

"Many men in history have thought that and yet their bodies lay six feet under. *LET. HIM. GO!*" My magic was aching to be used, the darkness taking hold. Malignus smiled as Nik grimaced, but not out of pain. It was concern that filled our bond. Malignus stepped on Nik as he moved toward me. I walked closer. "Are you ready?" A hand touched my arm, shocking my body as I looked over.

"Move away, Larissa." Katrina's voice was filled with motherly love as she stroked my cheek. "I will always be with you." She turned back. "Roman, take her and don't look back. Do you understand me?" I watched as he pounded his chest with flaring yellow eyes.

"Mum—" She placed her finger against my lips.

"This is not your fight. Not yet. You will live a long and happy life, Larissa. Carry me in your heart."

"Mum, no." Roman grabbed my arm, but I yanked out his grasp. "NO!"

Malignus seized my face, and he dragged me closer. His eyes glowed, but I was not afraid. The evil seeped from his pores as it attempted to enter mine. I threw up a shield before allowing a fireball to leave my chest. It threw him across the room, slamming him into the wall. Roman caught me before I hit the floor.

"Even if you manage to leave, I will always be inside you, Larissa. Your blood is mine, your power is mine, and one day you will release the darkness a—"

A shot of bright light hit him square in the chest as Katrina threw another at him. "*GET HER OUT OF HERE!*" she yelled as she threw more and more at Malignus, while he attempted to fight back. I moved to help her, but Nik whisked me into his arms and over his shoulder.

"Nik, put me down. I have to save her," I begged, but he ignored me as Roman followed behind in his wolf form. "Nik, please. We cannot leave her." Sadness filled the bond between us. "She is your friend, my mother. We cannot let her die." My words were no longer comprehensible as I blubbered with emotion. My mother would die. I had just broken her cage, and she sacrificed herself for me. Again. "Nik." I pounded against his hard body before he collapsed. Roman took over, carrying Nik on one shoulder and me on the other. I wanted to say that I hated them, that we could have saved her, but I knew deep down it would never have been possible. It would have meant the end of us all, but I wished I had more time with her. The woman who discovered a way to break the curse, the secret only her grave knew.

CHAPTER 17
TIME TO GRIEVE

Larissa

SINCE DISCOVERING THE IDENTITY OF MY FATHER AND KNOWING that Katrina sacrificed herself, the woman who had all the answers, I lay in bed with the sheets cocooning me with warmth. I never wanted to move. It had been a few days since Nik and Roman saved me from Malignus. Spending just over a week in literal Hell was more than enough time.

Nik entered the room as he did every day with a smile. "Good morning, beautiful." I covered my face, hoping to drown him out. I just wanted to be alone, but he pulled the blanket off me. "It has been three days of you wallowing. It is time to get up and move on." I sat up and yanked the blanket back to cover myself.

"Go away, Nik," I grumbled, before laying down once again. He pulled it off with more force, using his supernatural strength. My own power bubbled, the lid to keep it contained had vanished. I had to learn my triggers and how to control it. My fingers sparked, ready for an attack. Nik noticed as his eyes shone red. He prepared himself, but the idea of harming him brought me back to reality. Tears welled in my eyes as I sobbed. "I am a literal monster. I am the daughter of the Devil and a black magic witch. I always believed I was a good person, but how can I be good when my parents are evil? I was born to break a curse; I have no other purpose in life."

Nik growled, clenching his fist. He was restraining his beast. Another growl entered the room, and Roman forcefully hit Nik in the back. I had not even noticed, but my emotions were being projected onto Nik causing him to lose control of his own demons. I ran to the bathroom. Every person around me could be in danger. There was no limit to what I could do. These powers were evil in every sense of the word. I locked the door and leant against it, sparks continuing to light my fingertips. I closed my eyes and breathed out as my heart thumped in my chest.

"Larissa?" Roman's soft voice brought a calmness, but I did not speak. I feared whatever came from my mouth. I heard Roman sigh and a soft thud on the door. I could feel his wolf on the other side, trying to give me comfort. His voice was barely a whisper. "You are not evil, Larissa. My wolf wants only to give you comfort, not tear you to pieces. Stop thinking you are something you are not."

The soft animalistic moan seeped through the door, and I smiled. I had hurt Roman, but he would always be a constant comfort for me. I did not speak, simply waited, tingles erupting over my body. Nik leant against the door, and my body yearned for his touch, his comfort, his need. He did not speak but rather sat and waited for me to be ready.

It was a few hours before I stood and showered. It had been days, and I was starting to smell. The water cooled the burn inside my body. Since the spell was gone, my body was continually warmed by the fire that lay dormant just beneath my skin. It brought comfort but felt like a curse. Arms wrapped around my waist, and I let my head fall onto Nik's chest. His touch calmed the constant buzzing in my body.

"I have you, Larissa, and I will always protect you." His love surrounded me, and it was all I wanted, but it would never erase the knowledge that I was evil incarnates daughter. How could I ever get past this? Katrina never told me why she did this, and I would never discover why because she was dead. Nik kissed my head. "What's going on in there?" he asked as he lathered his hands with soap and scrubbed my body. He would be able to feel the desire I had to scrub the evil from my body. At least him doing it would not cause me any harm.

"How do you live every day knowing you have a darkness inside you? Knowing you are the daughter of evil?" My voice quiet as I spoke the words that filled my head.

Nik growled as he grasped my face to look at him, his blue eyes piercing my soul. "You have never been evil. You fill me with light, Larissa. You give me purpose." I pushed his hands away in frustration, but he slammed me against the wall. My power sparked, ready to ignite this whole room. "The day I sensed you, I saw your magic. It was magnificent and I detected no darkness, only love." He kissed me, his passion, emotions, and pent-up tension from not being near me spilling out. I wrapped my arms around him to bring him closer. I wanted a release, but I could not bring myself to have sex. "Let me please you, let me give you a release." The way he could somewhat hear my thoughts through our bond terrified me. He pushed me harder against the wall, but I could not do it. I needed to sort my own head out, as much as I was dying to feel him touch every inch of me.

"Nik..."

He put his finger to my lips and stroked my face. "You do not need to say anything. We have a lifetime together. I can wait until you sort out whatever is going on in there." He tapped my head before kissing it, then he stepped out of the shower while I perved on his sexy arse. He chuckled as he glanced back and winked at me.

"Will you ever not be cocky?" I asked as he wrapped a towel around me, rubbing the droplets from my skin.

"When I look this good? Nope. Now get dressed. We are going on a trip. Something to cheer you up, I promise." I sighed as he walked out wearing his towel around his waist. I almost regretted my decision to not sleep with him, but it would only cause more confusion. I left the bathroom to see clothes laid out on the bed, a charcoal cotton wrap dress and a pair of tan boots with a brown cloak. He had style, it was undeniable. I lay down on the bed to stare at the ceiling. I could never tell Nik the truth. I was Liyana, reborn, not reincarnated.

Chapter 18

The Secrets of Butterflies

Nik

I could understand Larissa's struggle, having felt the same when I changed from a wolf to this beast. She believed her demon half made her evil, but I only saw her beauty, her light, her innocence. She walked down the stairs, light surrounding her. I wished she could see her as I did. Her discovery of magic had twisted her up inside. She needed to find the strength I knew she had, deep inside. I held Larissa's hand as we rode the elevator to the ground floor. Our bond tingled with apprehension. She worried about our destination, but I knew it would bring a smile to her face. I opened the door to the luxury Mercedes as she slid in and buckled herself. The engine roared to life as we drove through the city, and Larissa stared out the window in silence. I could sense she needed time to process, my presence giving her comfort. We arrived at the Horniman Butterfly House, Larissa only noticing as I parked the car.

She looked at me. "Why are we here?"

I scratched my chin as I turned to see her properly. "I want you to understand that you are not evil."

She scoffed and motioned to the building before us. "Nik, how is this supposed to prove anything?"

I needed her open to this otherwise it would not work. I cleared my throat and put my hand on her leg, staring into her green eyes that were filled with so much confusion. "In every culture, there are stories about animals and their ability to sense whether a human is good or evil. There has always been a belief that butterflies have the same ability. Which is why they will land on some people and not others. I brought you here to prove to you that you are not evil." I could sense her body relax, opening up to the idea. I took her hand and brought it to my lips. "If you wish to leave, I will drive us back home."

"You brought us out here, we may as well explore. You have not really taken me on more than one date." A cheeky grin spread over her face. *There's my girl.* I opened the door and ran to her side to help her out, and she wrapped her arm around mine. While I bought tickets, she walked around the foyer, reading various signage, unaware that I had booked out the entire venue for the day to ensure we had privacy. I worried if I said the wrong thing, it could spiral her power. I had already called Sophia to beg for her help, which was beneath me, but I would do whatever I needed to ensure Larissa's safety. This time was different, but I couldn't explain how. I just felt it. The receptionist glanced at Larissa before her eyes trailed over me, and I smirked as her desire filled my nose. No woman could resist a god, but I enjoyed the stroke to my ego. Larissa cleared her throat, jealousy filling our bond. I snorted as I peered over my shoulder at her.

"The only eyes that still entrance me to this day are yours." The receptionist's young plump face fell, but I slid an extra hundred across the table toward her for the trouble.

I spun around and watched Larissa's every move. She bent over to read with a small smile on her face. Joy filled our bond, and I knew I had made the right decision. I wrapped my arms around her waist as she stood and kissed the back of her neck. My desire surged as I remembered all the times I had feasted on her while I fucked her from behind. The hardest part of her lack of memories was that I remembered her every weakness and where the best spots to seduce and distract her were. She barely knew anything other than who I was now. She chuckled before turning to face me, her lips meeting mine. Fuck, I loved this woman more than reason.

I took her hand and led her into the garden. The fresh smells of watered plants and wet dirt hit my nose. To humans, this was a pleasant smell, but for me, it was dreadful. Larissa's energy shifted, having calmed. I spun her in a circle and allowed her to fall into my arms, her laugh filling the space and warming my heart. I kissed her as I fought the need for more.

"I haven't seen any butterflies yet." I moved her hair from her face, her skin glowing with happiness.

"I need you to close your eyes and relax." She breathed out deeply as I watched her chest rise and fall, grateful her chest was covered, or I may have taken her in that moment.

"I am relaxed," she muttered with her eyes still closed.

"We both know you never relax. They can sense stress or apprehension, so stop the brain and just fill yourself with happy thoughts." The bond shifted as she did as I instructed, her eyes remained closed, and butterflies started to fly about. I removed her coat and put it on the closest chair. As I spun back toward her, butterflies had landed on her arms and head. I smiled. "Open your eyes, beautiful." She opened one eye at a time before a grin appeared.

"Nik, no way. You were not lying." Her eyes were the brightest I had ever seen.

"I never lie to you. I may omit certain truths, but I refuse to lie to you." I walked over and took her hands in mine as butterflies landed on me.

"But how?"

"I may be a monster, but it does not define who I am." I paused to take in how she looked. "You are a rose, perfect in every way. My *golden* rose."

"Roses have thorns, Nik," she said as a butterfly landed in her hair and lost its balance.

"Exactly, because sometimes, even perfection can cut you. You are the rose I would bleed for. A rose I would do anything for." I stroked her cheek, feeling the warmth of her skin on my fingers.

"Nik, there is one problem with your theory. I never said I was evil, just that this power is evil and can make me that."

"Tap into that magic, let the dark magic in only slightly."

"Nik, I cannot control it. What happens if—" I pressed my finger to her lips.

"I trust you. I could feel how you focused on love that day; our love." She closed her eyes as the bond strengthened between us, her power flowing freely. The butterflies did not move. "Open your eyes, Larissa." Her fear filled the bond, her worry. "Trust me." Her bright eyes found mine before they ran to her arms.

"Oh my God, Nik. They have not moved." Tears ran down her perfect cheeks and over her tiny freckle. I waved my arms to remove the butterflies and pulled her into me.

"You have never been, nor will you ever be evil, Larissa. You are my light, my reason to breathe, my love, my everything. We will learn to control your powers, and we will live a happy and long life together." She sobbed in my arms as I held her close. I never wanted her too far from where I was. I rejected the idea of losing her to this curse. She was *mine*.

CHAPTER 19
TIME TO GET OUT OF THE FUNK

Larissa

Nik was trying his best to get me out of this funk. Mainly over the limbo of what my future was going to hold. I was a half-demon, half-witch reincarnated thing. I sat in the penthouse and watched the day move slowly by. Since yesterday, I had less apprehension about being evil, but it still lingered in my mind.

Nik came out of his office and threw a dress at me. "Put it on, we are going out," he ordered in his stern voice that meant I should not question him.

"Nik, just stop, please," I mumbled as I ran my fingers through the silk dress.

"No, this is my last attempt to pull you out of this funk, get dressed. We are going to a vampire club."

He walked up the stairs, and I followed not long after him. I stood before the mirror and picked up the curler, fixing my hair. My makeup was easy, simple, with dark eyes to bring out the colour. I turned toward the dress and slid into it. The black fabric clung to my body, showing off my every curve. The long sleeves made it look elegant despite the length and the fact that it was backless to just above my behind. Nik picked it on purpose, no doubt. Simple yet sophisticated. I picked a pair of golden heels and paired them with thick gold hoops. I glided down the stairs to see Nik pacing on the phone, wearing black jeans and a sleeveless, buttoned blue top. His tanned, muscular arms were on full display, and I could not help but ogle him. It made sense, considering he was the son of a god. He stopped pacing and sniffed the air before turning his eyes toward me.

"We shall speak later." He hung up abruptly. We had not been intimate since my kidnapping, and the monster was here. He stalked my every move like prey, his desire coursed through our bond. It was overpowering, and I wanted to feel his touch, but I needed more time.

"Nik, I...I..." He sighed deeply, understanding as he hung his head for a moment.

"I know, Larissa. I am a patient man." I could not stop myself from laughing. Between every life we shared, he had been patient.

"Well, I am one in a million."

He put his arms around my waist and held me close. "One of a kind. Nobody compares to you."

The little voice in my head whispered, *"You were never supposed to meet."* I could not stop hearing those words from Katrina. It was never part of the plan, but someone had been behind Elizabeth's death; someone wanted me to find Nik. It was not Roman, but I prayed I would discover the answer one day. Nik's face grew concerned. I had not told him. I knew he would sense my lies, but I could not bring myself to tell him.

I plastered on a smile. "I am just nervous about tonight." I knew he would not believe me, but it was worth a shot. I gave him a quick kiss on the lips. "Who knows, maybe you will get lucky." I winked at him to try to lighten the mood, but he pulled back. His forehead creased, which was never a good sign.

"Wait." He paused and rubbed his neck. I could feel his worry.

"What is it?" The fear grew after I asked, and I knew he would sense it. "Nik," I put my hand on his face, "you can tell me."

"I want you to drink my blood," he whispered, avoiding looking in my direction.

"Ah..."

"Before you say no, I've explained to you before that the more of my blood in your system, the more I can feel you. If something were to happen, I want to be able to find you, unlike earlier. Yes, Malignus had charms up, but I could feel you because some blood still lingered. Please, can you have some?" I shuddered at the thought. I had never outright tasted him because he had always put it on a cut, or I had been unconscious. "I'll hide it in something, so you will barely taste it."

"Fine," I said begrudgingly. He smiled and walked to the kitchen, then mixed a cocktail and handed it to me. It was still red. "Could you not have changed the colour?" I grimaced and lifted the glass to my lips, noticing Nik's eyes flare and his teeth appear. He was enjoying this way too much. I closed my eyes and sculled it. I was not taking any chances and wanted it to be finished. Surprisingly, it tasted like a simple margarita. "That was delicious."

He sniggered at my comment. "That was all me." He fixed his collar in a cocky manner.

"That's gross!"

"And you loved it."

"Alright, don't let it go to your head. Are you ready?" He kissed my cheek and sniffed my neck before a growl vibrated through his chest.

"Yes, you smell like mine."

"Your possessiveness needs to come down a notch."

"That will never happen." He pulled me into his chest and moved the hair from my face. "You are the reason I breathe." Those words echoed once again, "*You were never supposed to meet.*" I shook it off.

"Let's go, Mr Dankworth," I said as I walked towards the elevator.

"It's *Lord* Dankworth."

"Does that make me a lady?" He chuckled as he pulled me close to his body.

The car ride was quiet, and I had to stop myself from looking over at him. Despite the limbo I was in, I could not stop myself from admiring just how sexy he was—the tanned skin, the dark hair, the blue eyes I melted over, his muscular physique. I bit my lip thinking of the few times he had touched me, and a growl filled the car. I cleared my throat. It was not a warning to me but towards his driver, whose fangs had descended. I sat up straighter, thinking of how Malignus had caused a fracture between us. I did not know how to overcome it.

We arrived, and Nik came around to open the door for me. The cameras flashed continually as he held me close and ignored the questions from the paparazzi. Everyone knew who I was now, and there was no way to avoid being his mate and eventually marrying per the council's instructions. I should have been used to having no control in my life from Mum, but I yearned for freedom. Nik squeezed me tighter, this bond between us a curse. I could not hide anything from him. I returned the squeeze as the lights dimmed and the music pumped. My senses were sharper with Nik's blood in my system and it made this place light up. I could feel the vibrations through everyone's body, it was electric. I shivered.

"Nothing like it, is there?" I shook my head as he took me upstairs to the VIP lounge. We spoke to several other vampires and humans, and I watched with intrigue at how they openly fed and the euphoric faces of the humans. They looked at peace or high, it was strange. Nik stayed close to my side the entire time.

"I need to use the bathroom." His eyes flashed before he scanned the crowd.

"Malignus cannot find me. It is just a wee." He escorted me to the door and waited. I stared in the mirror, my eyes were brighter, and my hair was shiny, an effect of the blood. Nik pulled for me, and my body ached for his touch. I put my hands on the sink as the sensation worked through me. I hated this need for him that I could not shake. I walked out and took his hand, deciding I would dance away this frustration. I had to do something with the excess energy and sexual desire, and those words that would not stop whispering to me.

CHAPTER 20
YOU WERE NEVER SUPPOSED TO MEET

Nik

Her smell was intoxicating. I could feel how badly she wanted it, but I didn't want to push her. She held a secret, something that happened with Malignus. I didn't wish to push her further away, so I would be patient. I had to be, and I would wait for her to be ready again.

She left the bathroom and dragged me to the dance floor. Her sexual desire leaked from her body, and my fangs were out and dying to sink into her. My cock was hard and uncomfortable in my tight pants. These were the days I missed togas. She swayed her body against me, every movement driving my own need further. I ran my hands up and down her side, all the supernatural creatures could smell her. Not just her desire, but the power she emanated. She didn't realise just how powerful she was. The daughter of a coven leader and a demon. It was never going to be good. I noticed the entire mood of the room change; everyone was grinding on one another. She had not meant to, but she had projected her feelings onto others. I held her closer. I wanted her to have my blood more for the fact that it would warn others away. My scent covered her, my mate, mine. The beat changed as she ground harder against me, and I struggled to contain the monster inside.

"Larissa, you need to stop." She laughed and leant her head against my chest. Her neck was in full view, with her veins pulsing at me. I needed relief of any kind. This was torture. My teeth throbbed as my monster beat against my skull, needing to taste her in whatever way she would give me. She rubbed her body up and down, and when a growl escaped my chest, she laughed. She was tipsy; I could feel it through the bond. She knew what she was doing, but I did not want to force her. The monster wanted her beyond reason.

"I need blood." I nodded to security to watch her as I moved to my office. I slammed the door, unzipping my pants for relief and opening the fridge. I kept it warm, so the blood could be consumed instantly. I ripped open the bag and poured it down my throat. I did not care for a cup, needing my fill now. "Fuck." As I threw it down and grabbed another, I could feel her coming. I smashed another three bags before she arrived, and my eyes found her instantly. They would have been flashing red, and she turned her head curiously. She wasn't scared, as she had been in the past. Her emotions were dark, and she tried to hide them. She didn't know what she wanted.

Her own eyes flashed red as she walked over. "Have you ever had anyone drink from you?" I stalked her every move, the rise of her chest, the shortness of that dress giving me a peak at what I desperately wanted.

"Yes, in your past lives." Her face flinched. She did not like hearing about the past since being held captive.

"What about Liyana?" I shook my head, she never mentioned Liyana, her first life.

"No, we did not understand our powers as such. Before she turned, I fed from her and it became our norm, even after the transition. What is it, Larissa?" Her eyes flashed again, and she flicked the lock to the door with a mischievous smile on her face.

"I assume this is soundproof?"

I raised an eyebrow at her. "Yes." Her heart pounded, not from fear but from exhilaration. It was driving me crazy.

"The worst part of this bond is I can feel the surge of power when you drink, and it is intoxicating." She ran her finger along the wall; the monster was holding himself back. She stood before me and lifted my finger, putting it in her mouth and biting down. My blood spilt into her mouth. She smiled and licked her lips before she shook. I could no longer hold back, needing to be inside her.

"Larissa, I want to be clear about something. If you leave now, nothing shall happen. But if you decide to stay, I will bend you over this desk and fuck you till the morning." Her eyes sparkled, the alcohol giving her courage. Her desire increased. I couldn't do this, I shouldn't. She was still trying to figure herself out. She moved closer and put her hands on my chest, her touch making my body ache for more. I wished she would drag them down and take my cock in her hand.

"Do not utter words you cannot fulfil." Her words unleashed the beast, and I crashed against her mouth. She didn't pull back or fight me, instead pushing harder. Her magic surrounded us, light and filled with love. I had never experienced this sensation. Her kiss took me to a level I had never known possible. As I stood back, her eyes glowed green, and I knew she felt it. She smiled and grabbed my top, ripping the buttons and running her fingers along my abs.

Her fingers found my zip already down. "Oh, really?" She looked down and licked her lips before glancing up again. I was starving for more as I kissed her again, deciding the dress was staying on and sliding my hand down and inside her underwear.

"Nik," she moaned, throwing her head back and revealing her throat. I was dying to feast on her. I ran my teeth along her neck, and she shivered with delight.

"One day, I will fuck and feed from you. But not today." I spun her around and pressed her against my desk. I plunged my fingers back inside her, and she groaned before a quick release. She was so easy to please. She came another two times before I dropped my pants and thrust inside her. Her pussy was perfect, her tightness clenching my cock harder. My eyes rolled back. This girl was something else. It had never felt this pure, this amazing. It was like our souls united as one. Her every breath was my own. She took it all and wanted more, the perfect mate.

"Nik, please." This moan was different, so I slowed as I pulled out of her. I turned her to see what it was. I felt it before she even uttered the words, her eyes avoided my gaze, and she bit her lip.

"What is it?" She needed to say it. I had to hear her say the words.

"I want to feel it," she whispered, her shyness filling the bond.

"Larissa, are you sure?"

"Yes, I want to be yours." I lifted her back onto the desk and placed myself directly at her entrance, waiting as I moved her hair to the side.

I kissed her lips and dressed myself quickly. "I won't do this here. We shall return home to finish this. It is an intimate act, and I would prefer you to be comfortable. Hold on." I pulled her close and whisked her from the room as I rushed us home to the penthouse.

The entire flight home, her laughter filled my ears. This was Larissa, the woman I loved, my mate. The one who found joy in the smallest things. I landed quickly as her grip loosened, and I forced her close against my body. She buried her head into my chest before glancing up, those green eyes taking my breath away.

"You are perfection, Larissa Solis." She stood back, taking my hand and leading me inside the penthouse. She removed her dress, throwing it to the floor. She stood before me naked; the alcohol may have given her courage, but she wanted this. I lifted her onto the dining table as I moved her hair to see her neck, the vein throbbing to be bitten, dying to feel my teeth sink into its flesh.

"At any time—" She put her finger over my lips.

"Shh." She stroked my face and put her finger against my tooth, cutting it slightly. It tasted surreal; her blood was so pure it electrified my senses. I threw my head back and growled before sinking my teeth into her flesh. She moaned as I thrust back inside her. My mate was perfection, she gave whatever she could before her body could give no more. There was no question that she was mine. She could not escape our bond now. The thought of claiming her drove me harder, thrusting deeper inside her. I wanted to claim every inch of her body, her moans growing louder, driving my own need further. The sounds were all mine. The body and tight pussy were mine. I licked my lips to taste her sweet blood. It tasted so perfect, so *her*. I never wanted to resist it again. I climaxed as she did and licked the wound to heal it. Words echoed in my head; the voice was clear. Katrina. *"You were never supposed to meet."*

"Why is Katrina saying those words?"

She froze. "What words?"

The secret she had been hiding, the one I felt since the day I rescued her. Now I had her blood, we would never be able to keep anything from one another. She was mine and I was hers until our last breath.

CHAPTER 21

I DID NOT WANT TO HURT YOU

Larissa

THE WORDS THAT HAUNTED ME, THE WORDS I BURIED, THE WORDS I never wanted him to hear and yet they came out of his mouth. The secret I was not ready to tell hung between us. I didn't know how to respond. I stood staring at him as he dressed himself, my perfect mate, but I could not tell him.

"Larissa!" My skin crawled with his annoyance; this was new. I guessed drinking my blood only made our bond stronger.

"Yes, Nik." I batted my eyes, my skin crawling at my failed attempt at seduction. He remained focused on those words. "You need a warning label," I mumbled.

He smirked. "I was hoping you would get your memories back." I winced internally; it would never happen. "What do you know?" He eyed me suspiciously, and I sighed, pulling the chair out for him.

"Katrina found a way to break the curse. I am not the reincarnated version like the others. I will never get any memories because…I am Liyana. I am her. Reborn in the twenty-first century." His fist clenched, his anger was palpable, and it was affecting my buzz from the alcohol.

"Explain, NOW!"

"You preserved her DNA. Katrina found it and with Malignus's sperm, she cast a spell to rebirth her. I will never have any memories because I—she has been born again. Malignus tried to torture me with memories, but I only felt Liyana's death, not her vampire death and not every death after. Only hers. She figured out how to break the curse." His face remained neutral, but his insides were churning with rage.

"Why is that saying in your blood?"

"That I don't know, but since she said those words, they are all I can hear. We were never supposed to meet. She designed it for me to live a full life without ever meeting you. It's why she hid me that day when you visited her. It's why Roman watched me grow up. We were never supposed to meet."

"Fate had other ideas," he scoffed. He had a low opinion of the gods, but I supposed if his mother was cast out, I could not blame him.

"Fate or someone else. I still do not know how Mum died. She knew, as did Luce. I'm starting to think there is more to Mum's death. The timing is too perfect. Luce was about to leave for London, so why not go with her?"

He stroked his chin in contemplation. "The offer at the marketing company. Why did Sara and Andrew hire you?"

"Hey, I *am* skilled." I was offended by his comment.

"Yes, but you had no experience, so why?" He was right. Had someone been manipulating us this whole time? "Malignus?" he asked, scratching his chin.

I shook my head. "He only knew I existed once I almost died, and you gave me your blood and I gained almost full access to my magic. He felt my heart, my power. Nik, I think someone did it to get rid of you. It is all I keep coming back to." I took the business card out of my pocket and put it beside him.

"Richard gave this to me before Luce and I left for London." He slid his hand over to inspect his business card with a tiny smirk on his lips.

"Richard knew who you were. That money was from me, but I didn't know it. He said he needed a loan, and he wanted to tell me something, but I answered abruptly, which caused him to end the call." He scrunched the card, there was silence between us. He sighed. "There is another reincarnation coming, isn't there?"

I shrugged. "Strong possibility of that. You would feel it. We are fated mates, we are bonded, but it was never supposed to happen. All I know is that Katrina said we were never supposed to meet."

He shook his head. "Tell me about the day of your mother's death, the explosion. I feel it is connected somehow." He shuffled in his chair, lifting his leg over the other and holding it, his eyes focusing intently on my every movement.

"I woke up and went for a run like I normally did. Mum had put balloons in my room and Luce had pissed her off, telling her she was planning on leaving. I knew it would end in an argument. I cut my finger on the latch as I walked inside, and I forgot to clean it. Richard reminded me later in the day about it when I was at work. I came home to see Luce and Mum fighting; Luce came outside after running out of the house. I watched as Mum returned to the kitchen before her face filled with fear and the house exploded. The fire did not burn me, a shield protected me, which I have always assumed was the start of my magic making its appearance. I went to the hospital and that was it."

"Something doesn't add up. How big was the cut? Did it bleed?"

"Only a little, not much. Maybe a drop of blood. Why?"

"Katrina spelled you to keep you safe from me, to ensure I couldn't find or sense you. I believe Elizabeth did the same and I am thinking that maybe whoever is pulling the strings finally found you when your blood hit the air. Did you have many cuts before then?"

I thought back to all the times I grew up and realised I never had. My mouth dropped open in shock. I had a literal bubble around me my whole life to protect me, but it was not just from Nik. "Nik, I-I...No, I never had another cut before." The realisation hit me that somebody else may have been pulling the strings since the day my mother died. Who had enough power to bend my life at their will, and for what gain?

"I need air." He stormed from the room. I went to chase him but stopped, knowing it was a lot to process and he would need time. I texted Roman the details about what had happened and sat down. The girl Nik loved was supposed to be hidden from him. That was a betrayal he would not accept. He never had in the past, so why would it change now?

I dragged myself upstairs to shower and get ready for bed. Nik needed space. I could sense his anger, his love, and his confusion. Having full access to my magic terrified me because there was no limit to what I could do. I did not think Katrina truly considered the ramifications of demon blood and witch blood. I sighed. I could never leave Nik, and he would never leave me. I wished Katrina had told me. Leaving her behind was torture. She did evil things, but she did not deserve that end. The thought rolled around in my head; the thought that terrified me. The curse would end with my death.

Nik came home in the early hours of the morning. I glanced at the clock as he snuck into the room, noting it was five o'clock. His emotions were still heightened from hearing those words from Katrina. He slid into the bed and wrapped his arms around me before smelling the crook of my neck, groaning in delight.

"All mine," he whispered as he took another sniff. "I know you are awake."

I rolled to look at him. "Are you alright?" I touched his face, and he closed his eyes as he leant into my hand.

"No, Roman is coming. We need to talk about this some more. For now, I just need you." He held me tighter, as he tried to process what I said. Even I did not understand it exactly. His breathing stilled. I touched my forehead to his before kissing him.

"Nik?" I had to say this before I lost the courage.

"Yes."

"I am sorry I kept it from you."

He sat up moving the hair from my face to see my eyes. "I understand why. You wanted to know and understand. You were processing. I realised once I left that you are not like Liyana and the others. A piece of her disappeared every time she returned. She became more dependent on me, more unsure of herself. The curse took pieces of her every time she came back. You are strong and fierce. You have the courage that...even Liyana did not have. I forgot that. It has been so long. I have seen civilisations rise and fall, the best and worst of humanity." He sighed. "I forgot just how much has changed. You have a light, a purity, a strength unlike anything. You are not her and there is no comparison. I have been living with the idea of her for so long, I had forgotten who she was. Liyana was strong but she never had the choice that you did. She never had the voice, and Katrina gave you that."

I giggled as I rolled to sit in his lap. His eyes lingered on my breasts, and my body ached for his touch. He ran his hands up and down my back, knowing just what I needed without ever having been asked.

"And I still picked you." I kissed his neck, taking a little nip of it.

"That's not what I mean," he grumbled.

"I know. I just wanted to lighten the intensity of the conversation."

He sniggered. "Alright, cheeky, let me get you some food. I am sure you are tired."

"No, I feel amazing. I thought you drinking from me would make me exhausted or depleted but honestly, I feel stronger." His brows drew closer together.

"I don't think Katrina thought about this." He ran his fingers through his hair as worry flooded our bond.

"We shall never know. She will be dead now. Malignus would not allow her to live a second time." Nik winced; guilt replaced the worry. He cared for Katrina, and based on the stories, they had known each other for a while.

"Hey, it isn't your fault."

"I should have known he would—"

"He would what? Keep her captive? You thought she was dead. You couldn't have known he had a spell cast over her. That was probably why he sent you to her. He knew and wanted her to be his magical slave. I pity the next witch who falls under his charms." I rubbed against his body, and he bit my lower lip. "Roman just got here." I groaned at the interruption.

"I am going to shower." I stood making my way to the bathroom. "I shall have pancakes, please, and coffee with—"

"Larissa" His tone was stern. He already knew my order. I lifted my nightie over my head and winked at him.

"Enjoy the view." I knew he would not while his brother was here. He respected him too much.

Feeling refreshed, I waltzed down the stairs, never having felt so much energy in my body. My magic brimmed with excitement. Roman looked up, as attractive as ever. Tall, broody, muscular, rugged. The two were polar opposites but both sexy as hell or heaven. That, I could not decide. I glanced between them before picturing them naked. I shook it away, but it was too late, they sniffed the air. Roman's eyes glowed golden yellow and Nik's grew brighter.

My cheeks flushed with embarrassment. "Don't ask," I said as I reached the bottom step and went for a pancake.

Roman laughed. "It was both, wasn't it?" Nik's eyes snapped at Roman, warning him to keep his mouth shut.

"Do I want to know if you guys have shared her?" They both smiled, and I got my answer. I clicked my tongue. "Well, this got awkward really fast." I cut into the pancake, popping it into my mouth. It tasted divine. Nik had two distinct skills, sex and cooking. I knew which one I preferred.

Chapter 22
My Own Secrets

Roman

Even after centuries, no beauty had ever compared to hers. Despite living as long as I had, I still had not found my mate. It was a commonality between vampires and wolves, but when your brother became the first ever vampire after transitioning from a wolf and had already found his mate, it made sense. I became friends with Liyana before they met. I watched her walk through the market, shopping. Her husband abused her, but shopping made her forget that and gave her freedom. She hated him, especially since her parents sold her to him. She was a princess of sorts; her family had money, but they used her as a bargaining tool for more power. Her husband wanted the perfect pretty wife and children, and she yearned to be a mother. Her smile drew me closer, her eyes taking in the food, the trinkets, the jewels and more importantly, the people. She was magnetic and people wanted to be around her. She had never lost that in any of her lives. The pull people felt in her presence. She dropped her coin purse, and I picked it up, still remembering her smile and her sweet words.

"And who is this?" I grinned, which made her eyes sparkle. I spent every day walking through the market with her. Nik grew suspicious and would question my whereabouts, but I prayed I would hear the mate calling with her. The day Nik decided to join me, I saw it happen. The instant connection between them. They stared into each other's eyes and walked toward one another. It was clear they both felt it. Liyana and I were drawn to one another in a different way. We had our own bond, but her mate was my twin. We would have always been friends. Even so, I regretted the day they met and wished it never happened. I should have fought harder to keep them apart. My brother loved her so much, so unconditionally, that he sold his soul for her, not caring about the repercussions.

"Roman?" Fingers snapped before my face and I looked at Larissa, the same smile spread over her beautiful face.

"Where did you go?"

I shook my head. "Honestly, I was thinking about the first time I met you. Sorry, Liyana."

Her laughter filled the room and brought a sense of calm over Nik and me.

"Yes, it is a little confusing. That is what we need to talk about." Nik cleared his throat as he cooked breakfast and made coffee. I was about to break my brother's heart, but I had no choice. I wanted him happy, that was all I cared about. It was Katrina's idea.

"I don't care for your name, I only care that you are mine." She threw a pen at him. She adored Nik. I cleared my throat, to steer the conversation in the right direction.

"What are we discussing?"

Larissa went pale and breathed out. "What did Katrina tell you?" Straight to the point.

"She told me she figured out how to break the curse. She had brought you back, but you had to be kept secret from Nik. I didn't question it, I—"

"Why not, brother?" His tone was blunt and filled with frustration.

"I wanted you happy and Katrina believed you could finally get your happy ending." He didn't answer, but Larissa reached over and squeezed my hand with reassurance. "She made me promise that if anything were to ever happen to her, I would look out for her. Elizabeth took her in, she was told the truth about how important Larissa was. Richard and Valerie were made aware too. It was all to keep her away from you. On the night of her death, the noise in the cupboard was Larissa, but I couldn't risk you finding out. The mate bond would have kicked in. It wasn't what Katrina wanted."

My brother paced the room. "WHAT?!" Nik was barely keeping control of the beast.

"I keep hearing Katrina saying, *'You were never supposed to meet,'*" Larissa explained, filling the gaps in my knowledge, but that did not deter my brother's anger.

"What the hell was Katrina's plan? Why did you go along with it? You watched her grow up, and you dated her. Isn't that against what Katrina wanted?"

"Nik, it is complicated." I rubbed the back of my neck, my wolf growing anxious from the change in energy. I could feel him pacing in my head.

"Explain it, Roman," Nik demanded. Larissa shook from the amount of emotion flowing through their bond.

"I was spelled to keep her safe. I dated her because you know I have always loved her, and I wanted her to know love outside of you." Nik growled. "Don't misinterpret that. It was my intention before she met you." He moved closer; Larissa's eyes were trained on him, and they weren't filled with love. "Katrina spelled Malignus to sleep with her. She laced her DNA with Liyana to create a baby. She wanted her to have magic, to have power."

"But why? You are hiding something." Larissa stood and moved closer to Nik, most likely feeling his anger as she touched his arm.

"Nik," she warned, but he yanked his arm away, turning to her but glaring at me.

"Don't start, he does this. He hides stuff from me, always. I won't tolerate it anymore." Larissa's magic seeped from her as she prepared herself.

"I am NOT hiding anything else. Katrina found a way to break the curse, and she wanted Larissa kept away from you. She said you were not to meet. Larissa was supposed to die an old lady in her bed." Nik charged at me but before his fist landed on my face, it stopped.

"Larissa," he snarled at her as she held up a shield to protect me.

"You said you would listen. You are not! Roman has told us everything. We were not supposed to meet, get over it. We have, and now the curse will not be broken." I flinched, and she noticed as her eyes flashed between her bright green to brilliant red.

"Roman?" she queried after my earlier action.

"She said it was to help break it because she didn't trust that Nik could do his part to stop the curse." My brother relaxed but she kept the shield up. I could feel her love radiating from it, and I smiled. She was more beautiful than all the previous versions.

Nik's head snapped at her. "What are you hiding?"

She lowered the shield, feeling that Nik had calmed. "Do not take that tone with me," she warned him, pointing her finger towards my brother.

"Those I love are keeping things from me. I believe the tone is warranted."

"I believe you are an arsehole, but I still love you. Now stop." Her magic surrounded the room, and she shook her head to bring it back under control. Nik moved closer, taking her hand and planting a soft kiss on it. "I believe she mated with Malignus because her spell was dark magic. It is why this power does not feel natural. It is hard to explain. I don't know her exact thoughts but when he was torturing me with my previous deaths, I only felt Liyana's, not any of the others."

"Wait, what?" I questioned. How was that possible?

"I do not know how or why, but she mentioned that history needed to repeat itself. I do not understand it exactly because I have no memories of that. I am certain she brought James back for a reason."

"I need a drink." Nik's fangs descended as his eyes stalked Larissa, and her own eyes flashed. They fed from one another.

"I'll give you space." The chair squeaked against the marble floor as I stood.

"Roman," she called. I turned with a smile. "Don't go far, please."

"I promise." Larissa could ask anything of me, and I would do it. She would always own a piece of my heart.

Blood sharing was intimate and always ended with them having sex. I rode the elevator to the ground floor; the wolf gave Nik stamina so it would be a while. We both weren't five-minute lovers, a blessing and a curse. We could give a woman immense pleasure, but human women would tire. They were more loving than wolves, who were rough. I chuckled as I walked to a local café; it was small and quaint. The wooden interior gave a fresh forest smell, the tables were white and metallic and bounced off the oak-coloured wood. It felt cosy but that could have been from my sheer size. I was not small. Nik and I may have been twins, but I towered over him even as wolves. It was why he threw the fight for one of us to rule.

"What's your poison?" the cute blonde server asked, her hazel eyes sparkling as she looked over my body. I leant on the counter towards her.

"You look to be poisonous. Maybe I should have a drink from you." She blushed. Finding a girl was easy but once they knew the real me, it always ended badly. Nik had to come in and compel them to forget before it got as bad as it did during the Salem witch trials. That was a story for another day.

"I finish in two hours."

"Well, today is my lucky day. I'll have a tropical juice on ice to go please." I winked at her, smelling her desire waft in the air.

"Sure thing, handsome." A familiar chuckle echoed behind me, and I smiled knowing who it was.

"You always were smooth." Larissa stood, glowing from the feed and the light surrounding her from behind. She appeared angelic and pure.

"That was quicker than I expected." I glanced at my watch; it had barely been ten minutes since I left.

"Why? It was just a feed." I never understood how she seemed so different to the others.

"When did that start?"

She looked away almost ashamed. "Last night, it just happened, and, well..."

"Larissa, you know that deepens the bond between you." She threw her arms up in frustration as she shook her head.

"I *don't* know anything, but my body was craving it. It's hard to explain" I walked over and put my hands on her shoulder, squeezing them gently. I chuckled at her. "Why are you laughing at me? That's not fair Roman." She was something else.

"I'm sorry. It makes me laugh how you talk."

"What is wrong with how I speak?" she asked putting her hands on her hips as I snorted.

"It's so formal. Are you aware you do not use contractions often? Rarely ever." She paused to think about it. "It makes sense now, knowing that you are the real Liyana, the soul born before they were really ever used. I think they only became popular shortly after you died. The first time." She opened her mouth to speak. "Yeah, I should have noticed it and put the puzzle together sooner, but it all makes sense now."

She playfully pushed my arm while shaking her head. "Can we get back to the topic of conversation?"

"What was that again?" I asked her as my pineapple juice was called up.

"Drinking each other's blood."

"Ah, that's right. I get it, it is fine. It's just..."

"You are hiding something" A sliver of her magic escaped as all the patrons snapped their heads in my direction.

"Wait, you can control others." I took her hand and left the store.

"Roman, I have no idea what I am capable of. Do not avoid my question."

"I truly am not sure, but if Katrina didn't want you to meet, I believe it has something more to do with Nik than you. I think it is because he chose to save you despite your protests. He has to let you go and if he never knew you existed, it would be possible. But now that he does, neither of you will be able to be parted. You can't stop a connection that strong." She sighed, dropping her head toward the floor.

"I had the same thought, but we really will never know. Katrina is dead and I will be one day as well." I lifted her chin to look at me, her eyes as bright as ever.

"It won't happen. This time is different, I can feel it." I thumped my chest, certain in my belief that I wasn't wrong. She was something else and it wasn't just the magic. I wasn't sure how else to explain it but this time, she was stronger. She buried her head into my chest, wrapping her arms around my body.

"Never make promises you cannot keep, Roman." Her voice was barely a whisper as she held her body tighter against my own. My wolf responded, wanting to comfort her, to rub himself all over her.

"I never have," I muttered into her hair and kissed it softly. It didn't matter if she wasn't mine. I would always love her.

"Roman, I have to ask this. I have to know the truth. Why did you let me go so easily?"

I exhaled. "You were my brother's mate. We have our own bond, with Nik being my twin. We will always be close, and I know you have always loved me. Every time you picked me, it never lasted. Your love for Nik has always been too strong. I am happy with the knowledge that you will always be in my life."

"I love you, Roman."

"I will always love you, Larissa Solis."

CHAPTER 23

A ROOM OF MEMORIES

Larissa

THE CONVERSATION BETWEEN NIK, ROMAN, AND I WENT nowhere, so I sent Roman home. After dissecting it over and over, we only knew two things: I was Liyana in the twenty-first century, and Nik and I were never supposed to meet in this life. We had no idea how to break the curse or if what Katrina did managed to break it. I buried myself in work to avoid thinking about my possible impending death. Nik refused to tell me how long I lived in each life, and when I asked Roman, he simply did not answer. I hated this limbo of not knowing anything.

Nik had designed a study for me in his mansion and told me to consider it *our* house, but it only reminded me of a past that no longer existed. The girl he thought would return and not the original. I put work aside, pulling out Elizabeth's grimoire and I slowly learnt how our family came into their magic. They were one of the oldest magical families in history, managing to survive the witch trials. All magic came from the earth, Mother Earth. She imbued it to any person who she thought deserved it. According to the grimoire, our family were farmers. We grew plants for food and medicine, which we used to help any person who needed it, and as such, we were rewarded with powers. Magic to manipulate anything that came from her. It was filled with warnings about how dangerous this power could be, and how it must never fall into the wrong hands. It was only passed down to one female within that bloodline. I contemplated how Elizabeth managed to have control of this power when it should have never been passed to her. My future child…I slammed the grimoire shut and threw it across the room. A child, an impossible idea.

My phone rang and I glanced to see Nik's name flash across the screen. This fucking bond. "I am fine," I answered, giving him a blunt tone, not wanting to talk about it.

"Are you sure?" His voice was filled with concern.

"Nik, sometimes there are moments when I don't wish to discuss things, and this is one of them."

"Larissa, you cannot shut me out."

"I'm not. I just…I cannot do this over the phone." How could I have a conversation telling him how I loved him, but I would never have the life I truly wanted?

"I will be home soon. We shall discuss this." I hung up on him as I made my way down the stairs and into the grand kitchen. I pulled a glass from the cupboard and opened a bottle of red wine. Nik entered; his eyes focused on my movements. He removed his navy suit jacket and rolled up his sleeves before taking the bottle and pouring a glass for us both. He took them into our lounge and lit a fire. I smiled before taking a sip. He did not pressure me to speak, only waited as he ran circles on my hand, his touch a constant comfort.

"Nik, I do not even know what to say or how to start. I love you with every fibre of my being. It doesn't make sense how much I love you and how your touch can bring about a calmness I have only read about in books, but…"

"You feel like you are living in a shadow." My eyes snapped to him as I took in his face. He put his glass down as he stood and leant against the fireplace. I moved forward to inspect the strange look on him. "You look around this house that you know is filled with memories; memories that you don't have, memories that won't return. You are almost living in a shrine dedicated to a girl you cannot relate to. Liyana had the same light and purity as you do but she was a woman stuck in the past. A woman raised to be a perfect wife, a perfect creature with no voice. You are born into a world where you are allowed to be whatever you wish, with no restraints. But you are living in her world." He walked over and wiped the tear from my cheek, a tear I did not feel fall, a tear representing the words I could not speak. Nik took my hands to help me stand. "You are the most precious thing in the world to me. I have sacrificed for you, and I will always do that. You are my mate. I want you to feel my love in every way. Come with me."

He led us to a room on the lower floor, a room I had never entered. He unlocked it with his thumbprint, and as it squeaked open, he stepped aside to allow me to enter. I hesitantly moved forward as the light turned on and found myself in a room of memories. A room of paintings, pictures, and items from our history. He walked over to a corner and picked up a golden bracelet to hand to me. He dropped it into my hand. I did not account for the weight and almost lost hold of it. I turned over the solid gold bracelet with a snake head holding it together.

"This was the first piece of jewellery I ever bought you. The snake was believed to represent immortality. On the day I gifted it to you..." He paused as I noticed his eyes well with emotion. I had never seen him show pain in this way, his blue eyes growing brighter from the shine of the tears he refused to let fall. I ran my finger over the snake with gems for eyes.

"I said it signified our love, which would be eternal," I muttered as I glanced back at the man who held my heart.

He tilted my head to look at him. "Do you remember?" he asked, his voice sounding hopeful. I shook my head, wishing I did.

"I heard the words in my head, but I do not remember, I am sorry. Actually, fuck no, I'm not sorry. I am not Liyana. You have a fucking shrine for the girl who is never coming back. The girl who died in your arms, begging you to let her go, and here I am begging you to do the same. Let Liyana go. I don't want a half-life with you, Nik. I want a whole life with you. I want to carry your children. I want to grow old with you. Liyana and I may share the same DNA, but I am not her and never will be. I need you to understand this. I want more than just pieces of you. I want to *live*. And not with the feeling of a clock hanging over my head as it counts down what time I have left. I—" He pulled me into his arms and kissed me hard, but I pushed against him and slapped his face. "This is my point."

"You are missing *my* point," he said. "I don't care about the past. Liyana did not want kids. She only cared about surviving and not what our life could hold. You see past that; you see us and what we could be. I wanted to show you this because I needed you to see...fucking hell. I am begging you to see, to listen to me. This means nothing because you mean everything to me. I will do whatever you ask of me."

"What are you saying?" I needed him to lay it all out.

"If you want to sell this house, to create a new one, done. If you want to pick your engagement ring, done. If you want to change jobs, do it. Whatever you want, let's do it." I stood dumbfounded. This man had treated me like the past for so long and here he was, willing to accept the future of my choice.

I noticed he didn't refer to children. I shook my head. "No, it is not supposed to be my choice."

"It will be our choice, our life, our future. Stop fighting me and listen, Larissa. It is *our* time." The words echoed through my head. Our time. Could it really be time for us to finally have our happy ending?

CHAPTER 24
VAMPIRE MEETING

Nik

I COULD FEEL HER NERVES AS SHE STRAIGHTENED THE BLACK AND gold gown along her beautiful figure. It highlighted the best aspects of her physique. Her breasts were covered in the silky gold fabric to show just a hint of her cleavage while the remainder of the gown flowed over her child-rearing hips. I watched as she pinned her waves off her face to highlight her delicate facial features. Her eyes more than anything; the green reminded me of a rainforest with the leaves brighter after a recent rainfall. She pursed her lips while applying gloss. I stood behind her, wrapping my arms around her waist.

"Why the nerves? Worried about being the most beautiful woman at this party?" Her body relaxed in my arms.

"Ha, ha, no." She rolled her eyes. "I am worried I may offend or not demonstrate proper etiquette for some of the vampire Lords. What if I do something wrong?"

I chuckled as I smelt the crook of her neck, her scent was a drug —the perfect mixture of sugar and spice. "Larissa, I don't care if you offend—"

"Nik, you cannot say that. I am human and—"

I interrupted her placing my finger against her lips that I wanted to puncture and suck on. "You are so much more than human, my little demon witch."

She turned in my arms and I stared into her green eyes. "But they do not know and what if I say or do something and it triggers this?" She held up her hand covered in fire. I placed my own around it, causing the flames to extinguish.

"I will be there to put out the metaphorical flames. You are mine to protect, mine to love, mine to keep, mine forever."

"Sometimes I hate your carefree attitude when I am freaking out." She reached over, grabbing her pills and popping them into her mouth.

"Do not mistake my attitude for carefree. I worry about this night. There are men I have no desire to see but it is how we hold ourselves that reveals true character. I aim to be better than most vampires. Do I have enemies? Yes, I have plenty. But do I care? No. The only care I have is keeping you safe. I cannot wait to show you off to the Lords. But keep in mind, you may be called various names by some of the older Lords."

She groaned as she dropped her head against my shirt. "Great." Annoyance vibrated through our bond. She hated being known as more than just Larissa. I understood, but nothing could be done. Her face had not changed, only her soul. Larissa was my light in the dark, my reason for breathing. She fluffed her hair one more time before spinning around. "Let's go." She waltzed over to our bed and swiped her gold-beaded clutch.

"Ah, excuse me." She tilted her head as I watched the waves cascade over her shoulder. She glanced down at herself, and I could not help but laugh. "You look beautiful, but it is more that I didn't get my kiss." I pursed my lips, ready to taste her sweetness.

"Come and get it." Her face lit up with a smile that matched the brightness in her eyes. I pulled her against my body and pressed my lips against hers, warmth and love filled my spirit as I licked her lips to allow entry. I dragged my tongue over hers as a moan erupted from her. I tightened my grip on her hips. "Nik." Her voice was barely a whisper as I kissed down her jaw to her neck, dragging my teeth to that special spot. "Do it." Her body ached for the rush, the desire to feed me and give me every part of her. I pierced her soft skin, groaning as the sweet taste of her blood filled my mouth. My own personal drug. My hand drifted down her body, gathering the soft material. I needed to feel her want for me. I reached under and ran my finger over her silky wet underwear. Another groan left my throat, as I slipped my fingers inside and through her wetness. "Nik." I plunged two fingers inside her, and she gasped as I drank from her again. The monster wanted more. He wanted to take every inch of her, but he never would. He needed to be contained, or he would terrify Larissa. She tightened around my fingers as my thumb rolled circles around her clit, and her breathing became ragged. I licked her neck before the orgasm ripped through her body. Her head landed on my shoulder, her breathing slowly normalising. I tasted her desire; this woman was perfection. She lowered her dress as she returned to the bathroom, and I sped from the room to make her a drink containing my blood. The blood sharing helped, and the more of my blood in her system, the more she smelt like me to all other predators. She scrunched her face, a look I loved.

"Bottoms up." She swallowed it in one. "At least, you are making it taste better. The metallic taste is almost non-existent."

I snorted as I put the glass down. "Now, we are ready to go."

"Wait, we need a photo." She chirped, batting her eyes at me.

"Yes, if I must." She pulled out her phone and flicked it to selfie mode. I kissed her cheek before smiling. I never liked the idea of pictures, but her life was vastly different from my own. She returned her phone to her clutch as I whisked her to the car. I buckled her belt before my own, the reminder that she had no immortality a constant in my mind. She hated it, but she allowed me to do it since our discussion the other night. She understood my need to have her safe.

I handed her a folder. "What's this?" she asked, hesitant to open it.

"Open it to find out."

She opened the black folder and flicked through the five selections. "Are these houses?"

"Yes. Let me know which one you would prefer, and I shall organise an inspection." Adoration filled our bond as I saw her eyes staring at me, filled with love.

"Someone will be getting lucky tonight."

"I already am. The most beautiful woman on the planet is my mate." She laughed as she read each of the descriptions and ran her fingers over the photos. I took out my phone to respond to business matters while we drove into the city, as it would be an hour-long drive. I had been running Refresh Marketing in her absence, refusing to let it go under as I knew it would devastate her. She had voiced that she felt ready to return and I organised extra security for my peace of mind. Peter remained incarcerated while Luce could not be found, and I had called off the search for her. I doubted she would hurt her sister without his influence anymore.

"This one." She handed me a picture of a two-story plantation-style house with a wraparound balcony on both stories.

"Done. I will set it up for Saturday morning." I sent a text to my receptionist to organise this tomorrow morning with a high-priority notification. I could always rely on her efficiency. I handed her one more folder.

"What is this? A car? An apartment? An engagement ring?" I chuckled at her attempts to be funny as she wriggled her eyebrows.

"No, but that reminds me to do something before you open that. You need a new ring. You have not worn one since your return." I opened the compartment before me and pulled out five rings, each vastly different. "Pick one." Her eyes were wide but did not look pleased. "What is it?"

"I kind of wanted to go to a store and pick it together. Something that represented us."

"I understand. I selected these as I enjoyed several features I believed represented your beauty, purity, and light. If you wish, I will put them away and we can visit the jewellers together."

"No, no. That's fine. You wanted to be more efficient." The words stung but at least she now understood why I did things a particular way. She opened every box and slid each onto her finger, one at a time, and held them up before selecting the one I did not expect.

"This one." She handed the remaining boxes back. She selected the princess-cut emerald stone ring in platinum with a twisted band containing tiny diamonds. It had elegance and beauty with a simplicity I believed was beneath her.

"Alright, open the other file." Her heart raced at the sight of Hector, and I placed my hand over hers, waiting as it slowed.

"He will be there tonight as well as another man." She turned the page over and her heart raced once more.

"Duzi. I have heard you mention him before, on the phone."

I glared at her. "You need to stop listening to my conversations."

She shrugged her shoulders. "What has he done?" I smirked at her question. It was a hard one to answer, as the list was endless.

"He simply doesn't like me."

"The man who is responsible for the entire creation of vampires." She nudged me playfully as I winked at her. "Anyone else?"

"Oh, there are multiple, but these are the two that may try or say something tonight," I explained, knowing she would feel more worried with these men.

"I shall just stay by your side." I cleared my throat. "What now?" She spun in her seat to look at me.

"There will be a time when I leave you alone to discuss business that is not appropriate or relevant to humans. It is when we discuss executions and—" She raised her hand, and I shut my mouth.

"Please stop. That is fine." The car slowed as I peered out the window. We had arrived. Highclere Castle was several hundred centuries old and made popular by various television shows. At least some old architecture had survived the nuclear war. Larissa's anxiety increased as her eyes took in the sheer size of the castle. Her door opened, which caused a small scream to escape her lips.

"Apologies, Miss, I did not mean to startle you." The young man's eyes swept over her, and I growled as I smelt his desire for my mate. She was mine to ogle, mine to adore. I moved around Larissa and exited the car while he bowed his head in submission.

"Lord Dankworth, I-I-I—" I seized him around the throat, squeezing slightly, relishing the feeling of his closing windpipe.

"If you look in her direction again, I shall remove your eyes from their sockets." His heart raced. If I fed from him now, I would not be able to stop myself. The taste of fear in blood was dangerous and led to our species becoming monsters; a monster I never wished to become.

"*Nik!*" Larissa screeched; she didn't understand the monster that took control when someone else wanted her. I let him go with a smirk and spun towards my mate, offering my hand. "Was that necessary?"

"I have claimed you as mine, so yes. No other man is allowed to crave you unless they wish to die."

"Riiight. Shall we go inside?" She wrapped her slender arm around mine and the monster calmed instantly, knowing I could protect her by my side. We entered as all the wait staff bowed their heads.

"Lord and Lady Nik Dankworth," the ageing butler announced. Larissa snorted.

"What is it?" I whispered, keeping a smile plastered on my face.

"A little old-fashioned, is it not? Lord and Lady Nik Dankworth. Should it not be Lord and Lady Nik and Larissa Dankworth?"

"The vampire world is old-fashioned. You are considered my property; however, if you were the Lady vampire, it would be the other way around."

"Sure, sure." The antique Corinthian-style doors opened to show the vast array of vampires and their mates. They raised their glasses with smiles out of respect, while some sneered in my direction. Now the games would begin. I questioned whether Larissa would survive the night.

CHAPTER 25
IN THE LION'S DEN

EVERY SET OF EYES SNAPPED IN OUR DIRECTION; SOME FLARED RED while others glared with hate. Nik kept a fake smile on his face, but mine had long disappeared. I distracted myself by staring at the handsome man beside me, wearing a matching black suit with golden lapels and cuffs. He could wear whatever he wanted and looked damn sexy. Every woman's eyes lingered a little too long on him and jealousy shot through me. Nik let go of my arm and placed his hand on my lower back, moving closer.

"Don't worry about them. I only care for you. Let's go." His warm hand slid into mine, bringing comfort. Nik made his way through the crowd, nodding and introducing me to different people. I remained polite, even with my anxiety teetering on the edge of a panic attack. The pills were not working. The idea of running into Hector terrified me. The man tried to kill me on top of trying to have me killed through the courts. Commotion ahead caused Nik to bring me to his side, his hand holding on tightly to my hip. A man in his forties appeared with mousey brown hair and an air of superiority to him, which did not suit his measly features. His eyes looked a little too close together, but his fat nose seemed to only aid in his ugliness.

"Ah, Lord Dankworth, you have graced us with your presence. We have not seen you at one of these events for some time." His eyes dragged over my body, and Nik's nails dug into my hip. I wanted to tell him off but the flash through our bond alerted him and he loosened his grip slightly. "This must be the girl I have heard so much about. I thought her to be a virgin. I see that is no more. What a pity. They always taste better. Who are you, human?" He spoke as if I was beneath him, that I had no place here and right now, I did not want it.

"My mate, Larissa Solis," Nik piped in, keeping his eyes trained on this man.

"Is she a mute? Does she not speak for herself?" The man extended his hand to shake mine. I moved slowly, not wanting to provoke either creature.

"Larissa." My voice remained clear despite the terror I felt inside. He yanked my hand forward to place a kiss while sniffing my skin.

"Ah, mate indeed. She smells of your dirty money. Where is your vermin brother?"

"He does not need to be among the filth of men that are here, Duzi. As there is no need for you to be here." I coughed to cover the laugh that wanted to escape.

"You forget yourself, young Lord. I started this. I am responsible for the way we can enjoy our lives as we deserve. We are the top of the food chain." I wanted to say something as I tilted my head up towards Nik. Young lord? Nik's eyes glared down at me in warning. Nobody knew who he was.

"As always, Duzi, it is a pleasure to speak with you. I would rather my mate be acclimated with those who are more civilised within our community. Come, Larissa, let us mingle with those who prefer to act as reasonable beings. We shall speak later, Duzi." Nik's eyes flared, and rage vibrated through his body. I had discovered two things since we had deepened our bond. The first was that his need to feed was linked to strong emotions and the second was that I could calm him down with a simple touch or kiss. Nik dragged me from the elegant room into a tiny drawing room. The walls were covered books, and a fireplace, a desk, and an old-fashioned floral couch sat beyond them. He slammed the door behind him. I put my hands on his shoulders and rubbed them up and down.

"Nik it is fine, he is gone. We are safe." He growled as he pushed himself back to pace the room. I moved my hair, turning my head to give him access.

"Fucking hell, I want to rip his head off. That piece of shit, that scum thinks he can speak to me like that." His rage filled the room, and it felt almost suffocating.

"Yeah, why do you allow it? He wouldn't exist without you."

"The moment people discover the truth, it would split our world apart. I am the son of gods; my head would be sought for power and control. Roman and I have always remained in the shadows to avoid being hunted."

"I cannot believe you just take his words and attitude. Who is his maker?" Nik laughed as he moved closer. I touched his face. His beast had settled, only slightly.

"You know his maker. She is an abrupt and cold woman who lives in a small town with her mate."

"Wait, Valerie? No way."

"Yes. He had been begging Richard to do it for years but tricked Valerie. Our rules changed not long after his trickery. A conversion must be consented to by both parties. Duzi drank more than his share of blood before taking his life and transitioning. He is a pig of a man."

"I could always just trick him into drinking my blood and bye-bye." I waved my hand with the same motion.

"Oh, my cheeky little demon witch." His fangs extended, and I could not explain the joy I felt seeing them. He was a drug to me, a drug I would never be able to quit. He flicked them away. "I need us both level-headed and not in a sex daze. As much as I want to rip off those panties and have everyone hear you screaming my name, it would not be wise. Let's continue to mingle."

"Come on." I groaned, knowing he made sense, but it didn't stop my body from wanting to give him more. He took my hand, placing a gentle kiss on it.

"Later, I promise." I rolled my eyes, which caused him to laugh. The door burst open as Nik spun around, ready for an attack.

"There you are!" the familiar voice shouted. "At least you still have your clothes on."

I peered around Nik to see the face. "Richard?"

"Hello, Larissa, you are looking wonderful as always. London seems to agree with you."

"Is that despite your warnings that I would die?" I lifted an eyebrow at him with a smile on my face.

"What, Richard?" Nik crossed his arms. Uh-oh, he wasn't happy.

"Well, am I wrong? Katrina informed me of the truth, and I knew if she came to London, she would meet you and eventually die as all versions do. Apologies for the bluntness, Larissa."

"It's fine. I have kind of accepted I am living on borrowed time."

"Did your memories return?" he asked as he leant on the doorframe, but his eyes stayed focused on Nik and his reactions.

"Where's Valerie?" Nik asked, purposely deflecting the question. I made a note to discuss this later.

"You know she hates this nonsense, the 'who has the bigger dick?' It doesn't matter if you are man or monster, it is always a pissing competition." I could not help but laugh because it did seem like that. Nik glanced at me, a slight warning to stop.

"Does he know the truth?" He shook his head, and I wondered who he trusted enough to tell. Had Roman truly been his only confidante his entire life? Was that why the betrayal was so hard for him to accept? He hid me for the sake of his brother and now he could barely look at him.

"What truth? The curse? You bet I do. I have met three versions of you. I like this one the most, but I disagreed with Elizabeth casting a spell to make you hate our species. Hate is not a trait you have ever had. You have always been loving, so it was strange to see, but my only task was to keep you safe."

"I've heard enough. We will have to discuss the rule breakers soon." Nik pushed himself off the desk and towards the door, pausing only for me to catch up to him. I slid my hand into his and we left the drawing room. He kissed the top of my head before leaving me to the various other mates of vampires in attendance. I was the sheep in the lion's den, and it terrified me.

Chapter 26

Time to Show Strength

Nik

I feared leaving Larissa alone with the other vampire mates, some vampire and some human. She would drift closer to her species. Richard stayed close, as did the other members who feared the power I held over the vampire race. I may not have been one of the men to make the decision to take over the world, but I fought hard to ensure humans were safe. If Duzi won, humans would be farmed for their blood and kept shackled for our delight. The monster would love to see Larissa in chains at my beck and call whenever he wanted her, but I pushed the thought away. I had to stay focused but since staking my claim on her, I found it harder to not think of her.

Daniel Wright entered with Duzi, and I clenched my fists. They had partnered; a dangerous liaison. Daniel may be a fellow Lord in London, but he treated women as dolls. He actively sought virgins to turn them into blood whores before selling them to the highest bidder. He had never been caught as the evidence never linked directly to him. Since his threat in the café that my time would be over soon, my search attempts for evidence had increased.

Richard nudged me. "Your eyes are flaring," he whispered, as my gaze stayed focused on my enemies.

"I am aware. Why is that pig here? When did he earn a seat?"

"It was recent. You have been distracted and Duzi took advantage. He is planning something, but he knows I am tied to you and his spies are not revealing anything. If only we could compel other vampires." I smirked, knowing it could be done by only me.

"Point them out to me later and I shall get the answers we want." Richard nodded as he moved to stand beside me. Duzi sat on his throne as I stood on the edge. I had more power than all combined in this room, but they would never know. Three vampires were escorted into the room with a human attached to one. I recognised her, the flaming red curly hair.

Richard held my arm. "Don't react, you can't. We will figure it out but stay hidden from her." Richard had a point. Luce would more than likely yell or scream. Larissa would sense the change and ask later. How could I lie to her? Fuck, this was about to get complicated. Duzi raised his hand to quieten the room.

"Gentlemen…" he had no women present in the council I formed centuries ago. He believed they were too emotional, but I had seen a different type of power from women; they were cunning, manipulative and beautiful, like snakes. "We have three vampires and a blood whore to sentence today." Richard moved closer so Luce could see him, her eyes registering through the haze. She had been fed from recently, and the drug-like effect lingered.

"What are the charges against this one? I know her family, they come from my town." His voice projected strength as he crossed his arms to glare at Duzi. Daniel moved forward, grabbing Luce by the throat and lifting her. I fought against my better judgement to save her.

He sniffed her neck. "She is a blood whore who killed one of our own with magic." Fuck, it would not end well for Luce but why was it behind closed doors? I questioned the motives of these men, but I trusted my friend to find the answers.

"Then it should be through the courts. Why is this human part of vampire judgement?" Richard stayed strong, and I knew he wouldn't accept any reason other than the truth. Duzi shifted as Hector came out of the dark. I sneered at the sight of the man who laid his hands on my mate. The man who still lived because of the laws I implemented.

"She is a witch from the bloodline of Katrina Solis, the High Priestess who killed our kind through manipulation and dark magic." He did not mention Larissa. Richard glanced briefly towards me. They were baiting me, and I had to hold myself back.

"She is not a direct link to Katrina. She had no children and the magic within her blood would not be as powerful. She is no threat to our people."

"She killed one of our own."

"How?" I admired Richard. He fought for the girl who spewed so much hatred toward him.

"She shot a burst of light, which caused the vampire to disintegrate." I stroked my chin. Luce should not be as powerful as that. She had bargained with the witches, so she would have to answer to them. The loss of her sister had affected her more than I wanted to admit. Larissa kept her focused, kept her strong.

"I reject this accusation. Luce does *not* hold magic." I closed my eyes. Richard made a grave error in mentioning that. Hector found me in the dark as a smile played on his lips. I moved forward, leaving the dark. Duzi, Daniel, and Hector all glanced at one another, pleased with themselves.

"What did the three vampires do?" I ordered, standing close to them, peering down at their shaking bodies. They disgusted me. I needed this judgement done to get to what these men wanted.

"The first massacred children in a school, the second raped, drained, and transformed three women turning them into the worst part of our species, and the last ate the hearts of his relatives after he turned." I had done the same after my transition but the first two deserved to die. I chose the first, lifting him to his feet with my eyes trained on the men before me.

"How do you plead to your crime?" I snarled, having no patience for men who hurt the innocent in the world. I paid no attention to his physical appearance, my eyes staying trained on my enemies. Their fangs descended as they relished in my harsh judgement.

"Guilty. I could not resist the taste of their innocence." My fangs tore into his throat and his blood spurted over the surrounding men. I dipped my hands into his neck and ripped his head from his body, throwing it across the room. The smell of vomit and urine reached my nose as I looked at the next victim.

"Did you enjoy raping women and turning them into creatures that would be destroyed? Or did you just enjoy getting your dick wet?" The man sobbed as I reached down, grabbing his cock in my hands and pulling it from his body. He screamed in agony before I slammed my hand into his back and ripped out his spine, holding it above my head as I bathed myself in his blood, allowing it to cover me. I wanted to show all the men present just how dangerous I could be. The last man, I took pity on him. I understood the pain of being alone, the pain of transition, the pain of keeping the monster at bay, the pain of losing what you love.

"Why did you kill?" I crouched beside him, glancing at the blood staining my suit. Maria would not be pleased with this in the laundry. Larissa flashed her apprehension through our bond, and I motioned for Richard. He followed my order, leaving to check on her. He was a boy, little more than eighteen with black hair and pale skin but his brown eyes were filled with innocence and a curious compass tattoo on his arm. It seemed oddly familiar, but his eyes; I knew that look, I had seen it before I took my first life.

"I couldn't help myself, the voice in my head told me I had to. I didn't want to," he cried, letting his head fall into his hands. My heart ached to help his poor soul. I stood, glaring at the men before me.

"I do not accept the judgement passed on this boy. He deserves a chance to learn control, to learn how to be a vampire. I will take him as my ward where he will receive proper training on how to control his beast. The man who should be judged is his maker." I turned back to the boy. "Do you know the man who turned you?" Richard re-entered the room and took in the blood covering my suit. My attention returned to the boy, his head shaking. I pulled him to his feet, yanking the chains from his wrists. Duzi's eyes flared with rage, knowing a vampire should not be able to touch those chains. I was not an ordinary vampire, and I wanted him to remember that. He would never discover my secret.

"I reject your sentencing," Duzi's voice shook. I spun around looking at the faces that surrounded us.

"Are we not a democracy? Do we not vote? All those who wish to help save this poor boy from the bad choices of his maker, raise your hands." I watched as nearly all hands shot to the sky. Duzi sped over and seized Luce by the throat before sinking his teeth into her. Her scream echoed through the room and Larissa registered who was attached to that voice. I ripped her from his arms as Richard grabbed her.

"EVERYONE OUT!" I shouted as Richard took the boy and Luce. "Keep her out of sight from Larissa." I watched all the men file out of the room with Duzi, Daniel, Richard, and I left. Hector had snuck out, and I knew he would go for her, but I couldn't allow the worry.

"This is not our way, Duzi, and you know it. We vote, we give chances, you have no right to make decisions."

"I have every right. This only works on respect for Elders. I am an Elder!" he shouted, trying to project strength.

"As am I."

"Your age has no significance to my own." I laughed at his stupidity, but I knew I could not reveal my truth.

"You were turned at the beginning of the Industrial Revolution. I was turned before the death of Christ. I am older than you can comprehend."

"You lie."

Larissa's fear increased as the door opened and she fell to her feet, tears filling her eyes.

"YOU DARE TOUCH MY MATE, HECTOR!" I roared as I ran for him, but Larissa put her hands on my chest to stop me. She glanced at the blood covering her hands but returned her focus to me.

"Nik, stop. You have to stop." Her eyes were flaring between green and red. Her emotions were muddled, and I couldn't make them out. I had never sensed this from her before.

"What the fuck did you do to her?" The monster beat against its cage, it wanted blood. Hector's blood.

CHAPTER 27

BLACKMAIL AND DEATH

Larissa

RICHARD HAD TOLD ME NOT TO WORRY BUT I COULD FEEL NIK'S anger, his power radiating through our bond. His bloodlust caused my own cravings to use my magic, but I struggled to hold on to normality as the demon voice whispered to me, '*Go save your mate,*' a scream echoed through the hall. Nobody else reacted, as if it was normal but I knew that scream. I had heard it before. Luce. My magic ached to be used, ached to save her, and the demon inside pounded against my skull. Time ticked by as I regained control over my body and mind before a nose sniffed my neck, but it was not Nik. I spun to see Hector.

"Glad to see he has claimed you, finally. I would have enjoyed tearing you to pieces. I dreamt of bathing in your blood and watching Nik cry over his lost mate."

"You are fucking sick. Get away from me." I pushed him away. Not the wisest choice but he made my skin crawl.

"You are coming with me." He pulled my hand, his touch causing my power to electrify.

"Like hell I am. You have no right to touch me. Get away." Warmth filled my hands, my body, my eyes, as the tingles started. I glanced down at my hands to see sparks flying before flame engulfed my hands. Hector smiled, the joy on his face made me feel sick. He provoked me on purpose. He wanted this to happen. I pushed the darkness away, focusing on the light inside as the flame extinguished.

"Tsk, tsk. Too late, little witch." His hand clasped around my arm with an iron grip. I knew I would be able to push him, but it would only prove his point further. He kicked doors open, throwing me inside the room and I fell to my knees as Nik roared. The room smelt of metal as lifted my bloodied hands.

"Nik, you have to stop." My hands touching his blood covered suit. I barely recognised my own voice. What the hell happened in this room? I noticed the body crumbled in the corner with no head, another with his back ripped open. I barely registered what anyone was saying as I took in the horrors surrounding me. The contents of my stomach chose that moment to come back up. Vomit covered the floor as a hand grasped the back of my neck, wrenching me to my feet, the thumb pushing too hard on the side. It triggered an odd bodily response, the pressure point in my neck. My eyes found Nik's, covered in blood, his eyes a shiny red with black replacing the white, his fangs fully extended but he had an extra set on the bottom. Despite how he looked, I knew he would never hurt me.

"Put her down." Hector brought me closer licking my cheek. "I will fucking kill you. Put her down."

Duzi stalked over, placing a hand on Hector, who put me down before Duzi yanked my hair back to reveal my neck. His breath lingered and the dark voice returned, whispering evil things. I wanted to give in to them. I could kill him, and I craved it. My darkness desired to dance in his blood. It wished for terror.

"What does she taste like, Nik? I hear her blood is so pure it is like the nectar of the gods. Why not share her around?" A deep rumble filled the room as it started to shake. "You don't wish to share your witch, fine. Let us talk." The vibrations in the room settled.

"What do you want?" Nik's eyes trained on me, focusing on my hands, my face. He forced a calmness through our bond, a way to say he had this under control, but I had no idea how.

"That is the important question, but I don't think I have your full attention," he said as he glanced at my mate.

"You have it, Duzi. Let Larissa go, let my mate go. I am outnumbered, you are in control. Give her back to me." A bright flash caused my eyes to blink as I noticed the knife he dragged up my body. "If you harm her, I cannot protect you," Nik warned. I knew my darkness would come out.

"Oh, ha ha ha, Nik. You are funny. You think this witch can harm me? She can only harm you." Time moved slowly as I watched the knife plunge towards my stomach. My body reacted, forcing a shield of protection. I couldn't afford to be injured. "Perfect, good girl, Larissa. You can return to your mate." He let me go and I ran into Nik's arms, wrapping myself in his warmth. He kissed the top of my head.

"The courts are already aware she is a witch. It is not a bargaining tool."

"Witches can no longer hide from us. I want your vote to implement a registrar."

"*WHAT?*" I shouted as Nik pulled me back into his arms

"Why?" Nik asked, pushing more calmness through our bond.

"You agree or I tell everyone that your precious mate is the daughter of the black magic High Priestess who slaughtered twenty vampires after controlling them to get what she wanted. She was a fugitive, she was dangerous. Magic is passed through generations. Lucky Larissa inherited it all."

I pulled on Nik's arm, but he refused to look at me. His jaw ticked, his eyes scanning the room before he shook his head.

"Do you honestly believe I will agree to this? That I can be blackmailed by false stories with no proof. Duzi, you are more insane than I thought you were."

"Your time is coming to an end, Nik. Everything is about to change. Vampires are at the top of the food chain, and it is time we claim our rights. That includes putting all others in their place."

"Witches will never bow down to vampires," I spat at him.

"Why? It is the natural order. We came first." Nik scoffed. He knew the beginning of all creatures; to have lived for this long and have his knowledge blew my mind. Nik poured love through the bond, his attempt to keep me calm, keep my magic contained.

"You have no idea about the history of supernatural beings. You are a minor. I know hundreds of vampires and other supernatural creatures who are older than you. I will leave with my mate, and if you try to blackmail me again, I will dig your grave myself." Nik's grip on my arm tightened. I would bruise but he did not care. He wanted us out of this room, more specifically, he wanted me safe. His anxiety increased my own, and my magic ached to be used, feeding on the fear, the anger.

"Keep your eyes to the ground. I can feel your magic. Don't worry, we will be out of here soon."

"Oh, Nik," I knew that voice, a voice that should have left well enough alone. Nik froze, the darkness licking at his anger. It shivered with delight, the part of Malignus's demon blood I wanted to bury, the evil I kept contained.

"Larissa, keep calm." He pushed me behind him as he spun to face Hector. "Yes, Hector, I believe I made my position known. I am leaving and you will allow it."

"You tried to get me killed." He pressed a finger into his chest, as Nik glanced down with a smirk.

"Only after you tried to harm my mate. Call it karma. You are alive, my mate is alive. We will be leaving now."

"You are not leaving until I get an apology from your witch bitch." Nik snarled; my magic responded as my hands illuminated.

"Larissa," he growled. "Trust me, I have this. Close your eyes," he ordered but part of me wanted to see this. I had to understand what this darkness really was. He kissed the top of my head before he took a deep breath, and I watched his shoulders rise and fall as his entire face changed into something monstrous. I glanced at Hector with a sly look. He should enjoy his last moments on earth. I waved at him as Nik moved supernaturally fast. In a flash, Nik's hand burst through his chest and Hector cried out. I could not take my eyes away from Nik. I had no fear, only admiration for the man who slaughtered the monster who hurt me. This man would always protect me. It was fucked up, but I loved him. Nik ripped Hector's heart out and took a bite out of it.

"Enjoy hell. I will see you there one day." Hector fell to his knees and Nik kicked him to the floor before throwing his heart into the fireplace. I held my hand up for him, and he whisked me into his arms and sped into the car. I observed my man covered in blood, his fingers pinching the bridge of his nose. He punched the seat in front of him and roared.

"We are getting married next week." He took my head in his hands and kissed me, leaving blood covering my cheeks. "I won't lose you to fucking politics. Buckle up princess, it is about to get bumpy."

CHAPTER 28
THE AFTERMATH

Nik

I waited until Larissa fell asleep. It did not take long after we returned home. She had retreated into her shell, her anxiety coursing through our bond. She didn't want to marry, and I was not thrilled about it either. Not the part about being tied to her forever or the idea of seeing her wear a white gown, no. This was more about having the romantic opportunity ruined by ridiculous blackmail and politics. I smashed another glass of whiskey before the door swung open.

"What did you do?" Roman growled. He would have heard about my antics tonight. I held up a glass of whiskey as he joined me on the black sofa in my den.

"They baited me," I muttered, unable to look at him.

"You fell for it?"

"*You fell for it?*" I mocked his tone in response. "Yes, I fucking did. They had Luce strung out from being a feeder. Duzi knew exactly what he was doing. Richard tried to protect me but with the combination of this bond strengthening and her power coursing through it, I lost my temper." My head fell backwards against the couch.

"Her power coursing through it?" Roman asked as I stood to put space between us.

"I don't understand it myself. Her moods are affecting my logic, the darkness in her magic whispers to me. It's evil." I shivered as it lingered in the recesses of my mind. The monster begged to be let out, the bloodlust threatening to take control. I dared not tell Larissa any of this. It would devastate her.

"Nik, this must be why Katrina never wanted you to meet. Maybe this version of Liyana is dangerous."

"Larissa is Liyana, there is no version, this is her. You know this. What did Katrina do?" My voice projected so loudly that I heard Larissa stir in her sleep.

"What do you need, brother?"

"Find a witch, someone you can trust. I need a dampening spell on her magic."

"You can't. She will hate you." I finished my glass of whiskey before pouring another.

"I know, but it is what has to be done, or we will both be killed." Roman put his glass down beside mine and sighed, slamming his hand on my shoulder. "Also, find a tux."

"Dare I ask why?"

"We are getting married next week. The only way to stop Duzi from executing her, yep."

"Can't I just wolf out and kill him by accident?" he asked. I enjoyed the idea of Roman tearing him to pieces.

"Trust me, he would know it came from me." Roman snorted. Duzi was sly. He may not be as powerful as us, but I feared what he could be capable of.

I was rattled by the events of the other night, but I needed to plan our wedding and keep her safe. It had never been like this in the past. I only had to worry about her inevitable death, but now I had to worry about so much more. The world had grown more complicated and with the rumours of other places still existing, I worried what it could mean for the future. I decided to check on Luce as Larissa's blood inside whispered for me to see if she was alright. I could not comprehend the strength of the bond this time. We were more in tune and could sense one another faster.

My feet broke the silence in the room, and Roman followed close behind. He hated her more than I did at this point. He never understood how one could betray their own family. I flicked on the light to reveal Luce, chains wrapped around her wrists, cuts and scrapes covering her body. She wore a flimsy black dress, which brought out the paleness of her skin. Her wavy red hair appeared knotted and covered her face. Small sobs echoed through the space. I walked over to set her free. She did not deserve this treatment. I knew this was Larissa's blood telling me to let her go.

"Nik," Roman growled and when I turned back to him, his eyes were flaring. I stopped and took a step back. "You know we cannot trust her. If she is tainted and truly addicted, there is no telling what she would do for another fix."

The sad reality of the bite was that the euphoria produced mass amounts of oxytocin, and the body enjoyed the high and craved more of it. The length of her recovery depended on how long she had been in this state. I squatted to my knees, moving forward, and slowly lifting her chin. Her green eyes met mine, but they didn't have the same sparkle as her sister's.

"Luce, are you there?" I asked, worried about what I would get in return.

She snarled and swiped at me. "I will fucking kill you. How dare you think you can place your hands on me? Do you think my sister would approve? You blood-sucking leech! You are nothing but a monster."

Roman laughed at her remarks, and I snorted in response.

"You kidnapped, drugged, and got your sister shot and I am the monster? I have done nothing but protect her from you and your warped boyfriend. How is Peter? I hope he is enjoying his cell," I snarled at her. I had ensured he would be kept with the worst prisoners, my own personal torture for him harming my Larissa. She lunged forward, and Roman and I both responded. His claws extended and his eyes glowed. My fangs descended. The room filled with the stench of her desire. The idea of touching her repulsed me but her addiction meant she no longer saw logic. I knew I could use this to my advantage, so I moved forward as Roman grunted his own warning. I glanced back at him and nodded.

I took a steadying breath. "Luce." I wanted to compel her, but I could almost hear Larissa screaming in my head. She consumed my every thought, becoming my own addiction.

Luce glanced up, her eyes registering the fangs as she whimpered with need, "Do you want a bite?" I chuckled as her eyes glistened, but I could see her fight. She didn't want this. I took another step to be sure of my convictions.

"Are you sure? A quick little high while I feast on your blood?" I questioned, her face scrunching up. Roman and I breathed out, realising how much we wanted this for Larissa.

I moved back toward my brother. "What do we do?" I asked him. I had never had to dry a person out or remove their addiction. The only thing I knew was that compulsion wouldn't work.

Roman sighed, moving closer to her. He grabbed her hair, yanking her head back to look at him. "I have one question for this maggot. If we save you, if we fix your mistake and help get a handle on your addiction, what becomes of you then? What do you want?" I clenched my fists to stop myself from hurling them at Roman.

Luce's eyes brimmed with tears, and her heart thrummed faster as Roman let her go.

"I...don't...know," she said between sobs, trying to cover her face and hide in shame. Roman strolled back over. "I never wanted to hurt my sister. I love her. I was raised to keep her safe, raised to keep her in the dark, all the secrets about Mum and Katrina and you." Her long slender finger pointed in my direction.

"Me? How?" She knew about me. Had Katrina revealed the truth to her sister?

"Mum told me who you were and why we had to keep her away from you," she croaked. I almost pitied her, seeing the shell of the person she had become.

"Why?" I moved closer. I had to know why Katrina wanted us to never meet. What was the reason behind her sacrificing herself to hide Larissa's very existence? Roman's hand landed on my shoulder, a warning and a comfort.

"You would be her doom."

"How?" I growled, wanting more. Why would she not give me the whole answer?

"I don't know!" she shouted at me, her eyes filling with fire. "I don't know. I only knew that if she ever met you, she would die. I never thought…" she exhaled, holding back her tears, "I never thought I could have almost killed her. The day you let me go, I knew that you weren't the monster I had been raised to hate. The one I swore I would protect her from."

"So, what about Peter?" I was curious how he played into all of this. She shook her head.

"He knew what to say, he manipulated me, and I saw a way to use him right back. He hated your kind, so it made sense to use him to try to kill you."

"The aim was my death."

"If it meant my sister lived, then yes." She loved Larissa but her actions spoke of something else entirely. I wondered if the root of all of this was another spell, but from whom? Larissa and I spoke of a puppet behind the scenes, but we never got to the bottom of who it was. Roman and I exchanged glances, not much more could be obtained from this topic. I sighed as I ran my fingers through my hair. I had a glimmer of hope that just diminished with yet another secret that yielded no answers.

"Luce, you will need to dry out. I will have someone bring you food when needed and water. You will always crave it, but right now, you need to remove the high from your system. You will suffer withdrawals, and they will be excruciating but necessary." I paused as I thought about how to word the next sentence. "Larissa will need her sister on her wedding day, she deserves that. And so much more." Luce's eyes met mine, they were filled with sadness and understanding. She nodded. I turned and left the room as Roman gripped my arm with force. I glanced down at his hold.

"You think it is wise to allow her to your wedding considering what she has done?" He let go, and I shook my head at him.

"I understand your reservations, but I also know my *mate* and what *she* would like on her special day," I said, emphasising select words for him to remember. He loved her but I knew her better than he ever would. He grumbled as he looked at the other door and sniffed the air.

"Who is in that one?"

"I rescued someone else that night. I saw..." I hesitated to say it out loud. "He reminded me of myself at the beginning. Of what I could have become if I didn't have you." My words were barely a whisper as Roman breathed out. The months after were hard for us and it tested the strength of our brotherly bond. "Roman, I couldn't leave him with no one. He had been alone; he killed his family because he couldn't control himself."

"I get it. You have not taken a ward for a long time. You always plan your life Nik but sometimes the best things appear when you least expect them. I will leave you to bond with him, but just promise me one thing." I waited for his response. "Bring me next time you want to go on a slaughter. It has been far too long since I let my own monster out." He winked before he slinked away into the darkness. I moved back towards the door.

This poor boy. I knocked on the door before I entered the silent room. He sat in the middle, looking out the small window with his legs crossed. The latch clicked on the door once it closed. I moved and sat beside him, observing his actions. He sat motionless, staring into the distance.

"Why did you save me?" he asked as he continued to gaze at the window.

I sighed. "Honestly, because you reminded me of myself after I was turned. It is difficult and you have so many emotions and sensations that you can often lose yourself to the monsters inside. I almost lost myself and if it wasn't for my brother, I would have." His eyes snapped in my direction.

"I don't remember seeing any information on you having a brother."

"I see you know who I am, but it is polite to introduce yourself to the man who saved your life."

He cleared his throat as his eyes fixated on his feet. "My name is Bodhi, Bodhi Evans." The name rang a bell, and he seemed to know me.

"How do you know of me, Bodhi?" He shook his head, worry carved into his young pale face. He moved his hair to try to hide from me. It was rather odd. I had never encountered this before. I could smell his fear in the room. "Bodhi, I have declared you my ward, do you understand what this means?" He shook his head before he exhaled.

"No, should I be worried?" his voice quivered.

I snorted at him. "It is a good thing. It means you are now under my protection. I will keep you safe and train you to hone your skills with vampirism. You were not given the proper training, which led to poor circumstances that are not a reflection of you, but rather your master. He shouldn't have left you with family. After transitioning, the call to blood is very strong and most are warned to stay away from loved ones. Some do it on purpose because they want to bathe in their relatives' blood."

"How do you know that wasn't me?"

"Your eyes. They were innocent and filled with regret. Your heart has remained this whole time, which indicates that you don't care they are dead, but you regret the fact that you took their lives. I am going to assume that they were not kind people."

He cleared his throat. "They were abusive, and they had rather extreme views." I connected the dots in my head.

"They did not agree with my leadership of the region, did they?"

"No, sir." His voice sounded clearer as he grew more comfortable with our conversation.

"Bodhi, you are my ward. It is more like a father-and-son relationship as such, so *sir* is not needed. Understood?"

"Understood."

"In the future, I will introduce you to my brother and my mate. Once I am sure you won't harm her, you will be placed as her primary protector. This is due to the hierarchy. You are my ward, and you protect what I declare is the most important and, in this case, it is her. When I am not around, you are to keep her safe from all perceived dangers." His heart beat a smidge faster. "There is no need to be afraid. She can hold her own and if you lost control, she would not hesitate to restrain you." He smirked but something in his face brought unease, and I couldn't understand why. For the next week, he would be working with Roman and me to control his new powers.

I glanced at my watch. I needed to alert my other allies to the issues of tonight and prepare for the aftermath of killing Hector, but based on his past indiscretions, I doubted there would be any repercussions. I knew I could not hide the truth about Luce from Larissa. As much as I wanted to; a little white lie wouldn't hurt.

CHAPTER 29
THE BLOOD AFFECT

Larissa

THE BED WAS COLD AND EMPTY AS I RAN MY FINGERS OVER THE silk sheets. I sat up, listening to the water in the shower, knowing Nik was close. Despite the three rounds last night, I needed more. My legs moved without thinking as I removed my pink floral nightie, throwing it to the floor. Nik's hands were braced on the wall when I slid in, my hands trailing over the bumps in his abs. His body was literally carved from the gods.

He laughed. "Did you not get enough last night?" His voice was smooth as it tickled my insides.

"What is it you once said? I could never get enough of you." He turned in my arms as I began to trace the lines of worry on his face. He did something last night. He hadn't explained much, only that we had to get married right away. Nik moved closer as I grabbed his hard length, pumping it up and down. My body ached with need. I stared into his eyes and said, "I think it is time I take care of you." Nik growled in response, his nostrils flaring as he tracked my every move. I moved to my knees, not daring to look away as I slid his cock into my mouth. I pulled it out, rolling my tongue over the tip as my free hand massaged his balls.

"Larissa," he moaned as I felt the stress leave his body. I pushed myself further as he hit the back of my throat. "Fuckkkkk," he groaned, grabbing my hair and twirling it into his fist. "That's a good girl." He swelled in size, a clear sign of enjoyment as I gathered rhythm. "No, stop." I sat dumbfounded as he lifted me into the air, my back hitting the cold tiles as he thrust inside me. "You are perfection."

"I…wanted…to…please…you." Every word was an effort to get out as he drove himself harder, his teeth biting my nipple. I screamed in a mixture of pleasure and pain.

"You are mine to please, mine to fuck, mine to love." I could feel my walls tightening before my orgasm ripped through my body, waves of pleasure rolling over me. The sensation in my own body mirrored Nik's as he came not long after me. He laid his head against mine. "I wish you could feel just how much I love every inch of you." He pulled himself out but didn't let me go.

"What happened last night? Other than the blackmail I witnessed and your execution of Hector." He groaned, letting my legs find the ground. Grabbing a towel, he wrapped it around himself before handing one to me, pulling it over my shoulders and kissing my forehead.

"Nothing you need to worry about." He turned to leave but I slammed the door shut with my magic.

"I may not be able to use my magic on you, but I can on my surroundings. Tell me. We are in this together."

"Larissa, let me out."

"No, tell me." His anger grew, his eyes flaring. "You can get shitty with me all you want but I deserve to know. I heard Luce, where is she?" His shoulders slumped, and I allowed the door to open.

"She is going through withdrawal." His eyes avoided looking in my direction.

"WHAT? HOW? Did you know?"

"Not until I saw her last night. Richard got her somewhere safe. She needs to get the drug out of her system."

"Hang on, why don't I suffer from the same effects that Luce does?"

"The venom in our teeth gives a high but it only lasts until your mate is satiated. If you have a vampire feed from you who is not your mate, it has a drug-like effect that brings on addiction. The more satisfied I am, the happier you are."

"That is kind of fucked up." His teeth flashed as I took note of desire running through me, he smirked. "That's why when a vampire loses its mate…"

"Yep, it feels as if you died." I touched his face, stroking my thumb on his cheek. I understood the pain of every death, why he called me his curse. The pain he endured, the loss, and for it to happen over and over again… I worried about my own death and the pain it would cause, even though Nik kept repeating this time was different. Would it hurt more for him?

"Hey, it won't happen again. Did she know?"

He moved my hand to kiss it. "She never asked." The more I got to know the reincarnated version of myself, the less I understood. She loved him but they had nothing in common.

"Nik, what was your relationship with her like?" I asked, grabbing a dress from our robe to place it on the bed.

"I told you already, Larissa. She became dependent on me, she lost the spark that Liyana had, that you have."

"What the hell is this curse?" He started to button his shirt, and I watched as he looked out the window, his face pensive. The face I enjoyed staring at more than anything, showing more worry lines.

Nik cleared his throat. "Are you excited to go back to work?" he asked to break the quiet in the room.

"Yes, I just worry about everything. Julian and Stuart booked a meeting about the TimeShaft app, they want to discuss its future. In other words, they are worried because of my absence."

"Julian and Stuart like money, they like good deals. You'll win them back." Nik folded his tie, straightening it before sliding his arms into his jacket. His movements were smooth, and I marvelled at him as he stalked over to the robe, scouring his selection of watches to wear. He held up each one, inspecting them until he found the watch he liked. He selected another and walked back over to me, sliding it onto my wrist. His stoic face filled with concentration as he pressed the clasp shut. His hand ran up my arm, my skin erupting in bumps before his warm lips crashed against mine. "Let's get you to work."

CHAPTER 30

WAREHOUSE OF CORPSES

Nik

I worried about Larissa's return to work, but I knew it would aid in her recovery. Her return to normality. She drank a fresh sample; it was no longer necessary, but I liked the idea of her smelling like mine. I had cameras installed in her office to watch her every move. If she discovered the truth, it would have dire consequences but only I could view them on my phone or tablet. I could feel her nerves in the car ride. Roman had requested to meet this morning, and I hadn't informed Larissa that she would be entering alone. She checked her emails before chewing her nails, and I watched her bite into one nail, ripping it down too far, causing her to bleed.

"Fuck," she muttered, holding another finger over the top. I held my hand up, cutting my thumb and healing her wound. She smirked. "I doubt I would have bled to death."

"No, more than likely an infection, and I don't wish for anything else to happen to my mate."

"Yes, sir." She saluted with her tongue poking out.

"Careful, I shall bite it off." She leant over, rubbing her hand on my leg.

"Careful, I may let you." Her sweet scent of desire filled the car before it consumed our bond. I noticed the roads.

"Larissa, I would love to get on my knees and eat your perfect pussy, but I don't have enough time for a proper feast. You will have to hold onto that thought until tonight." She grumbled, crossing her arms and turning away. I laughed at her childish protest. The car slowed as it pulled to the curb, and she sighed.

"Nik, you are not coming in?" her voice croaked.

"No, I have a meeting I must attend. I shall return within the hour, I promise." I tipped her chin to kiss her soft, full lips, wishing to pierce them with my fangs and suck them dry but I loved how perfect they were without fillers as used by most women at the turn of the twenty-first century. She leant closer before embracing me as I took in her delicious scent.

"I love you, Nik."

"Words cannot describe the love I have for you, Larissa."

"You should try." She winked as Andreas opened the door, offering his hand. I allowed him to touch her, knowing his tastes differed. Andreas entered the driver's side, clearing his throat.

"Are you ready, sir?" I ignored his question, my eyes trained solely on Larissa's entry into the building. She waltzed over to her friends who ran over to greet her. I exhaled, knowing she had arrived safely. "Sir?"

"Yes, let us meet with my brother on this urgent matter." I texted Roman to alert him to my imminent arrival. "Andreas, with haste."

"Yes, sir." Andreas had been part of my security detail for centuries. His master left him for dead and I brought him back to life before the monster took over. There were two types of vampires; the first was normal, living within society. The second were those who lost the fight between their humanity and their monster. Once the creature took over, it was rare for them to return to normality. They were the creatures written into horror movies, the ones who hid in the dark.

Larissa's nerves eased, as joy spread through the bond. My assistant had left a box of sweets on her desk as a return-to-work present. My phone beeped.

LARISSA

Should I thank you or your assistant?

ME

I did ask my assistant, but the idea was my own.

LARISSA

Thank you, Nik, but I shall email her as well. :P

My fingers tapped rhythmically on the car ledge, worried about what my brother had discovered. He didn't always request to meet, and this location was further away from the city.

"We have almost arrived, sir."

I took note of the change of scenery from urban buildings to industrialised. The warehouses were neatly packed against one another. The car rumbled on the uneven road and the side streets were filled with the homeless or drug-affected. This area would be a monster's playground for both supernatural creatures. Wolves did not attack humans unless they were within their territory. This location looked like an ideal training area for a wolf to gain control of their beast. Andreas pulled up to the dilapidated warehouse, and I tapped his seat.

"Stay in the car."

"Will you be safe?" I looked in the mirror as he avoided glancing in my direction. I exited the vehicle, buttoning my suit jacket. The air smelt of dirt and rotting flesh, an indication of a freshly murdered corpse. I walked toward the red rusted door, pushing it open, and the smell intensified as I covered my nose. A heightened sense of smell had advantages but at this moment, it was annoying. Roman stood surrounded by bodies. There were humans and wolves.

"What is this?" I scanned the area to see the room filled with various supernatural creatures. Roman bent down to move the hair from another's face. The boy looked no more than fourteen. Roman shook his head before standing.

"I don't know. I stumbled across it during the full moon. The smell alone worried my wolf." He sighed as he wandered over. "Nik, it smells like magic." I inhaled, focusing on each significant scent before I understood what he meant. The magic was powerful but not close to Larissa's or Katrina's.

"Are you saying all of these wolves were killed by witches? For what purpose?" Roman's eyes snapped back to the young boy. "Who was he?"

"Remember the day Aurora died? I told her I couldn't save her family, they had grounded all planes. She begged on the phone to do something, but I refused to help her. You called an hour later telling me she flew into the radioactive cloud and perished. My wolf rampaged, and that young boy was in the wrong place at the wrong time. I sliced him, watching him bleeding out as my wolf took pity on him. He bit him to save his life…" Roman's eyes welled with tears. I placed my hand on his shoulder.

"He became like a son to you." Roman's shoulders slumped, his eyes falling to the ground. "I will find out what happened. I swear to you, I will use every contact possible." I sensed he had not told me everything. "What else, brother?"

"I have heard the rumours for a while now, but since Peter's arrest, I began to investigate the validity of them. Nik, they are true."

"What?" How was it possible? The world had been destroyed. I saw the destruction. I saw the bombs fall. I watched Aurora perish before my eyes.

"I know. I am shocked, but it is true. There are places that are habitable, beyond this tiny island."

"But how has it been hidden, and by whom?"

"I am still trying to find the answers as was…" his eyes drifted to the young boy, "Sean. He called me to say he had found something, but I just discovered him dead. Nik, if the witches killed him, what else could they be hiding?"

I stroked my chin. I had to keep my head level or Larissa would sense my muddled emotions. Love drifted through the bond, her thoughts distracting me. I smiled at the idea of her sitting and chewing her pen as she flicked through her files.

"Nik." Roman brought my attention back to the room. "Who would have the power to hide this?" I pondered his question. I had been on the committee to create the rules for the new society. How did I know nothing about this? "Nik, the witches wanted to see Larissa. Maybe we allow them. To see if we can find more of this coverup?"

"Roman, they won't take kindly to Larissa when they discover her parentage. I cannot keep her safe. They will strip her of all her power, which is engrained within her blood. It will kill her. What do you think I should do?

"Nik, we need the answers."

"There is one other person we can ask or compel for answers." I glared at my brother, at his suggestion of putting my mate in the path of harm, but his eyes scanned the room filled with dead wolves and witches. I sighed; he was right. We needed answers.

CHAPTER 31

THE PAIN OF THE PAST

Larissa

I OPENED THE DOOR TO MY OFFICE, NOTHING HAD CHANGED. Piles of work, piles of bills, mass amount of work, but I couldn't wait to dive in. Nik gave me access to his accounts, which may have been driven by guilt. He tried to stay on top of all the work, but he had enough on his plate. My first task for the day —I needed an assistant. I had been doing it all by myself before my double kidnapping. Nik had organised for Maria to pack my lunch despite knowing he would bring me something, his own piece of control. I called the employment agency, asking them to send me five resumes for assistants. They were efficient, and I ended up calling them all for a phone interview before meeting them in person. I hired a young girl from a small town, her name was Mimi. I thought she reminded me of myself, the naivety, the innocence I once had before I discovered my demon witch heritage. I did not stop all day, but images of sex flashed through my mind as my phone rang. I checked the time, five. The day had flown by, and I barely achieved anything.

"Larissa Solis speaking."

"We never finished discussing the name change." The annoyance in his voice brought a smile to my face.

"It is the twenty-first century, you could always take mine. We are not wed either."

"True but we are mates and in vampire law, you are known as Larissa Dankworth. Also, my name will open more doors." I rolled my eyes at his ego but this time there was truth behind it.

"Why are you flashing images of sex into my head? Did you miss me today?" I bit my lip, twirling the phone cord between my fingers. He had been especially naughty with his thoughts.

"With the bullshit I had to deal with, you have no idea. How was your day? I see you hired a new employee," he said, brushing me off. I disliked when he tried to avoid certain topics. This had become the norm for him with the reincarnated versions of me who became yes people.

"Keeping tabs on me. Should I be worried?"

"Larissa, it is my job to keep you safe."

"Blah, blah, blah. What is the point of this call, Nik?"

"When are you thinking of finishing?" I sighed, rubbing my temple, my head hurting from the million things I had to do. The office had so much gossip and nobody seemed to work in unison.

"I had not thought about it, to be honest. Maybe within the next hour or two, why? Did you want to go home earlier?"

"No, I have a few more things to do. Shall we work through dinner together and sleep in tomorrow?" I groaned, thinking about him eating his breakfast between my legs. I squeezed them shut.

"No, I cannot sleep in, my assistant starts tomorrow. Happy to work through dinner but are you able to come down here?"

"I will on one condition. I cannot always see what you think. Tell me and I shall arrive promptly with a bowl of spaghetti marinara." My mouth salivated. He knew all the foods I loved. It made dating rather easy as I never had to tell him multiple times, he knew everything.

"I pictured you eating your breakfast in the morning."

"Which was what?" His voice sounded lighter, less serious, and more playful.

"I pictured you between my legs, eating my perfect pussy as you call it."

"Larissa, I only speak the truth, and it is perfect. How about I bring some food and feast on your dripping pussy after dinner?" My heart raced, my core pulsing with desire.

The words out of his mouth were pure sin. He would be the literal death of me. I set up the conference room for us to work in, knowing I could lock it overnight and only I had a key. This would help to keep any important documents safe and away from prying eyes. The view looked out onto the cityscape. London was beautiful at night. The lights lit up the city as I watched the cars and people float by. I wondered if they feared the darkness inside them, as I did. I shivered as the room grew colder, a shadow appeared behind me in the glass, its face unmistakable. Malignus. I turned to see the room was empty and only I stood there.

Nik entered shortly after. "Everything okay, my love?" I nodded, glancing back out to the city and the people moving about freely. "What is it?" He rubbed his hands up my arms, my body tingling from his touch. I leant my head against his chest. "I missed you too," he whispered into my ear as he kissed along my neck.

"Nik, please, as much as I seriously would love to lay on this table and have multiple orgasms, I am starving, and I want to finish this report." He chuckled as he moved to stand before me.

"Let us eat and work, and on the drive home I will give you those orgasms." I rolled my eyes at him before kissing his lips and unpacking the bag. Nik sat down and watched me, unbuttoning his suit jacket and placing his feet on the chair opposite him. I slid his food across the table. He ordered his favourite—a bloody steak with fresh vegetables. He had simple tastes. I removed my own jacket, picked up my fork, and ate my dinner while finalising my budget report. I had to work out the finances for the next month to remain afloat. We had a few projects I could bring closer, but my only worry was the discord between the employees. I swallowed a spoonful of pasta before looking at Nik.

"I had an idea," I chirped, pushing my bowl aside.

"Did we not say that we should work before any fun activities?" His eyebrow quirked at my statement.

"Nik." I glared at him to take me seriously, and he put his hands up.

"I am listening, what is it?" he said, resting his head on his hand.

"There is unhappiness amongst the staff after Andrew's firing, my appointment, and my disappearance. I think it would be best to organise a retreat with the staff. It was Stacey's idea, and I agree with her. I know this may interrupt our impending marital plans, but I believe this is important for Refresh Marketing's future success."

"You want to postpone your wedding to the most eligible bachelor in the world for a retreat with other people."

I raised my eyebrows at him. "Yes, I believe it is important to create unison amongst the staff." He stood, rolling up his sleeves, and I watched the muscles flex in his forearms. He walked around the table before stopping behind me. His strong hands massaged my shoulders before one slid into my bra, grasping my breast as he bent down.

"I just want to make sure I understand this correctly. You would prefer to spend the weekend with other men and women than marry the man you love." His fingers rolled my nipple, and I moaned from his touch.

"Yes…wait, no." I fumbled my words as he chuckled. He kissed along my neck, grazing his teeth.

"What do you desire, Larissa?" His fingers played with my breast, and I could barely think straight.

"You." Another moan escaped my lips as he pulled my hair back to look at him. His lips crashed against mine, his tongue invading my mouth. I forced myself away. "Don't distract me with sex. Do you care?"

He grumbled as he strode back to his seat, slumping into his chair. "No, Larissa, I can postpone our wedding by a couple of days."

"Days?"

"After the events at the meeting and the deaths of certain individuals, I have had to bring that timeline forward."

"To when?"

"I had planned to tell you tonight when you came home to see the wedding dresses around the house, but I suppose it is better now. I planned for it this coming weekend but I don't wish to stand on your toes when it comes to your career ambitions. I will push it until Tuesday or Wednesday at the latest. Think of your retreat as a bachelorette weekend. Take Travis and Alina with you."

"Nik…" My mouth sat open. He had taken it upon himself to plan our entire wedding. "Did you *not* think to discuss details with me sooner?"

"I informed you in the car that we were to be wed."

"You did not speak of it again and now you are saying you planned it for *this weekend*?! This is where you frustrate me!"

"I could say the same." I bit my lip, my anger radiating through myself and our bond, with Nik feeling his own. I leant back in my chair, crossing my arms.

"You could say the same about what?" I asked him, wanting to know where I had possibly frustrated him. Nik leant forward and I noticed his jaw tick.

"Larissa, this has been important since the trial after you killed a vampire. The decision to marry was made then, and I postponed it with the council for your benefit. So, you could adjust to this new life and all the expectations that come with it. While adjusting to the use of your magic, I have been understanding and thoughtful, but now I am telling you that it is happening, and you are abhorred by it? Please explain the thought process on how I frustrate you. I have always been clear with my intentions." He spoke sternly, his eyes boring into my own, wanting me to know it wasn't up for discussion.

I sighed and dropped my arms to the table. "I just assumed it would not happen, not that I didn't want it to, but…"

"I can feel it, Larissa, that is fine. You wanted choice, something that has been taken from you at every corner and I have done the same. I should have consulted you. I am not used to this version of you." He slammed his fist on the table, and I smirked at him.

"You mean the version who bites back when all others would just submit?" His eyes sparkled with desire. He may not enjoy that I was more vocal, but it did rile him up, which I found pleasure in.

"Yes, yes, Larissa. I will include you in all decisions for the wedding from this moment on," he exclaimed. I stood as I made my way over to his side, noticing the computer open to wedding locations, and smiled.

I sat on his lap and flicked through. "Which do you like more?" His fingers fumbled with my zip, but I shook my head. He was hungry and not for sex. I tilted my head to the side to allow him an opportunity to feed as I scrolled through his selections. He had created a presentation on all aspects of the wedding; the venue, flowers, dresses, suits, guests, cake, and food. I noticed he had no wedding reception, only a selection of churches.

"Why only churches? Are you even allowed inside a church? You won't burn up will...ooh." As his teeth sunk into my neck, euphoria spread through my body, and he groaned as I listened to him slurping my blood. I leant my head back for him to get a better reach. He growled, and in a flash, I was on the table with my legs spread, Nik's eyes glowing red with my blood dripping from his mouth. The sight would unnerve any normal person, but I had come to discover that I was born from darkness and Nik understood those quirks, helping me to accept the evil inside. He wiped his mouth before his lips crashed against mine, the metallic taste still lingering on his lips as he licked mine.

"Open," he ordered, and my legs spread without thought. His hand travelled up my thigh before his fingers hitched inside my underwear, ripping them from me.

"Nik, they were brand n—" I complained, but his lips stopped me, the taste of blood heightening my own desire. I wrapped my legs around him, forcing him closer, needing more. I fumbled with his pants, not able to wait a second longer. He thrust in and I moaned as the dark voices in my head whispered, *'Taste him. Do it.'* They grew louder as Nik increased his rhythm, and I looked into his eyes that flicked between their crystal blue and the red, his monster threatening to come forward. He slowed, touching his forehead to mine. The voice shouted at me, *'DO IT! Make him yours.'* I pulled Nik down and bit into his neck. His warm blood split into my mouth, the taste initially like iron before a sweetness overtook my senses. He moaned, and with one final drive, he finished, pulling me along with him. I let go, screaming with pleasure.

Nik took steps back, holding his neck. "What the fuck did you just do? Why did you do that?" His brow creased as he wiped away the blood from his neck, no bite detectable. I didn't understand what even happened. He zipped his pants back up, while I stared at the floor. Nik shook me, touching my face. "Are you ok?" His anger was gone, and emotions rushed through me that I had never felt before. The magnitude of his love hit me, the pain of all the losses, as I clutched my heart. He pulled me into his arms. "Breathe…it will pass."

I screamed as images flashed through my head of Nik holding my dead bodies of the past, the agony of every loss that moulded him into the person he was today before it stopped with an image of him holding me in a room filled with columns and covered in gold, the face of this body resonated with me. Was that me?

'Good girl,' the dark voice echoed as darkness enveloped my senses.

CHAPTER 32
YOU DARE SPEAK TO YOUR LORD THAT WAY

Nik

THE EMOTIONS I KEPT BURIED FOR SO LONG CAME TO THE surface as they rushed through our bond. Larissa could feel the pain and agony as I held her dead body. I held her tight as her own anguish filled her, and she shook her head. I had no idea why she drank from me; it was not typical for this to happen. She shouldn't have done it. Only a fellow vampire can drink, not a human. The rules of our bond were constantly changing, and I couldn't understand how she could feel what I felt without being a monster. She spoke about her own darkness, but had she buried a monster for so long that she had no idea? Was this a secret that Elizabeth spelled to keep her safe? Was this the reason why Katrina did not want us to meet? We were always doomed, but this time it had to be different. I knew in my soul she would survive but I didn't know how. She had to be kept from me. What was this curse? Larissa slumped against me as the bond grew quiet. I laid her down, unconscious.

I grabbed my phone as I walked to the window, dialling my brother. Larissa remained still as I listened to her breathing.

"Nik, is everything okay?" Roman's voice sounded croaky.

"Did I wake you?" I took note of the new moon. Roman always

felt the exhaustion from a new moon. I remembered that tiredness would consume my entire life.

"You know already. What is it?"

"Larissa bit me." The phone went quiet as I noticed bodies lying on the pavement, cars stationary. I glanced back at Larissa. Whatever had happened, she had projected it onto other people.

"Did you turn her?"

I banged my fist against the glass. "No, I didn't ask her, and I had no idea she was even planning this. Roman..." I couldn't bring myself to finish my sentence as even I was confused about why she felt all my pain.

"Nik, you are scaring me, what is it?"

"Roman, she experienced all of my pain..." I exhaled, containing my own emotions that threatened to spill out, "from her deaths." The words didn't sound real. I closed my heart to never feel the pain. She brought it all to the surface, everything I had lost with our lives that were constantly cut short.

"Where are you?" Roman sounded more awake. "I'll be at your penthouse in five minutes." Larissa had not moved by the time I hung up the phone. I sped and packed up the office, cleaning the mess and sending out the email for the company retreat. I would call on some contacts to fast-track this for her. I held Larissa close to my chest as I flew home, landing on the balcony as I heard Roman call for us. I slid the door open, laying her on the couch. He ran over, moving the hair from her face as he listened to her chest. He sniffed her neck before standing with his mouth open, scratching his chin.

"Roman, I don't like that face. What did you smell?" I moved closer, fearing the words that would come out of his mouth.

"She doesn't smell like herself. I can smell her power. Katrina was a High Priestess, could she have transitioned to one without the ceremony? If she drank from you, she could force something to happen without meaning to. Why would she drink from you?" Larissa stirred and we both froze, waiting for any sign from her. Roman's shoulders fell. "What would possess her to drink vampire blood? You said she hated it."

"The voices told me to do it," Larissa mumbled as she sat up, her eyes flicking between their green, red, and black before stopping on their signature colour that took my breath away. I rushed to her side and knelt before her. I searched her face for any sign of harm. Roman sat beside her, sniffing her once again. "Dare I ask why you are looking at me like that?" Roman was right, she did smell different. Those with immense power radiated it, and now so did Larissa. She had transitioned into something else. My phone rang and I noticed the caller. I dreaded this call.

"Who has you all churned up inside?"

"Juliet," I mumbled as Roman stiffened. The witches never called with good news. "Get her some water," I ordered my brother as I took the call on the balcony. The cool air brought the refreshment that I needed before listening to her inevitable demands.

I cleared my throat. "Juliet, how are you?"

"Do not be smart with me, Nik." Her rude response informed me that this call wouldn't be friendly.

"I believe it is Lord Dankworth to you." If she wished to speak with that tone, she would play the game that I set.

"Lord Dankworth, where is she?" she demanded down the

phone as I glanced over my shoulder at Roman handing Larissa a glass of water that I could feel going down my own throat.

"I am not sure of who you speak, Juliet. Please enlighten me. I know plenty of women in the world."

"Where is Larissa? Do you have any idea what she has done?"

"No, I am not aware. She has been with me all night, working. She couldn't have done anything."

"Don't you fucking hide behind her, and don't lie for her. Where the fuck is she?" Juliet shouted into the phone.

"YOU DARE SPEAK TO YOUR LORD THIS WAY. I have tolerated your attitude thus far, but you do not raise your voice to me and make demands. You live in my world, Juliet. You witches wanted to hide in the shadows, so this is what you get. I have the power; don't you forget that." Silence echoed down the phone before a deep sigh.

"I apologise for my actions, Lord Dankworth. Larissa has caused a disruption in our line. I am the Head Priestess but, in a blink, the power in our coven was disrupted. I took the role after the death of Katrina and, as you know, it generally flows down the generational line. Larissa can only claim that with a blessing from Katrina, but she is dead. She stole from my coven."

"I need to go." I hung up and rushed inside. Larissa was laughing as Roman cracked some jokes. She turned to look upon me, her eyes glowed a brighter green than usual.

"What is it?" she asked so sweetly, so innocent.

"You said the voices told you to do it. I need you to do something for me." I moved to sit beside her, her eyes tracking my movements. "I want you to think back to those voices that told you to bite me. I need to hear them."

"How is that possible? It is in the past," she asked as I noticed her sink further into the couch, fear filled the room and Roman growled before shaking his head.

"I need some air," he muttered as he left the room, her fear causing his wolf to want to offer protection. I could feel her influence, it was a reaction she didn't mean.

I cleared my throat. "I will be able to feel it in your blood if you focus on that moment. Can you do it?" She nodded as I slid my hand up her throat, turning her head and grazing my teeth along the nape of her neck. Her skin was so soft as I pierced it, listening for the voice. Darkness filled my mind as the voice echoed before I let go.

"What is it?" Larissa asked as she shivered. I had taken more than she should have given today. I would have to supplement with blood bags for a few days to allow her body to recuperate.

"I know that voice, but I can't place it," I whispered, almost ashamed that I had no answers to give her. The voice echoed in my head. I had heard it before, but my memories of that voice were fuzzy. Who was she?

CHAPTER 33

MORNING SEX

Larissa

A FEW DAYS PASSED SINCE I HAD TRANSITIONED INTO WHATEVER this was. I woke every morning with a freshness that I could not describe. I had never felt so happy, and I had no idea what drove it. I threw on Nik's shirt and waltzed down the stairs, the sun soaking into my skin and filling me with joy that I had a man I loved who would be marrying me within the next seven days. I danced around the kitchen as I made him a blood pancake with fresh blood from my wrist. I poured the batter onto the pan as I danced around the kitchen, making Nik the perfect breakfast. Since consuming his blood, our bond had never been stronger. I could feel his every thought, emotion, and sense where he was at all times. He walked down the stairs, trying to be quiet and sneak up on me. I spun before he had a chance and jumped on him. He laughed and sniffed my neck, making me groan.

"You smell like mine." I giggled as his beard tickled my neck. He kissed me before putting me on the bench, his hands on my thigh, his grip harsh as I stared into his eyes that flicked between red and blue.

"Sometimes, I wish you would let me see the monster inside. I am not scared of him. I know you would never hurt me," I said, stroking his face. He kissed my hand as his eyes settled on the familiar crystal blue. I sighed. "Why do you not ever let him out? Why are you so scared of it?"

"He is dangerous. When I swore to serve your father all those years ago, he discovered he couldn't remove my wolf as it was a blessing from my parents that even he couldn't go against. In order to turn me into his slave, he transformed me into a vampire with my wolf becoming a blood-thirsty monster. It was no different because wolves sought blood and destruction during a full moon." He took a deep breath. "There are two types of vampires, those that can control their instincts and those that become enslaved to the calling of the blood. If a vampire ever loses that battle, run. I am serious, Larissa, promise me. If you ever see that part of me, run." His fingers dug into my skin, and I gasped as he looked down.

"Nik, it doesn't make sense, but I *know* you will never hurt me," I said, lifting his chin to see his face. He pushed my hand away and took a step back.

"You don't get it!" he exclaimed, turning his back to me.

"Did your monster kill a version of me?" I asked, sliding off the bench, and running my hands up his back.

"No."

"Has he ever asked you to hurt me?" I prodded further, trying to understand the creature under the surface.

"No."

"Then what are you so scared of?" I questioned, unsure why he was so scared of his monster. I had never feared him even when I could feel his presence.

"Larissa, just stop it, please. Let us eat." He spun in the other direction, away from me. My anger radiated through our bond, and his eyes snapped to me.

"I want to know what you are scared of. Tell me the truth."

Nik's eyes flashed red as his chest puffed out. "Don't push anger through our bond. Don't force me to do something that I don't want to do," he warned, his fists clenching. He was holding himself back even as his fangs elongated.

"Just tell me the truth. What scares you?" I raised my voice slightly in frustration.

A growl escaped his lips as he stalked over to me, and I stepped backwards until I hit the wall. His hand ran up my neck and grasped the back of my head pulling it closer to him. "I am terrified of hurting you. I am terrified of losing you. I have slaughtered hundreds for you, and I would do it again, but the idea or the thought of harming you would kill me. You are the most precious thing in my world, the reason I exist, the reason I have done all this. If I lost you because of my inability to control my demons, I would burn the entire fucking world because I destroyed the single most precious thing in it. I love you with every fibre of my being. I love the glimmer in your green eyes, the innocence in your heart, even down to the mole on your backside, but if I destroyed or hurt any part of you. I…" He did not finish as he relaxed his hand on my head. "All I want is to worship you and give you everything you deserve. I took your life and your choices because of my own selfishness. There is no point living in a world where you don't exist."

"Nik, I may not remember the past, but I forgive you. I can feel the extent of your love for me. I experienced every ounce of pain from each death, feeling the anguish you endured and the shattering of your heart. I just want to understand why you fear the monster so much."

"What if he does hurt you?" Nik's voice was barely a whisper as he stared at the floor, his shoulders slumped.

"He won't because he has only ever protected me. I saw a glimpse of him at the castle when you tore Hector apart." A growl escaped his lips as he raised his head slowly, his eyes black with the blue iris visible. His fangs were dangerously long as he raised his hand, stroking my cheek with his claws threatening to cut me.

"Careful what you wish for, princess," he purred as he sniffed my neck, groaning. "All mine. Forever mine." He cut the buttons from my shirt, opening it up with my breasts on display. He dragged his finger down my chest, making a small cut, and I watched the blood trickle down my body. He kissed me harsher than ever before but all I could feel was his passion and love. He nibbled my neck, his hand playing with my breast, rolling my nipple between his fingers. "Perfect." He bent down and I watched him lick up my body, getting rid of the blood that spilt out while healing at the same time. He lifted my leg over his shoulder. "Your smell is intoxicating." His mouth covered me, his tongue delving inside, and my knees threatened to buckle. His hands held my body up as I glanced down to see his eyes focusing on my reactions. I looked towards the ceiling when he suddenly stopped, his hand slapping my thigh hard, the sting causing a mixture of pleasure and pain. "I want to see your eyes as I watch you come on my tongue."

"Holy fucking shit," I groaned, his words causing my body to erupt with a primal need.

"Good girl," he whispered between my legs as his tongue licked its entire way up and back. His eyes grew brighter, and I dared not look away. His fangs grazed along my folds as his tongue drew patterns. I could barely focus when I felt his finger thrust inside. I moaned, biting my lip, reminding myself to not look away.

"Nik," I whimpered. He stood in a flash, spinning me and forcing me down on the bench. The plates scattered all over the floor. His feet pushed my legs open, and he rubbed his dick through my wetness.

"Such a good girl for me." He spanked my arse, a new sensation that caused my body to ache for him. "It's coming, princess." He thrust inside me harshly, there was no gentle love this time with Nik. This was animalistic and fucking fantastic. He clasped the back of my neck, pulling my body up. "Who do you belong to?" he asked as he thrust faster, my eyes rolling to the back of my head.

"You," I answered.

"WHO?" he shouted.

"Nik Dankworth," I moaned as I came undone with the force of his movement. He roared as he let my neck go. My body sank to the floor, my breathing erratic, but I had never felt better. Nik bent down, his beautiful eyes watching me with his brow creased. "I am fine, more than fine, and you were worried that he would hurt me." Nik chuckled as he lifted me onto the bench before cutting his wrist and letting it drip into a glass.

"Have it, please. I think you may have some bruises later, and this will stop them and avoid unnecessary questions."

I wrapped my arms around his neck. "I love you, Nik."

He leant his head against mine. "As do I, Larissa. Don't make me bring out that part of me again."

I did not answer, feeling regret flood through our bond with a mixture of hate. He taught me to accept the darkest parts of me, but he couldn't do the same.

I ran upstairs to dress myself and heard him cleaning up the mess while muttering to himself. I pushed my adoration for him through the bond and listened to his reaction. His laugh filled the kitchen as he glanced up to see me watching him.

"If you are finished, you can help me clean up your mess."

"Only if we have a breakfast date. My first meeting is not until ten."

"Done, now get your sexy arse down here," he ordered as I rushed down the stairs to help him clean.

CHAPTER 34

A BREAKFAST OF WITCHES

Nik

After breakfast, I ventured to meet with Juliet as she requested. I hadn't told Larissa, but Roman agreed to come with me. We decided to make it public, where she would be less likely to attempt anything. I was protected from her magic but Roman did not have the same shield. It could be called a blessing, but it was simply part of the curse to avoid any witch trying to break it. The quaint café was hidden down a side street, its exterior covered with weathered brick and an awning that needed to be updated as the café name was obscured. As Roman and I entered, our noses were filled with the aroma of freshly brewed coffee intertwined with the scent of freshly baked goods. The interior had a cozy charm with mismatched wooden tables and chairs placed in a random arrangement that worked well with their functionality. The soft lighting gave the room a warmth that was sometimes missing from London and its cold weather. One signature wall had a black and white snapshot of London Bridge from centuries ago, which brought about nostalgia for the time that it had been built. Roman nodded his head to the left as I saw Juliet sitting with another witch.

We approached the blonde coven witch. I knew her to be around eighty years of age, but she barely looked a day over forty. Her associate must have been her apprentice, with mousey brown hair and eyes that showed an innocence that hadn't been tainted with black magic that all witches eventually dabbled in. I sat down, unbuttoning my suit jacket as a waitress walked over. I sensed her magic. We were not alone, as Roman confirmed by sniffing the air. He knew as he flashed a charming smile to the young brunette waitress.

"Two lattes, beautiful." His voice was filled with charm and I glanced out the window to hide my smirk.

I cleared my throat. "You called this meeting, Juliet. What do you want?" I asked, getting to the point as I leant forward in my chair.

"Do not attempt to intimidate me, vampire, I am stronger than you. I don't fear who you are." Her words were laced with hatred, and I chuckled. Roman crossed his arms, watching our interaction and the surroundings.

"I have no such desire. I only ask what you want," I said, picking up a sugar packet before placing it on the table. Her eyes watched my movements as I repeated my actions.

"I want Larissa. I want what is mine. She has to return the power to the coven," she asserted as I moved the sugar packets around.

"You want me to hand over my mate for what exactly? Please elaborate, Juliet," I demanded, not giving her the reaction she wanted as I avoided her eyes to show her how beneath me she was.

"She stole from me," she hissed, slamming her hands on the table. Roman growled but I put my hand on his knee to settle him. He might be the muscle, but I had the strategy.

"Forgive me, as I am a little rusty with witch politics, but is magic not passed down between mother and daughter? Same with titles? Or am I mistaken?" I tapped my chin, staring at the ceiling, feigning confusion. The young waitress brought the lattes over as I ripped a sugar open, tipping it into the warm coffee. I shuffled the other packets around in a pattern that she had yet to notice.

"You are correct, but Katrina skipped the line of succession, granting all her powers to the coven after her destruction." The lights flickered above as Juliet struggled to contain her anger.

"Ah, but at any stage Larissa can claim what is rightfully hers. Elizabeth kept Katrina's powers safe until her death. They have since transferred back to Larissa. Now, as the final part of the spell broke, the part that kept her powers contained, the title and all rights returned to the rightful bloodline, correct?" Shutters closed around the windows as the chanting grew louder. I snorted at their attempt to scare us. "Roman, leave now. They cannot harm me."

Roman stood and left the café as instructed. I would never put my brother's life at risk, as much as he annoyed me on occasion. I tipped the latte over, watching it soak into the packets I had placed strategically around the cup. I stood as Juliet tried to force her magic upon me, but it bounced off. I moved to the middle of the café to keep an eye on my surroundings.

"Juliet, I thought you were smarter than this. You came to a café with protection against a vampire that cannot be harmed by your trivial magic."

"I know who you are. I know what you are capable of." She stood smugly as her witches formed a circle around us.

"Juliet, did you notice the pattern on the table?" I questioned. She glanced over before shaking her head.

"It is irrelevant, it is a ploy to distract from the purpose of this meeting. You will hand Larissa over or we shall take her by force," she demanded as the lights flickered, a few blowing in a mystical wind.

"Ooh, I am terrified of your parlour tricks. That pattern is a reflection of what can happen today if I remove your head from your body. All those who are tied to you in this moment, who are lending you their power will also perish. Think about this before you make any drastic decisions. I will not be handing Larissa over. She has reclaimed her power. You will leave her alone or I will hunt you down." I turned to exit the café before spinning back. "I should add that when I hunt you down, that will include all those within your bloodline. So, your magic will disperse back into the earth where it belongs. If I sense a whiff of your presence, I will destroy your coven. If you attack her, I will kill your entire family line. Am I understood, Juliet?" She gritted her teeth, knowing she had lost. Her rage vibrated through the air as a smile covered my face. I left the café, the door slamming shut behind me.

Roman leant against the car with his arms crossed. "You look pleased with yourself," he noted as he stood up, walking over.

"I am. I didn't have to kill anyone." I shook off my anxieties as I opened the car door.

"But let me guess, a strong recommendation?" He chuckled as I nodded.

"Always." The car started and he drove towards Larissa. She would leave for her retreat tomorrow and had requested that I not linger. "Roman, I need a favour."

"You have been asking a few of them lately," he said as he turned the wheel.

"Could you watch over Larissa while she is on the retreat? I fear this is not over with the witches. We know they are crafty, and I doubt they will take this seriously." He cleared his throat, and I noticed him shifting in his seat. "What is it?" I asked, worried about his concerns.

"The retreat is on wolf land. I can, but I will need to remain hidden and if caught, we will need to explain ourselves."

"One day, you should claim your title as Alpha. But understood. I appreciate whatever protection you can provide." I stared out the window, focusing my attention on Larissa's emotions. They were jumbled and filled with stress. She needed this retreat to be over as well as the wedding. She had been barely sleeping since she ascended to High Priestess, and I could feel her apprehension as much as she tried to hide it. I knew she would open up soon enough.

CHAPTER 35
REALITY HITTING HOME

Larissa

I DELEGATED THE PLANNING OF THE RETREAT TO STACEY AND gave her the company credit card. Nik had selected three acceptable locations that would suit a company retreat and a bachelorette party. Stacey sought the help of Travis and Alina, but my heart yearned for my sister to be there. I knew it wasn't possible, but Nik had not spoken about Luce since he saved her. I clicked my pen against the wooden desk, glancing over the itinerary. Stacey had planned team-building activities on day one before a barbecue dinner. Day two, the focus would be on ideas and creations for the future. I liked the plan. My thoughts were interrupted by the office phone ringing.

"Larissa Solis," I answered, knowing this name was about to change.

"Why are you all jumbled up today?" Nik's voice purred down the phone and I breathed out in relief. I needed to hear his voice.

"Sorry, Nik, I am just stressed. I have so much to do before we leave tomorrow."

"Like what? Let me help. My day has slowed down, so I am available to help my fiancé." I smiled as I put the phone on speaker and let my head fall on the desk. He had left his office, already on the way down to me. "You know I can feel you coming."

"You are a little wrong. I have to get fitted for my wedding suit and check Roman's measurements before I can help you out. It should only be an hour."

"Can you organise for Maria to pack a suitcase for me?"

"Done, what else?"

"Sorry, Nik, I am just in a mood."

He sighed loudly down the phone. "You are due for your monthlies soon."

I stiffened at his comment. "Um, how did you know that?" How could he tell?

"Your smell changes as you produce different hormones. Not all vampires have this ability. It is more a lingering effect from my transition."

"Does that mean you can smell when the optimal moment is to conceive?"

"Yes, Larissa." My heart skipped a little before I remembered that children would never happen for us. He was the living, breathing dead and my life was doomed to end, shorter than the average life expectancy. I knew he would have felt my emotions, so I buried them.

"I need to get back to work, Nik, I will see you later tonight. Love you," I mumbled as I leant back in my chair, wondering what our children might have looked like. They would have dark hair and olive skin, and I hoped his eyes, but it was only a dream. A tear rolled down my cheek as a knock shook me from my dark thoughts.

I wiped it away. "Come in," I said cheerfully as Stacey entered with a smug look on her face.

"What are your thoughts on strippers?"

"NO!" My voice came out a little louder than intended. "Sorry, but no. Have you met my future husband? Not many compare to him and his perfection." We both laughed as she moved closer.

"What is it, Larissa?" she asked, but her question was devoid of emotion. It was odd.

"Just stressed about this retreat. I think I may head home early and pack." I started to clean up my desk and pack my bag, needing to get out of there, suddenly feeling claustrophobic. "I'll see you in the morning." I ran from my office, barely containing the emotions that threatened to spill out of me. I texted Andreas who waited outside with the car. I slid in, slamming the door closed behind me. My hands were shaking.

"What is it, Miss Solis?" he asked as I met his eyes in the mirror. I couldn't keep looking at him. I stared out the window, ignoring his question as my phone rang. Nik would have sensed my emotions, so I texted him to say I was fine before turning my phone off. My way of saying I needed some space but knowing he would sense where I was. I walked into our home. Our current home. After we were married, we would move into our new home. I found my way to the room with our history, and I turned the light on. I wondered if the past lives had this same feeling. I hated that my life would end. I hated the fact that I would never be able to have a baby, to feel it grow inside me, hold it for the first time as it cried, and snuggle with it when it was sick. Tears fell down my cheeks and they would not stop.

"Larissa!" I heard Nik shout as he rushed into the room. He

raced over, pulling me into his arms as we sat on the floor. He didn't ask, he simply let me cry.

As I woke the next morning, my arms searched the bed for him the moment I opened my eyes. The bedroom was empty, but I listened for any sound of him being around. I collected my pink robe from the end of the bed and headed out, sensing he was close.

"Nik!" I called out before I heard his voice. I moved closer, knowing he would feel me.

"...she has never been like this. I am worried. She always accepted this life, but Larissa is struggling. I don't know what to say to make her feel better...I know, brother. I know she loves me, but I can feel her keeping things from me...I don't know how to make it better for her." I moved to stand in the doorway as Nik glanced up, his hair dishevelled, rings around his eyes, and still wearing the same suit from yesterday. "She is awake. I'll talk to you later." He hung up as I walked over, sitting on his lap and burying my head in his chest.

"I am sorry."

He sighed as he wrapped his arms around me. "You have nothing to be sorry about, but I would like to know specifically what upset you."

"We can never have children. I am destined to die young, and I'll never be able to carry or hold my own child." Tears started once again, dropping onto his shirt.

"I am the one who is sorry. This is all my fault, Larissa. I never intended for this to happen. I couldn't imagine a life without you, and I sought help from the worst person and now we are cursed to live in this time loop where neither one of us will ever get what we want."

"Nik, just hold me, please. I just need you right now." He sped up to the bedroom, holding me against his chest before we snuggled into one another. "Did you ever picture them?"

"Every day, Larissa, every single day. I remember when I met you in one life, you were pregnant with your then-husband's child at the time. That relationship ended but you died in childbirth. You were twenty. Your memories returned and you were so happy because you thought we could finally have a family together even if it was not mine."

"How do you picture them?" I closed my eyes as Nik's power entered my mind, projecting images from Ancient Rome, our children running through the markets with my smile and his blue eyes. Our son was tall and strong while our daughter had long beautiful waves and eyes that could stop any man in his tracks.

"The moment I met you, I saw this. I saw our life together, our children. It was what made it so hard to lose you because this should have been our future. I wanted nothing more than to grow old with you and die holding your hand. I took it all from you and I wish I could take it back." I looked up at him, at the tears welling in his eyes. This fucking curse took everything from him and me. He chose to never lose me and instead lost what his life could have been. Nik cleared his throat. "Stacey is here. You had better shower and get yourself ready."

"Nik." The words stuck in my throat. I wanted to tell him it was alright, but I couldn't bring myself to say it. I barely believed it. How could I speak words that had no meaning to them?

"Larissa, I promise after we are married and we are on our honeymoon, I will tell you about all of our lives. Every heartache, every joy, all of it. You need to understand what has happened to understand how we move forward."

CHAPTER 36
WHAT COULD GO WRONG?

STACEY ORGANISED A STRETCH LIMOUSINE TO FIT ALL FIFTEEN OF the staff. Refresh Marketing did not have a vast number of employees despite its reputation, but still enough that there was disharmony among everyone; well maybe just towards me. My anxieties were hitting another level as the staff all spoke to one another, laughing and drinking the complimentary champagne. I stared at my engagement ring, conflicted about whether to remove it, but Travis and Alina would arrive later to have a mini bachelorette party. Stacey put her hands over mine and I looked up at her,

"Don't hide who you are. It will only make it worse," she whispered, glancing back towards everyone. She grabbed a glass and handed it to me. "Loosen up."

Nik warned me before leaving to keep the drinking to a minimum to avoid a flare of my emotions and triggering my magic. One glass would not hurt as I took it from Stacey, having a sip. Annoyance flared through our bond. Nik could feel the alcohol in my blood. I focused on him, closing my eyes and projecting myself into his head. It was hard to do but possible.

"It is only one, Nik. I am not stupid." I heard voices around us. *"Are*

you seriously in a meeting and sending your annoyance through the bond?"

"Larissa, just be wary. You are in an environment unknown with new powers and hormones fluctuating. Just be careful."

"If I am not, will I get a spanking?" He growled. "Fine, I promise. I will behave. Love you, Nik."

I shut down the projection and landed back in the limo. They were all singing to the latest tune as Mark stood and shuffled over, his eyes glassy. We had only been in the car for an hour, and he had clearly consumed enough alcohol that he was slightly intoxicated. Mark had grey hair from his age, roughly forty to fifty. His wedding ring dug into his finger, and I idly thought he must have put on weight since he initially wed years ago. We had only had one interaction in the past, the day that I met Nik. He was in the meeting to support Andrew but did not do anything.

"Helloo," he said, dragging out the word.

"Hey, Mark, how are you?" I asked politely, looking anywhere but directly at him.

"I knew the first day in that meeting that you and Nik would be together," he slurred.

I smirked as I eyed him suspiciously, wondering where he was going with this conversation. "Yeah, how is that?"

"The guy could not keep his eyes off you. I remember telling my wife, who has had a crush on Nik since I first introduced them at the yearly ball. She wanted to know everything, and she agreed, it was love at first sight." I cringed as I remembered exactly how awkward the meeting was, especially when he touched my hand and I almost moaned. He knew everything he was doing to me and enjoyed it while I struggled to stay composed.

"It was so awkward," I chuckled, the memories coming back to me.

"I knew you were destined for greatness even if everyone else here doubts your ability. Nik does not make stupid business decisions. If he appointed you, it is because he believes you can do it. Don't worry about the negativity from others here. You managed to figure out the finances to avoid making anyone redundant and keep us paid. Many won't admit it, but you will succeed even if there is a bet that you will fail." I kept my face neutral to not show how hurt I was that people were making bets to see me fail.

"What's the pool at?" I chuckled, trying to portray my strength to Mark.

"I think someone has it a thousand to fail within a year."

"Only got around nine more months then; enough time to have a baby and quit." I snorted as all eyes snapped in my direction. Mark laughed with me as Stacey leant closer to see what was being discussed. Mark pulled me into his chest and kissed my forehead.

"Careful now, you touched another's mate." I snorted as Mark laughed harder. He stayed by my side for the remainder of the car ride to Bath.

We turned down a gravel path, the car stopping as the divider slid down.

"I ain't driving down there. You lot can walk it." The driver's strong accent echoed through the car. As most were tipsy, they simply laughed. I sat forward.

"Thank you for driving us." As I headed for the door, I was grateful that I decided to wear jeans over a skirt or dress today. My staff did not need to see that much of me. I stepped out of the car and breathed in the crisp air. The forest was serene and enchanting with various tree limbs intertwined to create a mystical canopy. The ground was carpeted with ferns and moss, and I took in the beauty of my surroundings. Up ahead, I could see various huts; some were circular, triangular, and some the normal size for a cabin. It was perfect.

I turned to Stacey with a beaming smile. "This is perfect Stace, you have truly outdone yourself." The collective gasps of the staff highlighted their own love of the area. An elderly woman approached, wearing what could only be described as a hippie poncho with varying shades of orange and brown. Her wavy grey hair cascaded down her back to almost reach her bottom. She held her arms out in a welcoming gesture.

"Hello and welcome to your retreat. We are blessed to have you here to relax and reconnect with each other and nature." Stacey snorted behind me. I believe she polished off an entire bottle during the car ride, and I turned to glare at her. She stopped, casting her eyes to the ground. "Please select the cabin that calls to you the most." I turned to speak to the staff, noticing their eyes were wide with amazement at this location. Nik had done well to narrow it down. He truly had all the resources that I could ever need.

"You heard her, please select whichever you want. I will pick last." They all went their separate ways, selecting their cabins and those they wished to share with. I hoped they saw this as a kind gesture, but I doubted it. I noticed that nobody selected the cabin furthest away, so I wandered towards it, climbing the rickety stairs before pushing the creaky door open. The room smelt of pine and lavender. I closed the door, noticing the bed was located in the centre with a bear blanket that I found rather distasteful. I checked my phone and saw there was no reception. I closed my eyes to focus on Nik, and he soon came into view.

"Is everything okay?" he asked with worry in his voice.

"There is no phone reception, and I miss you. I dislike this bond. I feel so needy all the time."

He laughed. "How do you think I felt before you realised what it was?"

"Okay, I get it. Sorry for driving you insane. We arrived around ten minutes ago." I sighed as I projected the room to him.

"Looks cosy. I could imagine bending you over the wooden bed frame—"

A knock broke my focus, and I was thrust back to reality. I enjoyed the way I could speak to him in my head since drinking his blood directly from him. Apparently, I marked him, in a sense. Some special supernatural thing.

I walked over to the door. "Stacey, what's up?" I asked her, leaning against my door as exhaustion hit me hard. I yawned as she giggled.

"I am so tipsy, but we are about to sit down to eat morning tea before the first activity. Travis and Alina will arrive after dinner with more champagne and penis straws!" I rolled my eyes. Of course they were. You would think after centuries of being alive they would be a little more mature, but alas they took pleasure in silly antics.

"Yep, I'll be down soon." I closed the door before changing into more comfortable yoga pants and pushing love through the bond to Nik who returned it instantly. I sighed as I looked in the mirror at my messy hair and no makeup, about to head down and be a boss to people who had been in the business for decades. "You've got this," I said to myself as I headed out.

The afternoon was a success as we worked through our team-building activities and spoke about grievances with the sudden change of leadership. I happily discussed that I am open to changes within roles and recreating a new environment that would be more 'user friendly' as they explained. All my anxieties withered away as I discovered that most of the staff had a strong dislike of Andrew, and their only worry was my lack of knowledge. Today, I had proven the knowledge I did have and what I would be happy to work on for the success of the business. We all ate dinner before heading to our cabins for personal time. I sat on my bed and wrote down all the ideas and strategies to achieve them. I listened to my music with a singular focus on writing before I forgot or got distracted. My body tingled as I noticed my magic flare. I played with the fire in my hand as it flickered between blue, red, and gold. I didn't understand the change in colours. Nik explained that every colour represented something but there was no manual for this witch stuff, even Elizabeth's grimoire contained nothing important. I sighed as I clicked my fingers to diminish the flames.

"Where is the bride to be?" I heard Travis's cheerful voice as the stairs creaked outside. I packed up my work, stacking it neatly on the dresser as they burst into my room. "Excuse me, Lady Dankworth, it is time to celebrate your upcoming nuptials to London's most eligible bachelor. The man all women and men want." I snorted as he handed me a glass of champagne.

"Thank you, Travis. Dare I ask how much you went overboard?" He innocently tapped his chin.

"I was informed to not allow you to get too intoxicated. Nik came to see me and stated that he could feel it all through the bond and would be discussing a performance review if he deemed that I had been taking good care of my future lady boss."

"Oh, please do not use that word, it gives me the ick." I took a sip as I tasted the quality of the wine. It was not cheap. "Nik bought the champagne, right?" Alina and Stacey giggled, and I rolled my eyes. His own version of control, but I would speak to him about the performance stuff. Alina took my hand as we took a seat by the fire pit.

"I have to ask and spare no details please, how big is it?" Travis asked, moving forward in his seat eagerly.

"How big is what?" I wondered where he was going with this.

"Oh, my small country girl. I have fantasised about that man's dick on multiple occasions. I need to know if my imagination lives up to the reality." I choked on my wine through laughs.

"You know, I haven't seen many to know if it is big or not, but I would say about average. I mean I have only been with him or Roman and they are brothers." I internally chastised myself. That was something I was not supposed to say. They didn't want it outwardly known. They wanted the knowledge they were acquaintances to avoid any speculation.

"WHAT?" Travis yelled

"YOU ARE KIDDING ME!" Alina screamed.

I noticed that Stacey remained quiet, and I curiously watched her. I could spell her to tell me, but I dared not reveal the extent of my magic to them. Travis and Alina followed my gaze.

"Stacey, you are rather quiet," Travis noted as he stood to fill the glasses.

"Just not feeling the best."

"That is bullshit. You forget we have our own lie detectors. Did you know?" he asked, standing in front of her. She refused to look at him or even speak.

"Stacey, what is it?" Her eyes locked onto mine, and hate radiated from her.

"You think you are so perfect, don't you? Your perfect ring, your perfect job, your perfect partner. You have everything while some of us have nothing."

"Whoa," Alina whispered as the playful mood suddenly died.

"Stacey, I have no idea where this is coming from. I am sorry if I have upset you but maybe we should discuss this tomorrow when you are not so intoxicated." It only seemed to add to her anger.

"I have loved him for three years. I waited for him to notice me. Then you arrived and took him from me." If my mouth could hit the floor, it would have in this moment.

"Took him? Please tell me you are joking, Stacey. I had no control. He is my mate! I resisted him but, in my heart, I knew he was my future. I am sorry you are upset but you need to direct your hate elsewhere." She scoffed and stood, walking into the dark of the forest. "Fucking hell!" I shouted to the sky.

"Larissa, leave her. She is being a child!" Alina exclaimed, shaking her head as she watched Stacey walk away.

"I have a duty of care. She is my employee. I need to make sure she is safe. Even if it is pitch black outside and I do not have night vision." Travis and Alina stood, taking my hands.

"We will be your eyes," Travis said as we headed towards Stacey. "Best not to call out. There may be other creatures out here," he whispered, almost sounding scared.

"Are you guys not apex predators?" I questioned, noticing their eyes glowing in the dark.

"Yeah, but some things still scare us." The bushes rustled behind us, and we all froze.

"St…acey" My voice shook as two yellow eyes glowed. A small growl filled the space. Travis and Alina ran, leaving me all alone. Another sound came from behind me. I had been drinking, so my magic would not be the most reliable. I threw up a shield of protection but even I knew it would be weak. Nik entered my head, but I forced him out. I needed to focus. I turned to see more eyes on either side of me. I had two choices; run or die. I froze in place as all directions were blocked. One wolf charged, but he was thrown backwards from the power of my shield, which weakened slightly as all six attacked at once. What the hell had I done to piss off wolves? A monstrous roar filled the air. I knew that roar; Roman. He entered, still in his human form, his eyes glowing, his fangs and claws ready to attack.

"LEAVE!" he ordered as the wolves remained in position. One charged at me again but Roman rushed over, throwing him against a tree. It crumpled to the floor, whimpering. He roared once more, and I watched the remaining wolves submit in place. They transformed back to humans, kneeling on the ground.

"WE DO NOT ATTACK HUMANS. What is the meaning of this?" his voice boomed as I stepped closer for safety. His hand reached for mine, squeezing it before releasing.

"We were asked to attack her."

"By whom?" His voice was deeper than usual, a constant rumble coming from his chest as he puffed it out.

"The witches," the young boy answered as his eyes remained focused on the ground.

"Since when do witches ask for attacks on humans?"

"We didn't ask. We were only told that once the truth is revealed, we will be protected."

"What truth?"

"Of the world, but Alpha you need to know…we weren't the only pack asked." I peered at Roman curiously. He wasn't an Alpha. Was he? He had never ruled a pack and spoke of his distaste for leadership after what happened in Rome. But he did not correct the boy.

"She is *not* to be touched. Remember her scent and if I discover that any of you harmed her, I will eat your fucking hearts for breakfast." His voice boomed as they whimpered. "Larissa, let them smell you." He motioned for me to step forward, and I did as he asked. They each took a sniff. It was so strange. I scurried back to Roman, and he took my hand and raced me up the stairs. "Time to go home."

"Roman, I have no car," I said, trying not to fall over as he dragged me behind him.

"I brought one. Nik wanted you safe, so I followed you down and have been watching you all day."

"Not at all creepy, but fine. But my staff," I pointed towards their cabins, "I can't leave them."

"You can and you will. Fuck your staff. You know Nik will want you safe," he ordered as he stopped before his BMW, opening the door and motioning for me to enter.

"Yes, Alpha," I muttered sarcastically.

"Don't start, and call Nik. He will be fucking livid." Roman froze as I walked past him. "Wait." I stopped as he sniffed me, his eyes glowing brighter. He scoured my entire body, sniffing every part.

"Roman?" I questioned as I watched his animal side take over. Another growl escaped his lips, as he looked back at the cabins before he whimpered.

"Fucking hell, it will have to wait. Get in the car already," he grumbled, and I noticed the sad look in his eyes. My eyes grew fuzzy as I was filled with an unexplained buzz.

I paced the room after Larissa shut me out. She knew not to do that, that it only pissed me off further. But with her fear mixed with magic, I knew she did it for a reason. My phone rang and I noticed Roman's name.

"What the hell happened?" I screamed down the phone at him.

"Hey, honey." Her voice was soft and cheerful, an attempt to bring down my monster. I breathed out in relief. She was safe, he had her, he protected her.

"Come on, brother, you think I would let anything happen? We are on the way back. Talk to your fiancée, she had a bit of a scare."

"I am right here. Give me the phone." Roman laughed before his voice died down. "I am alright, Nik. Stacey got upset with me because she has been in love with you for three years." Her voice was extra cheerful from the wine in her system.

"Yes, I am aware. Her obsession seemed only minor," I grumbled as I remembered her incessant tricks to try to catch my eye. The worst was when she learnt the code to my penthouse, but Larissa didn't need to know any of this.

"Would have been nice to know, Nik, but moving on. She gave me a verbal lashing before storming off in the dark. I went after her with Travis and Alina but when they saw the wolves, they ran. I threw up a shield before the big strong Alpha came and commanded them to submit. Have you ever seen Roman use that power? Holy shit, it was incredible and terrifying." She continued to ramble into the phone, and I relaxed hearing how fine she seemed to be. Roman had done exactly as I asked, he kept her safe. He always would.

"Do you know why they attacked you?" I interrupted Larissa's tirade with my own need for answers.

"Apparently the witches ordered it. I didn't think I pissed them off that much, or did I? I truly cannot remember. The lights are so pretty in this car." Her voice slurred as unease developed through the bond.

"ROMAN STOP THE CAR!" I shouted. "Where are you?" I asked, knowing she had either been spelled or poisoned, but I needed her blood to know for sure.

"About an hour away from the retreat."

"Don't move. I am coming, keep her awake. Keep her talking." I grabbed a jacket and headed towards the balcony.

"Nik, I am exposed." Worry laced his voice.

"I will be there in ten minutes, find somewhere safe." I flew as fast as I could. The bond buzzed with sensations I had never experienced. It wasn't magic. I could taste the poison. I had bought the wine to avoid this, and Travis and Alina would not dare hurt the mate of their Lord. They knew the repercussions. Larissa stated that Stacey gave her a verbal lashing, but had her obsession gone too far? I had never sensed that she would dare hurt someone for me.

I landed in a field as Larissa danced around Roman, her heart racing as she sang at the top of her lungs. Roman stood with his arms crossed, his brow creased as he watched their surroundings. I stormed over, trying to contain my anger that she had once again been out of my sight and was harmed. I would need to attach a leash to her and pull her around all day.

"Nik!" She ran over, throwing her arms around my neck. "I missed you." She kissed me hard, and I tasted the poison, relieved that it would not harm her. Thankfully the only side effect would be the delirium she was currently in. Stacey, or the perpetrator, probably hoped it would have kicked in before the wolf attack, and her magic would have been useless against it. Her tongue licked my lips, and I wanted to throw her on the ground and take her right here. This woman is going to be my literal death if I could die. Roman growled and I glared at him.

"I know, Roman, I am not stupid. We need the drug to make its way out of her system. It is already dissipating and will be gone shortly." I glanced at his car. It wouldn't fit all three of us and Roman was particular about who drove his cars. "Should we stay or leave? I will not fly her, and I want her to stay awake until the drug passes."

He grumbled as he threw his hands in the air. "I have a cottage over the hill. I stopped here for a reason. I thought the fresh air would be good for her. I only worried about any other wolves searching for her scent as she pranced around like a fucking child." I laughed at his irritation as he stalked towards the cottage.

"Larissa." I whistled at her, her eyes flicking between red and green. "Jump on my back, we will race Roman."

"YES!" she squealed as she ran over, jumping as I caught her, gripping her legs tight. "Let's go, horsey." She laughed loudly as I proceeded to run.

"Catch us if you can, Roman!" I shouted as we ran past, and a monstrous roar echoed through the field.

"Oh no, we pissed off the Alpha." Larissa snorted as I ran quicker. Roman appeared beside me in seconds. He would be faster in his wolf form, and it hit me how much I missed running through fields with him. It strengthened our brotherly bond. "Why are you sad?" she asked, kissing the back of my neck.

"Nothing important, principessa." The cottage came into sight as Roman froze and shifted back to his human form. "Roman?" I questioned, already knowing the answer as he spun. I watched his gaze dart nervously around the open field, but he avoided meeting my eyes. His hands trembled slightly, betraying the fear that gripped him despite his attempts to remain composed. His eyes flickered with uncertainty as they searched the field. "ROMAN!" I shouted at him, and his eyes met mine.

"Nik, the keys are in the car." I shook my head. I would never leave my brother. "I know, but you said this time is different. I have only wanted your happiness, brother. Get her out of here. There are four Alphas." Roman had sacrificed so much for me, and I wasn't about to let him do it again. I ripped my wrist open, flooding Larissa's mouth with blood. She choked and coughed it up as I saw her eyes flick to their brilliant green. The drug was gone. She shook her head as realisation hit her.

"What happened? Where are we?" I kissed her lips hard, wanting her to feel the extent of my love for her. "Nik, why did that feel like a goodbye?" A tear rolled down her cheek as she saw Roman transform into his wolf, howling at the moon.

"What's happening?" I sensed her terror as her eyes searched me for answers.

"I need you to do this for me. Don't question it. When I tell you to run, I want you to throw up a shield and tap into every single bit of magic you own to run to Roman's car. When you get in, drive home, don't look back. Just drive. Can you do that?"

"Nik, let me help." I leant my forehead against hers, knowing she was not prepared for this fight.

"I can't. You aren't ready for this fight. You don't know how to fight wolves. I won't risk my safety, your safety, or my brother's. I need to be focused, and I can't do that with you here. I need you safe. I need my girl safe. Promise me, please," I begged as Roman prepared for the first attack. She nodded as she stood, taking a step back. I sensed her magic flow through us as she locked a shield in place. Her eyes shone red; they were beautiful. As she turned and ran, my heart ached. I turned, preparing myself for a fight.

"WHO'S READY?" I shouted as I stood next to Roman who flicked me with his tail. I smiled at him as the wolves ran at us. I had never seen so many in my life. My fangs and claws elongated, preparing for the first wolf. I spun to my brother and looked at him, his golden eyes glowing, his fangs sharper than ever. I grabbed his head in my hands. "You are and have always been the true Alpha. Time to accept it. I know you never wanted it, but I believe in you. Show them who you really are. Stop hiding and be who you were born to be."

A wolf bit into my leg as I spun around, punching him in the head. The wolf whimpered before standing and preparing his second attack. He launched himself and I wrapped my arms around his head, snapping his neck. He transformed back into a human as he landed on the ground. I hated this, but I would do it for Larissa. Another launched itself at my neck, but I blocked the attack with my arms, holding them up. Its teeth bit into my flesh, and its claws tore at my chest. I held the pain. Larissa would stop if she felt the intensity of it all. I punched my hand through the wolf's chest, tearing its heart out. The wolves howled as I saw another run in Larissa's direction. "ROMAN, NOW!" I screamed at him. I rushed after the wolf with every inch of my vampiric powers, projecting darkness into his eyesight, and blocking him from seeing her. It would only slow him down. Shivers ran up my spine as the ground shook, and I turned slowly, seeing Roman glowing from head to toe. He had almost doubled in size before he raised his head toward the moon and howled. The wolves that surrounded him fell to the ground. I smiled with pride at my big brother finally taking his position as the Alpha. I strode over to him as he turned back to human. I pulled him into my arms, holding him tight.

"I did it. I did it." His voice was so quiet, so weak, as he slumped against me. I lost my footing before bracing against the sheer size of him.

"You did it, big brother. I am so proud of you." He laughed as he stood taller. "What is it?" I asked him.

"She is different this time. The idea of her being hurt with a mixture of finding my mate, it helped me finally do it."

"Wait, you found her?" Roman had searched for centuries to find his girl. He sought comfort in versions of Liyana, but it never compared to the hole he never filled.

"Kind of. I smelt her on Larissa. She works at Refresh." I smacked my hand on his shoulder.

"I will invite all of them to our wedding. Surely, that will go off without a hitch, right?" We both laughed as I glanced towards the gods who had abandoned us over a millennia ago. I contemplated praying but they had always gone unanswered. What would change now?

CHAPTER 38

ARE THE TIMES CHANGING?

Larissa

I HAD NEVER DRIVEN SO FAST IN MY LIFE ON THE DRIVE TO THE penthouse. I leant my head against the cold elevator walls, waiting to reach the floor. It beeped open, the room was dark as I clapped my hands. The lights flickered, and I reached out for Nik. He was filled with terror, but I could not focus on him. I did as he asked. I entered the gym and punched the bag in anger. If only I were stronger. I could have helped. I was a weak person. I hit the bag harder, refusing to be this person, this damsel.

My body tingled as I ran to the balcony. Nik landed; his blue shirt ripped with blood smeared over his chest. I tore it from his body, checking for wounds. He kissed me, pulling me against his hard body.

"Nik, I...I..."

"Not now, Larissa. I need to feel you. I need to touch you. I need to be inside you." He growled as he lifted me into his arms and sped into the bedroom. He threw me onto the bed and grabbed my pants, pulling them from me. I squealed and laughed at him. "I need my mate, right now." He removed his pants as he climbed up the bed, removing my top as he kissed me. I ran my hands up his muscular back, enjoying the various grooves as I wrapped my legs around him. He tore the fabric from my bra and he bit my nipple, his touch gentle yet firm. He took control, his hand sliding down my leg, pulling me closer as he buried himself inside me. I moaned as his teeth grazed along my collarbone before sinking them into my neck.

"Fuck me," I moaned as euphoria spread through every inch of my body.

"I thought I already was." He chuckled as he thrust himself deeper, hitting my sweet spot as my body arched for more. "You are perfection," he whispered as he pulled out, grabbing my hip and flipping my body over like I was a doll. My back was against his front as he spread my legs a little wider. He pushed himself inside, his hands running up my body, grabbing my breasts and rolling my nipples between his fingers as his teeth sank into my neck once more. "Good girl," he purred as he licked my wound, his hands dancing along my skin before he found my clit.

"Nik," I whimpered, feeling my body clench around him. He paused inside me with an evil laugh.

"Not yet, princess. I want to hear you beg for it."

He forced my body onto all fours, smacking my arse. I cried out in a mixture of pleasure and pain. He lined himself up, rubbing his cock along my wet folds before sliding inside. I buried my head in the pillows. I needed a release as he pulled out the whole way, forcing himself in again. I wanted more; I craved it.

"You are so wet; I need to taste you. Stay still." I dared not move as his lips licked up and down. I groaned. He wanted me to beg but I refused to give him that satisfaction. His tongue delved deeper as another moan escaped my lips.

"I can taste how close you are. Just give in, Larissa." I lowered myself onto his face before swinging myself around and landing on his cock. He laughed as I rode him, gripping his legs as my release got closer. Nik held my hips, forcing me down, and groaned. He let go, spinning me around till my back landed on the bed. He thrust in once again, hitting that spot, again and again.

"Nik," I whimpered. "Please." He laughed, burying himself deeper. The orgasm tore through my body like never before. I lay there, panting as he found his own release. I moved to lie on his chest as I struggled to catch my breath.

"Are you two done yet?" I heard Roman call out. I closed my eyes, embarrassed that he heard us.

"Did you have to stay and listen?" Nik called out as he kissed my forehead before standing. "I'll meet you downstairs," he said, pulling on a pair of shorts and heading to his brother. I rolled out of bed and showered before dressing in a pair of denim shorts and a black tank top. Roman and Nik clinked their glasses together as I walked downstairs.

"What are we celebrating?" I asked, noticing Roman seemed lighter. His shoulders were no longer slumped, his eyes were brighter, and he wore a smile that reached them. Nik grasped his shoulder, seeming happy for his brother.

"I found my mate." The words were almost impossible to comprehend. I stood dumbfounded for a moment before running over to him.

"When? Where is she?" I was filled with elation. He finally found his partner after searching for centuries.

"Well, I haven't found her exactly, but I smelt her on you earlier. She works for you."

"Was that the reason for your weird smell thing earlier?" He chuckled as he finished his glass. He nodded with a proud smile.

"My wolf smelt her on you. Safe to say, I will be coming to your work until she realises."

"Wait, you have been around all those smells before. It may have been someone at the retre—" My brain clicked as I registered who his mate was. "No way! My assistant? My *nineteen-year-old* assistant is your mate? No way, Roman, she is a baby." I shook my head as Nik and Roman shrugged. "Does that not bother you?" I crossed my arms at the disregard for her age.

"Larissa, you are thousands of years younger than me. Has that ever bothered you?" Nik asked as he slid a glass of whiskey across the marble bench. He had a point. I never thought about it.

"Well, my soul is that old."

Roman snorted as he came over and pulled me tight. "Don't worry, you will always be my first love."

"Oh, come on." I pushed him away. "That is just gross." They laughed, both brothers way too happy. "Why are you so happy? You have both been moody for months." Nik wrapped his arms around my waist and lifted me from the ground.

"I am going to marry the love of my life in three days. My brother has found his mate and taken his rightful place as Alpha. Everything seems to be working out." A dark voice whispered in my head *'Except for the fact that the wolves tried to kill you.'*

"Nik, why did the wolves try to kill me?" He squeezed his drink so hard, that the glass broke in his grasp. I squealed from the shock and rushed over, but the wound had already healed.

"The witches," Roman muttered as he avoided meeting his brother's gaze. "They want you to return the power you stole from the coven."

"But I didn't steal anything. How? Why? What?" I scratched my head as Nik grabbed another glass.

"You ascended into your power. The one given by birthright from Katrina. You did not steal it, but they see it differently. I spoke to them already; however, it seems they didn't get the message. I will meet with Juliet again and discuss how we can come to a resolution."

"You spoke to them already?" The secrecy hit me suddenly, voices filled my head as well as an image of Roman and Nik sitting with unknown women in a café. I bent over the sink, emptying the contents of my stomach. As I wiped my mouth, I glared at Nik. "You met with them behind my back. You fucking arsehole. Let me guess, you threatened her. Did you stop to consider what I want? They can have my fucking powers. I am done with being this weak person. I want to be in control for once. Let me meet with this bitch."

"Larissa—"

"No, sleep on the couch tonight," I ordered, storming upstairs, away from my mate even as my heart yearned for him. I couldn't give in. I needed to send a message.

I WOKE TO AN EMPTY BED. NIK HAD DONE AS I REQUESTED, which honestly surprised me. I rubbed my eyes before seeing him asleep on the chaise lounge in the corner. I did say couch, but I did not exactly specify. I snuck into the closet, grabbing a pair of bike shorts and a black crop top. Nik still slept soundly as I took each step slowly to avoid any excess noise. I made my way into the gym. Today, I would no longer be weak. I wanted to be able to save myself from now on. I refused to be the damsel. The door creaked as I entered, and I closed it hoping to stop the noise. I spun to see Roman lifting a weight. His arms were on full display as I watched the muscles ripple from movement. It fascinated me how different they were for twins. Roman was built like a bear, whereas Nik had muscles and definition but nowhere near as large as his brother.

"Are you enjoying the perve?" Roman asked as he put it down.

I snorted at him. "For once, I wasn't perving. I was just thinking about how different the two of you are for twins. You are not identical, that much is clear."

"And yet we fooled you." He put the weights away as he rubbed the sweat from his face.

"Deceived, not fooled. I never wanted to think about the similarities between the two of you. I was trying to ignore the call for Nik."

He scoffed. "How did that work out for you?" I rolled my eyes and glanced around the room. I had no idea where to start. "Let me guess, you want to learn how to protect yourself."

"God, am I that transparent? Or did she do it in the past?" I groaned as I walked over to the treadmill.

"No, I just know you. What did you want to work on?" he asked as he strode over, standing beside me. I fiddled with the strings on my shorts. I had no idea.

"Self-defence." He squeezed my bicep and smirked. "Alright, I know I am weak, but will you help?"

"Have you asked his highness?" He flicked his head to the ceiling, where Nik was still sleeping. I crossed my arms.

"I *don't* need his permission for everything. He does not own me."

"Ah, Larissa, I love the way you challenge my brother. Let's get started. Come here." He walked over to the bag, holding up a pair of gloves. He slid them on and fastened them around my wrist before putting on his pads. "Alright, let's take it slow. This hand goes here, and this one goes here. When my hands are out wide, you need to swing like this, but you must keep your elbow locked in position. Then the uppercut is under while using your knees to drive upwards. Does that make sense?"

"I think so," I muttered as he tipped my chin to meet his gaze. His eyes challenged me. "Yes, I can do this," I said will a little more enthusiasm. Roman held up his pads and I struck them as he instructed. The more I did it, the better I became. My heart rate increased as I pushed myself to hit harder.

"There she is, my little tiger." I pumped harder again, and he started to brace himself against every attack. "Harder, Larissa." The intensity of his voice increased.

"WHAT THE HELL IS THIS?" Nik's voice boomed as he entered the gym wearing nothing but a pair of grey track shorts. I turned to glare at him as his rage flooded the bond. My eyes travelled down his body to the clear semi-erection in his pants. I licked my lips at the sight of him.

"I want to learn, and you don't get to tell me no." I held my ground as he smirked.

"Alright, principessa. Roman, give it to her. Let the beast out." Roman peered around me.

"Are you sure?" he questioned as he removed his pads.

"She wants to learn. She can tap into her power. Let her use her natural instinct for protection. She is fighting a god. Be prepared, Larissa." He sat down in the corner as Roman growled, his eyes glowing with pleasure. "You may want to take your gloves off." Nik walked over; his eyes trained on me. "Time to let the monster out of the cage." He kissed my hands as he gently nudged me forward.

Roman charged with a speed I wasn't ready for and tackled me to the ground. My body thumped on the floor while Nik laughed. I stood back up, reminding myself that I asked for this. Roman swung as I ducked and connected with his side. My magic tingled up my arms, and pride filled our bond as Roman increased the strength of his attack. His fist connected with my stomach, and I bent over in pain. He attempted another shot, but I blocked it with magic as I composed myself. But Roman continued.

I held my hand up to stop him. "Give me a moment." Instead of granting my request, Roman grabbed my hand, twisting it behind my back, forcing it higher as my shoulder threatened to pop. I threw my head back and it connected with him.

"The enemy doesn't give you a moment, Larissa. You asked for this," Nik reminded me, unhelpfully. These were the sons of Mars, the God of War. One inherited the muscular form, the other the strategy. Nik showed his own power as he stalked the fight between Roman and me, analysing our movements. I flicked my leg under Roman to trip him and he growled. My temper flared as I proceeded to use more magic with every hit. I ducked, twisted, and avoided his targeted attacks. My powers started to have a mind of their own, creating more force behind my swings and blocking Roman at every point. He picked me up, throwing me into the wall. My arm cracked as pain seared through it. I gritted my teeth against the pain and watched it heal instantly. *Holy shit!* I could heal. I charged at Roman as he lifted me above his head, tossing me into the air before he brought his foot out to hit me on the descent. Magic surged within me, a force guiding my every move, calculating whatever was needed to protect my fragile human form. Roman threw a sword at me as he swung, pushing all his strength onto me as I barely held up against him. My knees folded underneath, and I closed my eyes to focus my breath as the dark voices echoed.

A rush of power spread through me. I had never felt anything like it. My body was stronger, my senses heightened. I pushed against Roman as I rolled to move out of the way of his strike. He laughed. It only provoked more anger inside me and the determination that I had to win. An overwhelming urge to beat him came over me, and I craved his blood. The monster inside me was coming out. I started to shake with anticipation as I charged at Roman, swinging, stabbing him in any way I could. I failed to cause any wounds. I growled, wanting to tear him apart. I took a deep breath to centre myself as I threw up a shield to focus on my breathing for a moment. The voices grew louder, more demanding, they were darkness.

"Roman, get out," Nik ordered. "NOW!" he shouted as I opened my eyes to see my power enveloping the room. Nik ran over, holding my head in his hands. "Larissa, focus on my voice." His voice was a whisper against the voices in my head. He spun me around and I saw my face in the mirrors lining the walls, my eyes were black except for a red iris. I looked every bit the monster, a creature that children are taught to fear in the darkness. "There is my princess." My head cleared slowly, my heart no longer beating in my ears. He wrapped his arms around me tight. "Good girl," he muttered as he kissed the crook of my neck.

"What was that?" I asked him as I began to feel normal, turning to see his face.

"That is the reason why I was mad at you for training. We have no idea what you are truly capable of. Your powers are limitless. You transcended to another level, Larissa." I buried my head into his chest.

"I could have hurt you." Tears rolled down my cheeks as the gravity of everything hit me.

"Larissa, you could never hurt me. I am your mate and even in your darkest moments, you will see me. You heard my voice, didn't you?"

"Yes, I did. It was faint but I heard you. Why do you not trust your monster if you can trust mine?" He shook his head as sadness filled my body.

"I am a supernatural creature. I am cursed to live with a monster that craves destruction. You are human with a few extra spices thrown in." He winked at me, his attempt to lighten the mood.

"But you haven't answered my question. Why?" Nik sighed as he stepped away, running his fingers through his hair.

"I blacked out one night and tore through an entire village. It took centuries for me to make peace with the creature inside, to form a bond where I could stay in control. But this version of you has triggered something more primal. A darkness that wants to harm any who come near you, a darkness that wants control. If you are hurt, I want to hurt. If you are sad, I want to destroy. These are new sensations that scare me." I reached for his hand, bringing it to my lips.

"You say with confidence that I could never hurt you, but I know you would never hurt me either." I kissed him, pulling him against me in a tight embrace. He may not have been worried about my darkness, but I was terrified of it. "Will I need to find a way to control my beast?" He smiled and it seemed to light up the room and remove all my anxieties.

"You have to find your centre. The one thing that makes you who you are. Focus on that and the darkness will never win. You haven't lost control yet. I intervened because I worried that you may actually hurt my brother," Nik said, glancing over his shoulder to see Roman laughing.

"A tiny human could never hurt me." He peered at his fingers as if we were beneath him.

Nik smirked. "Next time, I won't intervene then. Let's get you some breakfast and discuss how I will never not sleep in our bed again." I snorted as I climbed the stairs to our room, covered in sweat. I wondered if I really could have harmed Roman if Nik had not interfered.

CHAPTER 40

A NICE DAY FOR A WEDDING

Nik

A wedding day was supposed to be the happiest day of a human's life, right? Nothing could go wrong. I had been getting Luce cleaned up so she could be part of Larissa's day. I wanted her far away from my mate, but Larissa had so much love and loyalty for her, and I didn't want to cause her any further harm. I sighed as I poured another glass of whiskey. I had nerves, actual nerves. This was a feeling I hadn't encountered for centuries. In two hours, Larissa would officially be my wife. Larissa Dankworth. I sighed.

"What is it, brother?" Roman asked as he entered, wearing a tailored black suit with red lapels, a black shirt, and a red floral tie. It matched Luce's bridesmaid outfit. He spoke of his disgust at having been partnered with her, but he knew Larissa would be ecstatic to have her there and see no disharmony between anyone.

"When we first wed, she took my name, and now…"

"Will she not be taking your name?" I glanced up, meeting his eyes in the mirror.

"She will not have our name, Silvia. Our mother's name."

Roman stalked over. "You can always return to your true name. Nik Silvia has a nice ring to it or even Remus." I shuddered at my true name. I never liked the name Remus. Nik was me; I was a phoenix who had evolved into Nik. I contemplated the idea of changing my name back.

"If I do, I wonder if any person will put together the fact that we are not exactly just an Alpha or just a vampire."

"Society is full of fucking idiots. I doubt anyone would make that connection." He snorted as he filled his glass again, we both had indulged a little too much this morning, but alcohol didn't have the same effect as it did on humans. I had encouraged Larissa to refrain from drinking after the last couple of days. I could sense her anxiety already. She had taken her pills, but they had done nothing to ease her worry.

"Yes, it is. I will discuss it with my new wife on our honeymoon. Did you finish organising it all?" Roman glared at me, finding the question to be an insult. I sniggered to myself.

"I need to finish getting dressed," I muttered, fastening the last few buttons of my black shirt. I wanted to keep it traditional for Larissa, but she made the point that neither of us were traditional. I wore a tuxedo with my usual flare; black pants and a shirt, with a black suit jacket that had deep green patterns woven into it. The pattern started as a flower with vines and leaves as it worked its way around the jacket. I requested that it symbolise our love. She was the flower, and the vines were the challenges that we encountered in our long lives. I pulled the jacket on as a cackle echoed around.

"Roman?" I called out as I turned around, finding I was alone. I picked up my glass to finish, spinning back to admire just how handsome I was, only to see those familiar red orbs staring back at me.

"Malignus." I turned, swinging my fist, but the space was empty. I looked back into the mirror to see his cocky face smiling at me.

"Hello, Remus." I shivered at the sound of my birth name. I reminded myself that he and I were nothing alike.

"How are you here?" He tapped the glass, and I moved closer. He was inside, he was not on the mortal plane. "Still not strong enough?" I smirked, causing his eyes to flare red.

"Tell me, Remus, how is the monster inside going? You know of the creature that I speak, the animal that you keep caged, the animal you keep satiated enough to never lose control. How is your leash on him going?" He spoke with an edge that highlighted he had the upper hand, and that I was missing something important.

"Just fine," I gritted out.

"I have doubts about that. How is my daughter going? I can feel her strength growing with every passing day." He licked his lips with delight, and I now understood why he wanted her.

"You can feed off her!" I exclaimed as the pieces started to click in my head; the reason why he kept her in hell.

"She is my blood; I do not need to feed. I absorb it through her blood, her power is magnificent and now that you have linked together, and she has transcended to a High Priestess; it is delicious. I had forgotten how gods tasted; it has been a few millennia since I have feasted on one."

"What?"

"Oh, you don't know. I forget our naïve you are, Remus. You feasted on her blood and continued to do so. She transfers a piece of herself into you every single bite. The more you take, the more you want and the more I indulge." It made sense why he spoke about my darkness; the more he took from me, the more I would lose control of the beast. My fists clenched as they landed on the mirror, projecting it across the room. His cackle filled the air, "Oh, Remus, so childish." I shook to contain myself; he would feed off this moment. Roman burst into the room, his growl echoing.

"What is it?" he asked as he stood on alert in the doorway.

"Yes, tell your brother, please, Remus." Roman stalked towards the mirror before a guttural noise escaped his throat. He lifted the mirror, leaving the room before tossing it out the window. I crossed my arms.

"Don't start. I am only returning him to the depths of hell where he belongs. What happened?"

I hesitated, not sure whether I should tell him, but I had no choice. "Malignus told me that the more blood I take from Larissa, the more chance I have of losing control of my beast. Malignus is manipulating us, and I am powerless to stop it."

"You were never supposed to meet," Roman repeated. The more we discovered, the more I understood why Katrina said it. We were dangerous to one another; the combination of our powers could destroy us both. Why had she done this?

CHAPTER 41
WEDDINGS AND FAMILY NEVER MIX

Larissa

I STARED AT THE CEILING. TODAY WAS THE DAY; THE DAY I married Nik. And while that fact alone should bring me joy, all I felt was impending doom. Your wedding day was supposed to be filled with happiness, surrounded by all the people that you love. But as I sat up, glancing around the room, I was struck by how alone I was. I dragged myself from the luxurious king-size bed toward the shower, remembering the hairdresser telling me that I must not wash my hair. It needed to be a little dirty. I pulled my hair into a high bun as the water warmed my skin. I missed Nik. I didn't like being away from him. He prodded the bond all night to ensure I was alright, which I found cute even if a tad annoying. I dried myself and dressed in just a white lacey bra and white G-string, pulling a large white robe over the top as I walked down the stairs of the penthouse. There were at least twenty people, all running around doing various jobs.

"What is all of this?" I asked as I reached the bottom step. A random person handed me a cup of coffee. I made my way over to the couch, in awe of the people rushing around.

"Who would have thought that my sister would be getting married today?" I looked up to see Luce standing before me, holding her arms out. I ran into them, holding her tight, and never wanting to let her go. She was alive, she was safe. Nik hadn't mentioned her since he encountered her at the vampire meeting.

"You're alive," I whispered. "I missed you." Tears fell from my eyes; I cried, holding her as if it did not seem real.

"Did you really think I would miss your wedding day?" I pulled back to look at her. "Okay, I probably would have but Nik had every chance to kill me that day at the warehouse. He also saved my life from being a blood whore. I may not agree but I can see how much he loves you and is willing to sacrifice for your happiness. I am beginning to understand this mate bond. You may need to fill in the blanks though."

"You have no idea how much it means to me to have you here. I thought that I would never see you again." Luce stared at the floor, her cheeks flushing red. "What is it?"

"I need to ask for your forgiveness. I couldn't see past my own hatred, my own jealousy, and Peter had this way of stoking it further. He fed it. I hate myself for the fact that I got you shot, that I attacked your mate, and I tried to steal your power. It was never mine, but I felt inferior to you. You seemed to have it all and I wanted something for me. I lost Mum, I kept your secrets, and I just..." She threw her hands in the air. I could see her anger and frustration. Right now, I saw a crossroads. Either I understood and forgave her, or held onto this betrayal forever.

"Larissa and Lucianna, we are ready for your hair and makeup." A beautiful blonde appeared, wearing a tight black dress, her perfect skin and body were evidence of her vampiric nature. Was it wise for Luce to be around vampires right now? "My name is Scarlet. I'll be doing your makeup, and Victor shall be doing your hair."

Scarlet took my hand as she led me over to a stool before a mirror surrounded by lights. Courage flooded the bond. Nik wanted me to enjoy the day, to stop worrying. I flicked out my phone.

ME

Thank you for Luce. I cannot put into words just how much it means to me.

NIK

I wish I could have seen your smile, it would have lit up the room.

ME

It still is. Only another three hours before I am officially your ball and chain.

NIK

Larissa, do not give me ideas. I rather like the thought of being tied to one another every day. :P

ME

Maybe only in the bedroom.

NIK

That can wait till after we are wed, we have a couple of days honeymoon then time to return to work.

ME

Some would call you a workaholic

NIK

I will be worse now, knowing that my wife is just a few floors below me.

Luce grabbed my phone and put it on the table.

"Luce," I grumbled at her. "I was texting Nik."

"You will see him in a few hours. Now is the time to spend with your sister...or cousin? What do we call ourselves now?" she asked as she handed me a bottle of water. I checked the lid, noting it had not been opened.

"You will always be my sister in my eyes, but it is up to you."

"Sisters it is. I only wish Mum was here to see this," she whispered as sadness tinged her voice, tears welling in her eyes. I reached for my anti-anxiety meds, the idea that both my mothers would not be here brought a tightness to my chest. Luce coughed and took the pill bottle from me.

"Luce, what the hell? Give it back!" I shouted after her as she stormed into the kitchen and threw them in the bin.

"Rissa, I can't believe you never realised. You never had anxiety. Mum tricked you. The pills were spelled. When you were twelve, she noticed your magic starting to appear. She didn't know how or why but it freaked her out. She went crazy. Remember the weekend when she had no sleep and became like a zombie?" I nodded. We thought about calling a psych hospital for her. "They were designed to dampen your powers."

"But what about the panic attacks and the racing heart?" My head was racing. Did my mother really drug me?

"The more you take, the more those symptoms occur. When you don't take them, it causes sickness, almost like a junkie needing a hit." Nausea swirled in my gut.

"Fuck, I am going to be sick." I held my mouth and ran to the bathroom, the contents of my stomach coming up. I sat beside the toilet for a moment before Luce arrived, holding my phone. I took it from her and Nik's face appeared on the screen.

"What the hell just happened?" There was hint of anger in his voice, but all I could focus on was the worry in his eyes.

"Just finding out more family secrets; it is fine."

"Did she hurt you? I warned her that I wo—" I glared at him, daring him to finish his sentence. Roman suddenly appeared behind him.

"Explain, Larissa, please," Roman pleaded. "Nik wants a reason to hurt someone today." He snorted to lighten the mood. I noticed that Nik had a little more anger than usual, but he attempted to hide it by pushing through his love.

"My anti-anxiety meds are not what they seem. I am going to be sick again." I handed the phone to Luce. "Tell them, please," I begged before I chucked again. How could my mother do this? Did she know the truth about my father? Luce re-entered the room, handing me the phone.

"He is demanding to speak with you," she snarled as I took the phone and sat up.

"Nik, how did you not smell it on me?" I questioned him, knowing he would have been able to sense anything off in my system through scent alone.

"I don't know, Larissa. Truly. You have always had a unique smell, but I never smelt anything peculiar about it." He rubbed the back of his neck, and I could feel his worry. "Let us just worry about it later. Today is supposed to be one of the happiest days of our lives and I am respecting your need to not see each other before we walk down the aisle." I chuckled at his annoyance. I knew it seemed so trivial, but I wanted some aspects of our wedding to remain traditional. He smiled, having achieved what he set out to do; to distract me.

"Fine, thank you for not racing over here. I appreciate it and I will show just how appreciative I am later tonight."

"As will I, Mrs Dankworth." His voice broke as he spoke. It was odd.

"Love you, Mr Solis."

Roman laughed in the background as Nik threw an object at him. He hung up the phone and I sighed before standing to wash my face and teeth. Luce reappeared, leaning in the doorway with her arms crossed.

"Are you alright?" she asked, her tone laced with concern. I turned to look at her, shaking my head as she held out her arms. I collapsed into her embrace.

"Luce, why did you never tell me the truth about any of it?" I whispered as her arms tightened around me. She sighed deeply.

"It probably isn't the best topic for your wedding day. I promise after you get back from your honeymoon, we will talk. We will have a nice long lunch or dinner together and I will tell you everything."

"You promise?"

"With everything I have, Larissa. With everything that I am. All my secrets will be laid bare." She kissed the top of my head. "Now, let's get you married to the monster of your dreams."

I snorted. I mean, she didn't lie. Nik *was* a monster, but he loved me as I loved him. I remembered back to the day Nik told me about the mate bond and I laughed at him. I chuckled to myself at how far we had come. How I hated him for how he made me feel and how persistent he was but now I could not imagine my life without him. I knew without a doubt that losing him would shatter my very existence. How the hell had he done this hundreds of times?

I sat down as the hairstylist and makeup artist worked their magic. Luce refused to let me see myself in the mirror until I wore my dress. I slid out of my robe as Luce held open the bottom of my silk wedding dress. I stepped in cautiously, not wanting to ruin it. Luce snapped her fingers at Maria to help. Her face tightened, lines of worry etched around her eyes, making me giggle softly. She was taking the role of Maid of Honour very seriously. Luce lifted the front as Maria brought it up my back. I slid my arms into the incredibly soft fabric. Nik told me my dress alone cost twenty thousand dollars. I did pick it, but never would have guessed that it had that price tag attached. But I fell in love with the dress and wasn't about to give it up, even though the idea of having that much money blew my mind. Maria fastened the band before Luce handed her the belt. I held onto the exquisite golden belt, mesmerised by the intricate floral patterns that danced and intertwined across its surface. Each delicate curve and twist sparked my imagination with tales of opulence and history. The gown revealed nothing at the front except my tiny waist. The dress stopped at the curve in my lower back revealing my olive complexion, which almost made the colour of the dress shine brighter. The cape covered my near nakedness only for the ceremony but once the formalities were removed, I could show more skin.

I ran my hands down the softness of the silk before glancing up to see myself in the mirror. I barely recognised the person looking back at me. I always wore demure clothing and kept my style simple yet sophisticated and right now, that wasn't me. I touched my face almost scared it would break as my skin shimmered from the blush. The golden headpiece sparkled from the sun's reflection. Its delicate filigree was adorned with tiny floral motifs. It nestled atop my head as waves cascaded down my shoulders. The headpiece had been specifically created by Nik to symbolise our love. I could not tear my eyes away from its beauty.

"Oh. My. God!" Luce exclaimed, as her face lit up. "You look amazing. Mum would be in tears right now." She raced over and held me tight, as if sensing my emotions were about to spill out. I wished more than anything that both Mum and Katrina could be here. I closed my eyes to stop myself from crying and felt Nik pushing through his own comfort to help. I sighed as I held my sister tighter. My only family left and even that was complicated.

I took a step back to look over my sister, her crimson-coloured gown highlighting her complexion and the brightness of her eyes. The long sleeves of sheer lace were woven with a tapestry of roses, their petals entwined with golden thread that shimmered under the lights. The dress hugged her tiny waist with a cinched satin ribbon that fastened at her back and flowed down her back. The dress had almost been designed for her.

I sighed, realising Nik had planned all of this to perfection. He was always going to let my sister be here, even with our rocky past. The man who murdered his enemies without a second thought, but here he was, allowing my sister, the one who tried to kill us both, to be here on our special day. I closed my eyes; he had thought of everything. I noticed Luce's concern, but I smiled.

"I am getting married to a man who would do literally anything for me. A man who has seen me die countless times, a man who waits forever to spend what little time he has with me. A man who loves me with every piece of his heart even when it breaks as he holds me in his arms in my last moments. He literally ripped Hector's body apart to stop him from coming near me again. He has done so much, and I mean, he has let you be here, and I am sorry he fucking hates you," I stopped to laugh, "but here you are, and he organised a gown that is perfect for you. I cannot believe this is my life."

Luce cleared her throat. "Wait. What? You died?" I snorted at her comment. I hadn't told her the truth about the curse.

"I thought you knew because Mum told you I had to be protected."

"I never knew what for. What is it?" She put her hands on her hips as she huffed out in frustration.

"When I get back from our honeymoon, I promise we will discuss all our secrets," I said as I kissed her cheek. "Are you ready to walk me down the aisle?"

"Abso-fucking-lutely." She beamed with pride as she took my hand, and we made our way to the door. For once, I did not feel nervous. I knew what was waiting for me. Nik would be standing there, as handsome and suave as ever. With that smile that could make butter melt, exuding sophistication and confidence. During the car ride, I watched the cityscape, and the blur of people speed past. When we pulled up at Kew Gardens, Luce squeezed my hand and opened the door.

"Let's get you married to your soulmate. I actually can't wait to see what he has done for you." Luce glanced over the venue before us. I steadied myself as my body tingled, a sign of just how close Nik was. I knew he would be watching for me before I walked down the aisle. He would not be able to help himself. He never liked surprises. I hooked my arm into Luce's as her other hand held onto her bouquet of red roses and white carnations. The wedding coordinator came rushing out, her blonde hair a mess atop her head. The wrinkles around her eyes showed her stress, and I wondered if Nik had been ordering her about. Her plump black dress was covered in pollen and a mixture of other stains. I smirked as she bowed her head.

"Lady Dankworth, you are late, and he is not too pleased." I chuckled as I put my hand up to silence her. She sighed and composed herself.

"Please, it is Larissa. And take a breath. I am here now. Let us head inside." The lines on her face disappeared as she relaxed. She stood aside and straightened her dress, then walked towards the door as we entered the tall building, which led us into another.

Luce whispered, "Are you alright?" I nodded as we were stopped. The blonde coordinator paused as she spoke in her headpiece. I paced a little, not from nerves but more from apprehension about what was behind those doors. What he had planned, what he had designed. He typically asked my preference when making decisions, but he had full control, which I favoured as I tried to get work under control.

The wedding march echoed through the doors before me. They swung open, and my eyes blinked to adjust to the light. The walls were glass from the floor to the roof and the sun reflected as green vines wrapped around and cascaded down. The aisles were lined with arrangements of roses and carnations to symbolise our relationship. The roses represented the love that we had for one another while the carnations signified eternity. He wanted everything to symbolise our love and devotion to one another. I looked at the petals that lined the floor and the multitude of guests with faces I didn't know. I noticed my new receptionist Mimi, her eyes solely focused on Roman whose eyes bore into hers. He had yet to speak with her, but I think the bond was already forming. My eyes were everywhere before I saw him, the man of my dreams, my monster. His eyes were brighter than ever, his suit fitting his frame perfectly. I thought about how good his arse would look in those pants. The green floral pattern, laced with gold reflected from the sun that shone through the glass. He took my breath away. I reached the end of the aisle and Luce kissed my cheek, lifting my veil.

Nik's hand wrapped around my own as he pulled me against his chest. "Screw tradition." His lips smashed against mine and he licked my lips to part them. He groaned as the crowd erupted in laughter. He let me go with a cheeky smile on his face. "You are more beautiful than the heavens. You have enchanted me to the point where I find it hard to breathe. I am the luckiest man in the world to have you beside me in this life." I grinned at his cheesy statement, wanting to kiss him again.

The celebrant cleared his throat. "Shall we get started?" We giggled at each other before turning to look at the elderly woman beside us in her grey wrap dress. Nik and I nodded, holding each other's hands tightly as if scared to let go. The celebrant proceeded with the ceremony, and I glanced around at the number of guests. I barely knew half of them, but I spotted Daniel and Duzi, who looked enraged. They whispered to one another as I met their eyes. Nik's thumb rubbed my knuckles, bringing my attention back to him. I gave him a small smile, despite the sudden unease filling my body. The hairs on my arms stood up and Nik's eyes flashed. He felt it too. The room began to shake.

"Is that you?" he asked but even I could tell from the worry etched into his face that he wasn't convinced. I shook my head, and he pushed me behind him, holding me close to his back. Roman stood closer and even Luce joined us. The doors burst open, and I noticed the familiar mop of hair.

"James," I said softly as I peered at Luce who nodded. "What the hell is he doing here?" I asked her as Nik's growl echoed through the space.

"LARISSA!" James shouted but he didn't look right. Something about him was off. I moved to step around Nik, but his head snapped in my direction, a clear warning that I had to stay exactly where I was.

"Nik, look at his eyes. Something is not right." He ignored me, so I glanced at Roman who stared intently at James before peeking back at me. He saw the same thing I did. He put his hand on his brother's shoulder.

"He has been spelled. This is not James, brother. We must tread carefully, as we don't know what could happen," Roman muttered to avoid others hearing. Nik straightened, plastering a smile on his face. He raised his hands to get everyone's attention.

"Apologies everyone but I believe someone may be a little lost. Just a momentary pause in the ceremony," he called out for all to hear. That didn't stop people from assuming the worst. James proceeded to cackle, and it echoed through the room as dark clouds rolled in, taking away the sun. Rain began to pound against the glass as the temperature dropped suddenly. Luce held my hand, her eyes widening, her pupils dilated as her breathing increased. Her body began to shake as small beads of sweat appeared on her forehead.

"Luce, it will be fine. Stay calm." I pulled her against my body and rubbed her back to soothe her. Roman placed his hand on my lower back, his warmth a comfort as I buried my own terror.

"Ah, Nik, did you really think that I would allow you to have a happy day?" I recognised the voice of my father coming from James's mouth. He had been possessed. I stood in horror. What was the point of this? I let go of Luce and placed her with Roman who held her close. I stepped up to Nik before clapping my hands to create a bubble around the three of us that only we could hear. At that moment, I didn't care about my secret. Most of those in attendance already knew. Nik glared at me before understanding that whatever came from my father's mouth would be worse than others discovering just how powerful I was. "Smart girl. You get your intelligence from me obviously." I wanted to tear him to pieces for harming my friend. James was innocent.

"Let. Him. Go." I gritted my teeth, emphasising every word. Malignus smiled, the creepy look on his face sent shivers down my spine.

"My lovely daughter, he is a pawn but a necessary one. I wanted to give you a gift and you made it so easy for me."

"Larissa!" Luce shouted as I turned to see the bubble being covered in blood.

"I may not be able to step foot on your earth just yet, but I can still use my powers to manipulate and torture. I will give you the choice that you never had. The choice of who you want your life to be with—Nik or your darling husband James, better known as Romulus Augustus in his first life. Choose wisely, my dear." He clapped his hands and a scream ripped from my throat. Darkness covered my vision and the world grew silent. I could no longer feel Nik.

CHAPTER 42
SPELLED TO REMEMBER
Nik

I stood over my soon-to-be wife, who lay unconscious on the floor. Malignus's eyes stared back at me through James's face. I wanted to murder him, to rip him to shreds. Luce screamed as she ran over, pounding against the spell that Larissa cast that kept us trapped in this bubble with him.

"ROMAN!" I shouted. "Can you hear me?" I prayed to whoever would listen that he could.

"I am here, Nik." Larissa spelled the bubble to avoid others hearing but was smart enough to keep Luce and Roman in the loop. I beamed with pride at her spell.

"Get Luce out of here. Get the guests out of here. I won't risk anyone's safety when she wakes from whatever he has done to her." Pain tore through my body as if every single wound had reopened. As if I was dying a thousand deaths at once. Malignus's cackle filled the space. My breath grew ragged.

"Do you think she will pick you again or will she return to her husband?" he hissed, the words echoing in my head. She had to pick me; we were mates. She loved me and always had. "Are you sure?" I forgot he could read minds; he also had the power to change fates. I fought against the pain, charging at the man who threatened to take away my one reason to live.

"I will fucking destroy you." My fist froze in the air as he held up his hand to stop it. I pushed with everything I had but it didn't move. He flung his wrist and I flew backwards, slamming against the wall of the bubble. I groaned.

"Nik? Nik? Are you okay?" Roman called out, worry lacing his voice.

"I am fine, is everyone safe?" I questioned as I stood, removing my suit jacket and rolling up my sleeves.

"Yes, but…uh Luce won't leave. She promises she will listen and is sitting with me." That I could deal with. Larissa may need her sister if she chose wrong. I shook away the thought. We had been through enough to know our love was eternal. Malignus smiled.

"You won't win. She will pick me."

"What happens when she discovers the truth?" I froze, remembering what I sacrificed to keep her alive. The blood I had to pay with. Would she forgive me?

CHAPTER 43
RELIVING LIYANA'S CHOICE

Larissa

"Time to wake from your slumber, my wife," the voice spoke, one that I didn't recognise. My eyes blinked awake as I took in the view above. The roof was built from stone. I lay in an impossibly large four-poster bed with a wolf's fur blanket. A hand lay on my stomach rubbing it in small circles, and I glanced down to see a swollen belly. I sat up quickly, feeling bubbles in my stomach.

"Holy shit," I gasped as I watched my own hand drift down to touch it. I wanted to cry. I had a baby growing inside me. I was pregnant. What type of dream was this?

"What is this holy shit that you speak of, wife?" I turned to see the man who called me wife.

"James?" I raised an eyebrow at him in confusion.

"Have you lain with another man? Who is this James that you speak of?" His voice grew louder as he stood from the bed. I rolled off, to stand opposite him. I was no longer in London. I wore a beautiful white toga with golden thread on the trim. I was living Liyana's life, and she was pregnant. But Nik and Roman told me that I never fell pregnant. Had they kept this a secret? And for what reason?

"Never, my love. I have only ever lain with my big, strong warrior husband, the greatest in all the lands, Romulus Augustus." He cocked his head in the air at the compliment. I was thankful that Nik had told me whom I had married before I met him. Romulus cleared his throat and held out his hand. I slid my hand into his, Malignus's words ringing through my head: '*I will give you the choice you never had.*'

"We must feed my son. You will eat." Nausea ate at me. I wanted to vomit at the idea of eating right now, but Romulus dragged me through the partitioned doors and into what could be considered a lounge area. There were daybeds laid out in the shape of a square with pillows on the end. He pointed and I sat down, grateful for a seat as the dizziness hit me. A plate was thrust into my hands, containing a variety of nuts and bread. The smell caused my stomach to turn, and I bent over and vomited. Romulus grabbed my face, his grasp tight as it pinched my skin. "I did not marry a weak wife. You will eat and you will keep it down or I shall make you eat everything you vomit." I nodded weakly.

I now understood why Nik hated him so much. A female slave sauntered past, making eyes at my husband. He cleared his throat. "I will return to ensure you have eaten." The anger in his eyes showed just how serious he was about his comment. I bit my tongue to avoid saying anything bad and possibly getting myself killed. Being pregnant would certainly help, as long as it was a boy.

"Princess Liyana." Another slave wandered over. She appeared to be in her thirties while I had no knowledge of my age, not having seen myself in the mirror yet. Did they have mirrors during this time? I tried to remember my history, but I focused more on the gods than the minor details. Her dark hair was pulled into a ponytail, and her gown was secured with clips unlike my own, which had golden clasps. Mine glowed in the light while hers was grey, I assumed from the dirt that she had to clean all day.

I smiled at her. "What can I help you with?" She rushed over to clean up my vomit. I reached for her, knowing I could do it before stopping. This was the expectation of slaves during that time. The nausea rolled again. "I am going to be sick again," I muttered as she handed me a bucket. The smell was rancid, which only made me want to vomit some more. I pulled the bucket away as the slave handed me a glass of water. "How long have my husband and that slave been rolling in the sheets together?" I asked as I took small sips to wash my mouth out.

"The idea was yours, princess."

"But…" I pondered why I would have asked someone to lay with my husband.

"Do you not remember?" She bent down to look at me as I shook my head.

"The master has become frustrated with your inability to keep food down. He has been forcing you to eat and swallow your own vomit. You asked for Octavia to distract him during times when you eat and times when his temper flares and he beats you."

"Oh my. I sent a woman to distract him for my safety while she receives his brutal hand." She nodded. How could I do that to a person?

"You promised her land and fortune if it is a son, or until *he* can save you." My ears perked up at the way she said *he*.

"He?" I queried, not wanting to say the name but thinking I may be on the right track.

"Remus." Her voice so quiet, it was barely a whisper.

"Who does the baby belong to?" I asked softly, unaware if I had even slept with Nik or Remus during this time. She shrugged her shoulders. If I seemed to be protecting this baby so much, I believed it may have been Nik's. Was that why he showed the dream of our children running around? Because we almost had it? But what happened to the baby?

"I need some air." I fanned my face, nibbling on nuts and a few pieces of bread before she took it away. Romulus returned, and I was glad to know he lasted long because it served its purpose. Octavia followed, covering her face with her hands. He had hit her. This was my fault. Romulus grabbed my face and kissed me as I smelt the stench of sex on him. "I ate as you requested. I would like to walk about in the gardens. Care to accompany me?" I asked him, but he shook his head.

"I have more pressing matters to attend to than a walk amongst flowers that inevitably die," he bit out with so much cruelty in his voice. "Go on your own, but you must return to eat soon. My son will be strong. It took you long enough to conceive my child." As he stormed away, I stood, dizziness hitting me again. I fumbled before the slave returned.

"I have you, princess." Her hand took mine and another landed on my back.

"I seem to be unsure of your name today. I do not feel like myself." I shook my head to get my bearings as I stared at the woman who seemed determined to protect me.

"Flavia."

"I thank you for your help, Flavia." A small smile crept over her face as I wandered into the garden, taking a seat on the stone bench that looked out to the town below. I held my stomach, thinking about what could happen from here. A light hit my eyes, and I closed them, squinting in that direction. My eyes found him. Nik. I stood and slowly walked over into the large bushes that formed a maze as he pulled me into his arms. His hair was longer and curly, but those eyes were just as beautiful as ever.

"I have missed you, my love," he whispered into my neck, taking a big sniff. I chuckled at how he had not changed. His lips crashed against mine as I felt myself getting poked by his erection. "I need you." He got on his knees, lifted my leg over his shoulder, and snuck under my gown and his tongue took one long lick, before nibbling on my sensitive clit.

"Holy fucking shit," I groaned out as Nik laughed. He knew what to do even back then.

"Princess?" a voice called out. I cleared my throat.

"I am fine, just tripped on a rock." I maintained a steadiness in my voice as Nik's tongue delved between my folds, licking as if I were his last meal. I tapped his head as I was about to come. I worried about how loud I would be. I bit my finger to block it out, moaning from sheer delight. He stood, lifting me, and I wrapped my legs around his waist as he lowered me onto his throbbing dick. I threw my head forward, landing on his shoulder. The same emotions and feelings floated between us, love and needing each other like it was our last breath.

"Liyana!" Romulus shouted, and we froze. Nik let me down before kissing my lips and running away. The man was a god, and he ran from a mere human. I chuckled as I pretended to do something in this maze. "Liyana!" he called out again, his footsteps crunching on the mixture of brown dirt and rocks. I turned to him with a smile as I placed a flower in my hair.

"Romulus, are the flowers not beautiful?" He crossed his arms, obviously displeased that I hadn't answered him immediately.

"They do not compare to how beautiful you look right now." My cheeks flushed with embarrassment. He had seemed so cruel and now he looked at me as if I was the most beautiful creature in the world. "Ah, that is even better, I love to see the blood rush to your face." He stepped closer as another bout of nausea hit me. I forced it away, fearing his reaction. "Come, I discovered something that I wish to tell you." I followed closely behind like a good wife till we reached his office, so to speak. A dark-coloured wooden desk stood in the middle, covered with maps of the city.

"I found them." He beamed with pride.

"Found who, Romulus?" I made sure to say his name rather than tripping up and calling him James.

"I found the brothers; the ones who created Rome." My heart sank.

"Oh, that is wonderful." I had to pretend to be happy at his information and I feared my voice would give away my true emotions. He slammed his fist down as he glared at me.

"I cannot wait to have them do my bidding, my own personal weapons. They will help me keep my city safe from any invader." I had missed so much; I had no idea what was about to happen.

"Yes, but you are strong enough without them." He stormed over, hitting me with the back of his hand as I fell to the floor.

"You are a fool! Your inability to secure my heir sooner has led to this unrest within our peaceful nation. Now my title and wealth are not safe as I wait for you to deliver my son. Until that happens, I need extra protection. Our enemy is advancing."

Flavia ran in to help me up, but I held up my hand to stop her. "Get out!" he shouted at her. Tears pricked my eyes. He relaxed his shoulders as he helped me to stand. "I shall extend an invitation to dinner tomorrow. You will enchant them with your beauty," he gripped my face, "do you understand?"

I nodded. "Yes, Romulus, I swear it." He pushed me away as I rushed from the room. How the hell was this happening?

———

The next day, as I sat, forcing myself to eat lunch for the day, Romulus entered with Roman and Nik, or Romulus and Remus. I chuckled at the fact that Romulus had his name sake from a god that he possessed no similar traits to.

"Liyana, I have found them. The men who shall protect us." Their eyes focused on me, eyes I already knew. They bowed their heads as I walked over, struggling to keep my food down and stay upright from the constant nausea. Nik's eyes lustfully peered over my body as I remembered the work of his tongue from yesterday. They brightened for a moment as I registered that he would smell my desire. I strode over to my husband.

"I am honoured to meet the brothers who founded our wonderful city." Nik took my hand, placing a kiss on it before Roman stepped forward to do the same.

"They are brilliant. Come, we shall speak and enjoy a feast tonight," Romulus said. I watched as they walked away, Nik glancing over his shoulder with a cocky smile. He hadn't changed at all.

Hours passed as I busied myself with menial tasks before changing into a red gown and adorning myself with golden jewels. The men laughed and enjoyed the spread of food as I excused myself for a moment to use the bathroom. I sat on the cold bench, perching myself perfectly over the hole before standing and leaving the room. Nik stood outside, pushing me against the wall without a word.

"Let's hope we are not interrupted today." He lifted my leg and thrust himself inside me. He clasped his hand over my mouth. He felt so good, filling me with every single inch of his throbbing cock. He groaned as he increased his pace, and I could feel my walls clenching as I bit into his hands to stop myself from moaning. The sensations were amazing as he nibbled into my neck. We climaxed together, my legs shaking from the shot of adrenaline. He leant his head against mine and lowered my leg. "You will be the death of me, Liyana. I promise we shall run away. We will be together soon. I swear it on my life." The words made my heart ache as I knew he meant it and he would risk his life for me. I wanted to warn him, to make him stop, but I couldn't bring myself to do it. I returned to the room without Nik, sitting beside my husband and offering him a goblet of wine. As he took the wine, he grabbed my face, planting a kiss on my lips.

"Is she not the most beautiful woman in the lands?" he asked as he finished his drink. They both nodded before he stood and took my hand. "I am glad to have your help, but I will retire for the night. You are welcome to spend time with whomever you please while you stay within my compound." Nik and Roman nodded as Romulus dragged me to the bedroom. I suddenly felt like a whore as he removed the clasps on my gown, letting it fall to the floor. Nik's semen still lingered, some dripping to the floor.

"So pleased that the thought of me makes you drip with need." I cringed, wondering how many other women had to do this. "Get on the bed on your knees." I did as he asked, hearing him place his clothes and jewels down before the bed sunk under his weight. His fingers teased my entrance as he coaxed a moan out of me. My body was sensitive enough, with all the hormones, but he knew exactly what he was doing. He slid his dick into my wetness, as he called it. A sense of satisfaction filled me, knowing it was another man's sperm. He pushed himself in slowly, groaning at the feeling of my tightness around him. "Utter perfection." He picked up a solid rhythm before he sat on his legs and lifted my body to sit upright. I knew this meant I would have to do most of the work as I bounced on his erection. The feeling didn't compare to Nik. Romulus's fingers reached around, rubbing circles into my clit. I moaned, enjoying the sensations, but as I opened my eyes, I saw red glowing eyes before me. Romulus finished, pushing me off him as he climbed into bed.

"I will go and clean myself," I spoke softly as I gathered my gown and wandered over to the bowl, wiping what remained of the two different seeds between my legs. I hung my head in shame. I really was a whore in this time. I had slept with two men in the space of an hour. The red eyes remained as I dressed myself and followed them.

My father stood before me, a devilish smile upon his face. "Hello, Larissa, enjoying your trip to the past?" I wanted to hit him, but I was in a body that had no power. He laughed. "Always eager for a fight."

"Why did you do this?" I asked him, cautious about who may see us.

"I thought, considering I took your life from you, that I would offer you a choice."

"What choice?"

"The life you wish to live without the complications of being fated to one of them. I will ask you this question and you will have till the morning to answer it. If you could make Liyana's choice all over again, who would you pick? Romulus or your precious Nik? You should think about it as that baby is Romulus's and you know of Nik's dislike of your husband. Will you raise your son, or will you risk his life by going on the run with the man who cannot offer you everything you want? Romulus can give you wealth, power, and stability. Nik has nothing more to offer than his love. Which is worth more to you? Time is ticking, Larissa, make your choice."

I pondered his question; he had a point. Nik would never be kind to my son knowing who his father was, but he wanted children. It begged the question of why he never told me the truth. I was pregnant when I died. Why had the baby never come up? What happened? Romulus, despite being an arsehole, could be manipulated and give me a life of stability. I did not care for the money or jewels or the roughness of him, but I had to consider the security he would give me during this time. There were so many questions that I had to think about. I dragged myself to bed, pulling the blanket over me as Romulus snored beside me. What did I want?

I woke the next morning with the same questions running through my head. Romulus rubbed my stomach, and I heard him speaking to it. "You will be big and strong like your father, a fierce warrior, and will cut down all your enemies." In these moments, he seemed sweet and loving.

"Romulus," I interrupted him, "do you love me?" I wanted to know what I was to him. He peered at me curiously as his brow creased.

"You are my wife. Yes, I do. Our marriage may have been for political reasons, but you are my partner," he answered with tender words, but they seemed almost devoid of emotion. I smiled as he rolled out of bed. "If you are finished with nonsense questions, we have breakfast with our guests." I dressed myself and ventured out, pushing the nausea aside once again. I feared the abuse I would receive if I vomited in front of guests. Nik glared at me, his eyes brighter than usual. He would have felt and heard our sex last night. I hung my head in shame. I needed to speak with him. I motioned for him to join me, noting how Roman distracted Romulus, allowing us to speak.

"You dare lay with him while I am within these walls," he spat at me, his body vibrating with a deep guttural sound.

"I cannot deny my husband, Remus, despite what I feel for you. I need to ask you a question." He waited as I took a breath. "If I run away with you, what happens to the child?"

"We shall find it a proper home, where it will be loved and cared for, and we will try for our own." My heart sank. This baby was a piece of me, and he couldn't put his hatred aside. The thought of leaving this baby behind made me want to cry. He rubbed my arms. "What is it?" I wondered if, as a wolf, he could sense my emotions.

"You would expect me to give up a piece of me for a life of uncertainty?" I asked him, barely holding myself together.

"Do you not love me as I love you?"

"Of course I do, but this child is part of me. I cannot be parted from it. You must understand that."

He growled, shaking his head. "I will not raise a pup that is not my own. It is not my responsibility."

"Leave now." I pointed behind him. "I do not wish to see you any longer."

"Liyana," he pleaded as I turned away from him.

"What is the meaning of this?" Romulus's voice boomed in the space as he saw Nik's hand on my hip. I stood frozen in fear as he stormed over, grabbing my hair and pulling me toward him. I yelped with the pain as Nik and Roman stood beside one another, growls escaping their chests.

"You will unhand my mate," Nik threatened him, stepping closer.

"Remus, you are a fool if you believe I will hand over my wife to you. She is mine, I own her, she carries my son in her womb." Romulus held up a sword as guards swarmed them. Nik's eyes darted between his brother, the guards, and my husband who yanked on my head. "You believe you can take my wife from me? I bought her and all her wealth and lands. She will not leave with you."

"Remus, we are outnumbered, we need to leave." Roman grabbed his brother's arm, pulling him back.

"This is not over!" Nik shouted as they ran away, the guards chasing him from the castle. Romulus dragged me to our room and threw me onto the bed. My pregnancy was still early enough, only around sixteen weeks, I guessed. I cradled my belly in fear as I moved away from him.

"You let another man touch you." I shook my head, smelling the saltiness of my tears as they streamed down my face.

"No, never Romulus, I have only been faithful to you. Remus and I only met yesterday; I swear it. I promise you. He only spoke of my beauty and that no one could compare." I crawled over and got on my knees before the man who could kill me if he so wished. He stroked my face as his red face settled.

"Stand," he ordered, and I slowly rose to stand before him. He held the sword to my throat. "You belong to me, do you understand?" I nodded as he pushed me onto the bed. He stormed from the room, but I couldn't fall apart even though I wanted to.

Romulus did not return for the night as I lay on the bed, stroking my belly. The next morning, my sister arrived. She had the same features as me. The dark hair, green eyes, and olive skin but she had more beauty marks on her face. We were both beautiful and would have been sought after during this time.

"Ah, my baby sister." She kissed my cheek on either side. "How is the future leader of Rome going?" My eyes were sore from crying all night, but she did not ask.

"He is fine, thank you, Cecilia." I turned away from her, glancing out the window at the garden where the man I loved had kissed me. And now I stood in a castle guarded by more men than needed. Romulus wanted to keep me contained or, as he suggested, safe. I sighed as more tears fell. "What is it, Liyana?" my sister asked as she ran over, running her hand up my arm.

"Cecilia, I lost him." She reached for my baby, but I pushed her hand away, "No, not the baby. My soul mate, the man who makes my heart ache when he is not near, the man who makes me feel more beautiful than the sunrise or the sunset or the flowers in the garden."

"Have you slept with another?" Her tone changed. "Does Romulus know?" I ran over, taking her hand in my own. I shook my head.

"Cecilia, you cannot tell anyone. He will kill me. The child is Romulus's but yes, I love Remus. I cannot live without him. What do I do?" I asked her, knowing I had no choice. I had to stay here and pray that he would return for me. Cecilia stood and walked backward towards the door before tearing it open. "No!" I shouted as she ran from the room. "Cecilia"

It was too late. My own sister had betrayed me. I ran for the maze in the garden, hearing Romulus yelling my name. I couldn't stop. I had to keep running or he would kill me. My feet grew heavy as every corner I seemed to turn led me to another dead end.

"You have lain with another man, you filthy whore!" he yelled from behind me. I turned slowly to face him. "I loved you, I stayed with you despite your womb lacking in its duty. I told my men that you would be worth it because of your father. I made allowances for you. By the gods, I even loved you, yet you slept with another man. You disgust me."

"Romulus, please, the child is yours. I could not help that I found my mate, we are fated to be together by the gods."

"Do you know what he is? Do you know that he turns into a wolf and tears people to pieces?" I nodded, which only seemed to anger him further. "I swear on everything that I hold dear, I will kill him, and I will dance in his blood. You will watch as I slaughter the man you love."

"Romulus, please," I begged as he stormed over, grabbing me and dragging me back into the compound. The guards gasped as did the servants. I refused to scream, even as the threat of my death loomed. "Tie her hands together and attach them to my horse." Tears brimmed my eyes as I glared at my sister.

"You deserve this," she whispered as she walked away from me. She was leaving me to die.

Romulus rode into the city centre as I barely kept the same pace as the horse. I kept a mask on my face as I dodged the food thrown at me before we reached the city centre. I didn't look up or listen to any words that he spoke as he held a sword to my throat, yelling as the crowd shouted in response. I scanned the area for those familiar blue eyes and curly hair, but I couldn't see him. I was all alone. I glanced up at Romulus, now understanding why Liyana made the choice she did. I knew why she never wanted Nik to resurrect her. She didn't wish to live a life on the run, for him to be hunted. She knew with her death, Romulus would let it go. She wanted to make the ultimate sacrifice for him. I closed my eyes before grabbing the sword and thrusting it into my body. I screamed, knowing this would end not only my life but the life of my unborn child. I made my choice, and it was Nik.

CHAPTER 44
WOULD SHE ACCEPT THE TRUTH?

Nik

I paced the area for what seemed like hours as I waited for Larissa to wake. Her body twitched as pain and euphoria seeped through the bond. Malignus sat with a smug look on his face as he pushed dark thoughts into my mind. *'Would she accept the truth?'* and *'Will she still love you after?'* I focused on the single point that we were fated to be with one another. That would not change the love that we shared. I leant against the bubble, facing away from them, but I could still feel his eyes boring into me. A sharp pain tore through my chest as she gasped behind me. I spun to see Larissa lying on her stomach, her eyes flaring red. She sat up as Malignus snapped his fingers, disappearing into thin air with James's skin. Her anger vibrated through the bond. I held my hands up to her.

"Larissa, let me explain."

"Oh, trust me, you will be explaining all of it." The bubble dispersed as Luce ran over, embracing her sister. She moved her hair from her face and Larissa glared at me.

"She knows, doesn't she?" Roman asked as a growl came from Larissa.

"You fucking knew! You knew and you decided not to tell me." Her fists clenched as the air grew thin. Luce dropped to her knees in submission, bowing her head. Roman clutched his stomach as he fell to the floor.

"Larissa!" I shouted, but she was in her own world of anger. I rushed over, pulling her against my body and planting a kiss on her lips. Her body relaxed instantly as she breathed out. Roman helped Luce to her feet. "Can you give us a moment and find the priest for me?" They nodded as Luce held onto my brother's arm for support. Larissa stepped away from me, shaking her head. Her emotions were all over the place. I waited for her to say anything, even if it was to shout.

"I am just not sure what to even say or ask right now. I want you to tell me everything about that deal. What happened to my baby?" she choked on her words as a tear rolled down her cheek. The one secret that I never wanted her to know. It always caused conflict in our relationship, especially when her memories resurfaced. I thought I could hide it this time.

"When you were stabbed, I rushed to your aid. I carried you while you were bleeding to death before I arrived at his cave, den, whatever you want to call it. He wanted a sacrifice in response, and I only thought of bringing you back, I only thought for myself. My exact words were, 'Take the baby, just bring my mate back.' It was all I cared about. All I wanted was you. I had no thought about the consequences after. I never processed that it would mean we would never have children in the future. I never contemplated that I would become this monster. I couldn't lose you; the thought was ripping my heart in half."

Larissa crossed her arms over her chest, shaking her head in disbelief. I could feel her understanding and her anger. She threw her hands up in the air as tears fell down her cheeks, smudging her perfect makeup.

"I thought we said no more secrets. It is our wedding day. You rushed through this ceremony, and for some stupid reason, I thought that maybe once we were wed, you would stop this. On the one day that is supposed to be the happiest for a couple, I find out that you took something from me. Something that I can never ever get back. I have been grappling with the thought of kids since the start, and I discover that the man who warms my heart, who brings me constant love and affection, a man I stood in front of a fucking gun for, took that chance away from me. I don't even know how to process this, Nik. I love you but, fuck, you are an arsehole." She proceeded to walk away before turning back around. "I begged you, I fucking begged you to let me die. I wanted to die to save you, those were my final thoughts before I stabbed myself. Romulus didn't stab me. I did it myself. For *you*."

"Larissa, please…" The doors swung open as Roman returned with the priest and Luce. She cried harder as she looked between the both of us.

"I *can't* do this, Nik. I am sorry, but I need to go. If you love me at all, let me leave." My heart ached to chase her as she ran up the aisle, clutching her dress. I wanted to hold her and make her pain go away, the same pain that I had caused her. I always hurt her. When would I stop and just give her the life she deserved? Luce ran after her sister as I sat on the floor, burying my head in my knees.

"She will come back, brother. You know she will." His hand landed on my shoulder with a soft reassuring squeeze. I knew he was right, but something about this time seemed almost final.

———

I refused to leave the reception hall. I watched the sun move across the sky, and with every passing minute, it almost seemed like my heart would stop beating. My ears pricked up at the sound of heels clicking against the tiled floor. I sat up as the doors opened and Larissa walked in, her head hanging low before her eyes found mine. I exhaled deeply, the sight of her making my heart feel lighter. She brought colour to my dark world.

"I don't forgive you for yet another lie, but we pledged to make a vow today to each other and I do not go back on my word. Especially since this gives me protection and ensures the curse does not activate and I won't die young." The priest entered after her as Luce beamed, nodding in my direction. I found her action curious as she waltzed over to grab her bouquet.

She whispered, "You're welcome," as she took her place by Larissa, who snatched the bouquet from her hands and turned back towards me. Roman laughed at the obvious annoyance of my future wife having to do this when she was irritated at her future husband. I smiled, knowing she would soon be mine. She would take my name and officially be recognised as my mate and my wife until the day that we died. I only hoped to convince her to transition in the near future.

The priest cleared his throat. "Today, we witness the marriage of Phoenix Dankworth and Larissa Solis…"

"Can we skip ahead? I truly don't want to be near this man for much longer than I need to be. The very sight of him is pissing me off." Roman sniggered as I waved my hand, hitting him in the gut. She didn't need the encouragement.

"Let us skip to the vows. I believe you have written your own. Nik, would you like to start?"

I removed them from my suit jacket as I hooked my finger into my collar to loosen it slightly. "Larissa Solis, from the moment you poured coffee all over me, I knew you would be my wife. You are the reason that I wake up every morning. You bring light into my dark heart, and you bring me joy I thought I no longer deserved. My only desire is to fall asleep with you in my arms and wake up to your smile. I love you with every fibre of my being and I cannot wait for our life together. I am the luckiest man in the world."

Larissa dabbed her eyes with a tissue, struggling to contain her emotions. Pain spread through the bond as I noticed her biting the side of her mouth to stop the smile that wanted to spread over her beautiful face. She turned, grabbing the cards from Luce before turning back towards me, her eyes slightly glassy with tears.

"Nik, I may not be as old or as wise as you, but I know this. Sometimes I can be hot-headed and stubborn, I am not a perfect person but...I have found the perfect person for me. Your very touch can calm the noise when it gets too loud, and your smile makes my knees weak. I love you more than words can express, and it does not matter what gets between us, I will always choose you. I'd choose you in a hundred lifetimes, in a hundred worlds, even on the days when we struggle to understand each other, I'd still find you and choose you because I love you with all that I am. I always will."

I pulled her into my arms, dipping her down to avoid squirming as I planted a kiss on her lips. I could feel her smile underneath as she wrapped her arms around my neck. "You may kiss the bride!" Roman shouted behind us, which caused the priest to say the words as I stood her up, moving the hair from her face. I leant my forehead against hers, my mate, my wife, my love.

"I am sorry for lying to you," I whispered, inhaling at the crook of her neck. Her scent wrapped around mine as I bit into her neck, sealing the deal between us. I could almost feel the final threads of our bond snap into place as she did the same.

"This does *not* change the fact that you will be sleeping on the couch tonight and no marital sex for you," she muttered against my lips as I groaned. At least she was mine in all the ways that mattered.

CHAPTER 45

FIRST DAY OF MARITAL BLISS

Larissa

THE NIGHT OF OUR WEDDING, WE SLEPT APART. I SUPPOSE YOU could say it was a great start to our married life. The bed felt cold without him, and I found myself reaching over to the absence of his body. I spent the entire night grieving this curse that had been laid upon us. He couldn't bear to live without me and sacrificed my unborn child to save me. I was not Liyana, but no part of me agreed to this. He took it away so easily as if it didn't matter. I could understand his point. He would prefer to have me than a piece of me. It could be classed as romantic, but I saw it as a betrayal, especially after discovering it from another, rather than his own mouth. I sat up, wrapping my arms around my legs as I glanced around our room. I looked forward to moving into our new house, to the feeling of no longer living with a ghost. Some boxes still needed to be packed, and furniture needed to be bubble-wrapped. I sighed, pulling my hair from my face as I strode towards our bathroom. I could feel Nik downstairs. He was awake, and he would know that I was too. I missed his touch, the warmth of it against my skin, the way he brought my body to life. This mate thing sucked. I wanted to be mad at him, but my body just craved the feel of him.

I removed my silky black nightie and turned on the taps, letting the warm water spread through my fingers as I became transfixed by the way it moved around. I manipulated the water to form shapes on my hand, which made me giggle. I stepped in, the touch burning my skin a little, but I preferred the water scalding hot. I closed my eyes, letting my head fall under the water to block out the noise, which in turn silenced the thoughts running through my head.

"I miss you," Nik's voice whispered in my head, and I couldn't help but smile as I missed him also.

"I am naked," I returned to him with a cheeky laugh.

"Don't tease me. The fact that we did not consummate on our wedding night doesn't sit well with me."

"I'm not going to keep speaking in my head to you. Either come up here or go away."

A cold breeze hardened my nipples as Nik's hands grasped my hips pulling me against his body.

"I missed you too." He kissed my forehead as I wrapped my arms around him.

"I needed time to process. I am frustrated you hid the truth, annoyed that you kept it a secret, and fucking angry that you made that choice. As much as I understand the reasons, it's just...you took away a piece of me. You said I never had children in any life and even when I was pregnant in one, I died while birthing it. You added another factor to this curse. I love you, Nik, but you can be so selfish and that's not who I am."

He sighed as he grabbed the soap, lathering it into my hair and massaging my scalp. "I am not a perfect person, Larissa, I know that, but my love for you is stronger than all reasoning. The idea of living eternity without you tore my heart to pieces. I didn't think about what you would want. I was selfish and thought of myself. I never imagined the repercussions would be never having a child of our own. Even if I had known this, I wouldn't have cared. I would pick you and only you in every lifetime." I exhaled as he washed the soap from my hair. "You are all I think about, you're all I will ever need. Your beauty, your purity, and your heart give me hope that one day, I can return to the man I once was. I've often wondered whether, if I had the choice again, would I choose the same? And every single time, I would. I want all of you. I wouldn't survive without you." His love covered us in a bubble that could not be penetrated.

"I know, Nik. I don't hate you. I am just disappointed that yet again, you kept another secret."

"Did I not promise before our wedding that I would tell you all my secrets on our honeymoon?" He chuckled as he wiped the soap from my face. I watched his jaw tick, the water running between us, and desire flared through the bond as my eyes swept over his body, focusing on the delicious abs that I would enjoy licking the water off. I reached over, taking hold of his erection, stroking it slowly. I rubbed my thumb over the head, causing him to shiver as he stepped forward. I raised my other hand as I stopped stroking him and flicked my tongue out to taste his come.

I stepped out of the shower, grabbing a towel to wrap around my body. I glanced over my shoulder to see him standing there, his eyes flaring. I chuckled, spinning around and dropping the towel, then curled my finger for him to come closer. He sped over, wrapping his arms around me and pressing a harsh kiss to my lips. God, I loved this man with every fibre of my being. I wished I could explain how he became my everything. He set my body on fire with his touch and challenged me, just as I challenged him. We were not a perfect couple; we were complicated, we fought, we fucked, but at the end of the day, we would do anything for each other. His hands drifted around me, lifting me so I could wrap my legs around him.

"Fuck, I love you so fucking much Larissa S…" He said every word between a quick peck of my lips before he paused and dropped me on the bed. He ran his fingers through his hair. I reached up, taking his hand in mine and kissing it.

"Where did you go?" I got on my knees to be closer to his face, and he smiled. I watched as it reached his eyes and his whole face lit up with a level of happiness I had never seen before.

"Yesterday, I had an internal conflict," he began, "I never considered marrying you again after we did in the past. We never discussed it because you were already mine and you remembered our day but yesterday…it triggered thoughts I hadn't had for centuries. As I held you in my arms, it all clicked into place. I want you to have it."

I laughed awkwardly, putting my arms around his neck. "Nik, you might need to be more specific about what the hell you are talking about."

"Take my name."

"Is that not custom for me with your ridiculous rules?"

"No, my real name. Silvia. I want you to have my mother's name." I gasped, so shocked I froze in place. He had never mentioned this. "Larissa, are you still with me?" He chuckled as he rubbed his nose against my own.

"Ye-yeah, I…uh, are you sure? I mean you are Nik Dankworth. Will it not confuse others with my name being different?"

"Legally and in private you will be Silvia but in public, you will be Dankworth. I told you this time it is different. I can't explain it. You complete me in ways I never expected. I want this. I want you to have my real name."

"Then yes, I would be honoured." I pulled him in for a kiss as we fell onto the bed. Nik was careful not to land on me to cause any harm.

"I love you, Mrs Larissa Silvia."

"I love you, Nik," I stroked his face, his eyes the brightest they had ever been. He kissed me as his hand explored my body, taking my breast and rolling my nipple between his fingers as I moaned. His mouth found my neck and inhaled deeply, groaning before his teeth sank in, taking their feed. His hand travelled further south as he plunged two fingers inside, curling them at the right angle, hitting that special spot as euphoria spread through my body.

I moaned at the multiple sensations as his thumb circled my clit. "Fuck, Nik." He increased his speed as a growl roared from his throat.

"Mine, all fucking mine." As I screamed in pleasure, he rolled on top of me, pushing my orgasm to continue as he thrust harder. When he kissed me, the metallic taste of my blood was still on his lips, and the voice in my head whispered to bite him again. "Do it." He turned his head as I bit down hard into his skin, licking the small amount of blood and driving Nik to his own orgasm.

"Well, that was quick," I remarked as I tapped his shoulder, his hands resting on either side of my body as he got to his knees.

"Oh, really?" I noticed the position of his hands, ready for their attack.

"Don't even think about it," I warned him between giggles as he started to tickle me. I thrashed to get out of his arms before he rolled me on top of him. I could not stop laughing as he moved my hair from my face. I had completely forgotten that it was still wet, so I snapped my fingers to dry it. He glared at me with annoyance, never liking it when I used my magic without a decent reason. "What? I don't want to catch a cold." I kissed his lips just as my stomach grumbled.

"Come, I need to get my wife fed." I stood, heading to the robe to put on some clothes as Nik wandered towards the kitchen.

"What should I wear?" I called out for him as I finished fastening my bra, glancing around at the multitude of clothes that I now owned.

"Preferably nothing, but I cannot afford for my wife to be arrested for public nudity," he called from downstairs. I shook my head at his remark. "A nice dress. We are going somewhere warm."

"Wait, how?" I asked as I quickly chose a dress and headed downstairs. I pulled the white dress with pink roses over my head as I stopped at the bottom of the stairs. I couldn't believe the sight before me. The room was covered in red and gold rose petals and the table was filled with a selection of breakfast foods. "You didn't cook all of that. H-how?" I stuttered as I approached the buffet of food.

"Maria. I didn't even need to ask her. She did it…" he walked over, handing me a note, "because she saw how much of a good influence you are on me." I wrapped my arms around his bare chest. He kissed the top of my head before tapping my bottom. "Now, go eat while I get dressed and pack our suitcases," he said as he began to walk up the stairs

"Nik, I can pack my own bag." I crossed my arms at him in defiance, and he spun to look at me.

"Oh, I am aware, but you don't know what clothes to pack," he said smugly, his signature smirk on his face.

"But I feel like you might pack nothing, which would be problematic." The smile on his face only grew wider as I snorted at the cheeky grin. "Fine, go. But I want to know where we are going."

"Surprises are exactly that wifey, surprises."

I grumbled as he ran up the stairs, picking at the food, and eventually deciding on fresh fruit and a warm croissant. I stared out at the city below us. When we returned from our honeymoon, we would officially be able to enjoy our new house. We would move in after the renovations were complete. I reflected on the last couple of months. I had been kidnapped and almost killed by my sister and then my father before being drugged. I was attacked at my wedding. I breathed out, hoping it would be easier, at least soon. I worried about what Luce and Nik would tell me over the next couple of weeks, and I only prayed it wouldn't destroy my entire life or soul.

The rustling of wheels behind me distracted my thoughts as I spun to see Nik wearing cream cotton shorts and a matching, unbuttoned linen shirt that made my imagination run wild. His hair was perfectly styled, and his glasses sat on the bridge of his nose.

"If you are finished checking me out, let's get on the road. After I give you your wedding present."

"I thought that was this morning." I winked at him.

"Oh wifey, you have no idea just how sore and satisfied you will be after our honeymoon." My pussy clenched in worry and anticipation of what the next four days would hold. We couldn't risk being away from work for too long, with all the troubles lately, but Nik was adamant we both needed a break from life and time to reset as a couple.

259

CHAPTER 46

ROMANTIC HONEYMOON

Larissa

Nik held my hand as we rode the elevator. He seemed so unnaturally happy that it was almost disturbing. The doors opened and our steps echoed through the garage. It was quiet, except for us.

"Nik, where are we going? Are you planning on driving us?" I asked him, noticing how he hadn't brought the bags down with us. He spun me into his arms, placing a kiss on my forehead.

"Do me a favour."

"Uh-oh, what?" I rolled my eyes at him playfully, and he tightened his grip on my waist while he laughed.

"Please." He pursed his lips, and I closed my eyes as he wrapped a piece of cloth around my eyes. "Now, hold my hand."

I giggled, quick and high-pitched, ignoring the fluttery feeling in my stomach. Nik held my hands tight in his as I stepped cautiously before he suddenly stopped and let me go. I reached for him, but his hands returned to me, rubbed up and down my arms. "I've got you, principessa," he whispered in my ear from behind. "Now, keep your eyes closed." He maneuvered me around some more before he untied the cloth obscuring my vision. "Open those beautiful eyes to your wedding present."

I waited a moment before opening my eyes. A green car with a matte finish was before me, and I couldn't help my awed gasp. I glanced at Nik who nodded in the car's direction. I strode over, taking in the four circles connected in a line. "It is an Audi R8 with a V10 engine. Considering the end of the world happened, it is a unique vehicle, and it now belongs solely to you." I ran my finger along the brass wheels. It was surreal.

"What, wait? What do you mean solely belongs to me?" I asked, registering what he said.

"You are now a secondary account holder to all my finances." He handed me an envelope, which I opened to find the keys to the car, around five hundred in cash, and a black American Express card with the name Larissa Dankworth on it. My heart began to race as I took in the fact that I had access to millions of dollars.

"Nik, this is…this is way too much." He covered my hands with one of his, tipping my chin to meet his gaze. I stared into his stunning blue eyes as he placed a gentle kiss on my lips.

"It is nothing less than my beautiful wife deserves. I won't control our finances. You are my wife, my mate, and you deserve nothing but the best."

"But…but I have no idea how much you are even worth. I mean, I know it is *A LOT*, like a million or more but…but I… that is so much to comprehend. What would I even do with this? I have my own money, which is tiny in comparison to…to yours but —" He pressed a finger to my lips to silence my thoughts.

"No more rambling. Do you want to drive your new present?" I stood dumbfounded, looking between Nik and the car. Nerves bubbled in my stomach; I shook my head.

"No…no, I'm not ready for that. I have never driven a car with that much power. Maybe I should start small for now." He chuckled, taking the keys from my hands and opening the passenger door. "Hop in, principessa mia." He closed the door, and I got comfortable in the leather seat as the engine roared to life.

"Where are we off to?" I asked as he slowly drove out of the parking garage. "It is a secret, right?" He took my hand with his signature smirk, and he kissed it.

———

Nik promised to reveal secrets during our honeymoon, and I worried about what would be said. The awkward tension between us led to silence for the entire car ride. I watched the surroundings change from the cityscape to the vast landscape, before stopping at a large dome-shaped *thing* covered in cloudy hexagon shapes. I had never seen or heard of anything like this. I turned towards Nik, who had been watching me with interest, propping his head on his hand, his index finger draped over his chin. His eyes showed an eagerness to see what I would do next.

"What the hell is this?" I asked, pointing at the strange object before me. He chuckled as he unbuckled his belt and then stepped from the car. I watched as he moved around the car, opening my door and offering his hand. I slid mine into his warmth, allowing him to pull me from the car. "Nik, are you going to explain?" He simply shook his head as he led me toward a clear glass door. He pushed it open, and we walked through the corridor. The interior changed slightly the further we walked. The floor changed to beautiful oak herringbone, and the walls were no longer plastic-like but actual plasterboard with floor-to-ceiling panelling that led to a double door entry. Nik pushed the doors open to reveal a hostess standing at a desk, a smile plastered on her face. Her blonde hair was in a tight bun, her makeup immaculate. She wore a white blouse with a tight black skirt, and she bowed her head as she saw Nik.

"Lord and Mrs Dankworth, welcome to EcoEden Retreat. The largest created biosphere to make dreams a reality."

I gasped at the realisation that it was a *created* honeymoon. "This is amazing. Who the hell thought to create this?" Nik beamed beside me, and I snorted. "You designed this? When? Why? How?"

"I started the idea just before Aurora died. She loved the beach and when the world was destroyed, I wanted the next you to have exactly what you wanted. Technology took a while to catch up and the environment creation took time to grow naturally. The point of the biosphere is to sustain the life that lives inside. We are the first to ever visit and stay the night, the testers to see what works and what doesn't. We will have the entire island all to ourselves for the next couple of days." He moved closer, pressing his lips to my ear. "Which I will enjoy because no one else will hear you screaming my name." I clenched my legs together in need. He fucked me no less than three hours ago, yet I craved more. He chuckled, feeling exactly what my body wanted.

He turned back toward the hostess. "Thank you, Arabella, we are excited to test out the EcoEden Retreat. We cannot wait to see our room." She slid the key over the counter as she pulled out a map of the retreat. She explained where our room was located, and which facilities were close by as well as the attractions that we could visit. I honestly couldn't stop thinking about seeing a beach. Not an English beach with stones, but a beach with sand and crystal blue waters.

Nik whisked me into his arms and down the hallway towards our room. He pressed the key to the door and as it beeped open, he kicked the door gently with his foot. "Are you seriously carrying me over the threshold?" I chuckled covering my mouth. He smiled like a cheeky boy as he let me find my feet.

He spun me around. "Now enjoy the view." I had never seen anything more beautiful in the world. The blue sky with speckled clouds, the crystal blue waters as the waves crashed onto the shore. The whiteish-yellow sand looked too perfect to be real.

"Nik, it is stunning." He moved my hair to rest his head on my shoulder, wrapping his arms around my waist. I could not tear my eyes away from the picturesque sight. "Is that real? Like not a fake picture, it is really real?"

"Yes, would you like to go outside and find out?" His words were hoarse as I felt his erection poking into my back. I chuckled at the fact that our need for each other just never dissipated. We were quite literally born for one another. I wriggled my bottom against him and he groaned before I peeled myself out of his grip.

"I am going to change into something more comfortable or maybe I will run down there completely nude." I raised my eyebrows at him suggestively as he looked down at his erection. I followed his eyes, my hand and mouth aching to touch it. He raised his finger, curling it toward him. I removed my cardigan, throwing it on the floor. His eyes flared as I ran for the door, giggling as I did. Nik sped and stopped before me as he threw me over his shoulder, smacking my arse.

"I can already smell how wet you are. I will be feasting on that dripping pussy soon enough." He ran to the bedroom and threw me onto the bed before lying beside me. I found his strength and speed to be an even bigger turn-on as he ripped the dress and underwear from my body.

"Oh, I liked th—" His tongue delved between my folds, licking slowly up and down as a moan escaped my lips. He groaned as he pulled my legs to him and pushed them wider, his teeth grazing over my throbbing clit. "Nik," I gasped as he continued to nibble, his finger plunging inside, and my body arched over the bed for more, wanting that release. He curled his fingers inside, hitting that spot as I orgasmed, causing my entire body to tremble. His fangs bit into my thigh as his fingers continued to move in and out, his thumb circling my clit. I could barely form a coherent thought as the euphoria from the bite filled my body. My body shook with another release as he got on his knees beside my face.

"Suck it, princess." I opened my mouth, rolling my tongue around as he threw his head back. His fingers found my entrance once again. "Look at me, I want to watch your eyes glow as you come while you suck my cock." My eyes focused on his face as he bit his lip, and his thumb continued to circle, which he would intensify before painfully slowing down once again. I wanted the release. I nibbled softly on his knob as I licked the tiny drop of precum. "Who's a good girl?" He spun me onto all fours in seconds as he thrust inside, lifting me so my back was pressed against his chest. He bit into the back of my neck, having another drink, as a growl escaped his lips. "You are mine, Larissa Silvia, fucking mine. Say it."

"I am yours."

"Who's?"

"Yours, Nik Dankworth, I am all yours."

"Yes, you are, my fucking mate, my fucking wife." He forced himself deeper and deeper, his fingers reaching around to play with my nipples.

"Nik, fuck yes!" I screamed as another orgasm tore through my body.

"Hold on, princess," his voice strained as he finished, licking the bite at the back of my neck to heal it as he laid me back down. I had never felt more exhausted and satisfied in my entire life. "Have a little sleep, and I will get some food brought in." His voice was barely a whisper as my eyes grew heavy very quickly. "Fuck, you are an idiot, Nik." The last words I heard before sleep took over.

Chapter 47

Secrets and Feasts

Nik

Malignus's warning played through my head. The more I took from Larissa, the more I would want. I craved more blood than I needed; she tasted so divine, and she was becoming my addiction. I slammed my hand against the wall, barely registering that her heart had started to slow during her orgasm. I couldn't take any more from her this entire trip; she would either die or end up in hospital with a transfusion. I ran my hands over my face as I strolled into the kitchen, which had been filled with fresh tropical fruit. I doubted she had tasted half of these delicacies. Many were grown in tropical areas, as they needed heat and continual rain to survive. When the end of the world began, I proceeded to harvest the seeds from whatever plants I could get my hands on. I always planned on creating a biosphere, as humans were hopeless. If it wasn't a world war, I am sure there would have been some other extinction-level event.

Larissa would sleep for maybe an hour if not longer for her body to recuperate what I had taken from her. I pulled my laptop from the suitcase, replying to work emails and asking my private investigator if he had any news on the whereabouts of Duzi, Daniel, and the wolves. I knew more was happening behind the scenes, but I had yet to piece it together. My body still thrummed with excess energy from the power within Larissa's blood as I picked a pair of basketball shorts and walked to the gym that was attached to our room. I started up the treadmill, knowing I could easily beat the top speed, but it was more about burning the energy than winning the race. A sense of doom spread through my body, an unease that I couldn't explain, something was coming but I didn't know when, where, or what.

I had been so focused on my thoughts that I hadn't registered that she woke up, only noticing when she leant against the doorframe, wearing my cotton shirt. My dick twitched in my pants, wanting her again. The sight of her tanned, muscular legs that felt perfect when wrapped around my body and neck, her skin had a softness that was incomparable. I would never even dream of comparing it to a baby's bottom because it never came close. She was the perfect woman, my princess, my wife. I pressed pause on the treadmill.

"What are you doing up?" I asked, panting to catch my breath. I may have been an immortal son of a god, but I didn't always have the best stamina when it came to running. Sex, on the other hand, I could go all night long. I mean, especially with Larissa. She was flawless.

"I had a bad dream." I thought back to my thoughts of doom and shook my head. I was so prepared to accept something was coming rather than the idea of her having a bad dream. She walked over, wrapping her arms around my body and burying her head in my chest.

"You know I will do everything to protect you." I tilted her head to look at me.

"Nik, I just have this feeling that whatever is coming is something you won't be able to protect me from. I know it probably makes absolutely no sense but—" I pressed my finger to her lips, silencing her rambling thoughts, her anxiety flaring between our bond with a small amount of panic. I wanted to ask her to take one of her pills, but we now knew that they were magical dampeners meant to keep her safe. I sighed, pulling her back into my arms. She relaxed and in turn, the hum in the bond relaxed.

"Let's get you something to eat because I don't need to be a supernatural creature to hear your stomach right now." She squeezed me tightly one more time as I took her hand in mine, kissing it, and dragging her to the kitchen. I placed her on the bench as I cut up the fruit, organising it onto a platter.

"That vision in the hospital, it was Aurora, yeah?" she asked as she picked up a piece of pineapple, popping it into her mouth. "God that is juicy." She took the towel from my shoulder to wipe the juices away.

"Yes, why do you ask?"

"You are in the kitchen prepping me food and it was the same as that, except for that apron. Let me guess, Roman bought that for you." I chuckled, thinking back to the day he gave it to me as a joke that I would always be the weaker brother. I rather enjoyed the insult and wearing it, as did Aurora.

"He most certainly did, and you thought it was hilarious." I handed her a piece of mango and she popped it into her mouth, her eyes brightening slightly. "Do you like that one?"

"What is it called?"

"Mango." I stabbed another piece with the knife, holding it up for her. She stole it quickly as if I would run away with it.

"What else can you tell me about Liyana or the others?" I sighed at her question. I promised this, but now the moment was here, and I feared it, especially after Malignus dropped that bombshell. I finished organising the fruit, took the tray and my sunglasses, and opened the door. The warmth hit my skin, and it made me think of how I missed the full strength of the sun on me. I could tolerate it more than other vampires could.

"I would recommend putting on a bikini set or light dress. It is a warm one today." She ran into our room before returning with a black bikini and a light breathable top. I adjusted myself in my pants, sitting up straighter as she plopped into the seat opposite me, pulling the wicker chair out to put her feet on it. Her bikini rode up slightly, revealing hints of that perfect fucking pussy. I cleared my throat as I chastised myself, a reminder that she wanted to talk. Her eyes flared with desire as she registered my own need for her.

I ran my fingers through my hair. This would hurt. "As we have already established, you and Liyana are the exact same person, at least physically, but she was restricted in ways that you are not. She was fierce and strong, but she never spoke up to a male, it was forbidden. And men had no issues raising their hands to their wives during that time. Romulus made it a point to smack Liyana into line. It took her years to fall pregnant with their first and I know she only did after she met me. When a human female is mated with a wolf, their body will go into overdrive with a need to mate with them, it would be all they think about because her eggs are literally craving her wolf's sperm." She shuddered with disgust. "Don't like talking about sperm?" I asked her, grabbing a piece of dragon fruit and enjoying the flavours I hadn't tasted in decades.

"No, it isn't that, more the thought of Liyana's body doing that. Let me guess, she fell pregnant a week later. I am guessing that was before you had been intimate with her." I nodded, remembering how she had resisted my touch, fearing her death.

I understood it now more than I did then. I was no longer the person from that time. I had grown and changed with the times.

"Yes, she did. Romulus was thrilled, as was Liyana. She wanted a baby, craved being a mother, and she had the gentlest touch. She would have been one of those women who were born to stay home and look after her children. It's interesting how you are the same person and yet society has shaped both of you differently." She sighed as she reached over, grabbing another piece of fruit. I stood from the chair, grabbing a bottle of wine from the fridge before returning and pouring her a glass.

"Why did she not immediately run away with you? She would have felt the bond. I mean, I did even if I tried to fight the constant pull to you."

"Her fear. Romulus had resources everywhere and she was a known princess for her beauty. Romulus would kill her entire family before hunting her down and torturing her endlessly. She figured it was best to hide our love until we figured out a plan to disappear." Larissa snorted as she took a sip of wine. "What is so funny?"

"She still hasn't quite figured out how to disappear yet." I laughed at her remark as it was the truth, she still remained, unable to do what she originally wanted.

"I suppose you are right."

"What else? I mean I saw a few deaths while I was tortured by Malignus. Did you notice a difference?" Her voice was quiet, but her question spoke volumes.

"Yes, I didn't want to admit it at the time but yes. She lost the spark that made her, well *her*. She would no longer fight me on decisions, she would just agree, she didn't want to work, she just wanted to please me. She had no ambition or drive, she just existed, and I truly don't know if it was because of the circumstances or because she was tired of reliving her life only as a temporary. Aurora and the version before her, Eliana, seemed to just want to please me. They isolated themselves and did anything I asked even if it wasn't on purpose." I laughed. "Almost like what you have done to me on a few occasions. Don't think I haven't noticed."

Her cheeks flushed with embarrassment. I was sure she would have noticed that even if it wasn't on purpose. "I don't know how to control it." I reached over to touch her hand as she stood, moving to sit on my lap. "Nik, I...am worried about this life. It almost seems final. There is a pit in my stomach that will not go away." I pulled her down, kissing her luscious lips, nipping at them playfully.

"I will do everything in my power to protect you. Now, what is your next question?"

CHAPTER 48

STUBBORN

Larissa

NIK DID AS HE PROMISED AND TOLD ME EVERYTHING HE HAD KEPT from me. I knew everything about each of my past lives. None of the memories returned, unfortunately, but I had a better understanding of why he acted the way that he did. One question plagued me the most. He told me that Aurora's death had hurt the least of all, but Katrina spoke about how devastated he had been. I wondered why it had been different, and what occurred for that to change. Had he grown tired of her constant need to please him? Or was it something else entirely? I lay on the beach holding a book in my hand, staring out at the beautiful beach before me and yet my mind focused on that one sentence.

'After Aurora's death, I wanted the curse to be finished as I barely felt the pain I had in the past.'

Nik had been tortured for centuries. I wondered if he was just tired of feeling the constant pain of my death, the constant loss of his mate. I sighed before Nik appeared out of the water, wearing nothing but his tight black speedos, water dripping off his delicious six-pack leading to the bulge in his bathers. My mouth watered at the perfect sight before me. He flicked his head as water sprung from his hair. I watched each of his calculated movements as my legs clenched together with need.

The man had no flaws, and I wished I could hate him for it. He crooked an eyebrow at me as I chuckled.

"Just admiring the view of my sexy husband." He proceeded to flex his arms to show off his biceps and spun around to shake his amazing arse. I laughed so hard, falling off the beach chair onto the sand. He ran over, scooping me into his arms, and I stroked his face. The man warmed my heart in ways I never thought possible. It hadn't even been a year since my mother died and, in that time, I had managed to go from hating his kind to looking at this man with an adoration I barely thought was possible.

"I love you too, Larissa Solis." He kissed my forehead as he placed me back onto the beach chair, lying beside me. "Now, what were you reading and why were you not enjoying the sun?" He already knew the answer as I glanced away from him. "Stop overthinking it all."

I wanted to tell him the truth, to let him know that this dream seemed to haunt me now. I had it a while ago and now it was constant; the white room with golden pillars and the figure in the corner, shrouded in darkness. I knew it signified my death and each time, I tried to take in more features for any type of clue of when the end was near.

I had to say this. "Nik, I want you to do me a favour. I know it will not make any sense, but I have to say it. When it is my time, you need to let me go. Katrina never wanted us to meet, maybe breaking the curse is as simple as finally moving on, but something inside is telling me that only you can break it."

He sat up, pushing my body down. "You are asking something that I would never do. I love you with every fibre of my being and you want me to just move on and forget you? I have fought for you for centuries. What the hell is this crap, Larissa?" He stood up, scratching his chin. "That is so selfish. Are you saying that you won't fight for us?"

"I never said that. I just feel it, Nik. Maybe the gods are trying to tell us something, maybe it is fate, maybe it is a sixth sense from my magic. Do you think it doesn't hurt me to say this? Do you think that I want you to move on? It pains me to think that I will break your heart again one day, soon or in a year, who fucking knows, but Roman has claimed his position, he has found his mate. I can't explain it, but something is shifting, and I think you need to learn to let me go."

He threw his hands up in the air. "Centuries of fighting for you and you say this bullshit. Fuck you, Larissa." He sped off into the water as I sat dumbfounded on the chair.

I wish I knew why I had this feeling but maybe I shouldn't have spoken those words. I picked up my book as I strolled back to our room.

'*Yes, he had to hear them*,' the dark voice whispered in my head, but I shook them off. I knew they weren't Katrina, but I wished I knew who they were if only to tell them to leave me alone. I could feel Nik's anger through our bond as I slowed my pace towards the house. I stopped myself, spinning back around and walking to the water. His tantrum would not ruin my day. I threw my book onto the beach chair as I dipped into the water, holding my head under and screaming my frustrations for a moment. I loved the man, but his temper and selfishness would forever be the one constant that caused us to fight.

I floated on my back as I looked at the beautiful sky above me. I played with my magic, creating shapes in the clouds for fun. I loved how Malignus taught me particular tricks with my magic. It had far more reach than simple witchcraft. There had been so many blocks on my magic, but I finally felt like I had more control over it lately even after the revelation from Luce during our wedding. I wondered how Luce was going with her addiction. Nik mentioned that Roman would be keeping a close eye on her, but I worried that she may fall back into old habits. That was my sister; she did not have the resilience to keep pushing through, always choosing the easy way out. Hence the reason she stayed with Peter. A splash close by broke my focus as I dropped my legs into the water. Nik stood on the sand.

"I'm sorry, but I am also not sorry." He walked slowly into the water before reaching me and wrapping his arms around my waist. "I know what you are saying but to hear you say those words makes it hard to accept. I have fought for us for so long. I helped to shape the world into what it is today and now you are asking me to let you go. That's not something I can even consider doing especially not this version of you. I don't think you understand, Larissa. I feel it inside, especially after Aurora's death. You are different and I wish I could explain how, but you have something they never had. You will never accept your end, and you will fight till your last breath. No version before you has ever fought like that, you just accepted it and let yourself die. Malignus tortured you but you kept going, your sister kidnapped you and you refused to give up. You are so tenacious and strong that even though you feel like it is the end for you, I feel like it is the beginning of the rest of our lives. I know this time, we will win."

"Nik, the voice is telling me that I will not survive, the drea—" His lips crashed against mine, his need filling my body as he wrapped his arms tighter around me. My legs circled his waist as we bobbed in the water. He licked my lips to part them, exploring my mouth. He groaned at my taste, his erection pressing into my stomach.

"Losing you this time will actually destroy me."

"I do not believe that. I think it will only make you stronger for what comes after."

"I hope you are right." He leant his forehead against mine. "You need to eat, come inside and I shall cook you dinner."

I cleared my throat. "Have we ever cooked dinner together?" He shook his head. "Then I shall help you this time."

Nik snorted. "You cannot cook to my standards," he said as I splashed him playfully, kicking back from his embrace.

"True, but my standards are really low in food and men." I winked at him as he swam after me. I ducked under the water to avoid his grasp, swimming back to shore. He laughed as he sped after me, and I whispered a spell, turning myself invisible. He froze in place, closing his eyes to focus on the noises in the area. I refused to move as I saw my feet in the sand. My heart hitched slightly as his eyes snapped open.

"I've got you now. You had better run because when I catch you, I will make sure you are on your knees." The dirty words out of his mouth sent my body into overdrive. As he sniffed the air, he stepped closer, even as I stayed still, not moving, as he would see the new spots in the sand. An idea came to mind as I looked above me to the clouds in the sky, the wind around us picking up. He laughed. "Smart girl." The wind would hide my steps if I ran quick enough, not that I minded being on my knees for him. I bolted towards our hotel room, manipulating the wind to hide my steps as I took them. Nik raced ahead to the door and waited with his predatory eyes scanning the area. I snuck around behind him, jumping on his back and kissing his cheek. "You are in so much trouble."

"Sorry, hubby." I flicked my fingers together so he could see my face. My eyes flared as did his. Our combined darkness should be feared by others as together we would be volatile. I feared whoever would dare take on the both of us together.

Nik laughed, "I know, I do pity the people who would dare challenge us together, especially after a fresh intake of each other's blood. I must say, I never feel more powerful when your magic thrums through our bond."

"Interesting. You feel that? Like, the strength or just the power?"

"Not sure, to be honest. I think it is a combination of both, depending on when I last fed from you."

"We shall have to test that theory later. For now, we need to test how our marriage holds up as we cook together. It could be a make-or-break situation for us today." Nik burst out laughing as I slid from his back and into the house.

———

The next day, I woke again to an empty bed. I noticed how he did not feed from me last night, and that he was drinking more than usual. I put that thought away for now, needing to remember to ask him later. I could sense that he wasn't in the room. I pulled on his beige cotton shirt, wrapping myself in his smell. I ventured out.

"Nik!" I called for him, knowing he would use his supernatural hearing to listen for me. He would also be aware that I had woken up. A cup of coffee was on the counter with a note.

I have gone for a ride to check on our activities for today. I will be back soon with breakfast. Enjoy your coffee and the quiet for now.

My mind raced at the word 'activities', wondering what he possibly had planned. I honestly would prefer to spend the entire day in bed or spend another day down at the beach, watching his muscles flex while he swam in the crystal-clear water. It seemed to make his eyes glow brighter than usual. I took the coffee off the bench and walked to the balcony, leaning on it and taking in the sounds of the water lapping the shore. It was peaceful, serene. I could live here forever. I wondered why humans had to destroy the world. I heard an engine roaring, and I looked in the distance to see a dune buggy flying through the sand. The bond alerted me to the fact that he was getting close, and the car spun around in the sand as elation floated between us. I smiled when I saw the binoculars on the table beside me. He always thought of everything. I picked them up to see the smile on his face, showing a level of happiness I had never seen from him before. *'You will break his heart again,'* the dark voices whispered as my heart sank, knowing it was the truth.

The buggy stopped, and Nik stepped out, my mouth salivated at the sight of his denim shorts hanging so low I could see the outline of his pubic area. His muscles flexed and relaxed as he walked up the beach towards me. I kept my eyes trained on him intently before he stood before me. He pulled his glasses from his face.

"Why the sadness?" he asked, rubbing his thumb on my cheek before placing a kiss on it.

"Sadness because I wasn't sitting in that lap." He smirked, knowing that I was lying, but I refused to let him know about the voices again. I could not help but notice the correlation between their return and the fact that I had stopped taking my medication.

"Larissa," he growled. I sighed, knowing that he would push for the truth, but I wanted to feel like a normal couple on their honeymoon, who would drink and fuck all day long.

"Nik, can we just have a day of fun? Please. I promise to tell you tomorrow." He held my face in his hands and nodded.

"Get dressed, we are going exploring. Put on some comfortable walking shoes, shorts, and a top. Or you can always go topless," he said, winking at me. I slapped him playfully before finishing my coffee and heading inside to dress myself.

Once I was done, I found Nik leaning on the balcony with his head in his hands. I rubbed my hand over his back, and I could feel how hungry he was. I put my wrist in front of him, but he pushed it away, instead grabbing the glass of blood beside him.

"I don't need my wife ending up in a hospital because I took too much."

"Ah, makes sense," I glanced over at the buggy. "Are you going to let me drive?" He handed me the keys and motioned his head for me to walk over. I did, but while he finished his glass, I had time to think about my choices and chickened out, handing him the keys as I leant against the door. His eyes draped over my outfit, with my shorts showing a little too much of my bottom and my shirt left little to his imagination with my black bra showing through the white tank top. He grumbled as he slid into the buggy.

He drove like a madman, flicking the sand up and all around us. I screamed in delight and held on for dear life, but the thrill of it excited me more than I ever thought possible. I had never had this much fun before. As the engine roared, he drove up an incline and we stopped at the top of a hill crest. He cut the engine; I shook out my legs from the buggy's vibrations. A picnic basket on the edge, showing the entire area in all its beauty, came into view. I smiled as I wrapped my arms around his neck, kissing him as his hands ran up and down my back before his fingers dug into my behind, lifting me. My legs circled his waist as he laid me down on the picnic rug, his eyes showing only his love as the bond filled with his adoration.

"I love you with all my heart, Larissa."

"As do I." His lips crashed against mine again as he ripped my top from my body.

"I don't even know why you wore this; the bikini top would have sufficed." I chuckled as he pulled the strings, letting my breasts fall out of the top. There was no roughness in his actions, his touch tender and delicate as he brought my nipple into his mouth, biting it as the pleasure and pain shot through my body and I moaned. He unbuttoned my shorts, his fingers slipping between my folds. He pulled them out, licking off my juices. "Fuck, you are always so wet and ready for me. You are so perfect." He kissed me again as his fingers thrust inside. I groaned at his touch and as I rolled over on top of him. I pulled his pants down, letting his cock spring free. I licked up his shaft before Nik shook his head. "I want to make love to you, not fuck you, love you." He rolled back on top and moved the hair from my face, his eyes never straying from mine as he entered me. His rhythm was slow and calculated and he rotated his hips in ways that heightened the pleasure. I threw my head back as he hit that one spot, and my body threatened to explode. His mouth found mine again. "You are all I will ever need, principessa." We found our relief at the same time, but Nik did not move as we held each other.

He finally rolled off, pulling up his pants as he sat up, tapping his leg so I lay down in his lap. "Nik, has it ever been like this before?" I asked him, curious because he had spoken about the difference between each of my past lives and a few select memories, but not much about other stuff.

"In what way?" He handed me another grape and I plopped it on my mouth, the juices splashing around my mouth. I chuckled as he licked them up.

"Did we ever have this?" He scratched his chin as he took in the view, his eyes squinting.

He cleared his throat. "No, we had times together, but you have a spirit that wants to explore, and you make me want to give you that. I want to help you be the person that you always should have been."

I sat up and reached for his face. "That is not your responsibility. It is on me to become the person that I am destined to be. I look forward to seeing where this life takes me, however long or short it is, but at least I can say I am married to an absolute god." He laughed as he pulled me back into his arms, kissing my neck, and my body ached to give him that pleasure of feeding him. His teeth dragged along my throat, and I pushed my neck towards him. His teeth sank in, and he groaned at the taste of my blood. I ran my fingers through his hair as he bit a little harder. "Nik, that hurt." He pulled back, his eyes glowing with ecstasy as he licked the area.

"Sorry, I didn't mean to. You taste so very good. We should head back." He moved to sit up, but I pulled him back down.

"Can we watch the fake sunset before we head back? The buggy has lights, and you have night vision, so we can stay. I want to watch it with you." He nodded as he kissed my cheek, wrapping the blanket over my body as he brought his closer for warmth.

"Whatever you want, my love."

CHAPTER 49

NEVER FELT MORE AT PEACE

Nik

By our last day, I had thoroughly enjoyed the peace and quiet of our time together. We lay on the bed, atop the ocean, and I watched the waves crash as she slept in my arms. I forgot that she needed rest. Pleasuring her all night as well as feeding had led to an exhausted wife. Wife, a word I had not used in centuries. I had only referred to her as my mate, my love, but now, here in my arms, lay the woman of my dreams, my wife. My fingers ran up and down the soft skin on her leg. Her body melded to my own as the sun warmed our bodies. My dick was hard at the touch of it, and I wanted to be deep inside her once again. I glanced at the sky, missing the sun on those small tropical islands. We had ventured everywhere in the past. Her preferences were always the small romantic islands, fewer people, less drama, and more time for just us.

She sighed before a whisper left her luscious lips, words I hadn't heard for centuries. My ears perked up; she spoke Latin. A language barely spoken, a language she did not know fully, and her enunciation was perfect. I wanted to wake her, to see her face, but I feared what it could mean. If she remembered, would she hate me for all the monstrous acts I had committed in the past? Larissa had something the others didn't, a compassionate heart and an ability to see the person behind the scars, behind the pain. She could see the real them. My life had taken me down a road of black and white, but she saw the grey. She was making me a better person. She was pushing me to see the light. I couldn't love her more if I tried.

"Nik." Her voice was croaky from sleep. She coughed to clear her throat as she snuggled tighter. "How long did I sleep?" She sat up. "Did we miss the sail?"

I chuckled as I pulled her back into my arms and kissed the top of her head. "I own this place. We did not miss anything, and you needed the sleep. You had been awake for fourteen hours and I had drank a little too much from you." After watching the sunset, we stayed up and spoke about the house, what renovations we wanted to do when we returned, and her direction for Refresh Marketing.

"Were we seriously awake for that long? It is a blur. You *have* been drinking more than usual. Do I need to worry?" I avoided glancing in her direction as *his* warning rang in my ears. The more you take, the more you will want. She was the perfect drug. I needed her. She clasped my face, forcing me to look at her. "Don't hide from me. What is it?"

"Before he joined the ceremony, Malignus visited me in the mirror with a warning. He said the more blood I take from you, the more I will want." Confusion flickered through our bond, and even I didn't understand it. She sat up as I moved to the side to see her face. "Larissa, I don't know. He just said the more I take, the more I will want, and he isn't wrong. Since the moment I met you, the monster has been banging in my head. He wants to constantly sink his teeth into you. I have found my control getting weaker." She wasn't scared, more worried, as the bond alerted me to her true feelings. Her brow creased before she moved forward and brushed her lips against my own. My cock hardened once more; this woman was an addiction.

"We will figure it out. I did notice yesterday that your bite was a little more rough than usual and the fact that you drank blood from a cup and pushed my wrist away. Thank you for telling me, it is the first step to admitting you have a problem." She tried to make light of the situation, and I shook my head at her attempt at a joke.

"Larissa, this is serious. What if I lose control and kill you?" I asked, letting her know what could happen and the fears I had.

She scoffed. "Nik, if I know anything, it's that you cannot and will not hurt me. I am your mate, and it isn't possible to kill your mate." She sounded so certain, and I thought back to her intense research after the attack during the retreat.

"You started looking into old myths, didn't you?" She shrugged her shoulders. "I told you not to do that."

"I am trying to understand it more, Nik. You weren't giving me answers. I got a little impatient and tried to find the information for myself."

. . .

"That information is not the most reliable source. I have told you this. I mean, I am supposedly dead according to Roman mythology and yet here I am. The stories are twisted to keep people guessing because if the world knew the truth about the gods, it would tear open the human psyche, they would never understand the purpose of life, not that they do now."

Larissa groaned. "I thought we moved past this cryptic bullshit." She stood up, brushing the sand off her dress. Her anger thrummed in the bond as my own monster banged against the cage.

"Just stop, it is our last day. Do we have to argue about specifics? Can we not just enjoy a sail together?" I sighed, which prompted the same response from Larissa. We had amazing moments and then arguments. Her stubbornness, as well as my own, made it difficult to not lose my temper plus her magic amplified hers. I ran my fingers through my hair as she sat back down. She didn't speak, she simply wrapped her arms around herself. I inhaled at the crook of her neck, loving how she smelt of me with her signature sweetness.

We spent the rest of the day holding one another as we rode the waves, the best part of the biosphere was the manipulation we could achieve. We were able to change the scenery as needed, the mountains that we rode on yesterday did not exist today, instead that space appeared as water. My team and I wanted to create a location that could be suitable for any person, but in that lay the difficulty, as it would depend on the bookings for that timeframe. We still had a few errors to fix but as I held my wife in my arms, stroking her head and watching the awe in her eyes at the magnificence of the sunset, I never wanted to forget this moment with her in my lap and the peace we both felt in each other's arms.

CHAPTER 50

NEW HOUSE

Nik

The honeymoon seemed to be exactly what we needed but it failed to stop our arguments, which only heightened our already magnificent sex life. Larissa finished packing her suitcase as I checked in with reception. I knew that we would not pay anything, but I wanted to tip the staff for working diligently around the clock. All staff were given a significant bonus and signed an NDA to avoid anyone speaking of particular acts that occurred over the weekend. As I returned to our room, I heard Larissa muttering to herself.

"How is nothing fitting now? It all fit to begin with. Argh! So frustrating." Her white and pink sundress highlighted her olive complexion and beautiful brown waves as her green eyes found mine.

"Have you finished blaming the suitcase for your inability to fold clothes properly?"

"Or maybe I just need my big strong husband to push it closed with his super strength," she said, batting her eyes at me. I chuckled as I strolled over, doing exactly as she asked.

"It would be easy if you were no longer human." She groaned at my remark. I had brought up the discussion with her recently, but she asked to pass on it for now.

"Seriously, Nik, we are leaving our honeymoon to head towards our new home and you wanted to bring this up now?"

I sighed, knowing her to be right as I picked the suitcase from the bed. "Sorry, maybe I was hopeful that you had thought about it some more."

"I put that thought away in the dark recesses of my mind, *for now*," she said, emphasising the last two words. We both knew that her transition was inevitable, but she didn't want to let me know the truth about why she hesitated. I wanted her safe as a vampire who could heal, rather than a human who could not understand her own healing power.

I held my hand out for her, and she slid her own into mine. We walked to the entrance as she spun around, a bright smile crossing her face. "I want to remember this exact moment that we officially start our lives as husband and wife." She closed her eyes and inhaled before she wrapped her arms around my waist. "Are you ready for our next adventure, renovating a mansion?" She chuckled as I kissed the top of her head.

"Oh, I am aware that the arguments may get worse during this time, but I am actually looking forward to it."

"Let the fun begin." Larissa snuck the keys from my pocket as I carried our luggage to the car. I had become a typical human male, left with all the literal heavy items to carry as my wife swayed her arse seductively in front of me. I cleared my throat as she peeked over her shoulder at me, her eyes shining brightly as the sun hit them. She was an image, and it may be cliché, but I really was the luckiest man in the world.

Larissa drove a little too fast through the countryside for my taste as I put the address of our new house in the navigation system. Her heart raced, excited to see our new house that we would transform it into our new home together. I enjoyed this.

In the past, we had never been completely together. There had always been this slight divide in the power dynamics of our relationship. With Larissa, this did not exist, and I found it challenging, but incredibly refreshing.

'Turn left and you have arrived at your destination.' The navigation system spoke as Larissa bounced in her seat. I reached over, placing my hand on her thigh as the tyres rolled over the rocky driveway. The house was only a thirty-minute drive from the city, which made our commute to work easier than the other house. Larissa looked at the house in awe as the car continued to roll, turning to stop at the front door. We stepped from the car, and I jiggled the keys in my hands.

"Am I carrying you over this threshold?" She giggled and jumped onto my back. Not what I had in mind, but I didn't care when I felt the pure joy move between us through our bond. I unlocked the door, and I pushed it open, the age of the house showing in the creaking that followed. It was built in the 1800s, with no significant renovations since then, and only had minor upgrades. It would be a massive project. The house had six bedrooms, four living areas, and space for plenty more things to create. The house smelt mouldy and dirty, with dust and plants growing inside, signs of how long it had been since anyone lived here. Larissa moved through the house in glee as I waited for her in the foyer. This place would take forever to fix up. I flipped out my phone, texting my assistant to find me an army of workers. I wanted to move in properly within the next month or two and refused to take no for an answer. She knew what to do.

Larissa skipped down the stairs. "Why are you still standing here? Did you not look around?" I shook my head, and she groaned as she pulled my arm. She dragged me through the house, explaining what she thought about each room and its potential. I stopped her, covering her mouth as she nipped at my hand. I glared at her and she shrugged her shoulders.

"I am over the moon that you are planning all of this but why don't we secure a builder and team of experts first before we make any decisions?" My phone beeped. "See, my assistant is already working on this. Shall I set up a meeting for tomorrow, where we can show the plans and work through the ideas of what will work best for both of us?" She clapped her hands together before jumping on me, wrapping her legs around my body.

"I have one more question, will we christen it now or later?" I chuckled as I kissed her, knowing I needed a feed and refused to take more from her. I nibbled her bottom lip as she ground against me.

"Larissa, I am starving, we can christen it later. I promise. For now, I have a doctor's appointment for you. I want to check your iron and blood levels after the last couple of days."

"Fine, I get it. Do I have to go back to work tomorrow? I want to enjoy just us for a couple more days."

"Trust me, I understand, but you especially have missed a lot of work. At least Duzi and Daniel will get off our backs for the time being. One threat neutralised."

"Don't be naïve, Nik, it has not been neutralised. They will always be a threat." She was not wrong. Duzi had been a threat for his entire life, and I doubted he would go away quietly despite being present for some of our wedding. I was sure he would be planning another attack soon enough.

CHAPTER 51
LUNCH WITH LUCE

TWO WEEKS HAD PASSED SINCE NIK AND I WED IN OUR DRAMATIC ceremony. I feel like it wouldn't have been *us* without some type of incident occurring. That seemed to be our entire relationship so far; I had been attacked more times than I could count. Although, I was grateful that I was still alive, and my life hadn't been cut short. Yet.

"Are you still meeting Luce today?" Nik called out from inside the bathroom as he brushed his teeth. I found it funny that he brushed his teeth, as they didn't age. They did not disintegrate, they stayed in perfect condition. Thinking about his teeth led to thoughts of them piercing my skin. A growl filled the bathroom.

I chuckled. "Sorry, my mind began to wander. Yes, I am meeting Luce today. I am out most of the day for meetings, so I blocked out a couple of hours to spend with her." I paused as I pulled up my stockings. "Wait, do I need to check that with you?" I stood up, my gaze meeting Nik's as he leant casually against the door frame. Fuck, he was hot. His sleeves were rolled up to reveal his muscular forearms and enough buttons undone to show off his body that my thoughts returned to the fuck-fest that was our honeymoon. Nik's laughter shook me from my head, and I smirked at him.

"You are something else, Larissa Dankworth." The sparkle in his eyes dulled for a moment as I felt disheartenment flicker through the bond.

"Nik?" As I moved closer, he plastered a smile on his face. I wrapped my arms around his waist, and he pulled me closer, planting a kiss on my lips. "Talk to me, what is it?" He leant his forehead against mine. I knew since the honeymoon that he was struggling with his inner demons. He wanted to pretend everything was fine, but I knew it wasn't.

He sighed. "I have never wanted this before but for some reason, I want you to have *her* name." I lifted his chin to look at him, his eyes filled with something I could not place and emotions I had never felt before flooded our bond. "I know we spoke about this already, but I started the paperwork for your official name to be Larissa Silvia."

My heart doubled in size. The idea of having his name, the name he had been born with, filled with me immense pride. "I cannot wait to have her name, your name." He picked me up and spun me around in his arms before his lips crashed against my own, our lips parting and my desire increasing in the process. I wanted him but I couldn't be late to work. I groaned, detangling myself from him and taking a step back. "I cannot be late, but I am happy to become Mrs Larissa Silvia." He beamed as I walked into our robe to select a sophisticated work dress, which I could convert into a lunch outfit. I flicked through my robe. Nik had filled it with so many designer dresses, and some were absolutely hideous. I reached for a maroon dress with a cardigan that would easily transform into something a little more casual. I selected a pair of black ankle boots as I admired myself in the mirror. My hair shined in the light, and my eyes were brighter than usual. The combination of a relaxing holiday and being in love with my literal soulmate.

"Hurry up, principessa, we don't want to be late." I smiled at his nickname for me, which had more truth to it than I initially thought. After seeing how we met and who I was in my first life, I now understood some of his actions, even with his lies. I cleared my throat at the one lie that hurt me the most, his sacrifice of my unborn child, the baby I never got to have. My one desire that I would never be able to fulfil. I picked up the frame before me, a picture of Nik and I from our wedding day. My face was alight with pure joy as Nik gazed at me with adoration. I had the love I always wanted, a man who would burn the entire world to the ground for me. I mean he did. He burnt Rome down to save my life. The tiny voice in my head whispered, *'But will he ever know true happiness?'* I shook my head. The whispers were growing louder, wanting to tell me *something*, but I was too scared to listen

---

My meetings with several companies went smoothly and I managed to secure three more marketing accounts. A self-conscious person would be worried that it was due to Nik, but I didn't tell them that. I wanted to earn their business and respect on my own merit, and I had. I could do this job. I sent off another email to another client with a list of ideas for their future marketing campaign before Andreas cleared his throat. I had not even noticed that he had pulled up to the kerb. "Sorry, Andreas," I said with a soft smile.

"It is fine, Larissa. I have stationed two men inside to watch you during your lunch, but they are undercover for your comfort. You will be safe and protected if anything were to happen."

I glanced up at him. "Do I need to be worried that something may happen?" I raised my eyebrow at him. He chuckled and shook his head. I enjoyed the relationship that was blossoming between us. He had always been true to his word, an old-school gentleman, but refused to tell me just how old he was. I stepped out of the car and walked towards the restaurant.

"Rissa!" Luce shouted from behind me. I spun on my heels and held my arms out for her. She ran into them and held me tightly. "I missed you, sis." I closed my eyes at her words, the softness in them. I had missed her and our relationship, and I hoped that since she was clean, we could return to what we had. *Hoped.*

"I missed you too." She pushed back, holding my arms out and looking me over.

"Sex agrees with you." She winked as I snorted at her.

"You can be so crass sometimes. Come on, I am starving." The glass doors to the restaurant were opened for us upon arrival; the room was filled with the hum of multiple conversations. The interior shouted elegance with their deep mahogany flooring and plush velvet navy armchairs. The warm glow from the chandeliers filled the space with opulence and class. Luce's eyes glanced around the room, taking in the sheer beauty of it. The waiter headed over and bowed his head.

"Mrs Dankworth, right this way."

"Is this your life now?" Luce whispered, holding tightly onto my arm.

"Yes, I am recognised as Nik's mate. It has some perks to it." We were led into a private dining area where he pulled out my chair before walking away. I noticed he didn't pull Luce's chair out but decided against addressing it. I worried the answer may upset Luce and I wanted to have her in my life again. I didn't want to fight with her anymore.

"It has perks indeed but where are the menus?" she asked as she picked her glass of water up to search underneath it.

"Please do not be silly," I scolded her, worrying about who could be watching for any ammunition to be used against Nik. She put the glass down and raised her hands in a *I will stop* motion. "They will bring out food for us. Don't ask, they just do it. I am still getting used to the idea but this whole thing seems to be over my head."

She laughed and reached across the table. "I can't imagine how hard it must be for you. I am sorry I haven't been here for you." Her eyes welled with tears, and I squeezed her hand in comfort.

"I know, Luce, I know." I let go and clapped my hands. "Now, what do you have to tell me? What do you know?"

Luce cleared her throat, pulling out a letter and fiddling with it. "I only know that you were never supposed to meet Nik. You were supposed to live a whole life without ever meeting him. Mum and Katrina wanted you safe, but I don't understand why. I tried to find the answers for *you,* I wanted you to be happy and experience life as I do but Mum forbade it." She slid the letter across the table, and my hand shook as I reached for it. I worried about what was inside, what secrets this would reveal. My finger slid underneath and opened the envelope before pulling the letter out.

My dearest Elizabeth,

I know you refused to help me in the past, as you did not agree with my choices. You did not agree with helping the monsters *as you call them. We have lived long enough that I hoped your prejudice would die down, but I was wrong. We are very different people. You see the world in black and white, and I see the grey. I choose to see the best in people and I did with Nik. He isn't like the others. He has suffered more than any one person deserves. I had to help him, to give him the peace he deserves. I know you will never understand why but my heart told me it was the right thing to do.*

I sought help from a divine creature, and she gave me more power than I ever dreamed possible. It was something else. She wanted to help give Nik peace, not wanting to torture him anymore. I figured out how to break the curse, and Larissa is the key. Larissa is innocent in all of this, and I may have started her life with selfish intentions, but I love her with every piece of my heart, and I want her happiness.

If you are reading this letter, then I am already dead and I failed in my attempt to keep her hidden because, Elizabeth, she must stay hidden. She has more power than the average witch. She was blessed at birth by a divine creature who swore to keep her safe. As the days went on, this creature requested that Larissa meet Nik, but I refused to let her. I told her that to break the curse, she must be kept from him. She must live a whole life and die an old lady in her bed surrounded by family. She ordered me against this, insisting she meet Nik, wanting the curse to be activated again. Larissa was mine. I couldn't sign her death warrant. I ran and hid, even from you, and I am sorry for this, but I had to protect my daughter. She is innocent. I regret many decisions in my life, but I would never regret her.

Promise me, Elizabeth, promise me on my deathbed. She must never go to London, she must stay in your small town of Shaftesbury, she must live a mundane life, a hidden existence from even the witches. If they knew what she was, they would kill her. She is a threat to their powers. She was born to stand out, she was born to lead, but she mustn't. If the divine creature finds her, I don't know what she will do. I have created a spell to keep her hidden. They are pills; they dampen her power. You must find a reason for her to continue to take them, it is the only way she will never be found.

I am sorry for all the pain I caused you, Elizabeth. I will live with the regrets even in the afterlife. I only hope when we meet again, you can forgive me.

Forever yours,

Katrina Solis

I breathed out as I noticed another letter behind it. I placed the one letter down before reading the next.

My beautiful daughter,

I am sorry to have left you so early in this life. I never expected it to happen. I wanted to see you grow up. I wanted to walk you down the aisle, to hold your hand as you birthed new life, but I will only be there in spirit. For this, I am sorry. I could have been a better mother to you. I should have been.

*My life was cut short. I crossed people I shouldn't have to give peace to my friend, your soulmate, Phoenix, as I knew him. He only allowed me to call him that. I loved him and his mate. I asked **her** for help, and it was my one mistake. She wasn't who I thought she was. She poisoned my plan and placed her poison inside you.*

Larissa, you are more than a witch. You have the sliver of a god's power running through your veins and by this, I don't mean your father. I brokered a deal, and I lost my life protecting you, but I would do it again. I am sure if you are reading this, you discovered the pills. Larissa, I beg of you, you must continue to take them. They—

The letter stopped, with the last word smudged. She had been interrupted. I had to keep taking them, but why? I met Luce's gaze, knowing she would have read them.

"But why? What do the pills do?" I asked her, folding the letters up and placing them back into the envelope, allowing it to sit on the table between us.

"Mum said they dampened powers."

"But why, Luce?" I pleaded, even though I suspected she didn't have the answers I wanted. But I hoped she did. I needed to know why. Who was this divine creature? Was it the same person behind the whispers? Is that why the whispers grew louder when I stopped taking my medication as often? Were they able to communicate with me?

"They kept you safe from *her*." I clenched my fist in frustration. I had been so close and yet I hit another wall. "Larissa, I searched for clues in Mum's grimoire growing up. I wanted to know for you. *She* is a god. I don't know which one, but she blessed you with life and power. But I can't understand why she wanted the curse activated when she helped Katrina to birth you to break it. I tried to decipher why, but I never got the answer, only more questions. I am sorry, sister, I wish I had more."

"Did you at least discover what her powers were or what she looks like or anything?" My voice croaked, holding back the emotions that threatened to spill out. Luce shook her head and shrugged her shoulders. I sighed, letting my head fall into my hands. My mother was scared of this god and wanted to keep me hidden but the reason was unknown. My phone rang and I saw Nik's name flash across the screen. I turned it over, needing a moment to process. My head was filled with too much information at the moment. The world could be bigger than we originally thought and now a god had helped to ensure I was born to break the curse but revoked what they said and wanted me to activate it instead. The god got what she wanted, surely that would mean I could stop taking the pills, but what if she required more from me? Something that Katrina had promised that I would have to follow up on. My phone buzzed again, and I flipped it over.

NIK

Please answer, I have to know you are alright.

ME

I am fine, just processing. I will call you soon, I promise.

I clicked the phone closed as I tapped it against my chin, contemplating no longer taking my pills, but I feared what it would look like. I pushed the letters away as I picked at my food.

"How is work, Luce?" I wanted to change the subject, to focus on something other than the Rubik's cube that was my life. Luce prattled on about her work and how she managed to keep her job after her disappearing act. I suspected Nik might have been behind this. I closed my eyes to focus on the voices in my head. I didn't take a pill this morning, and struggled to remember when I last had one. The more I focused on the voices, the more I could hear them.

'Hello, Larissa. Go see Roman.' The voice was as clear, as if they were sitting right beside me. I spun my head around the room, standing up to scan the area as a whisper of a touch against my skin caused shivers to erupt.

"Show yourself," I demanded as my magic brimmed at the surface, ready to explode.

"Larissa?" Luce's eyes squinted as confusion settled across her face. I shook it off as I sat back down. "What happened?"

"Have you ever felt the presence of another, but nobody was around?"

"Like a ghost?"

"Kind of, yes."

"Nope." She plopped another cherry tomato into her mouth and the juice ran down her chin. She wiped it away. I wasn't going crazy, but I could almost feel a hand on my shoulder.

CHAPTER 52

MY SECRETS REVEALED

Roman

I COULD FEEL THE EFFECTS OF THE FULL MOON ALREADY: THE exhaustion, the mood swings, the thirst for blood. I hated the creature that lived beneath my skin, the wolf that had the power to kill without a second thought. Since I claimed my rightful position as Alpha, he had been rather irritating, wanting to secure his mate. I swore to Larissa that I wouldn't until she was sure my mate had settled into London. I knew she was right. I couldn't rush it and terrify the poor girl. I was thousands of years old. I had seen empires rise and fall but all I wanted was to hold my mate in my arms, to smell her delicious scent of jasmine. I now understood why Nik had been so fiercely protective of Liyana since the start, even now with Larissa, and his constant need to know where she was despite being able to sense her. I wanted to never be apart from her. I watched her from the distance, determined to ensure her safety. My hand trembled as my claws extended, and I ran my tongue over my gums as my teeth bulged inside my mouth. The Alpha called to claim her tonight, but I had to resist.

A knock broke my focus and I moved to the door, looking through the peephole to see Larissa. Her hands fidgeted before she brought one hand to her mouth to chew her nail. I opened the door.

"That is a terrible habit," I said with a smirk, but she shook her head. In no mood to joke.

"I don't know why I am here, I...I... just left lunch and headed towards Andreas in the car before I arrived here. I cannot remember getting here, I..." She spun around to glance behind her, the area devoid of cars as even I didn't hear one arrive.

"Larissa," I put my hands over hers, "come inside." I pulled her inside, sitting her on the couch as I and handed her a glass of water. She didn't move. "I'll be back in a moment." I left her alone as I flipped out my phone.

"Nik."

"I am about to head into a meeting. Everything alright?"

"Larissa is here."

"Wait? What? Why?"

"I don't know. Did you not sense her?" Silence came down the end of the phone.

"Roman, I cannot sense her at all. Keep her with you, there is something in the bond. I...can't explain it. I must go to this meeting; it is vampire related. I am trying to find answers to these secrets about the parts of the world that may still exist. Keep her safe."

"I will, brother, I promise." I hung up the phone and returned to the living room. Larissa had a knife and was cutting into the brick walls inside the chimney.

"Larissa!" I shouted, but she didn't stop. She continued to cut into the mortar as if she did not hear me. I rushed over, grabbing her arm, but she blasted me with her magic. Her eyes flared red, and her hands were covered in small red cuts. Her heart beat steadily. I sniffed the air to assess the situation, but there was no hint of magic. What was this?

I walked back over to her, leaning in close and reaching around to take her hands. "Larissa." I kept my voice soft to avoid another reaction from her. "You are safe, listen to my voice. What are you doing?" I asked, watching her eyes focus solely on the brick that she cut around.

"The voice keeps telling me to cut." Determination filled her voice and she refused to look anywhere else but the brick and mortar before her. "I have to. I must *not* stop."

"Larissa, where is Nik? Can you reach him?" I needed her to sense her mate and the worry he would be feeling. I needed her to see reason from whatever was happening. She stopped for a moment as her eyes closed, her shoulders rose and fell as a deep breath escaped her lips.

"Nik." Her voice was soft as the room filled with love. Her power continued to grow as it covered my own senses, making my inner wolf go crazy with the need for his own mate. "Nik," she called for him again as her magic began to diminish. Her eyes burst open, glowing green as they flickered between worry and confusion. "Roman, what…what happened?" she stuttered, glancing around the room before turning back to the wall she had been cutting into. I took her hands in my own, dragging her to the couch.

She sat in silence as she stared at the wall, while I watched from a distance, as being close to her brought an odd sensation to my body that I couldn't handle. It almost seemed like she was twisting a knife in my gut. I heard Nik before he landed at the door. As I opened it, he ran over, moving the hair from her face and smelling the crook of her neck. His eyes found mine, but all I could do was shrug my shoulders.

"Larissa, my principessa, my love. Are you with me?"

"Did you find it?" She touched Nik's face as he kissed her hand.

"Find what?"

She pointed toward the brick. "Find the answers." Nik glared at me as he stood, punching through the wall. I knew he wouldn't be pleased with what he was about to discover.

"Nik, just listen. I can explain." He reached in and pulled out the weapon I had been hiding for centuries. A piece of our father, a piece of our past.

"You…you said you didn't know where this was." He turned the golden spear in his hand and when he clicked the button, it extended to its full height of six feet. The top had four edges, and with the press of another button, they would extend out to cause more damage to its victims. Nik twirled it in his hands before throwing it toward me. "You hid this from me?" he shouted as I pulled the spear from the wall.

"You can be pissed at me all you want, but it doesn't change what happened."

"How the fuck does it not change anything? He gave us the chance; he gave me the chance to break the curse. All I had to do was hand over our father's weapon, and I would never lose her again. You told me you lost it and this whole time you had it."

I hung my shoulders. I couldn't let him have it. "Father entrusted it to me."

Nik scoffed. "You fucked me. He wanted this to bring her back to life. I had to sacrifice her baby. I had a chance! Is this why you have fought so hard this time? Was guilt eating away at you because you had the key to stop it all and refused to hand it over?" His voice grew louder and angrier with every word.

"Nik, I can't explain it, but I couldn't. She wouldn't have wanted this."

"She, who? Liyana, Larissa, Aurora, or any version of them wouldn't have wanted this?"

"No, our mother. Rhea wouldn't have wanted me to hand it over. Mars told her to gift it to her firstborn, to pass to his child." Nik paced the room as his eyes flared red. Larissa stood, putting her hand on Nik's chest, settling him instantly.

"She wanted me to find it." She spoke so directly that it almost seemed robotic.

"Who?"

"Rhea. She was the voice in my head, she told me to bite you. She is the person Katrina went to for help."

"What?!" Nik and I yelled in unison.

"Rhea gave her power."

"Mum had no real power other than birthing us, how did she give Larissa the power to do this and why?" I asked as I moved closer. Nik's eyes watched me intently for any sign of weakness. His fist clenched.

"Go on, take your shot, brother. You always were one to take a cheap sho—" Before I could finish my sentence, his fist connected with my jaw, clicking it out of place. He didn't hold back but I couldn't allow Malignus to get the spear. He would ruin its beauty. I hoped when Nik calmed down, he would understand.

"Nik, stop!" Larissa shouted, and his fist stopped mid-air. He turned to look at her, waiting for her to say anything else. I saw the same look in his eyes as I did from those people in the café. Larissa could control Nik. Did she even realise this?

"What reason could you possibly ask for me to stop? You would have had your baby. You called me selfish when this man could have stopped it. He had what I needed."

"There is something else in the wall, it is calling to me." She moved closer as I sped toward the wall to block her. She couldn't see it, she couldn't know I had it, she would hate me. Nik noticed and moved closer.

"Move, now."

"Nik, brother, please. You can't know what else is in there, it will destroy her." He pushed me aside as I kept my back turned, hearing her gasp at the realisation of what it was.

"Wait, how?" Larissa's voice croaked with sadness. I had to turn and see, but I knew her face would tear my heart to pieces.

"Katrina spelled me. After she died, her ghost called to me and told me to collect it before Elizabeth could. I have had it hidden ever since."

"Not only did you know about Larissa being alive, but you also kept Katrina a secret. Is there anything else?" Nik's voice was strained as he tried to keep his monster contained.

"I was spelled, Nik. Please see reason," I pleaded with him, trying to make him understand that I had no choice. I remembered that night like it was yesterday. Her voice called to me, begging me to keep it from her sister's hands until Larissa needed it. "Larissa, it is yours to keep as it always was. I had the task of keeping it safe." Larissa beamed as she held it close to her chest. A piece of her mother, the woman taken from her too early.

"This isn't over, brother." Nik pointed in my direction with a glare and snarl on his face. He whisked Larissa into his arms and left my apartment as quickly as he arrived. I picked up the spear, twirling it in my hands. I could feel the power it contained, and I thought about where I could hide it next. Although if Larissa knew where it was, I doubted I could truly keep its power contained any longer. Somebody wanted it found.

CHAPTER 53
INTRODUCTION TO MY WARD

Nik

Larissa hadn't experienced any more possessions since the other day. She believed the pills stopped the whispers from the gods, in particular, my mother. I didn't know if she was right or wrong, but I hoped with everything she was wrong. If the gods were involved, it would not end well for us. We were slowly discovering more answers, and what she said on our honeymoon had merit. Katrina created her daughter to never know me, and it was key to breaking the curse. We should never have had our love, so we could move on. It still didn't make any sense to me how that would work. I knew we were missing one piece. Larissa kept having the same nightmare of the room with golden pillars that glowed so brighter she could barely see.

"Larissa!" I called out for her as I stood at the bottom of our staircase. Bodhi nervously stood beside me. He had done well with his training. Roman had a skill in teaching control, having taught most people I knew how to control their urges. We shared similarities in that vampires wanted to rip into throats for our enjoyment and wolves, like Roman, wanted to rip into throats out of anger.

"Coming," her angelic voice carried down the stairs as I heard the click of her heels on the tiled floor. "Do you have an early meeting?" she called out before stopping at the top and looking down. "Is this Bodhi?" she asked with a bright smile on her face. I swung on my heels and smiled at just how beautiful she was. Her auburn hair framed her delicate features, her green eyes glowing with love.

"Yes ma'am." Bodhi bowed his head out of respect, causing both Larissa and me to chuckle.

"Please, it isn't needed. I do not carry a title as my husband does. I am just Larissa, simple Larissa." Bodhi extended his hand, and she froze in place. Her eyes glazed with fear and her heart pounded in her chest. Her hands began to shake and as Bodhi reached to help her, she screamed, falling onto the stairs behind her.

"Larissa, what is it?" I scooped her into my arms, holding her close to my chest. Panic ripped through the bond, and I stroked her hair as I pushed calmness through to her. Her heart began to slow, her tremors abating.

"Nik, he...he...he was there."

"He was where, my love?" I whispered in response to her soft voice.

"He brought me food at the warehouse where Peter planned to sacrifice me." I found it interesting that she didn't mention her sister, but it *was* his plan. I placed her on the stairs as I stood taller than before.

"YOU WERE PART OF THAT GROUP" my voice echoed through the foyer, and Bodhi whimpered, falling to his knees and holding his hands up for forgiveness.

"I... was. I told you I had done horrible things. I disagreed with their actions. I brought her food when they wanted to starve her. I felt pity for her. She didn't deserve to die because of my cousin."

"Your cousin?" The one time I didn't bother to check an individual's background. I internally chastised myself for having missed this and putting her in jeopardy.

"I told you…I told you that they were cruel, that we spoke of you. I disagree with their way of life; it was why I killed them. I needed to rid myself of their darkness. You have shown me more kindness in a month than they did my whole life." His voice quivered, and I raised my hand, ready to strike, when Larissa stood, wrapping her fingers around my bicep.

"Nik, stop." Her eyes focused on Bodhi, who began to cry in his hands. "He never harmed me, and he did bring me food. You can compel other vampires. Do it to know the truth, but I feel it in my heart that he is not lying." She walked over and got on her knees, lifting his chin to look at her. "Did you mean to harm me at all?" He shook his head, tears staining his pale face.

"Fuck me." My monster wanted to rip him apart for being part of that group. They wanted to destroy me and almost took her life, and I wasn't able to stop them, not finding her until after. I breathed out. "Stand. Now," I ordered, and Bodhi did as instructed. Larissa slipped her hand into his, holding it tight as she stood beside him. I allowed my power to flow freely as I held his gaze. "Did you have intentions to harm my mate, Larissa Solis?"

"No, sir. I did not."

"Do you have any intentions to harm her now?"

"No sir, I will protect her till my death as she is my ward's mate." Larissa smiled and stroked his shoulder. The monster inside didn't like seeing her touch another, but I pushed the anger aside.

"Do you promise to reveal all the secrets of this group?"

"Yes, I swear." I blinked to allow the compulsion to stop and he shook his head. Larissa walked over as if reading my mind, slicing her wrist with a simple spell and holding it up to my mouth. I licked the wound to heal it but pushed it away as the warning played through my head. I promised not to drink as much from her as the more I took, the more I wanted.

CHAPTER 54
BROTHERLY FIGHT

Larissa

I HAD NEVER SEEN A VAMPIRE SWEAT BEFORE TODAY AND HERE WAS Bodhi, absolutely terrified with his forehead glistening from the sun shining through the glass ceiling. I placed my hand on his arm, giving it a gentle squeeze for encouragement. He feared Nik more than me, which I don't blame him for. He *did* help keep his mate captive and I did almost die.

"Speak," Nik ordered as I glared at him.

"Nik, he is terrified. I am sure you can sense it as I can see it." His eyes flared, and I wished I could control mine to do the same, hoping it would come one day.

"I know you understand my anger. This should have been discussed from the beginning. Instead, I brought him into our home and aided in his recovery. My brother has given him tools to control his thirst, but I have left him in this house with you *alone*. He *should* be fucking terrified because I want nothing more than to rip his head from his fucking shoulders."

I snorted. I could not help it, but I actually laughed. "Do you not think you are being a little ridiculous? He killed his family. If he had an inkling to harm me, he would have done it already, no?" A growl echoed through the space, and I stood up as the ground trembled. "I have had enough of your alpha bullshit. Go for a fucking walk and calm down. Bodhi will not hurt me. I can feel it. GO!" I shouted at him. His temper flared so easily lately. I knew it was due to my blood, but it seemed to be affecting him more than he would dare admit to me. Nik stormed from the room, making it a point to slam the door behind him.

I turned back to Bodhi, putting my arm through his and lifting him to his feet. We walked together in silence to the kitchen as I made him a bloodcino and a cappuccino for myself. He sat on the stool at the island, and I watched as he fiddled with his fingers, the familiar compass tattoo showing its head. I shook away the fear, remembering that he never harmed me during my time in captivity.

"You don't need to fear me. I-I did what was asked of me." His voice sounded so meek, so broken, that I wondered what his family had done to perpetuate his anger to the point where he killed them.

"I do not necessarily fear you; it's more remembering the circumstances of how we met. The fact that my own family orchestrated it, as well as your own. But I do have a question. What does the compass mean? I figured you would have like, 'I hate fangers' or 'death to vamps' or something like that. Not a compass, which has so many different meanings."

He rolled his sleeve up slightly to show me the full ink on his forearm. I slid the cup towards him, taking his arm in my hands and rubbing my thumb over the design. The circle contained a map of the world with a small red speck on London. The arrows pointed in the typical directions, with the longest higher on his arm stating FMP. I smiled, understanding his reason for this mark on his skin.

"Find my path. You never wanted the life you were born into, did you?" A single tear rolled down his cheek and I wiped it away. "Sometimes we have to go through the struggles to find the person we are meant to be. I learnt that the hard way. I had been so sheltered with my mother and I only truly found who I was as a person when I arrived in London. Even now, I am still discovering more about myself. What did your family say about it when they saw it?"

"They didn't understand what FMP stood for so I lied and said it was fangs must perish. They were too stupid to realise it had a larger meaning. You aren't who I expected you to be."

"Let me guess, you only heard about how I was a blood whore hypnotised by Nik to be his blood bag. Oh wait, and I stole magic from Luce." He laughed out loud, holding his chest and throwing his head back. I took a sip of my cappuccino, enjoying the sight. His youthfulness showed in the way he moved. The poor boy had barely experienced life before his world was turned upside down.

"Yes, among other things." I sensed Nik's return when my body tingled for his touch. I watched the door. "He is coming, isn't he?" I nodded and prepared another cup for Nik to drink from. He didn't drink from me as often anymore.

He pushed the door open in a huff and glanced between the two of us. "This isn't a laughing matter," he snapped.

"Oh sorry, we were only trading stories about what a big, strong vampire Lord you are," I teased while pushing my chest out as monkeys would do to show their strength. A smirk played on his lips as he sat beside Bodhi, his nerves calming. "Bodhi has settled, and I think he is ready to tell us what he knows, right Bodhi?"

Bodhi nodded, taking a deep breath and centring himself as he finished his bloodcino. "My family has connections all over the world and before you say it was destroyed, that is a lie. I don't know where it started but the world is still alive." Nik and I waited patiently for him to continue. "When the bombs fell, not all of them were nuclear. Some countries were wiped from existence while others survived. From the eight billion population that we had; it was reduced to one. Many were killed, and when the vampires sought control, the humans fought back. London had too many to even consider fighting back, as the weather is ideal for your species. The rest of the vampire population was spread out, they used the cover of night to try to coordinate their attacks, but we had sunlight, and we used it to our advantage. England became the only country that couldn't fight and when you became the face of the New World Order, I honestly believe most people just stopped trying." Bodhi gave me a wink, letting me know he wanted to see what Nik did.

"I am rather charming and attractive." Nik straightened himself and took a sip of his drink, while Bodhi and I exchanged glances before laughing. "You were messing me with, weren't you?" We both nodded as he put the cup down. "I don't know if I like this growing friendship between my mate and my ward."

"We still love you. Now keep going, Bodhi, please. Do you know who was behind any of it? Or anything else? Any information will help."

He ran his fingers through his black hair. "I heard a couple of names from my family, and Nik was one. They thought removing the face would bring hope back to the people, but you were harder to kill than they anticipated." I wondered if Nik had told him the truth about his identity. I made a note to ask later. "Then another was Ducky or Duki..."

"Duzi," Nik growled, his fists clenching in anger. I reached over, giving them a gentle touch to contain the monster inside. He relaxed slightly as he took a deep breath to calm himself down.

Duzi. One of the men who wanted me dead. He seriously needed to just die already. Nik's anger flared again as he stood abruptly, his chair falling to the ground before he picked it up and threw it at the door. It crumpled into pieces as the door flung from its hinges.

"NIK!" I shouted at him, getting his eyes to focus on me, the bright red letting me know that he was livid.

"No, Larissa, this man has plagued me since he was turned centuries ago. He tricked a vampire into turning him, he has been a fucking pest since the start and does what he can for power. Now it all makes sense why he didn't want me to help and why he kept trying to push me further away from power. He is plotting another move as we speak. I should have registered this. He has been censoring the news and keeping all this to himself. This goes deeper than I initially thought. I am such a fucking idiot! I had a chance to kill him when he tricked Valerie, but he sobbed, and my kind heart gave him fucking leniency. I will fucking bury him for this." He moved towards the entrance.

I blasted a spell to keep him in the house. "Nik, you are not thinking straight. He is a step ahead, and we need to be smarter than him. We need to find out who his people are, and who gives him intel. We need to figure out what else *The People's Revolution* know. If we want the world to be at peace again, we need to do it properly and not go off half-cocked in a rage. We need to get the people onto our side to overthrow the corrupt parties within the government."

"Open the fucking door, Larissa."

"No, I don't trust you to be out there right now."

"Larissa, I need to let him out."

"Then get in the fucking gym and I will throw you around. I will not let you out of this house to hurt someone," I ordered as his face screwed up in resistance, trying to reason with himself on what was the right choice. He stormed towards the gym, and I followed, quickly texting Roman.

ME
How far are you from home?

ROMAN

For you, five minutes.

ME
Get here NOW

I put the phone away, knowing Roman would do as I asked. I slammed the door closed as Nik removed his suit jacket and tie.

"What the hell is that shit? Get a hold of yourself." I crossed my arms as I watched him pace the room, a roar escaping his mouth.

"That piece of shit is behind all of it. I had the chance to kill him, and I didn't. Instead, I allowed him to live, and he threatened to kill you. How could I have been so stupid?"

"You cannot predict the future. Nobody could have known this would happen." Another roar echoed through the room as he tore his shirt from his body, his chest rising and falling with every pant. His fangs were ready to attack, his eyes black and red. I very subtly threw up a protection shield over half the room. The dark voices returned, whispering to fight him. It was a fight I would lose, as I knew he would be able to kill me. We didn't understand how I managed to heal that one time, thinking it was perhaps from activating the 'god' part of my body, but I was not sure how to trigger it. Nik's eyes were hyper-focused on my every move, his monster taking full control. The door creaked open, and I turned to see Bodhi. Nik growled.

"Bodhi, get out, slowly. Don't turn your back to him."

"Miss Larissa, I don't want you alone with him."

"You are more at risk, so it does not matter. He still registers me as his mate, even on a predatory level. You are more of a threat to me and him, so go." He left slowly as Roman entered, panting and shirtless. Nik's eyes registered his brother as Roman howled. I closed my eyes, knowing these two were about to fight. "Roman, please."

"I won't, I promise." His eyes followed Nik's every move.

Nik charged at Roman, whose fist connected to Nik's face, blood spilling from his nose. He stumbled back before finding his feet and charging once again.

"Brother, you know not to let the monster win. You are in control, not him." Nik roared louder. I knew this was the consequence of my blood, and guilt ripped through my body. The sustenance my mate needed also caused him more damage. I stared at the floor, unable to look at what I had done to the man I loved. We were truly cursed in every way possible. I wanted to sink to the floor and cry over the fact that we were no closer to breaking this curse. The sounds of punches and groans filled my head as the room disappeared. I no longer sat in the gym; I was in the room that had been plaguing my dreams lately. The large room with golden pillars and the glowing body in front of me. I still couldn't make out any features. A hand landed on my shoulder, and the room was gone as I saw Nik on the floor. Roman stood above me, covered in blood, and breathing erratically, his own eyes going between yellow and their distinct hazel. I pulled my phone out to call Mimi, thinking that his wolf would want to hear her voice.

"Hey, I just wanted to check on the Rysteen report?"

"Hey," she sounded suspicious, "yeah, it is all filed, and I am waiting for them to send back the signed copies."

"Excellent, will you let me know how you go with it?"

"Absolutely, what time are you coming in?"

"Probably in a couple of hours, just finalising some meetings with prospective clients. Let me know if you need anything else."

"Will do, ciao."

Roman relaxed at hearing her voice through the phone, bringing his wolf back to reality. He glanced down at his body as I walked over, handing him a towel before kneeling beside Nik and wiping the blood from his face.

"What happened?" Roman asked as he sat down beside me, rubbing my back in comfort. I sighed as I leant against his chest. He held me tight and kissed the top of my head.

"Has he told you about my blood making him sicker?" I asked, peering up at him, worried about how he might react. He nodded with a small smile. "His monster has been threatening to come out for a while now, but today, the information we gathered about Duzi tipped him over the edge."

"What about Duzi?"

"We discovered that the world hasn't been completely destroyed, that there is much more beyond London, and Duzi has been using this to his advantage. He has been censoring the news and covering up the truth. We are the only country under the control of vampires, and he has orchestrated it all."

"Fuck me. Nik's guilt would be eating at him. He kept him alive after he manipulated Valerie. It is no wonder his monster came out. Who told you?"

"His new ward, Bodhi. His family is part of the revolution. He knew about all of it. How has this been hidden for so long, Roman? Nik has his hand in everything, so how did he or you not know?"

"We had heard rumours for ages, but we never found any evidence. Lately, those rumours have amplified, especially after the wolves attacked you. The witches planned it, but we can't figure out how. They have nothing to gain regarding you."

Nik mumbled incoherently, and I sat up to stroke his face. "Nik, I am here. You're alright."

"Principessa." He brought my head down, sniffing the crook of my neck. "There is my love." He opened his eyes, moving the hair from my face before kissing me. "I'm sorry. I just felt like I had failed you again."

"Nik, we never could have known about that snake. We just need to work on the plan to kill him." Roman spoke behind me as Nik stroked my face, his eyes assessing every part of me. He sat up, looking at his chest covered in blood.

"You got a few good hits, brother." He noticed the towel in his hand. "So did I. I let you win." He winked as he stood up, offering his hand to me. "I need a feed. Can you get me a couple of cups of blood, please?" he asked as he looked at his brother.

"I'm not your slave. You know that, right?"

"Yes, but I need to speak to Roman about something and apologise to him."

"I thought we had no secrets." My own frustration grew, even after he had told me everything during our honeymoon.

"Larissa." I crossed my arms at him, and Nik sighed. "I need you to bring Bodhi in. I have to ask him a question and I want Roman here to listen in."

I glared at Nik for a moment longer before I stood, walked to the door and called out for him. Bodhi sped over quickly and knelt before me, bowing his head. I snorted at his action as he peered up at me curiously before he stood up. I shook my head to let him know that it wasn't necessary before I moved aside for him to enter the room. I flicked on the fans; the metallic smell of blood might irritate Bodhi and his newfound control over his bloodlust. Or maybe that was Nik's intention, to test his limits. Nik continued to wipe the blood from his chest, and I found myself envying the towel and the way it drifted over his abs. He glanced around Bodhi with his signature smirk as I rolled my eyes and went fetch his cup of blood.

I honestly couldn't explain why I left to collect it, but Nik had that serious, angry face on when I returned to the gym and saw Bodhi on his knees. Nik's emotions hit me hard, but Bodhi was terrified, his soft sobs hitting my ears. I rushed over, forcing the cup into Nik's hands.

"Larissa, he is fine. Don't baby him."

"Nik, he is a child, and his whole life has been changed. What did you ask of him?" Bodhi's head sank onto my shoulder, as he inhaled. I froze I had been so focused on comfort that I forgot he was no longer a human.

"A little frightened now, aren't you?" Nik crossed his arms as Bodhi relaxed. "For your reference, to other vampires, you will smell like me and because we have fed from one another, we carry a special mate smell. Bodhi is my ward, and he would never dare to drink from you. He may attack you, but to drink from you would cause him extreme harm even without your special blood."

"So, my scent will relax him because it smells like his master, so to speak. That is creepy. This supernatural world is bloody weird. No pun intended."

"Larissa, you are a supernatural creature, never forget that." Nik helped me to my feet and sniffed my neck, his own body relaxing. I pushed him away playfully. "Bodhi, I understand your distress, but I want to speak to whoever is in charge of *The People's Revolution*. I want to bring the world back together. Can you organise it or not?"

"Nik, my Lord, you are asking something that…that may not end the way that you desire." I glanced at Nik, wondering if he told him the truth about his real identity.

"Should you not inform him of your real identity?" Nik and Roman locked eyes with one another, having a silent conversation before both nodded.

"Bodhi," he sat down before him, "I need you to understand that it is near impossible for me to be killed. I am the son of Mars, the God of War from Roman mythology. Only particular weapons can kill me, and I doubt that any of them would know what they would look like. I can take my chances, but I would like to return the world to its former glory as much as we can. Can you do what I ask or not?" Bodhi nodded as Nik held me tight and kissed my forehead.

My nose turned up at the stench of blood. "Can you go shower now?"

CHAPTER 55

DESIGNS FOR THE FUTURE

Nik

It had been a week since discovering the world still existed. I felt relieved that Bodhi had been working on a way to speak with this group of people for the last week. I hated the fact that I had been used as the face of the New World Order. I never wanted to abuse humans despite their general incompetence, but why would Duzi want this? Larissa and I had been planning ideas to take him by surprise. Larissa was running late, but I could sense her presence closing in as my foot tapped on the concrete floor of our house. Our builders had a few questions about what we planned for our future. The car pulled up and Larissa jogged into the house, her heels tapping on the rocky driveway.

"I'm sorry! I am so sorry. The meeting ran late, and Julian didn't want to stop talking and he oddly kept asking questions about our relationship despite the number of times I redirected the conversation." My ears perked up at her comment. Julian had never asked those questions before, so I wondered why he would be now. I pulled out my phone, setting an alarm to call him later as I cleared my throat, brushing it off. Larissa laughed. "Nik, I can tell when you hide things, remember? You are frustrated and irritated. Just leave it alone with Julian. I don't think he had any ulterior motive, he only asked after I mentioned that I had to leave for a meeting at the house and with you for the blood magazine."

I shuddered at the thought. I had done the magazine interview to get a step ahead of Duzi. I had every intention of dropping the bomb that the world still existed, and I began to investigate how it came to be. I knew it would put more targets on our backs, but we discussed it at length, and we now knew how to break the curse. We didn't know how to overcome the curse for now, but we would get there. She put her hand on my shoulder as she removed her heels, sliding her feet into flat shoes as our builder, Tim, appeared. Even though I preferred to hire supernatural beings, as they would complete the work faster, we compromised. Tim understood our vision, more so than some of the supernatural creatures. He had spunk, as Larissa stated.

Timothy McCalk was in his early forties with thick black hair and a stocky build. He was what you would expect from a carpenter. He bowed his head out of respect and took Larissa's hand, placing a gentle kiss on it. A soft rumble left my chest as she giggled to play off the monster trying not to rip him apart for touching what was mine.

"Lord and Mrs Dankworth, tha—"

"Tim, I told you to call us Nik and Larissa. You are building our house, please." Her voice was light but stern to show him that she didn't like the formality.

"Nik and Larissa, can you follow me to the kitchen area, please?" I took Larissa's hand, guiding her through the house to avoid any possible injuries. I missed her touch. Lately, she had thrown herself into work and along with trying to figure out how to break this curse, I barely saw her leave in the morning. I knew she would eventually break, but she was avoiding accepting the truth that she would have to die once more before we could ever end up together. I knew her dreams were getting worse. The entire room would shake at night. She kept pushing for more answers but only ever saw the bright room with golden pillars and the ethereal figure standing in the distance. Roman and I had an idea of what it could be, but we refused to say the words out loud.

Tim rolled out the plans for the house for the first floor as he spoke about knocking down walls and creating others, the overall design for the house, and bringing in extra workers. My phone beeped with a message.

UNKNOWN

Don't reveal the truth about the world. It will not end well.

An ominous threat. This person didn't think about the consequences of sending me a text. I had enough power to discover who would have sent it.

"Nik," Larissa called out as I pocketed my phone, and I walked over to her as she leant towards my touch. She had her period right now and my thirst for her had reached astronomical levels. I had to order triple the amount of blood that I normally would to avoid drinking from her. "What do you think of knocking this wall out instead of the original plan? It will double the size of our wardrobe and make the bathroom a touch smaller."

"Definitely the bigger wardrobe, as you will need it for your shoe collection alone." She nudged me playfully as I pulled her into my chest. "Will it detract from the overall plan of the house?" I asked Tim, noticing the moment Larissa's mood shifted, the bond darkening for a moment as she cleared her throat.

"No, it won't. If anything, it will benefit us. Do you like the idea?" she asked as I kissed her forehead and nodded. An alarm buzzed on her phone. "Is there anything else, Tim?"

"No, that is all. I will hire ten more men as you stated, a couple of them supernatural, but that will increase my insurance costs." His eyes were glued in my direction as if a warning that nothing had better happen.

"Tim, I can assure you if any man or woman is attacked, I will be following it up personally. Please don't hesitate to alert me to any of your concerns, *instantly*." I emphasised the word for him to understand that I would never tolerate any abuse from my kind. He nodded and returned to work, pulling his phone out.

Larissa walked slowly through the house, taking in the renovations that had already taken place. "What are you thinking about?" I asked, knowing we had around five minutes before we had to get back in the car and drive to the interview.

"Just about how much this has changed and how much it is still about to change." She avoided looking at me.

"And what about those dark thoughts? What was that about?"

"Nik, can we not, please?"

"Larissa, I am your husband, please don't shut me out."

She spun on her heel and sighed as she ran her fingers through her hair. "I had a thought that I may not be alive to see the house finished. Happy now?"

I pulled her into my arms, holding her flush against my chest as I bent to her neck, inhaling her familiar scent. Her body relaxed as her arms wrapped around my waist and we stood for a moment in silence to stop her brain from overthinking.

"Now that I have your full attention, to avoid your death being premature, we have a solution for that."

"Come on, don't start with that, Nik." She shook her head. "I will never allow that to happen. I want to die as the person that I am. I want the choice to turn when I feel I am ready, not for some protection that we know won't work."

"Do you ever consider my needs? Do you ever consider that I don't want to lose my fucking wife, or do you only ever think of yourself?"

"Nik, can we fight about this later, please? We have the interview to get ready for." I threw my hands up in the air, everything had been on her schedule lately and I grew tired of it. She needed to understand that I had lived this so many times and I only wanted her safe. I wanted her in my fucking arms until the day that we both died.

"Yes, absolutely, whatever you fucking want. Let's go, we don't want to be late." I motioned toward the car as she strolled past with a snarky look on her face that said this wasn't over, and I agreed. It most definitely was not over.

THE CAR RIDE WAS QUIET AS NIK DROVE INTO THE CITY. HE SENT Andreas to wait for me at work so he could drive me home later. The interview would take place in Nik's office, even though I requested that we do it at the penthouse, but he explained that he wanted distance, so nobody knew where we lived. I snuck into his office bathroom to change into matching outfits. Nik's public relations manager wanted us to portray that we were a power couple. I rolled my eyes as I lifted the dress up and over my hips, noticing the bruise on my upper thigh. I didn't remember where it came from, and I tried to recall when I hurt myself, but I had no memory of it. From the purple and blue colouring, I could tell that the bruise was at least a couple of days old. When I applied pressure, the pain caused me to wince.

"Larissa, everything alright in there?" I sighed. This bond infuriated me sometimes.

"Yes, just putting my dress on."

"Don't lie to me," he growled through the door, and I heard his steps echo on the marble floor. The door swung open as I pulled the blue and black dress up my body, trying to hide the mark on my thigh.

"I am fine." He crossed his arms as he leant on the frame, giving me his signature smirk as his eyes grazed over my body. I pulled on my dress to hide it. I wasn't even sure why I felt the need to hide it, as I had not done anything wrong, but it seemed odd how I had a bruise with no knowledge of how it got there. His eyes stopped at my hand holding the dress, and he strolled over, lifting my hand. "I have no idea how I got it." He cut his thumb, rubbing it over the area, and it disappeared instantly.

"I think we need to go and get your blood levels checked. You may need another transfusion."

"You have barely fed from me lately. You only do it once every couple of days." Nik shivered at my words, taking a step back. His eyes flared as his desire for blood flooded the bond, the need was so great that I dropped to my knees.

"Shit," Nik muttered as he spun around, lifting me to my feet. "I apologise, I didn't mean that. I told you that you taste amazing and any thought I have about it seems to bring the monster one step closer to the surface. The bond felt the desire and you dropped to your knees in a submissive position. I am sorry, it wasn't on purpose."

The daze swarmed my head as Nik gripped my arms, shaking me back to reality. "Are you losing control of your own powers?" He hung his head at my question, and that gesture alone told me everything. We were literally becoming a ticking time bomb to one another. Nik helped me with control while he lost it with me. He leant his forehead on mine before he pulled me against his body.

"I did in that moment, but it is fine. I would never hurt you. I just need you…" He hesitated as words caught in his throat.

"What is it?" I lifted his chin for his eyes to meet mine.

"If you transition, this will no longer be an issue." I pushed his chest with all of my human strength, wary not to use my magic in this small space where I could possibly make the window burst open and throw him from the window. I didn't mind that idea.

"I told you, I'm not ready for that. What happened to me having a choice? You have always been mister consent, and now you are pushing an issue. I have given you my answer. I have more that I want to achieve in my life, can you not accept that?"

"I can accept that it is a stupid decision!" Nik roared, his voice booming through his office. "I cannot accept that you are willingly cutting your life short. Do you not want more time together?"

"Do not *dare* manipulate me in that way! I told you, I would prefer to live a whole life with you than a half life. I never got the choice in the past and I will be making sure that I will make *every choice* that I want now." I wanted him to understand that I may not have my memories, but I wanted to live the life that I deserved and not what I should just accept.

A knock at his door broke our focus. Nik fixed his tie and cuffs as he strolled over to the door. He opened it while I returned to the bathroom. My hair and face were all over the place. I exhaled quickly, focusing on what I wanted before snapping my fingers, making my makeup and face utter perfection. One of the few perks of being the daughter of a god, I could do whatever I wanted. I stepped out, fixing my shoe to see a tall, slender woman with black hair. Her hand was on Nik's arm, which he barely noticed, but my eyes glared at her touching my husband. She smiled once I entered the room.

"Larissa Dankworth, it is a pleasure to meet you." She sashayed over, holding her hand out. "I am Chloe Shark, and I will be conducting your interview today."

"Pleasure to meet you, Chloe." I made sure to put a little more force behind the handshake as a warning to not lay hands on my husband again. "Please take a seat. Would you like a coffee, tea, water, or even juice?" I asked her politely as Nik took a seat on his leather couch, moving a pillow to sit upright for when I sat beside him. A small smile spread over my lips. Even though we fought, he always put my needs first.

"I would love a tea, please. One sugar." Her eyes focused on Nik as she pulled her notepad and recorder from bag. I watched as she slyly lifted her skirt a tiny bit higher before my eyes focused on Nik. He stared at his hand as if bored of this interview already. I never had to worry about him cheating. I supposed it made sense, as we had literally been together for millennia. I opened the door to his office, asking his assistant, Laura, to organise the tea. I liked her, I always had.

I sat beside Nik, his hand landing on my thigh while the other wrapped around my back. I leant into him, my nerves calming instantly. He kissed the back of my ear.

"Let us begin," Chloe said as she started the recorder. "I am here with Nik and his mate, Larissa Dankworth. Tell me how, did the two of you meet? As a human, I can't quite understand the whole attraction in that way."

"You haven't found your person then," Nick said without hesitation. "It will happen for you." He spoke clearly, his way of saying stop eye fucking me and search for your partner.

"The day we met, I spilt my coffee on him. Pure accident. He knew who I was at the beginning, but I had no idea about this mate stuff." Nik laughed at the memory of our first encounter.

"Now, Larissa is leaving out the most important aspect. It was not a *little* amount. She dropped the cup on the floor due to a hangover, was it?" he asked and I nodded. "When I offered her a napkin to clean the mess, she took it standing and dropped the rest of it on my suit." He paused for a moment. "I have never washed that suit." I turned to look at him, not knowing this.

"Wait, why?" I asked him as I stared into his beautiful blue eyes, remembering the day fondly.

"I relived the moment for months until you finally accepted that we were fated to one another. I thoroughly enjoyed the smell of your desire during that meeting and the blushing of your cheeks."

"I take it you couldn't look away from her?" Chloe asked as she scribbled more notes onto her pad.

"Yes, and I still struggle to do that, Miss Shark." He kept it as impersonal as possible with her.

"Mr Dankworth, I find it interesting that you have been asked for interviews in the past and have never spoken of your personal life. Yet you requested this meeting today. May I inquire as to why?" she asked, tapping the pencil on her chin while she waited for him to answer.

Nik cleared his throat. "That is correct. I preferred to keep it strictly business until now. I have lived for so long that I have seen the worst of humanity but she, my love, my mate, has reminded me of everything that is good in this world. She has brought a new light into my life, a new focus."

Where was he going with this? I worried about what he had planned. We had barely spoken about this interview other than the stupidity of it. I shuffled in my seat and took a sip of water as Laura entered with the tea for Chloe and a whiskey for Nik.

"A little early to be drinking, isn't it?" Chloe asked, her eyes flaring with lust as he lifted the glass to his lips, his muscles flexing beneath his perfectly tailored suit.

"Miss Shark, what I do or drink is of no concern to you, understood? We are here to discuss my mate, my business choices, and the future."

"Yes, apologies. As a couple, what are your plans for the future? Your wedding seemed to be filled with scandal but not one person is speaking about it. I find that rather curious. What is there to hide?"

"I fainted at the altar. I had dieted a little too hard in the lead-up and fainted. It was so embarrassing. I was so focused on being immaculate that I forgot to eat and drink. It is silly, every person had to sign an NDA, and that is the only reason that it isn't spoken about. There was no ulterior motive." I hoped saying this would stop her from snooping further, for Nik's and my own safety. Witches were still hidden for now. Duzi hadn't followed through with his threat just yet.

Nik tapped my arm as he moved closer. "Larissa, I think we should tell the truth." My brows creased in confusion. What was he talking about? We decided that would be the story. "My beautiful wife is a witch and yes, they exist. We were forced to marry, but neither of us cared as we were already committed to one another. I married Larissa for her protection in both the human and vampire world as she had been threatened for what she is. There is more to the world than you are aware of, Miss Shark. Are you ready for this interview? What is that saying? It will blow your socks off."

I snorted at his comment, as he never spoke like that. He always had that proper tone with the rich English accent and a hint of his Roman one. His voice was just downright sexy, and I shifted in my seat thinking of the way his words set my body on fire. Wrong place, Larissa, wrong time.

"Witches are real? Larissa, can you show us a demonstration?" Chloe appeared amused, as if Nik was lying. I snapped my fingers, making her recorder break into a million pieces. She gasped in horror as I repeated the same action but returning it to its original state. She picked it up, turning it over in her hands. "How the hell did you do that?"

"More than just vampires exist in this world, Miss Shark." I winked at her as Nik smirked, his hand rubbing up and down my arm.

"Wh-what else?" Her words fumbled as she furiously scribbled on her notepad.

"Vampires, witches, and werewolves, but I think we shall leave the rest for now," Nik stated as if it meant nothing.

"Wolves exist? Holy fuck." She had lost her professional façade. "I need...do you know a wolf that would be willing to speak about this? Larissa, do you speak for the witch community?"

"Wolves will always keep to themselves," Nik said as he took another sip of his whiskey. "There is another matter that I think is more important though, Miss Shark."

"What the hell could be more important than this?" Her eyes widened in shock, and I could almost hear her brain exploding with this new information. I wondered what Nik's plan was. Why had he thought it was smart to reveal this right now?

"The world is not dead." She dropped her notepad. "I believed it to be, as did you, but I have recently discovered that this isn't true."

"Weren't you behind the revolution of your species taking over? Why are you revealing the truth now? What is happening for this to be told now?" She spoke so fast as her tiny brain tried to register what this could mean.

"Yes, I was behind it, and this is the reason for my truth. I had no knowledge of the truth, and I refuse to keep up the pretence about it. The world deserves to know. Bombs were dropped but they weren't all nuclear, and I will be hunting those responsible as it is my duty as lord of the region. I will find the perpetrators and I shall have them punished for this gross mistake against the human population."

"Mr Dankworth, how will the world survive with this knowledge? The United Kingdom has lived like this for over fifty years. It will be hard to come back from this. What happened to other countries?"

"Those are very good questions, Miss Shark, and once I discover more about this, I will happily share it with you. But for now, that is all that I am willing to relay." She scribbled more onto her notepad as she peered up at the both of us.

"Larissa, can you snap your fingers and kill a person?"

"Don't be stupid, witches do not harm people," Nik spat out. I could if I wanted to, but it was better not to tell her just how powerful I was.

"Won't the witch and wolf community be unimpressed that you have revealed this information?"

"Maybe, but I honestly don't care. I want the truth to come out and I want the world and those responsible to be held to account. Am I understood?" he asked as he stood, offering his hand to her. She packed her bag, taking his hand and offering a business card.

"If you wish to divulge any further information, please do not hesitate to give me a call." She nodded in my direction. "Larissa, same to you, if you wish to speak about the witch community." I waved her goodbye as Nik walked her to the door. I waited a couple of minutes before I threw a pillow at him.

"Was I not supposed to be laying low with the witch community? I think you just put a huge target on my back. Juliet is going to be furious. She has wanted me to visit her for months and I have been putting it off." My voice was a little louder than usual, thanks to all the stress.

Nik shrugged. "Who the fuck cares? Juliet cannot hurt you. You could literally wipe her from the planet if you wanted to. Don't worry."

"What is the purpose of that? Care to let me in on your plan?" He handed me a glass of whiskey, which I finished in one large gulp.

"I want to flush those people out. I do feel a little sorry for Miss Shark, as she will not live to survive the night. She will tell her editor who will run it up the approval chain before she is killed."

"So, the story will never reach the papers. What was the point then?"

"I want to know how long until it is passed onto someone. I tapped her phone and her laptop. It was why she was so close to me at the start of the interview when you came out all jealous that another was touching your mate."

"Sometimes you can be really annoying."

"Yes, but that is why you love me because I will always keep you guessing. Now, shall we continue with our transition talk?" This would be fun.

Chapter 57
THE ULTIMATUM

Nik

Larissa had been awake since early morning, visiting the gym to work off her frustration over our continued argument for her to transition. This conversation had been going for a few days since the magazine interview. I knew it would never be possible to wear her down with just how stubborn she could be. She had a strength I admired, a tenacity like no other. As I showered, I listened to her thundering heart as she punched the bag relentlessly. We argued until the early hours of the morning, yet she refused to transition. I understood her reasons, but she refused to acknowledge my own. I sighed as desire briefly flitted through our bond, as she would know I was in the shower and her thoughts would have drifted to my naked body. I stepped from the shower, drying myself before heading to join her in the gym. I put on a singlet top to show off the body of her god-like husband. I pushed the door open, admiring her arse as it moved with every punch. Fuck, she was perfection. My cock twitched, wanting to bury itself inside her. We hadn't been intimate for a couple of days, as she denied me after all the bickering we endured.

"Either work out or go away, but don't stand there and gawk at me," she mumbled between her punches.

"Why? I don't need a television when I have you to stare at all day," I rebutted as she turned her body. I watched her chest pant as my eyes focused on her breasts, which looked as if they would spill out of her top. She had been stress eating for the past week as she had just finished her period, and they always grew slightly at this time. I would never complain about it.

"Have you come to apologise?" she snapped as she removed her gloves before chugging water from her bottle.

"Apologise for wanting to keep my mate safe? No, I have not nor will I ever. Have you come to your senses and realised that I'm asking for you to do it simply for your protection?"

She rolled her eyes and allowed her head to fall backwards before replacing the glove. I knew this was her way of saying, *I am done with this*. I pushed myself from the wall and wandered over to the weights in her eyeline. I placed two hundred onto the bar before lying on the bench and gripping the bar. I lowered it, holding it for a moment, before lifting it once again. I continued this for twenty reps as I sensed and smelt her desire grow.

I placed my bar above my head. "I don't need to see you to know that you are staring." I sat up, removing my top to give her a better view. Annoyance flashed through the bond, and I laughed at her denial.

"Do you have to be such an arse?"

"For you, always, my wife." I sat up, watching her twist and turn, and lifting her leg to connect with the bag. I wanted desperately to get on my knees and worship her with my tongue, but I had to keep my resolve. I would use sex if I had to for her to see reason.

"Stop it, Nik, I cannot concentrate." She threw her gloves away as I stood up, stalking over to her.

"That bag will not get your frustrations out. Go for a round in the ring with me. Let us see what skills my brother has taught you." My eyes flared as did hers. "No magic either and I will avoid using my full strength to make it more of a fair fight."

She snorted. "You wouldn't know the meaning of the word." As she crossed her arms, I stepped back, gesturing her towards the ring. "Gloves on or off?" she asked as she took another sip of water, some of it dripping onto her already sweat-covered chest. I shook thoughts of licking those droplets away.

"Gloves off. Are you ready?" I waited for her to remove them, and as she glanced over her shoulder, a sly smile crept over her lips. She threw the glove in my direction with magic before sliding along the floor and kicking my abdomen. I was not prepared for it and groaned in pain. "You got me there," I said with a strained voice.

She chuckled, and as she turned her back, I wrapped my arms around her neck and waist, pinning her arms down as I breathed in the crook of her neck. I loved her scent, and I moaned knowing it was all mine. She struggled in my arms, and she tried to move in different directions before swinging her head back. I moved just in time, joy flicking through our bond. I had done as she wanted, and I knew what that joy signified as she brought her fist down onto my groin. I let her go instantly, the air was knocked from my lungs. Roman had been teaching her well, which meant I had to step my game up. I growled as her steps faltered, seeing my eyes flare brighter than usual.

"Now you are going to get it," I growled as I stormed towards her. She raised her hands in preparation as she swung, but I blocked her attack, so she attempted another to my side. I moved aside. She had already taken those two shots, and I wouldn't allow another. She continued her attack, and I blocked every single one, which only fuelled her anger. I grabbed her fist, spinning her into my arms, my hand drifting over her breast and kneading. I missed the feel of her skin against mine. Her body relaxed as a soft moan left her luscious lips. "Ready to yield?" I asked her, my fangs grazing along her neck. I had not drunk from her for a few days, and I was dying for a taste.

"Please," she whimpered as my hand drifted lower, rubbing over the top of her pants. She was already wet for me. I sank my teeth into her neck, enjoying the taste of her sweet elixir as I fumbled down the front of her pants to her wetness. I slid a finger across her throbbing clit as she groaned, her body relaxing at the euphoria that spread through her. I made sure to not take too much from her as she needed another transfusion. I licked over the wound, watching it heal as I plunged my fingers inside her, rubbing my erection into the crease of her arse. Her body responded, grinding against me.

"Nik." Her voice begged for relief, and I pulled my fingers away, sucking the juices from my fingers. "Why did you stop?" she asked, her face flushed as her fingers played with my abs, running them up and down.

"Did you not say that we wouldn't have any more sex until I agreed to stop with the transition question?"

"Yes," her voice elevated with anger as she registered where I was going with this.

"No sex until you agree." I took a step back, pulling my shirt over my head as she threw her hands up in the air. She flung her drink bottle at my head before storming from the room. I glanced down at my erection. "You won't get any either," I said to myself. I had to keep my resolve and my head prepared to win this argument.

CHAPTER 58
SISTER IN TROUBLE

Larissa

SINCE NIK DENIED SEX THIS MORNING FOR THE MOST RIDICULOUS reason, thinking he could manipulate me, I had been doing the same to him. My frustration grew throughout the day as the need to feel his touch became so overpowering, I could barely focus on work. Nik called a department head meeting at three, and even though everyone knew who I was, they no longer cared. I had earnt my right to be here after turning the small company into one of the most sought-after marketing houses. The TimeShaft app had excelled beyond my expectations. I rode the elevator to the top floor, and Nik's assistant bowed her head at me, making me chuckle.

"Laura, you do not need to do that." A perky smile filled her plump cheeks, lighting up her brown eyes.

"I know, but you are so kind compared to him." She averted her eyes as she continued to sort through the mound of paperwork on her desk.

I sighed, wondering how hard he worked this poor girl. "Is he still being an arsehole?" I asked her, pointing towards all the work.

"Not as much, but yep." She shrugged her shoulder as if she didn't care.

"I'll sort him out." I winked as her cheeks flushed with embarrassment. I entered without knocking, finding Nik leaning on the glass, the phone pressed to his ear. He would have already sensed my entrance, so I sat on the black leather couch and waited. There was an oak table between the two couches. The desk sat on a ledge, the windows showing the London cityscape. It was breathtaking but I only stared at his perfect arse. A man that attractive should look ugly in something, but he never did. He had no faults other than his possessiveness. A thump broke my perve session as I focused on Nik's conversation.

"He has no leg to stand on or rather he won't soon." His voice was deep and threatening. "I don't care. Nobody threatens my mate and lives to talk about it. I will fucking kill him."

I paid attention now. I swear, every week somebody wanted me dead but when your husband held the keys to the literal kingdom, it was hard to not be a target. I played with my fire magic to remind him that I had plenty of protection. He smirked, shaking his head. He didn't care. This was part of his old-fashioned values. He was my protector, and I would be his constant damsel. I hoped one day to show him that I could save *him*. Nik threw the phone across the room, and I sent a bubble to surround it. He snorted as he slumped into his chair.

"You don't need another broken phone. That will be the fourth this month."

"I don't need a dead mate," he whispered, sighing. I walked over and rubbed his shoulders. His muscles flexed underneath, which increased my desire to fuck him on this chair.

"Nik, I may be Liyana but I'm also not. Can you trust me?" He forced himself from the chair.

"I can't lose you again and you refuse to listen to reason."

"We have had this discussion. It isn't going to happen. I'm not a reincarnation. I'm her but improved. Katrina did us a favour by giving me this. Just trust that it will work out for us. I do not need to transition. I have powers to protect me. You saw what they did when Roman and I fought. They literally had a mind of their own. Can you just trust me?" I pleaded with him as I stroked his face, and he relaxed slightly at my touch.

"How? We are still figuring out how your death breaks the curse. We have no clue about the finer details of it all. It's my fault. I should have listened. I should have let you die." He stormed away, I threw a fireball at him, to which he appeared dumbfounded. "What the hell?"

"You did what you did, move on. Sit your arse down now." I pointed to his chair as he shook his head.

"Don't you—" I raised my hand in preparation, so he grumbled and sat. I spun his chair around.

"What happened?" He avoided my gaze, his typical avoidance technique.

"Larissa, I have made enemies in the past and some still have grudges. Plus, the article. Someone attacked her last night. Only two people were told, and I cannot find a link to any vampires from there," he grumbled as I noticed his gaze fixate on my breasts. I moved closer and his body began to relax as he reached out and pulled me onto his lap. His hands ran up and down my sides, an instant calmness enveloped my body.

I exhaled in relief. "That's cheating."

"Is it though?" I groaned as he nibbled my neck, and pushed myself back. He had already teased me this morning with his stupid ultimatum.

"Did I not say no touching, no kissing, no sex, and now no blood until you stop this talk?" His eyes flashed in anger.

"You would deny your mate *his* meal?" His red pupils fixated on my every move, and I contemplated running but I knew the predator in him would pounce. He stopped, sensing my fear. "Larissa, I would never harm you."

"I know. I pushed fear through on purpose. Now *that's* cheating." I winked at him. I had been working on ways to shut some of the emotions down between us. I found it hard to concentrate some days, especially when he was stressed.

"Time for the meeting," he mumbled, making his way to the door and holding it open for me. We rode the elevator in silence, and I thought about how I would get him to tell me who his enemies were even if he didn't want to. I entered before him, taking my seat as he pushed it in. Always the gentleman. He took his seat at the other end and the meeting began. My period had just finished and not having sex for the last couple of days had been a real tease. I glanced over his appearance, taking in all of the sex appeal he exuded. Having Nik as a mate made it difficult to concentrate on anything that was being said. I started to nibble on my pen in frustration and when I glanced up at Nik, his eyes were zeroed in on my mouth. I smiled. This would be fun. I threw up a shield to hide the smell of my desire before I thought of every single dark and dirty thought. Nik's hands gripped his chair tighter, and he shifted in his seat before grabbing a pen and clicking it. His eyes found mine as I pushed the pen further into my mouth and undid a button on my shirt.

"Meeting is over. I need to speak with my wife." The department heads glanced around, their faces screwed up in confusion. "NOW!" he shouted, his voice rumbling through the room. They exited swiftly, and as he stood, his desire was evident from the obvious tent in his pants. He pressed a button on the table, and the glass surrounding the room frosted.

"What's wrong, sweetheart?" A dark chuckle escaped his lips, causing a shiver down my spine.

"My wife needs to be taught a lesson." His eyes darkened with desire as his eyes focused on my breasts in full view.

"Oh really? What for?" I said, acting innocent, tapping the pen to my chin.

"Oh, she knows. Stand up." He leant against the wall with his arms and legs crossed. I tapped my fingers on the table, ignoring him as I forced more dirty thoughts through our bond. He growled before he lifted me over his shoulder and spanked my arse. I giggled like a child. "You are going to get it." He headed for the door,

"Nik, put me down, they will see."

"Exactly." I did not plan for this. Shit. I locked the door with magic and forced a blocking shield around the room. "Ah, smart girl." He dropped me on the table, then got on his knees.

"Nik, what are you doing?"

"Worshipping my wife as she comes on my tongue. Screw the no-sex policy, I need to feast on the delicious taste of your pussy. I could die between your legs, and I would be a happy man." Fucking hell, this man was a sinner and a saint. He ripped my undies off as he kissed up my leg. My breathing became erratic, and I could barely focus before his fangs sank into my thigh. I moaned as I felt his needs being satiated. The tie between us, the need to keep each other happy, blew my mind. Nik plunged two fingers inside me, and my body arched for more. My climax grew, waiting for that perfect spot to be hit as his thumb circled my clit. They say men can't do two things at once, but he was doing three. My body erupted, and my vision went dark.

Nik was gone and I stood in a blacked-out room, cold and alone.

"Larissa." A hand gripped my arm, and I spun to see Luce. Her face was covered in blood, her eye was bruised, and her clothes were in tatters.

"Luce, what happened?"

Her eyes welled with tears. "I'm sorry. I am so sorry for everything. I was wrong, and I fucked up." A loud thud echoed through the room, "They are coming. I know I don't deserve this after what I did to you but please, Larissa. They are going to kill me."

"Who?" I grasped her shoulders, shaking her for the answer. I tried to push against the force pulling me back to reality. "Luce, tell me."

"The witches." Her voice was a whisper, and I found myself back with Nik, his face crinkled, and his hands on my face, his eyes black with worry.

"Larissa, what the hell happened?" I followed his eyes to the black mark on my arm.

"Luce, I need to find her." I jumped from the table, collecting my shoes.

"The hell you do. She tried to kill you." Nik forced his hand on the door.

"That is in the past. She is my sister."

"Your cousin," he corrected. "She tried to remove your magic. It would have killed you."

"We moved past this. I mean, you helped her to get clean for our wedding. She needs my help, Nik. They are going to kill her."

"Good. She should burn for her sins."

"Nik! How many times have you and Roman fought?"

"Not the same. He is my blood, my twin. We shared a womb."

"We shared a room. She is my only relative. You can object or you can help, but I will save my sister from the witches."

"It's a trap. You know they want you. Think about this, Larissa." He gripped my arm tighter as I flinched from his strength.

"I don't care. I will not lose her."

"Larissa, I need you to see reason. I'm begging you. If we go there, it won't end the way you want. They tried to stop our wedding. Do you not realise that Malignus never would have gotten his claws into James without their help. Fucking hell. You want to go running for the piece of shit who would have killed you?"

"Yes! You may never understand, but she is my only family. She is my blood, and I can't lose her. I will never forgive myself. Has she fucked up? Yes! Does she deserve my forgiveness? No! But the only one who is allowed to torture her is me and I'll be damned if I let them harm another hair on her head." He stared at the ground, his hands on his hips, a look of contemplation on his face. I tipped his face to meet his gaze. "They tortured her, Nik. I won't be able to live with myself if I leave her to die."

"You are asking me to put you in harm's way. The curse waits for these opportunities, and you want to walk into one. This is why I have been asking you to transition." He turned away from me, trying to control his rage as his body shook.

I wrapped my arms around his waist, knowing I was about to put myself in a situation that could cause my death. "The curse has never had a half-demon, half-witch to fight against. Fate be damned. I won't be dying today. I promise."

He turned in my arms, holding my face in his hands as he kissed me. "I will hold you to that. If you are going, I am coming with you."

Chapter 59
It Came Crashing Down

Nik

She could hate me all she wanted but I wouldn't let her go to see the witches without my protection. They had been asking to see her since our wedding and we had been postponing it, so why the sudden urgency to see her now that they kidnapped Luce? We rode the elevator together, and as I held her hand, I could hear her heart thumping in her chest with a mixture of fear and anxiety. I reached over, squeezing her hand for assurance. She smiled gently, but it didn't reach her eyes. She slid into the car; I watched as she buckled her seatbelt before the car roared to life.

"Larissa, you need to have a level head when we reach the destination. You cannot run in on pure emotion. The witches will sense it, and they will tear you apart. You have to lock your emotions down."

"Nik, she is my sister, my only living family member. I cannot lose her. You are asking me to do the impossible right now. How do I shut my emotions off?" Tears brimmed her eyes at the thought of losing Luce, even after all the hurt she had caused. Larissa only saw the good in people. I weaved in and out of traffic as I tried to call Roman, wanting the wolves, or at least some, close by in case they were needed. I knew it would be difficult as they had already allied with the witches. I only hoped with Roman as the Alpha, they would listen to reason rather than possible threats, which is what witches were good at. They pretended to have more power than they believed and would use this guise to get whatever they wanted. They feared Larissa as she actually had the power to destroy all of them.

"I swear on everything I am, I will not let anything happen to her or you." She breathed out in relief at the fact that I put Luce before her but in reality, it would be vastly different. "Now, we need a plan of attack."

"We go in and save Luce. I honestly don't know, Nik. I am not the Son of Mars; I don't have the blood from the God of War running in my veins. I don't have strategies; I have no idea. I have never had to fight like this before, and I am terrified that I will lose her. I am terrified that I will lose control of my magic and hurt them. It makes absolutely no sense why I would even care about hurting them when...when Luce was bloodied and beaten."

"It is because you are a good person, and you don't want to kill. It isn't your first instinct, and it never will be. You try to see the good in every person you know, and you want to believe that there is a way out of this. But Larissa, my love, I need you to understand that not everyone has your beautiful heart and soul. Some people just want to take and take until there is nothing left. You may not get what you want from today. I need you to understand this, and I need you to process that Luce may not be coming home or," the next words would hurt her, "or you may have to hurt someone. They want your power. They believe you stole it and now that you have Katrina's grimoire, they will only see blood. They are incapable of seeing reason."

"Nik, what if you are hurt?" she asked, her eyes relaxing, understanding my words despite how hard they were to hear.

"Larissa, you know that I am more powerful than most. My bloodline is older than witches, so they will not be able to directly harm me. The witches will use the same techniques that you do—misdirection and blocking—but after a while, I can break through those as well. I don't want you worrying about me at all. I want you to focus on your task and how to overcome the power of an entire coven. You will need to tap into your father's power as well as your mother's dark magic."

Her breathing trembled as she shook her head. She understood but she wouldn't want to use it. A storm hit the car hard, the rain pelting unnaturally hard against the windscreen. Larissa touched the car as her eyes flared. I sensed it before anything else happened.

"Larissa, throw up a shield now." The witches had been smart enough to spell the car, and the rain seemed to be attacking it. It was their attempt to make us crash, but I held onto the wheel and focused with all my might on keeping the car on course. I wouldn't let my wife die in a car accident, but I knew this was to keep me contained. The witches planned to remove her protector, wanting her on her own where she would be more vulnerable. Fuck! I could not let this happen. Larissa had a shield up, which only made the car tremble more. Her eyes widened in shock.

"Whatever happens, I want you to know that I love you and I have always loved you."

"No, this isn't your end." I roared as a wheel burst, and the car began to swerve violently with the lack of traction. The brakes were not working, and the gears refused to change. The car continued at its speed of over ninety kilometres an hour. I glanced at Larissa, knowing this would hurt, but I would do my best to protect her with every fibre of my being. I turned the wheel, making the car spin continually in the hopes of slowing it down. The barrier came into view on Larissa's side. "Blast it!" I shouted at her as her powers shattered the glass, but her magic barely touched it. The coven had used its full force of magic. They wanted this crash to injure me, to remove me from helping her.

"Nik." Her voice was soft as the barrier came closer. I sped, unbuttoning my seat belt and throwing my body over hers to take the full brunt of the crash. I could survive this, but she wouldn't. The car crashed into the barrier, and her screams echoed before darkness crossed my vision and pain erupted through my body.

———

I woke to intense pain shattering through the bond. "Larissa." My voice was groggy as I reached to touch her. The space was empty, and my eyes shot open as I remembered the accident. Her scream echoed once again as I shifted in my seat, unable to move. "Larissa!" I shouted louder, hoping she would be close. But I knew from the bond that she wasn't. I barely felt her. I roared once more, "Larissa!" A small flicker vibrated through my chest, and I glanced down to see a street pole impaling my chest, just missing my heart. I smiled despite my predicament, knowing that I had saved her life even if it had cost me this much damage to my body. I tried to move again to no avail. Fuck. I was stuck. I looked for my phone, but I couldn't see it anywhere. More pain seared through the bond as Larissa's scream echoed in my head. She was being tortured. I would fucking kill them all. I did not care for the consequences. She didn't deserve this. I needed to contact Roman. We used to be able to communicate through a mind-link, but we had not used it since I had transitioned into a different kind of monster. I needed help. I needed my brother. I could hear sirens in the distance, but the last thing I wanted was to stay and be forced to give interviews about how a magical car crash occurred.

I closed my eyes to focus on my brother and solely my brother, pushing away the pain that Larissa was currently enduring. Something snapped inside my head as Roman's rough voice echoed in my mind.

"Nik, is that you? How is this possible?"

"Brother, I need you." It was our way of saying drop everything and come to me. We never used our names, only *brother*.

"Where are you?" he asked, the stress in his voice coming through clearly.

"I am on the highway out of the city. Listen for the sirens. I need you here now, brother."

"I am on my way."

"Roman, I need blood and lots of it. Bring it all."

"What the hell has happened?" he asked, as I felt him getting closer.

"I will tell you when I see you," I mumbled as the car shifted, the pole scratching more of my heart. I had to focus on Larissa, or I would lose consciousness again. I refused to lose the feel of her. I had to find her. I had to save her. I had to protect my wife.

Time seemed to drag on as I manoeuvred, pulling the pole from my body. It ached with every movement, causing Larissa to feel the same. I hated this. They had done this on purpose, separating us with pain. I wanted to rip them apart, and I would. I would drain their pathetic bodies dry. Fuck the alliances to never harm one another, I only saw blood for what they were doing. And what they did to Katrina. The car thumped as Roman jumped onto the bonnet, causing me to gasp in pain.

"Fucking hell, Roman! Use some logic in that wolf brain of yours." His golden eyes took in the scene as colour drained from his face. He pulled the door open, smelling her blood.

"Her wounds are superficial. Nik, how the fuck did you let this happen? I can smell other wolves," he growled. "They shall be dealt with." He walked around to the other side of the car, opening the door as a piece of metal tore further into my leg and it grew warm with the fresh blood that split from the wound. I had to close off the bond for a moment to avoid Larissa feeling more pain than she could handle. "Sorry, brother."

"It is fine. Just get me out of here. I lost my control on the bond and Larissa is feeling all of this. And to answer your other question, witches."

Roman growled. "Fucking witches," he mumbled as he evaluated the situation with the pole.

"Glad to see that you didn't continue the deal with them when you took control as Alpha."

"Come on, Remus, I am insulted that you even thought I would." Now it was my turn to growl at him and I could not return the favour in any way with my current predicament. "Lost for words, are you?"

I snorted. "When I get out of here, I swear I will give you a black eye."

"Yeah, sure you will, little brother. I am always cleaning up your messes." He moved around the car for the best vantage point as he mumbled to himself and gripped the pole, moving it in various directions as I winced, the pain annoying more than anything.

A scream ripped out of my throat, but it was not my own, it was Larissa's. These fucking witches had done it on purpose. They would know that I shut it down for a moment. Roman's hands gripped my shoulders.

"We will get her, I swear to you, brother. Remember what you said. This time is different. She is stronger. Hold onto that hope. Are you ready?" He gripped the pole in front of me. I took his hand and stared at my brother. "This is not our end. We swore to each other that we would be there for one another until the moment we died. I am not dying when I just found my mate, and it is not your time either. Hold on a little longer. I have blood when you are ready."

I took a deep breath, and I nodded, holding onto the seat, my fingers ripping into the leather as I bit into my bottom lip. Pain seared through my entire body as I did everything I could to block it from Larissa. I didn't need her feeling any of it. I needed her head clear, and if she knew what was happening, she would not be at her strongest. Her attention would be divided, and I didn't want to be the reason that I lost her, not again. The pole scraped against my heart as Roman adjusted the angle to minimise the damage as much as he could. Once it was out, my body slumped into the seat. I needed a vein, but a blood bag would do. Roman threw ten bags at me and I tore into each of them, my monster banging against the cage. It wanted Larissa's blood, which would return us to our full monster capacity. I stood from the car as flashing lights appeared in the distance.

"Thank you, Roman, go to your mate."

"Nik, let me help," he pleaded, his hand landing on my shoulder.

"As much as I want the help, I will not risk the fact that you found your mate. You deserve the time with her. Go and be with her or rather go and stalk her. I can handle a coven of witches. I just hope Larissa doesn't lose control of her magic and kill them all before I can help her."

Roman chuckled. "We both know she won't handle that, but it would be a sight to see her reach her full potential. Keep the link open if you need me." He turned to walk away before he paused, turning back. "I missed hearing you in my head, brother. It has been too long." I sighed. He was right. It had been way too long.

CHAPTER 60
TAKEN AND TORTURED

Larissa

"NIK! NIK! NIK, WAKE UP!" I SCREAMED OVER AND OVER AS I SAW his body impaled on a street pole. He moved at the last minute to protect me, and his body took the brunt of the hit. He saved my life. Again. Tears rolled down my cheeks as I continued to shout into the abyss, while he remained unresponsive. I barely felt him through the bond; it was barely a flicker. The door opened as two large men appeared, their eyes glowing yellow. Wolves.

"Does your Alpha know that you are traitors?" I spat at them as their claws dug into my arm, pulling me from my seat. "Nik!" I yelled, but he didn't move. Was he dead? How could the son of a god die? I did not think it was possible. He had to be alive. I fought against the wolf's hold as he tightened his grip on my arm. "You will let me go." I threatened, my eyes flaring at him, using what magic I could without weakening myself. I forced an explosive spell from my body, blowing them both away. I ran as far as my legs could take me, glancing down at the minor scrapes covering my torn and tattered clothes. My legs grew heavy as my vision blurred, and I touched my forehead, feeling a sticky substance. I pulled my hand away to look at it. Blood.

'There is no point running. You won't get very far.' A voice echoed in my head, then it cackled.

"Let me guess, you are Juliet, the coven leader, who has decided I am a traitor to my kind," I responded with sass to annoy her.

'You are a traitor, and you will pay for your crimes.' As a sharp pain tore through my body, my knees gave out and I dropped to the floor. *'That is just a touch of what I have planned for you.'* I gritted my teeth as I forced myself to stand. She wouldn't win this. I had to fight for Nik and Luce. I refused to let this curse beat me. I wanted to be the one who survived, the one who changed it all.

"Good luck. Tell me where you are, and we can fight this out like you had planned. I hope you are ready because I am going to destroy your pathetic fucking coven for what you have done to me, my family, and my mate," I snarled at her in my head. As I stood, electric pain shot through me, my body wanting to quit. But I would not yield to her. Nik was right, there were times when you had to kill, and this was it. At the end of this, it would either be Juliet or I left standing.

'Go with the wolves. I will see you soon.'

"Looking forward to it." I shut her out of my mind, turning to see the wolves running towards me with their teeth bared and growling. I knew this was going to hurt. A fist connected to my face as my body fell backwards. I didn't feel myself hit the ground.

———

I woke to sharp pain shooting through me once again, and I let out a small scream before clamping my mouth shut. I opened my eyes, focusing on my surrounding. I was chained to a chair in the middle of a warehouse and fourteen women surrounded me, wearing black cloaks and masks to hide their faces. Luce sat before me, her foot chained to the beam outside the circle, her face bruised. I took a deep steadying breath, remembering Nik's words. I had to keep my head straight. The chains were iron with markings that were designed to keep witches locked up, but my father was a god. I pulled my arms apart, the chains disintegrating in seconds. The witches collectively gasped as I stood, walking towards my sister. Juliet moved in front of me. Her smile reminded me of a serial killer.

"Get out of my way." I bared my teeth at her as she pushed me back with mere human strength.

"You are my prisoner," she snarled as I focused on the movements around me. The witches closed in together.

"That is what you think. You will let me check on my sister or I will snap your neck like a fucking bug." I never knew I had this confidence, but I could feel Nik in my veins, in my head, in my body. He was somehow giving me strength, which I knew meant he was alive. My eyes flared as she stepped aside. I strolled closer to Luce, but she held up her hand.

"Stop, Rissa, look up." I followed her finger to see a spell written in what could be blood on the roof. I stormed back over to Juliet, ripping her hood from her head, pulling her hair with it as her body bent backwards.

"You think you can trap me? You really have no understanding of what I am. You saw my eyes and yet you are foolish enough to not fear me. You obviously have no care of your coven at all." I spun around to look at each of the innocent women in the circle. "I will give you this choice, the one that Juliet didn't. I am the daughter of High Priestess Katrina Solis and the God Pluto. I have more power than you will ever comprehend. If you leave now, I will not seek revenge for your attack on my family. If you stay, I cannot be held accountable for what will happen to you." Whispers filled the room as they spoke to one another. Four women dropped their cloaks as they exited the warehouse.

"You traitors! She is an abomination; she must be destroyed."

"No," I looked at my nails as if I had no time for her, "they just have common sense unlike the rest of you. Nik warned me that I would have to do terrible things to save my sister today and honestly, I have no fear. You attacked me, you attacked my mate, you forced our car to crash, and you beat my sister. For that, you will pay the ultimate price. You were right to be scared of me."

"You shouldn't have taken what was never yours, nor should you have taken the title as a witch advocate." She bared her teeth at me, her face flushed in rage. I had really pissed her off.

"I never took your power. You know how the lines of power work. I didn't care about taking it, it just happened. Also, I had no say in it that article and I am not an advocate for witches. I have never wanted to be. Get over yourself. You can be the fucking advocate if you want."

"Stop sprouting your lies!" she shouted as she pointed a finger at me, a magical tether spurted from it, heading in my direction. I stepped to the side to avoid it hitting me.

"I am not lying. A voice in my head told me to bite my mate. I did and I got more power. I had no intention of taking from the coven's collective power. I am not even part of one."

"Katrina lied all the time. She was evil and manipulative," she spat her words in my direction as she started to circle me, touching each of her fellow witches' hands. This was going to hurt. "Katrina gave us all a bad name; she befriended those pathetic creatures. She saw them as people, but they are nothing but blood-sucking beasts. Your supposed mate is the worst of them all." I clenched my fists, trying not to lose my temper. She was prodding to find a weakness. Nik warned me of this. "But then we have Luce, your darling back-stabbing sister. The one who came to us for help, the one who traded secrets for more power before she became a blood whore for a quick fix."

My ears perked up as my eyes connected with my sister, who hung her head low. Juliet hadn't lied about this. Luce had betrayed me again. I had been careful since we repaired our relationship to not tell her too much, but I never thought of what she could have already told others who wished to harm me.

"I am sorry, Rissa, I never meant to hurt you. I deserve this. I earnt this punishment. Go home and save yourself. I deserve to die for my betrayal against you."

"She is not wrong, she told us all about your mate. And where you lived. But the best part is that she told us which spells she had seen you cast, in particular how you managed to break down a blocking spell. Not many young and inexperienced witches are able to do this and yet you did without breaking a sweat. I know you have *her* grimoire."

I froze, nobody should know I had it. I kept it hidden. I hadn't told anyone. Only Roman, Nik, and I knew about this. How the fuck did she know? I kept my emotions locked down; any hint would alert her to the truth. I had to be a statue. My eyes locked back onto my sister's as she sobbed. I wanted to hurt her, but my pure heart only wanted to hold her. I hung my head. Nik was right. I could spout all the words that I wanted, but could I actually take a life? Luce had been heavily influenced by someone else. How could I hate her for this? How could I punish her for what she thought was love?

"Yes, I have Elizabeth's grimoire. I found it in the ashes after she died, that isn't a secret. Luce never wanted it. You are welcome to have it if you wish. There is nothing of importance that you probably don't already know." I turned my back on Luce, keeping my eyes trained on Juliet. I barely noticed that she had been circling me, and that all the witches were joined by a thin golden chain. Juliet joined the link.

"More lies, just like your mother. She never deserved to be High Priestess, and you don't deserve the power you have."

"You know, I truly do not understand the point of this shit. You attacked my wedding, you sought help from the God of Hell, you sent wolves to kill me, and you kidnapped my sister to lure me into a trap, but *I* am the one lying when I just admitted to having Elizabeth's grimoire? Can you not see just how hypocritical she is?" I said, trying to reason with the remaining witches.

"I wasn't referring to Elizabeth's grimoire. I want Katrina's." Juliet smirked. How the hell did she know the truth?

The witches began to chant, and I knew this was about to hurt. I held up a small shield spell as my own magic bubbled in retaliation. I refused to attack first.

"Rissa, you need to get out of there!" Luce shouted. I spun to see her standing, her frantic eyes scanning those around her. She was terrified. I held my hand up to her with a small smile. I couldn't escape, and I knew it, but I would not let the witches be my end. If I died, I would take them all with me.

"Oh, Juliet." I cleared my throat as she opened her eyes. "Just one question, you know that you linked each other, right? So, if one dies, bye bye to your coven."

"Your point?"

"When my mate arrives, and he *will* because I think you underestimate him, he will simply only need to kill one of you to destroy the whole coven. Have you thought about that?" I asked her, putting on a brave face to hide the fear that my life would be ending soon. This fucking curse, yet again. Only this time, I never got my memories.

"He won't arrive in time, I made sure of that."

"You truly underestimated him then, and for that I am sorry. He will kill all of you and I think I will actually enjoy watching him bathe in your blood."

Their chanting grew louder as their magic hit me. I bent over from the pain. Small knives seemed to hit all over my body in random spots, the pain causing an echo in the large space. I gritted my teeth, trying to bare it. I wanted to scream but I held it inside, trying not to lose control of my power.

"Give me the grimoire, Larissa." Her voice grew deeper as the coven's magic channelled through her.

"You can have Elizabeth's grimoire, I already said that." I would never reveal the truth that I found Katrina's recently and only through a possession.

"Stop lying. I want Katrina's. It went missing the day she died. I want it. Hand it over."

More pain shot through me, and I dropped to my knees as I tried to keep my head from wanting to explode. My power was teetering on the edge of chaos. My hands landed on the ground as I made the entire warehouse shake. My eyes flared as I found my footing, my magic starting to form its own protective barrier around me.

"I don't have it and even if I did, that would never happen. You do not deserve to know her secrets. You tried to banish her, or did you forget that?" My voice grew deeper as my inner darkness started to take control.

"She wanted an alliance between us and those creatures! She was a fool to think they would help us. They only wanted to kill us; they wanted the special elixir of our blood. We give vampires that temporary reprieve, and they will want to take our power away."

"You seem a little power hungry yourself. Do I need to be worried?" More attacks hit my shield; the pain numbed by the lightness that returned to my heart. Nik was alive. I hadn't lost him.

"Give the power back to the coven or I will forcefully remove it."

"Good luck." I rubbed my hands together, ready for what would the fight of my life. Each witch forced a magical tether toward me, and I blocked many of them, but some wrapped their magical fingers around what they could. It burnt against my skin, the pain excruciating. I reminded myself to remain in control, that they would not win, they could not win. They sent out more, and I watched the threads move towards me, dodging as many as I could. I spun to see Luce. Her foot was still chained to the pole, so I snapped my fingers, lighting it on fire to break her free. The chain snapped as another tether stabbed into my back. A scream escaped my lips. I could feel them slowly ripping tiny pieces of my soul away. I had to be stronger than them, I had to survive. This curse would not win. I closed my eyes as I shook my body, causing some of the weaker strands to fall away while others seemed to tighten their grip.

Luce charged at the circle, trying to use her own magic against it. The power bounced off, and she shook her head.

CHAPTER 61
TIME TO DO THE RIGHT THING

Luce

I HAD NEVER DONE RIGHT BY LARISSA. I HAD BEEN JEALOUS OF HER since I was a child. She had a beauty and grace to her that could not be replicated. Her soul had been alive since almost the beginning of time, but it wasn't tainted by the mistakes of the past. She always saw the good in people, including me, yet I constantly tried to bring her down. My own insecurities brought that forward. It started when I told teachers that she would cheat on tests, then it turned into stealing the boys who found her attractive. It got worse as I grew older. I found out the hate I harboured towards my sister had been a spell. Our mother cast the spell on us to instinctually hate vampires, and after a while, it started to darken and spread. It became poisoned, and my hate started to direct itself at her. I had to do right by her now, to show her that I was the person she thought I could be, the person she always saw me as, even when I never did.

She crossed her arms over her chest as she mouthed, 'I love you and I forgive you.' How could she after I had betrayed her again? I was foolish enough to think the witches would help me, but magic had been nothing but my own curse. Larissa screamed as I scoured my brain trying to think of how to break this spell, how to save her from the death she didn't deserve. The door to the warehouse burst open and suddenly, Nik stood beside me, his eyes red and flaring. His head snapped in my direction.

I hung my head. "I didn't plan this, Nik. I wanted to be better after you saved my life. They used me and I fell for it." He moved towards the circle, which had created its own protection shield to ensure nobody could enter to save her. He reached a point, and as he raised his hand, trying to penetrate the shield, his skin began to burn. I grabbed him, pulling him back to safety.

"If she survives this, she will need her mate."

"Then what the hell do you suggest we do? That magic is not trivial witch magic, they are siphoning it from somewhere else." Nik stared at his mate as he paced the circle a few times.

I thought back to the conversation I had with Juliet.

"Leave Larissa alone. She hasn't done anything wrong, and you won't have the power to take her on." I tried to warn her, but it only seemed to fuel her more.

"No, I will have my power back. She cannot win this. I have a friend who has agreed to help. They are extremely powerful. Nothing will be able to stop me. She will make sure of it."

Witches were blessed with power from the gods and from the earth. The 'she' could be any number of things, but my instinct told me it would be the gods. Juliet could only siphon so much from the earth before it would demand a sacrifice, and as much as Juliet hated Larissa, she would never do that. I turned back to Nik, steadying my breath. "I need your blood. I need a supernatural boost. Trust me. I hate myself for asking this, but if you cannot help her, I have a solution."

Another scream echoed in the warehouse as Larissa's body rose in the air. All the witches had their tethers in her as they slowly pulled magic from her body. Nik bit into his wrist, not taking his eyes away from his mate as I fed on his blood. I could taste the power inside it as it filled me, supercharging my body with not just Nik's power but whatever power he had ingested from Larissa. I had never had such a rush in my life, this was barely a touch of my sister's power. My body shivered from having something that was never designed for me. Larissa was born to be this powerful creature, I wasn't, and I knew it. I knew what was coming for me.

"I am sorry for doubting you and keeping you apart. I wish I could take it back. I wish I could reverse it all and do better for her. She deserves it and more. I love my sister. I know my actions have spoken otherwise, but I love her. Can you do me one favour?"

"I will tell her, and I am sorry that I cannot do more. You don't deserve this, Luce."

I chuckled. "I do though, I really do. Take care of my sister." The words choked in my throat as I stepped closer to the circle. Being a witch, I could enter the shield, so I took their hands, joining the group. I spun my own weave, directing all the magic from Larissa into me. Larissa's body grew limp and fell to the ground. The magic strands latched onto my own body, and I screamed. My body was being ripped to pieces, torn apart in every sense of the word. I bore it for her, and I would never regret this decision. Larissa's eyes opened and she rolled toward me.

A glow surrounded me, and I could no longer feel anything. "I… am…sorry." I struggled to say the words as Larissa raised her hand, her magic trying to stop my sacrifice. I closed my eyes, welcoming my inevitable death as lightning tore into the building. At least I could see our mother again and hold her once more until Larissa joined us in the afterlife. I could feel my body falling, but instead of it growing lighter, it grew hot as it began to burn my skin. An evil cackle echoed in the darkness.

CHAPTER 62
THE DARKNESS TAKES OVER

Larissa

MY SISTER WAS DEAD. HER BODY LITERALLY EXPLODED INTO THE bright light. My rage vibrated through me. She had sacrificed herself and the horror of it all showed on Nik's face, his mouth hanging open, covered in blood that was not his own. The witches were all sitting on the ground. Luce had managed to break the spell, transferring it into herself, killing her instantly. It would have been excruciating. I stood up and glared at the witches who surrounded me, my vision clouded by a red haze. My purity was gone, rage was all I saw. I heard shuffling noises and snapped my head to see Juliet running away. I snapped my fingers, breaking her legs in seconds as she fell to the ground, screaming. I was done playing games with her. I swung my hands in the air as if I had an invisible lasso swinging it to drag her body back to me.

"No, please. I never meant for this to happen," she whimpered as I stood over her. The dark voices wanted me to rip her heart out of her chest.

"You should have stopped when you were told. Now, I will enjoy watching the light leave your eyes." My voice sounded alien, almost possessed with darkness.

"Larissa, please. I'm sorry."

"Bit late for that. Stand up." The voices grew louder in my head. I tried to shake them off, but they threatened to take control, they wanted blood and not just Juliet's. *'Kill them, they took your sister, destroy the coven.'*

Nik strolled over, rubbing my back as I glared at all the witches who surrounded me. Juliet clapped her hands together before grabbing those beside her as all of them joined as one. I shook my head as I looked into Nik's blue eyes. My source of comfort. I wrapped my arms around his chest, and he kissed the top of my head.

"Whatever you decide, I will be right beside you every step of the way." He lifted my head to look at him once more, moving the hair from my face with a small smile. The witches began to chant. I spun around, twisting my wrists and I cracked my neck. I used my magic to raise myself from the ground as the witches began to shout in my direction. I closed my eyes and threw my own tethers toward each of the witches, striking each in the heart. *'Give me control,'* the dark voice purred in my ear, it wanted to destroy them, but I didn't know if I could live with that decision. *'I will only destroy those who deserve it.'*

I glanced down at Nik and the pool of blood, the only thing left of my sister's dead body, and my emotions threatened to spill from me. "No, I will do it. I will be their judge, jury, and executioner." I pulled on each individual thread, listening to the voice of their souls, and deciding who lived and who died. Each tether vibrated with their truth, and as I forced pain through to each of them, the witches dropped in unison, screaming. I relished the noise, knowing they deserved this. They should feel it all. I replicated the pain that I felt as they tried to rip my magic from my body. I pulled their magic into my own body as my magic grew. The entire warehouse shook as I gathered all the energy from the universe.

"This is nothing more than you deserve!" I yelled at Juliet, forcing my fire magic out and engulfing the remaining witches that my magic believed deserved this end. Eight women burst into flames, their screams echoing through the space as they writhed in pain. They attempted to cast spells to put the fire out, but I counteracted with another spell, amplifying the fire that was already present. The remaining four witches ran for safety as I tortured those who took my sister, those who wished Nik and me harm. Those who deserved nothing more than to be swept into the dirt and be reborn as better people. The screams slowly died down as I lowered myself, walking over to Juliet whose face was blackened and peeling. I bent down to her level. "Say hello to my father. He will enjoy tearing you to pieces and putting you back together. He will swim in your blood and record your screams for his enjoyment and when it is my time, I will join him to do the same. You will never know peace for this. You fucked with the wrong girl. Enjoy your last breaths knowing you killed your entire coven for nothing."

CHAPTER 63

WHAT HAPPENS NOW?

Nik

Larissa fell to the floor, and I rushed over, wrapping my arms around her body. I held her tight against my chest, noticing her breathing was erratic. I never thought Luce would be capable of self-sacrifice, especially in the way she died. It wouldn't have been peaceful. Her death would have been agony until the last minute. She wanted to repent for all the pain that she caused her sister, and I understood that. But I'd never felt more powerless than I did in that moment. I couldn't protect her. I couldn't pierce the shield they created. I was older than most magic, which meant the magic they used came from the gods. I glanced up at the sky, at the bastards who had subjected me to this life, who had abandoned me, and they had helped torture the most beautiful creature on this planet. Larissa's emotions were all over the place, her mind flitting between reliving the death of Luce and the death of Juliet.

I kissed the top of her head. "Let it all out, my love." She buried her head into my chest as she howled in pain, roaring over the loss of her last loved one. I could sense she felt alone even though she knew she never would be. Roman and I were her family. Always. I held her tighter until the cries died down to nothing. Larissa passed out from emotional exhaustion. I picked her up and flew us home, landing on the balcony of the penthouse. As I tucked her into bed, I noticed that her hair was no longer a beautiful chocolate brown, but now contained red highlights. Her eyes, despite being closed, glowed with the power she had absorbed.

I left the room, closing the door behind me, and messaged Andreas to pick up the car before calling Roman.

"What happened?" his frantic voice answered the phone.

"Luce is dead. She…uh…she sacrificed herself for Larissa. She saved her life."

"Holy shit. How is Larissa?"

"She is asleep now. She passed out, she cried herself to sleep. Roman, I don't know how she will recover from this. Luce literally burst into a pool of blood before her eyes."

"She has us and always will. What happened to Juliet and the witches?" I breathed out as I replayed the sheer power she used. She was a sight, and it was amazing, but I doubt she would see it as that.

"She tortured them before burning them alive. Some were left alive, and I didn't ask her why, but I am sure there was a reason for it. Roman, I don't know what will happen when she wakes up. The bond is filled with so many emotions that I can barely contain my own anger and rage."

Roman was silent for a while. "Nik, could you not help?"

I dreaded answering this particular question. "No, I couldn't. The magic came from the gods." More silence.

"Nik, what does this mean?"

Tears fell down my cheek, tears that I could barely contain. I had been terrified on a few occasions but now, I had no idea how to process this. "Roman, I don't know. We cannot fight two battles."

How the hell could I fix the world if the gods were against us?